The Business of Life

By

Robert W. Chambers

CHAPTER I

"A lady to see you, sir," said Farris., lying on the sofa, glanced up over his book.

"A lady?"

"Yes, sir."

"Well, who is she, Farris?"

"She refused her name, Mr. James."

Desboro swung his legs to the carpet and sat up.

"What kind of lady is she?" he asked; "a perfect one, or the real thing?"

"I don't know, sir. It's hard to tell these days; one dresses like t'other."

Desboro laid aside his book and arose leisurely.

"Where is she?"

"In the reception room, sir."

"Did you ever before see her?"

"I don't know, Mr. James—what with her veil and furs——"

"How did she come?"

"In one of Ransom's hacks from the station. There's a trunk outside, too."

"What the devil——"

"Yes, sir. That's what made me go to the door. Nobody rang. I heard the stompin' and the noise; and I went out, and she just kind of walked in. Yes, sir."

"Is the hack out there yet?"

"No, sir. Ransom's man he left the trunk and drove off. I heard her tell him he could go."

Desboro remained silent for a few moments, looking hard at the fireplace; then he tossed his cigarette onto the embers, dropped the amber mouthpiece into the pocket of his dinner jacket, dismissed Farris with a pleasant nod, and walked very slowly along the hall, as though in no haste to meet his visitor before he could come to some conclusion concerning her identity. For among all the women he had known, intimately or otherwise, he could remember very few reckless enough, or brainless enough, or sufficiently self-assured, to pay him an impromptu visit in the country at such an hour of the night.

The reception room, with its early Victorian furniture, appeared to be empty, at first glance; but the next instant he saw somebody in the curtained embrasure of a window—a shadowy figure which did not seem inclined to leave obscurity—the figure of a woman in veil and furs, her face half hidden in her muff.

He hesitated a second, then walked toward her; and she lifted her head.

"Elena!" he said, astonished.

"Are you angry, Jim?"

"What are you doing here?"

"I didn't know what to do," said Mrs. Clydesdale, wearily, "and it came over me all at once that I couldn't stand him any longer."

"What has he done?"

"Nothing. He's just the same—never quite sober—always following me about, always under foot, always grinning—and buying sixteenth century enamels—and—I can't stand it! I——" Her voice broke.

"Come into the library," he said curtly.

She found her handkerchief, held it tightly against her eyes, and reached out toward him to be guided.

In the library fireplace a few embers were still alive. He laid a log across the coals and used the bellows until the flames started. After that he dusted his hands, lighted a cigarette, and stood for a moment watching the mounting blaze.

She had cast aside her furs and was resting on one elbow, twisting her handkerchief to rags between her gloved hands, and staring at the fire. One or two tears gathered and fell.

"He'll divorce me now, won't he?" she asked unsteadily.

"Why?"

"Because nobody would believe the truth—after this."

She rested her pretty cheek against the cushion and gazed at the fire with wide eyes still tearfully brilliant.

"You have me on your hands," she said. "What are you going to do with me?"

"Send you home."

"You can't. I've disgraced myself. Won't you stand by me, Jim?"

"I can't stand by you if I let you stay here."

"Why not?"

"Because that would be destroying you."

"Are you going to send me away?"

"Certainly."

"Where are you going to send me?"

"Home."

"Home!" she repeated, beginning to cry again. "Why do you call his house 'home'? It's no more my home than he is my husband——"

"He is your husband! What do you mean by talking this way?"

"He isn't my husband. I told him I didn't care for him when he asked me to marry him. He only grinned. It was a perfectly cold-blooded bargain. I didn't sell him everything!"

"You married him."

"Partly."

"What!"

She flushed crimson.

"I sold him the right to call me his wife and to—to make me so if I ever came to—care for him. That was the bargain—if you've got to know. The clergy did their part——"

"Do you mean——"

"Yes!" she said, exasperated. "I mean that it is no marriage, in spite of law and clergy. And it never will be, because I hate him!"

Desboro looked at her in utter contempt.

"Do you know," he said, "what a rotten thing you have done?"

"Rotten!"

"Do you think it admirable?"

"I didn't sell myself wholesale. It might have been worse."

"You are wrong. Nothing worse could have happened."

"Then I don't care what else happens to me," she said, drawing off her gloves and unpinning her hat. "I shall not go back to him."

"You can't stay here."

"I will," she said excitedly. "I'm going to break with him—whether or not I can count on your loyalty to me———" Her voice broke childishly, and she bowed her head.

He caught his lip between his teeth for a moment. Then he said savagely:

"You ought not to have come here. There isn't one single thing to excuse it. Besides, you have just reminded me of my loyalty to you. Can't you understand that that includes your husband? Also, it isn't in me to forget that I once asked you to be my wife. Do you think I'd let you stand for anything less after that? Do you think I'm going to blacken my own face? I never asked any other woman to marry me, and this settles it—I never will! You've finished yourself and your sex for me!"

She was crying now, her head in her hands, and the bronze-red hair dishevelled, sagging between her long, white fingers.

He remained aloof, knowing her, and always afraid of her and of himself together—a very deadly combination for mischief. And she remained bowed in the attitude of despair, her lithe young body shaken.

His was naturally a lightly irresponsible disposition, and it came very easily for him to console beauty in distress—or out of it, for that matter. Why he was now so fastidious with his conscience in regard to Mrs. Clydesdale he himself scarcely understood, except that he had once asked her to marry him; and that he knew her husband. These two facts seemed to keep him steady. Also, he rather liked her burly husband; and he had almost recovered from the very real pangs which had pierced him when she suddenly flung him over and married Clydesdale's millions.

One of the logs had burned out. He rose to replace it with another. When he returned to the sofa, she looked up at him so pitifully that he bent over and caressed her hair. And she put one arm around his neck, crying, uncomforted.

"It won't do," he said; "it won't do. And you know it won't, don't you? This whole business is dead wrong—dead rotten. But you mustn't cry, do you hear? Don't be frightened. If there's trouble, I'll stand by you, of course. Hush, dear, the house is full of servants. Loosen your arms, Elena! It isn't a square deal to your husband—or to you, or even to me. Unless people have an even chance with me—men or women—there's nothing dangerous about me. I never dealt with any man whose eyes were not wide open—nor with any woman, either. Cary's are shut; yours are blinded."

She sprang up and walked to the fire and stood there, her hands nervously clenching and unclenching.

"When I tell you that my eyes are wide open—that I don't care what I do——"

"But your husband's eyes are not open!"

"They ought to be. I left a note saying where I was going—that rather than be his wife I'd prefer to be your——"

"Stop! You don't know what you're talking about—you little idiot!" he broke out, furious. "The very words you use don't mean anything to you—except that you've read them in some fool's novel, or heard them on a degenerate stage——"

"My words will mean something to him, if I can make them!" she retorted hysterically, "—and if you really care for me——"

Through the throbbing silence Desboro seemed to see Clydesdale, bulky, partly sober, with his eternal grin and permanently-flushed skin, rambling about among his porcelains and enamels and jades and ivories, like a drugged elephant in a bric-a-brac shop. And yet, there had always been a certain kindly harmlessness and good nature about him that had always appealed to men.

He said, incredulously: "Did you write to him what you have just said to me?"

"Yes."

"You actually left such a note for him?"

"Yes, I did."

The silence lasted long enough for her to become uneasy. Again and again she lifted her tear-swollen face to look at him, where he stood before the fire, but he did not even glance at her; and at last she murmured his name, and he turned.

"I guess you've done for us both," he said. "You're probably right; nobody would believe the truth after this."

She began to cry again silently.

He said: "You never gave your husband a chance. He was in love with you and you never gave him a chance. And you're giving yourself none, now. And as for me"—he laughed unpleasantly—"well, I'll leave it to you, Elena."

"I—I thought—if I burned my bridges and came to you——"

"What did you think?"

"That you'd stand by me, Jim."

"Have I any other choice?" he asked, with a laugh. "We seem to be a properly damned couple."

"Do—do you care for any other woman?"

"No."

"Then—then——"

"Oh, I am quite free to stand the consequences with you."

"Will you?"

"Can we escape them?"

"You could."

"I'm not in the habit of leaving a sinking ship," he said curtly.

"Then—you will marry me—when——" She stopped short and turned very white. After a moment the doorbell rang again.

Desboro glanced at the clock, then shrugged.

"Wh—who is it?" she faltered.

"It's probably somebody after you, Elena."

"It can't be. He wouldn't come, would he?"

The bell sounded again.

"What are you going to do?" she breathed.

"Do? Let him in."

"Who do you think it is?"

"Your husband, of course."

"Then—why are you going to let him in?"

"To talk it over with him."

"But—but I don't know what he'll do. I don't know him, I tell you. What do I know about him—except that he's big and red? How do I know what might be hidden behind that fixed grin of his?"

"Well, we'll find out in a minute or two," said Desboro coolly.

"Jim! You must stand by me now!"

"I've done it so far, haven't I? You needn't worry."

"You won't let him take me back! He can't, can he?"

"Not if you refuse to go. But you won't refuse—if he's man enough to ask you to return."

"But—suppose he won't ask me to go back?"

"In that case I'll stand for what you've done. I'll marry you if he means to disgrace you. Now let's see what he does mean."

She caught his sleeve as he passed her, then let it go. The steady ringing of the bell was confusing and terrifying her, and she glanced about her like a trapped creature, listening to the distant jingling of chains and the click of bolts as Desboro undid the outer door.

Silence, then a far sound in the hall, footsteps coming nearer, nearer; and she dropped stiffly on the sofa as Desboro entered, followed by Cary Clydesdale in fur motor cap, coat and steaming goggles.

Desboro motioned her husband to a chair, but the man stood looking at his wife through his goggles, with a silly, fixed grin stamped on his features. Then he drew off the goggles and one fur gauntlet, fumbled in his overcoat, produced the crumpled note which she had left for him, laid it on the table between them, and sat down heavily, filling the leather armchair with his bulk. His bare red hand steamed. After a moment's silence, he pointed at the note.

"Well," she said, with an effort, "what of it! It's true—what this letter says."

"It isn't true yet, is it?" asked Clydesdale simply.

"What do you mean?"

But Desboro understood him, and answered for her with a calm shake of his head. Then the wife understood, too, and the deep colour dyed her skin from throat to brow.

"Why do you come here—after reading that?" She pointed at the letter. "Didn't you read it?"

Clydesdale passed his hand slowly over his perplexed eyes.

"I came to take you home. The car is here."

"Didn't you understand what I wrote? Isn't it plain enough?" she demanded excitedly.

"No. You'd better get ready, Elena."

"Is that as much of a man as you are—when I tell you I'd rather be Mr. Desboro's——"

Something behind the fixed grin on her husband's face made her hesitate and falter. Then he swung heavily around and looked at Desboro.

"How much are you in this, anyway?" he asked, still grinning.

"Do you expect an answer?"

"I think I'll get one."

"I think you won't get one out of me."

"Oh. So you're at the bottom of it all, are you?"

"No doubt. A woman doesn't do such a thing unpersuaded. If you don't know enough to look after your own wife, there are plenty of men who'll apply for the job—as I did."

"You're a very rotten scoundrel, aren't you?" said Clydesdale, grinning.

"Oh, so-so."

Clydesdale sat very still, his grin unchanged, and Desboro looked him over coolly.

"Now, what do you want to do? You and Mrs. Clydesdale can remain here to-night if you wish. There are plenty of bedrooms——"

Clydesdale rose, bulking huge and menacing in his furs; but Desboro, sitting on the edge of the table, continued to swing one foot gently, smiling at danger.

And Clydesdale hesitated, then veered around toward his wife, with the heavy movement of a perplexed and tortured bear.

"Get your furs on," he said, in a dull voice.

"Do you wish me to go home?"

"Get your furs on!"

"Do you wish me to go home, Cary?"

"Yes. Good God! What do you suppose I came here for?"

She walked over to Desboro and held out her hand:

"No wonder women like you. Good-bye—and if I come again—may I remain?"

"Don't come," he said, smiling, and holding her coat for her.

Clydesdale strode forward, took the fur garment from Desboro's hands, and held it open. His wife looked up at him, shrugged her shoulders, and suffered him to invest her with the coat.

After a moment Desboro said:

"Clydesdale, I am not your enemy. I wish you good luck."

"You go to hell," said Clydesdale thickly.

Mrs. Clydesdale moved toward the door, her husband on one side, Desboro on the other, and so, along the hall in silence, and out to the porch, where the glare of the acetylenes lighted up the frozen drive.

"It feels like rain," observed Desboro. "Not a very gay outlook for Christmas. All the same, I wish you a happy one, Elena. And, really, I believe you could have it if you cared to."

"Thank you, Jim. You have been mistakenly kind to me. I am afraid you will have to be crueller some day. Good-bye—till then."

Clydesdale had descended to the drive and was conferring with the chauffeur. Now he turned and looked up at his wife. She went down the steps beside Desboro, and he nodded good-night. Clydesdale put her into the limousine and then got in after her.

A few moments later the red tail-lamp of the motor disappeared among the trees bordering the drive, and Desboro turned and walked back into the house.

"That," he said aloud to himself, "settles the damned species for me! Let the next one look out for herself!"

He sauntered back into the library. The letter that she had left for her husband still lay on the table, apparently forgotten.

"A fine specimen of logic," he said. "She doesn't get on with him, so she decides to use Jim to jimmy the lock of wedlock! A white man can understand the Orientals better."

He glanced at the clock, and decided that there was no sense in going to bed, so he composed himself on the haircloth sofa once more, lighted a cigarette, and began to read, coolly using the note she had left, as a bookmark.

It was dawn before he closed the book and went away to bathe and change his attire.

While breakfasting he glanced out and saw that it had begun to rain. A green Christmas for day after to-morrow! And, thinking of Christmas, he thought of a girl he knew who usually wore blue, and what sort of a gift he had better send her when he went to the city that morning.

But he didn't go. He called up a jeweler and gave directions what to send and where to send it.

Then, listless, depressed, he idled about the great house, putting off instinctively the paramount issue—the necessary investigation of his finances. But he had evaded it too long to attempt it lightly now. It was only a question of days before he'd have to take up in deadly earnest the question of how to pay his debts. He knew it; and it made him yawn with disgust.

After luncheon he wrote a letter to one Jean Louis Nevers, a New York dealer in antiques, saying that he would drop in some day after Christmas to consult Mr. Nevers on a matter of private business.

And that is as far as he got with his very vague plan for paying off an accumulation of debts which, at last, were seriously annoying him.

The remainder of the day he spent tramping about the woods of Westchester with a pack of nondescript dogs belonging to him. He liked to walk in the rain; he liked his mongrels.

In the evening he resumed his attitude of unstudied elegance on the sofa, also his book, using Mrs. Clydesdale's note again to mark his place.

Mrs. Quant ventured to knock, bringing some "magic drops," which he smilingly refused. Farris announced dinner, and he dined as usual, surrounded by dogs and cats, all very cordial toward the master of Silverwood, who was unvaryingly so just and so kind to them.

After dinner he lighted a pipe, thought idly of the girl in blue, hoped she'd like his gift of aquamarines, and picked up his book again, yawning.

He had had about enough of Silverwood, and he was realising it. He had had more than enough of women, too.

The next day, riding one of his weedy hunters over Silverwood estate, he encountered the daughter of a neighbor, an old playmate of his when summer days were half a year long, and yesterdays immediately became embedded in the middle of the middle ages.

She was riding a fretful, handsome Kentucky three-year-old, and sitting nonchalantly to his exasperating and jiggling gait.

The girl was one Daisy Hammerton—the sort men call "square" and "white," and a "good fellow"; but she was softly rounded and dark, and very feminine.

She bade him good morning in a friendly voice; and her voice and manner might well have been different, for Desboro had not behaved very civilly toward her or toward her family, or to any of his Westchester neighbors for that matter; and the rumours of his behaviour in New York were anything but pleasant to a young girl's ears. So her cordiality was the more to her credit.

He made rather shame-faced inquiries about her and her parents, but she lightly put him at his ease, and they turned into the woods together on the old and unembarrassed terms of comradeship.

"Captain Herrendene is back. Did you know it?" she asked.

"Nice old bird," commented Desboro. "I must look him up. Where did he come from—Luzon?"

"Yes. He wrote us. Why don't you ask him up for the skating, Jim?"

"What skating?" said Desboro, with a laugh. "It will be a green Christmas, Daisy—it's going to rain again. Besides," he added, "I shan't be here much longer."

"Oh, I'm sorry."

He reddened. "You always were the sweetest thing in Westchester. Fancy your being sorry that I'm going back to town when I've never once ridden over to see you as long as I've been here!"

She laughed. "We've known each other too long to let such things make any real difference. But you have been a trifle negligent."

"Daisy, dear, I'm that way in everything. If anybody asked me to name the one person I would not neglect, I'd name you. But you see what happens—even to you! I don't know—I don't seem to have any character. I don't know what's the matter with me——"

"I'm afraid that you have no beliefs, Jim."

"How can I have any when the world is so rotten after nineteen hundred years of Christianity?"

"I have not found it rotten."

"No, because you live in a clean and wholesome circle."

"Why don't you, too? You can live where you please, can't you?"

He laughed and waved his hand toward the horizon.

"You know what the Desboros have always been. You needn't pretend you don't. All Westchester has it in for us. But relief is in sight," he added, with mock seriousness. "I'm the last of 'em, and your children, Daisy, won't have to endure the morally painful necessity of tolerating anybody of my name in the county."

She smiled: "Jim, you could be so nice if you only would."

"What! With no beliefs?"

"They're so easily acquired."

"Not in New York town, Daisy."

"Perhaps not among the people you affect. But such people really count for so little—they are only a small but noisy section of a vast and quiet and wholesome community. And the noise and cynicism are both based on idleness, Jim. Nobody who is busy is destitute of beliefs. Nobody who is responsible can avoid ideals."

"Quite right," he said. "I am idle and irresponsible. But, Daisy, it's as much part of me as are my legs and arms, and head and body. I am not stupid; I have plenty of mental resources; I am never bored; I enjoy my drift through life in an empty tub as much as the man who pulls furiously through it in a rowboat loaded with ambitions, ballasted with brightly moral resolves, and buffeted by the cross seas of duty and conscience. That's rather neat, isn't it?"

"You can't drift safely very long without ballast," said the girl, smiling.

"Watch me."

She did not answer that she had been watching him for the last few years, or tell him how it had hurt her to hear his name linked with the gossip of fashionably vapid doings among idle and vapid people. For his had been an inheritance of ability and culture, and the leisure to develop both. Out of idleness and easy virtue had at last emerged three generations of Desboros full of energy and almost ruthless ability—his great-grandfather, grandfather and father—but he, the fourth generation, was throwing back into the melting pot all that his father and grandfathers had carried from it—even the material part of it. Land and fortune, were beginning to disappear, together with the sturdy mental and moral qualities of a race that had almost overcome its vicious origin under the vicious Stuarts. Only the physical stamina as yet seemed to remain intact; for Desboro was good to look upon.

"An odd thing happened the other night—or, rather, early in the morning," she said. "We were awakened by a hammering at the door and a horn blowing—and guess who it was?"

"Not Gabriel—though you look immortally angelic to-day——"

"Thank you, Jim. No; it was Cary and Elena Clydesdale, saying that their car had broken down. What a ridiculous hour to be motoring! Elena was half dead with the cold, too. It seems they'd been to a party somewhere and were foolish enough to try to motor back to town. They stopped with us and took the noon train to town. Elena told me to give you her love; that's what reminded me."

"Give her mine when you see her," he said pleasantly.

When he returned to his house he sat down with a notion of trying to bring order out of the chaos into which his affairs had tumbled. But the mere sight of his desk, choked with unanswered letters and unpaid bills, sickened him, and he threw himself on the sofa and picked up his book, determined to rid himself of Silverwood House and all its curious, astonishing and costly contents.

"Tell Riley to be on hand Monday," he said to Mrs. Quant that evening. "I want the cases in the wing rooms and the stuff in the armoury cleaned up, because I expect a Mr. Nevers to come here and recatalogue the entire collection next week."

"Will you be at home, Mr. James?" she asked anxiously.

"No. I'm going South, duck-shooting. See that Mr. Nevers is comfortable if he chooses to remain here; for it will take him a week or two to do his work in the armoury, I suppose. So you'll have to start both furnaces to-morrow, and keep open fires going, or the man will freeze solid. You understand, don't you?"

"Yes, sir. And if you are going away, Mr. James, I could pack a little bottle of 'magic drops'——"

"By all means," he said, with good-humoured resignation.

He spent the evening fussing over his guns and ammunition, determined to go to New York in the morning. But he didn't; indecision had become a habit; he knew it, wondered a little at himself for his lack of decision.

He was deadly weary of Silverwood, but too lazy to leave; and it made him think of the laziest dog on record, who yelped all day because he had sat down on a tack and was too lazy to get up.

So it was not until the middle of Christmas week that Desboro summoned up sufficient energy to start for New York. And when at last he was on the train, he made up his mind that he wouldn't return to Silverwood in a hurry.

But that plan was one of the mice-like plans men make so confidently under the eternal skies.

CHAPTER II

Desboro arrived in town on a late train. It was raining, so he drove to his rooms, exchanged his overcoat for a raincoat, and went out into the downpour again, undisturbed, disdaining an umbrella.

In a quarter of an hour's vigorous walking he came to the celebrated antique shop of Louis Nevers, and entered, letting in a gust of wind and rain at his heels.

Everywhere in the semi-gloom of the place objects loomed mysteriously, their outlines lost in shadow except where, here and there, a gleam of wintry daylight touched a jewel or fell across some gilded god, lotus-throned, brooding alone.

When Desboro's eyes became accustomed to the obscurity, he saw that there was armour there, complete suits, Spanish and Milanese, and an odd Morion or two; and there were jewels in old-time settings, tapestries, silver, ivories, Hispano-Moresque lustre, jades, crystals.

The subdued splendour of Chinese and Japanese armour, lacquered in turquoise, and scarlet and gold, glimmered on lay figures masked by grotesque helmets; an Ispahan rug, softly luminous, trailed across a table beside him, and on it lay a dead Sultan's scimitar, curved like the new moon, its slim blade inset with magic characters, the hilt wrought as delicately as the folded frond of a fern, graceful, exquisite, gem-incrusted.

There were a few people about the shop, customers and clerks, moving shapes in the dull light. Presently a little old salesman wearing a skull cap approached him.

"Rainy weather for Christmas week, sir. Can I be of service?"

"Thanks," said Desboro. "I came here by appointment on a matter of private business."

"Certainly, sir. I think Miss Nevers is not engaged. Kindly give me your card and I will find out."

"But I wish to see Mr. Nevers himself."

"Mr. Nevers is dead, sir."

"Oh! I didn't know——"

"Yes, sir. Mr. Nevers died two years ago." And, as Desboro remained silent and thoughtful: "Perhaps you might wish to see Miss Nevers? She has charge of everything now, including all our confidential affairs."

"No doubt," said Desboro pleasantly, "but this is an affair requiring personal judgment and expert advice——"

"I understand, sir. The gentlemen who came to see Mr. Nevers about matters requiring expert opinions now consult Miss Nevers personally."

"Who is Miss Nevers?"

"His daughter, sir." He added, with quaint pride: "The great jewelers of Fifth Avenue consult her; experts in our business often seek her advice. The Museum authorities have been pleased to speak highly of her monograph on Hurtado de Mendoza."

Desboro hesitated for a moment, then gave his card to the old salesman, who trotted away with it down the unlighted vista of the shop.

The young man's pleasantly indifferent glance rested on one object after another, not unintelligently, but without particular interest. Yet there were some very wonderful and very rare and beautiful things to be seen in the celebrated shop of the late Jean Louis Nevers.

So he stood, leaning on his walking stick, the upturned collar of his raincoat framing a face which was too colourless and worn for a man of his age; and presently the little old salesman came trotting back, the tassel on his neat silk cap bobbing with every step.

"Miss Nevers will be very glad to see you in her private office. This way, if you please, sir."

Desboro followed to the rear of the long, dusky shop, turned to the left through two more rooms full of shadowy objects dimly discerned, then traversed a tiled passage to where electric lights burned over a doorway.

The old man opened the door; Desboro entered and found himself in a square picture gallery, lighted from above, and hung all around with dark velvet curtains to protect the pictures on sale. As he closed the door behind him a woman at a distant desk turned her head, but remained seated, pen poised, looking across the room at him as he advanced. Her black gown blended so deceptively with the hangings that at first he could distinguish only the white face and throat and hands against the shadows behind her.

"Will you kindly announce me to Miss Nevers?" he said, looking around for a chair.

"I am Miss Nevers."

She closed the ledger in which she had been writing, laid aside her pen and rose. As she came forward he found himself looking at a tall girl, slim to thinness, except for the rounded oval of her face under a loose crown of yellow hair, from which a stray lock sagged untidily, curling across her cheek.

He thought: "A blue-stocking prodigy of learning, with her hair in a mess, and painted at that." But he said politely, yet with that hint of idle amusement in his voice which often sounded through his speech with women:

"Are you the Miss Nevers who has taken over this antique business, and who writes monographs on Hurtado de Mendoza?"

"Yes."

"You appear to be very young to succeed such a distinguished authority as your father, Miss Nevers."

His observation did not seem to disturb her, nor did the faintest hint of mockery in his pleasant voice. She waited quietly for him to state his business.

He said: "I came here to ask somebody's advice about engaging an expert to appraise and catalogue my collection."

And even while he was speaking he was conscious that never before had he seen such a white skin and such red lips—if they were natural. And he began to think that they might be.

He said, noticing the bright lock astray on her cheek once more:

"I suppose that I may speak to you in confidence—just as I would have spoken to your father."

She was still looking at him with the charm of youthful inquiry in her eyes.

"Certainly," she said.

She glanced down at his card which still lay on her blotter, stood a moment with her hand resting on the desk, then indicated a chair at her elbow and seated herself.

He took the chair.

"I wrote you that I'd drop in sometime this week. The note was directed to your father. I did not know he was not living."

"You are the Mr. Desboro who owns the collection of armour?" she asked.

"I am that James Philip Desboro who lives at Silverwood," he said. "Evidently you have heard of the Desboro collection of arms and armour."

"Everybody has, I think."

He said, carelessly: "Museums, amateur collectors, and students know it, and I suppose most dealers in antiques have heard of it."

"Yes, all of them, I believe."

"My house," he went on, "Silverwood, is in darkest Westchester, and my recent grandfather, who made the collection, built a wing to contain it. It's there as he left it. My father made no additions to it. Nor," he added, "have I. Now I want to ask you whether a lot of those things have not increased in value since my grandfather's day?"

"No doubt."

"And the collection is valuable?"

"I think it must be—very."

"And to determine its value I ought to have an expert go there and catalogue it and appraise it?"

"Certainly."

"Who? That's what I've come here to find out."

"Perhaps you might wish us to do it."

"Is that still part of your business?"

"It is."

"Well," he said, after a moment's thought, "I am going to sell the Desboro collection."

"Oh, I'm sorry!" she exclaimed, under her breath; and looked up to find him surprised and beginning to be amused again.

"Your attitude is not very professional—for a dealer in antiques," he said quizzically.

"I am something else, too, Mr. Desboro." She had flushed a little, not responding to his lighter tone.

"I am very sure you are," he said. "Those who really know about and care for such collections must feel sorry to see them dispersed."

"I had hoped that the Museum might have the Desboro collection some day," she said, in a low voice.

He said: "I am sorry it is not to be so," and had the grace to redden a trifle.

She played with her pen, waiting for him to continue; and she was so young, and fresh, and pretty that he was in no hurry to finish. Besides, there was something about her face that had been interesting him—an expression which made him think sometimes that she was smiling, or on the verge of it. But the slightly upcurled corners of her mouth had been fashioned so by her Maker, or perhaps had become so from some inborn gaiety of heart, leaving a faint, sweet imprint on her lips.

To watch her was becoming a pleasure. He wondered what her smile might be like—all the while pretending an absent-minded air which cloaked his idle curiosity.

She waited, undisturbed, for him to come to some conclusion. And all the while he was thinking that her lips were perhaps just a trifle too full—that there was more of Aphrodite in her face than of any saint he remembered; but her figure was thin enough for any saint. Perhaps a course of banquets— perhaps a régime under a diet list warranted to improve——

"Did you ever see the Desboro collection, Miss Nevers?" he asked vaguely.

"No."

"What expert will you send to catalogue and appraise it?"

"I could go."

"You!" he said, surprised and smiling.

"That is my profession."

"I knew, of course, that it was your father's. But I never supposed that you ____"

"Did you wish to have an appraisement made, Mr. Desboro?" she interrupted dryly.

"Why, yes, I suppose so. Otherwise, I wouldn't know what to ask for anything."

"Have you really decided to sell that superb collection?" she demanded.

"What else can I do?" he inquired gayly. "I suppose the Museum ought to have it, but I can't afford to give it away or to keep it. In other words—and brutal ones—I need money."

She said gravely: "I am sorry."

And he knew she didn't mean that she was sorry because he needed money, but because the Museum was not to have the arms, armour, jades, and ivories. Yet, somehow, her "I am sorry" sounded rather sweet to him.

For a while he sat silent, one knee crossed over the other, twisting the silver crook of his stick. From moment to moment she raised her eyes from the blotter to let them rest inquiringly on him, then went on tracing arabesques over her blotter with an inkless pen. One slender hand was bracketed on her hip, and he noticed the fingers, smooth and rounded as a child's. Nor could he keep his eyes from her profile, with its delicate, short nose, ever so slightly arched, and its lips, just a trifle too sensuous—and that soft lock astray again against her cheek. No, her hair was not dyed, either. And it was as though she divined his thought, for she looked up suddenly from her blotter and he instantly gazed elsewhere, feeling guilty and impertinent—sentiments not often experienced by that young man.

"I'll tell you what I'll do, Miss Nevers," he concluded, "I'll write you a letter to my housekeeper, Mrs. Quant. Shall I? And you'll go up and look over the collection and let me know what you think of it!"

"Do you not expect to be there?"

"Ought I to be?"

"I really can't answer you, but it seems to me rather important that the owner of a collection should be present when the appraiser begins work."

"The fact is," he said, "I'm booked for a silly shooting trip. I'm supposed to start to-morrow."

"Then perhaps you had better write the letter. My full name is Jacqueline Nevers—if you require it. You may use my desk."

She rose; he thanked her, seated himself, and began a letter to Mrs. Quant, charging her to admit, entertain, and otherwise particularly cherish one Miss Jacqueline Nevers, and give her the keys to the armoury.

While he was busy, Jacqueline Nevers paced the room backward and forward, her pretty head thoughtfully bent, hands clasped behind her, moving leisurely, absorbed in her cogitations.

Desboro ended his letter and sat for a moment watching her until, happening to glance at him, she discovered his idleness.

"Have you finished?" she asked.

A trifle out of countenance he rose and explained that he had, and laid the letter on her blotter. Realising that she was expecting him to take his leave, he also realised that he didn't want to. And he began to spar with Destiny for time.

"I suppose this matter will require several visits from you," he inquired.

"Yes, several."

"It takes some time to catalogue and appraise such a collection, doesn't it?"

"Yes."

She answered him very sweetly but impersonally, and there seemed to be in her brief replies no encouragement for him to linger. So he started to pick up his hat, thinking as fast as he could all the while; and his facile wits saved him at the last moment.

"Well, upon my word!" he exclaimed. "Do you know that you and I have not yet discussed terms?"

"We make our usual charges," she said.

"And what are those?"

She explained briefly.

"That is for cataloguing and appraising only?"

"Yes."

"And if you sell the collection?"

"We take our usual commission."

"And you think you can sell it for me?"

"I'll have to—won't I?"

He laughed. "But can you?"

"Yes."

As the curt affirmative fell from her lips, suddenly, under all her delicate, youthful charm, Desboro divined the note of hidden strength, the self-confidence of capability—oddly at variance with her allure of lovely immaturity. Yet he might have surmised it, for though her figure was that of a girl, her face, for all its soft, fresh beauty, was a woman's, and already firmly moulded in noble lines which even the scarlet fulness of the lips could not deny. For if she had the mouth of Aphrodite, she had her brow, also.

He had not been able to make her smile, although the upcurled corners of her mouth seemed always to promise something. He wondered what her expression might be like when animated—even annoyed. And his idle curiosity led him on to the edges of impertinence.

"May I say something that I have in mind and not offend you?" he asked.

"Yes—if you wish." She lifted her eyes.

"Do you think you are old enough and experienced enough to catalogue and appraise such an important collection as this one? I thought perhaps you might prefer not to take such a responsibility upon yourself, but would rather choose to employ some veteran expert."

She was silent.

"Have I offended you?"

She walked slowly to the end of the room, turned, and, passing him a third time, looked up at him and laughed—a most enchanting little laugh—a revelation as delightful as it was unexpected.

"I believe you really want to do it yourself!" he exclaimed.

"Want to? I'm dying to! I don't think there is anything in the world I had rather try!" she said, with a sudden flush and sparkle of recklessness that transfigured her. "Do you suppose anybody in my business would willingly miss the chance of personally handling such a transaction? Of course I want to. Not only because it would be a most creditable transaction for this house—not only because it would be a profitable business undertaking, but"—and the swift, engaging smile parted her lips once more—"in a way I feel as though my own ability had been questioned———"

"By me?" he protested. "Did I actually dare question your ability?"

"Something very like it. So, naturally, I would seize an opportunity to vindicate myself—if you offer it———"

"I do offer it," he said.

"I accept."

There was a moment's indecisive silence. He picked up his hat and stick, lingering still; then:

"Good-bye, Miss Nevers. When are you going up to Silverwood?"

"To-morrow, if it is quite convenient."

"Entirely. I may be there. Perhaps I can fix it—put off that shooting party for a day or two."

"I hope so."

"I hope so, too."

He walked reluctantly toward the door, turned and came all the way back.

"Perhaps you had rather I remained away from Silverwood."

"Why?"

"But, of course," he said, "there is a nice old housekeeper there, and a lot of servants———"

She laughed. "Thank you very much, Mr. Desboro. It is very nice of you, but I had not considered that at all. Business women must disregard such conventions, if they're to compete with men. I'd like you to be there, because I may have questions to ask."

"Certainly—it's very good of you. I—I'll try to be there——"

"Because I might have some very important questions to ask you," she repeated.

"Of course. I've got to be there. Haven't I?"

"It might be better for your interests."

"Then I'll be there. Well, good-bye, Miss Nevers."

"Good-bye, Mr. Desboro."

"And thank you for undertaking it," he said cordially.

"Thank you for asking me."

"Oh, I'm—I'm really delighted. It's most kind of you. Good-bye, Miss Nevers."

"Good-bye, Mr. Desboro."

He had to go that time; and he went still retaining a confused vision of blue eyes and vivid lips, and of a single lock of hair astray once more across a smooth, white cheek.

When he had gone, Jacqueline seated herself at her desk and picked up her pen. She remained so for a while, then emerged abruptly from a fit of abstraction and sorted some papers unnecessarily. When she had arranged them to her fancy, she rearranged them. Then the little Louis XVI desk interested her, and she examined the inset placques of flowered Sèvres in detail, as though the little desk of tulip, satinwood and walnut had not stood there since she was a child.

Later she noticed his card on her blotter; and, face framed in her hands, she studied it so long that the card became a glimmering white patch and vanished; and before her remote gaze his phantom grew out of space, seated there in the empty chair beside her—the loosened collar of his raincoat revealing to her the most attractive face of any man she had ever looked upon in her twenty-two years of life.

Toward evening the electric lamps were lighted in the shop; rain fell more heavily outside; few people entered. She was busy with ledgers and files of old catalogues recording auction sales, the name of the purchaser and the prices pencilled on the margins in her father's curious handwriting. Also her card index aided her. Under the head of "Desboro" she was able to note what objects of interest or of art her father had bought for her recent visitor's grandfather, and the prices paid—little, indeed, in those days, compared with what the same objects would now bring. And, continuing her search, she finally came upon an uncompleted catalogue of the Desboro collection. It was in manuscript—her father's peculiar French chirography—neat and accurate as far as it went.

Everything bearing upon the Desboro collection she bundled together and strapped with rubber bands; then, one by one, the clerks and salesmen came to report to her before closing up. She locked the safe, shut her desk, and went out to the shop, where she remained until the shutters were clamped and the last salesman had bade her a cheery good night. Then, bolting the door and double-locking it, she went back along the passage and up the stairs, where she had the two upper floors to herself, and a cook and chambermaid to keep house for her.

In the gaslight of the upper apartment she seemed even more slender than by daylight—her eyes bluer, her lips more scarlet. She glanced into the mirror of her dresser as she passed, pausing to twist up the unruly lock that had defied her since childhood.

Everywhere in the room Christmas was still in evidence—a tiny tree, with frivolous, glittering things still twisted and suspended among the branches, calendars, sachets, handkerchiefs still gaily tied in ribbons, flowering shrubs swathed in tissue and bows of tulle—these from her salesmen, and she had carefully but pleasantly maintained the line of demarcation by presenting each with a gold piece.

But there were other gifts—gloves and stockings, and bon-bons, and books, from the friends who were girls when she too was a child at school; and a set of volumes from Cary Clydesdale whose collection of jades she was cataloguing. The volumes were very beautiful and expensive. The gift had surprised her.

Among her childhood friends was her social niche; the circumference of their circle the limits of her social environment. They came to her and she went to them; their pastimes and pleasures were hers; and if there was not, perhaps, among them her intellectual equal, she had not yet felt the need of such companionship, but had been satisfied to have them hold her as a good companion who otherwise possessed much strange and perhaps useless knowledge quite beyond their compass. And she was shyly content with her intellectual isolation.

So, amid these people, she had found a place prepared for her when she emerged from childhood. What lay outside of this circle she surmised with the intermittent curiosity of ignorance, or of a bystander who watches a pageant for a moment and hastens on, preoccupied with matters more familiar.

All young girls think of pleasures; she had thought of them always when the day's task was ended, and she had sought them with all the ardour of youth, with a desire unwearied, and a thirst unquenched.

In her, mental and physical pleasure were wholesomely balanced; the keen delight of intellectual experience, the happiness of research and attainment, went hand in hand with a rather fastidious appetite for having the best time that circumstances permitted.

She danced when she had a chance, went to theatres and restaurants with her friends, bathed at Manhattan in summer, when gay parties were organised, and did the thousand innocent things that thousands of young business girls do whose lines are cast in the metropolis.

Since her father's death she had been intensely lonely; only a desperate and steady application to business had pulled her through the first year without a breakdown.

The second year she rejoined her friends and went about again with them. Now, the third year since her father's death was already dawning; and her last prayer as the old year died had been that the new one would bring her friends and happiness.

Seated before the wood fire in her bedroom, leisurely undressing, she thought of Desboro and the business that concerned him. He was so very good looking —in the out-world manner—the manner of those who dwelt outside her orbit.

She had not been very friendly with him at first. She had wanted to be; instinct counselled reserve, and she had listened—until the very last. He had a way of laughing at her in every word—in even an ordinary business conversation. She had been conscious all the while of his half-listless interest in her, of an idle curiosity, which, before it had grown offensive, had become friendly and at times almost boyish in its naïve self-disclosure. And it made her smile to remember how very long it took him to take his leave.

But—a man of that kind—a man of the out-world—with the something in his face that betrays shadows which she had never seen cast—and never would see—he was no boy. For in his face was the faint imprint of that pallid wisdom which warned. Women in his own world might ignore the warning; perhaps it did not menace them. But instinct told her that it might be different outside that world.

She nestled into her fire-warmed bath-robe and sat pensively fitting and refitting her bare feet into her slippers.

Men were odd; alike and unalike. Since her father's death, she had had to be careful. Wealthy gentlemen, old and young, amateurs of armour, ivories, porcelains, jewels, all clients of her father, had sometimes sent for her too many times on too many pretexts; and sometimes their paternal manner toward her had made her uncomfortable. Desboro was of that same caste. Perhaps he was not like them otherwise.

When she had bathed and dressed, she dined alone, not having any invitation for the evening. After dinner she talked on the telephone to her little friend, Cynthia Lessler, whose late father's business had been to set jewels and repair antique watches and clocks. Incidentally, he drank and chased his daughter about with a hatchet until she fled for good one evening, which afforded him an opportunity to drink himself very comfortably to death in six months.

"Hello, Cynthia!" called Jacqueline, softly.

"Hello! Is it you, Jacqueline, dear?"

"Yes. Don't you want to come over and eat chocolates and gossip?"

"Can't do it. I'm just starting for the hall."

"I thought you'd finished rehearsing."

"I've got to be on hand all the same. How are you, sweetness, anyway?"

"Blooming, my dear. I'm crazy to tell you about my good luck. I have a splendid commission with which to begin the new year."

"Good for you! What is it?"

"I can't tell you yet"—laughingly—"it's confidential business——"

"Oh, I know. Some old, fat man wants you to catalogue his collection."

"No! He isn't fat, either. You are the limit, Cynthia!"

"All the same, look out for him," retorted Cynthia. "I know man and his kind. Office experience is a liberal education; the theatre a post-graduate course.

Are you coming to the dance to-morrow night?"

"Yes. I suppose the usual people will be there?"

"Some new ones. There's an awfully good-looking newspaper man from Yonkers. He has a car in town, too."

Something—some new and unaccustomed impatience—she did not understand exactly what—prompted Jacqueline to say scornfully:

"His name is Eddie, isn't it?"

"No. Why do you ask?"

A sudden vision of Desboro, laughing at her under every word of an unsmiling and commonplace conversation, annoyed her.

"Oh, Cynthia, dear, every good-looking man we meet is usually named Ed and comes from places like Yonkers."

Cynthia, slightly perplexed, said slangily that she didn't "get" her; and Jacqueline admitted that she herself didn't know what she had meant.

They gossiped for a while, then Cynthia ended:

"I'll see you to-morrow night, won't I? And listen, you little white mouse, I get what you mean by 'Eddie'."

"Do you?"

"Yes. Shall I see you at the dance?"

"Yes, and 'Eddie,' too. Good-bye."

Jacqueline laughed again, then shivered slightly and hung up the receiver.

Back before her bedroom fire once more, Grenville's volume on ancient armour across her knees, she turned the illuminated pages absently, and gazed into the flames. What she saw among them apparently did not amuse her, for after a while she frowned, shrugged her shoulders, and resumed her reading.

But the XV century knights, in their gilded or silvered harness, had Desboro's lithe figure, and the lifted vizors of their helmets always disclosed his face. Shields emblazoned with quarterings, plumed armets, the golden morions, banner, pennon, embroidered surtout, and the brilliant trappings of battle horse and palfry, became only a confused blur of colour under her eyes, framing a face that looked back at her out of youthful eyes, marred by the shadow of a wisdom she knew about—alas—but did not know.

The man of whom she was thinking had walked back to the club through a driving rain, still under the fascination of the interview, still excited by its novelty and by her unusual beauty. He could not quite account for his exhilaration either, because, in New York, beauty is anything but unusual among the hundreds of thousands of young women who work for a living—for that is one of the seven wonders of the city—and it is the rule rather than the exception that, in this new race which is evolving itself out of an unknown amalgam, there is scarcely a young face in which some trace of it is not apparent at a glance.

Which is why, perhaps, he regarded his present exhilaration humorously, or meant to; perhaps why he chose to think of her as "Stray Lock," instead of Miss Nevers, and why he repeated confidently to himself: "She's thin as a Virgin by the 'Master of the Death of Mary'." And yet that haunting expression of her face—the sweetness of the lips upcurled at the corners—the surprising and lovely revelation of her laughter—these impressions persisted as he swung on through the rain, through the hurrying throngs just released from shops and great department stores, and onward up the wet and glimmering avenue to his destination, which was the Olympian Club.

In the cloak room there were men he knew, being divested of wet hats and coats; in reading room, card room, lounge, billiard hall, squash court, and gymnasium, men greeted him with that friendly punctiliousness which indicates popularity; from the splashed edge of the great swimming pool men hailed him; clerks and club servants saluted him smilingly as he sauntered about through the place, still driven into motion by an inexplicable and unaccustomed restlessness. Cairns discovered him coming out of the billiard room:

"Have a snifter?" he suggested affably. "I'll find Ledyard and play you 'nigger' or 'rabbit' afterward, if you like."

Desboro laid a hand on his friend's shoulder:

"Jack, I've a business engagement at Silverwood to-morrow, and I believe I'd better go home to-night."

"Heavens! You've just been there! And what about the shooting trip?"

"I can join you day after to-morrow."

"Oh, come, Jim, are you going to spoil our card quartette on the train? Reggie Ledyard will kill you."

"He might, at that," said Desboro pleasantly. "But I've got to be at Silverwood to-morrow. It's a matter of business, Jack."

"You and business! Lord! The amazing alliance! What are you going to do—sell a few superannuated Westchester hens at auction? By heck! You're a fake farmer and a pitiable piker, that's what you are. And Stuyve Van Alstyne had a wire to-night that the ducks and geese are coming in to the guns by millions ——"

"Go ahead and shoot 'em, then! I'll probably be along in time to pick up the game for you."

"You won't go with us?"

"Not to-morrow. A man can't neglect his own business every day in the year."

"Then you won't be in Baltimore for the Assembly, and you won't go to Georgia, and you won't do a thing that you expected to. Oh, you're the gay, quick-change artist! And don't tell me it's business, either," he added suspiciously.

"I do tell you exactly that."

"You mean to say that nothing except sheer, dry business keeps you here?"

The colour slowly settled under Desboro's cheek bones:

"It's a matter with enough serious business in it to keep me busy to-morrow ——"

"Selecting pearls? In which show and which row does she cavort, dear friend —speaking in an exquisitely colloquial metaphor!"

Desboro shrugged: "I'll play you a dozen games of rabbit before we dress for dinner. Come on, you suspicious sport!"

"Which show?" repeated Cairns obstinately. He did not mean it literally, footlight affairs being unfashionable. But Desboro's easy popularity with women originated continual gossip, friendly and otherwise; and his name was often connected harmlessly with that of some attractive woman in his own class—like Mrs. Clydesdale, for instance—and sometimes with some pretty unknown in some class not specified. But the surmise was idle, and the gossip vague, and neither the one nor the other disturbed Desboro, who continued to saunter through life keeping his personal affairs pleasantly to himself.

He linked his arm in Cairns's and guided him toward the billiard room. But there were no tables vacant for rabbit, which absurd game, being hard on the cloth, was limited to two decrepit pool tables.

So Cairns again suggested his celebrated "snifter," and then the young men separated, Desboro to go across the street to his elaborate rooms and dress, already a little less interested in his business trip to Silverwood, already regretting the gay party bound South for two weeks of pleasure.

And when he had emerged from a cold shower which, with the exception of sleep, is the wisest counsellor in the world, now that he stood in fresh linen and evening dress on the threshold of another night, he began to wonder at his late exhilaration.

To him the approach of every night was always fraught with mysterious possibilities, and with a belief in Chance forever new. Adventure dawned with the electric lights; opportunity awoke with the evening whistles warning all labourers to rest. Opportunity for what? He did not know; he had not even surmised; but perhaps it was that something, that subtle, evanescent, volatile something for which the world itself waits instinctively, and has been waiting since the first day dawned. Maybe it is happiness for which the world has waited with patient instinct uneradicated; maybe it is death; and after all, the two may be inseparable.

Desboro, looking into the coals of a dying fire, heard the clock striking the hour. The night was before him—those strange hours in which anything could happen before another sun gilded the sky pinnacles of the earth.

Another hour sounded and found him listless, absent-eyed, still gazing into a dying fire.

CHAPTER III

At eleven o'clock the next morning Miss Nevers had not arrived at Silverwood.

It was still raining hard, the brown Westchester fields, the leafless trees, hedges, paths, roads, were soaked; pools stood in hollows with the dead grass awash; ditches brimmed, river and brook ran amber riot, and alder swamps widened into lakes.

The chances were now that she would not come at all. Desboro had met both morning trains, but she was not visible, and all the passengers had departed leaving him wandering alone along the dripping platform.

For a while he stood moodily on the village bridge beyond, listening to the noisy racket of the swollen brook; and after a little it occurred to him that there was laughter in the noises of the water, like the mirth of the gods mocking him.

"Laugh on, high ones!" he said. "I begin to believe myself the ass that I appear to you."

Presently he wandered back to the station platform, where he idled about, playing with a stray and nondescript dog or two, and caressing the station-master's cat; then, when he had about decided to get into his car and go home, it suddenly occurred to him that he might telephone to New York for information. And he did so, and learned that Miss Nevers had departed that morning on business, for a destination unknown, and would not return before evening.

Also, the station-master informed him that the morning express now deposited passengers at Silverwood Station, on request—an innovation of which he had not before heard; and this put him into excellent spirits.

"Aha!" he said to himself, considerably elated. "Perhaps I'm not such an ass as I appear. Let the high gods laugh!"

So he lighted a cigarette, played with the wastrel dogs some more, flattered the cat till she nearly rubbed her head off against his legs, took a small and solemn child onto his knee and presented it with a silver dollar, while its overburdened German mother publicly nourished another.

"You are really a remarkable child," he gravely assured the infant on his knee. "You possess a most extraordinary mind!"—the child not having uttered a word or betrayed a vestige of human expression upon its slightly soiled features.

Presently the near whistle of the Connecticut Express brought him to his feet. He lifted the astonishingly gifted infant and walked out; and when the express rolled past and stopped, he set it on the day-coach platform beside its stolid parent, and waved to it an impressive adieu.

At the same moment, descending from the train, a tall young girl, in waterproofs, witnessed the proceedings, recognised Desboro, and smiled at the little ceremony taking place.

"Yours?" she inquired, as, hat off, hand extended, he came forward to welcome her—and the next moment blushed at her impulsive informality.

"Oh, all kids seem to be mine, somehow or other," he said. "I'm awfully glad you came. I was afraid you wouldn't."

"Why?"

"Because I didn't believe you really existed, for one thing. And then the weather——"

"Do you suppose mere weather could keep me from the Desboro collection? You have much to learn about me."

"I'll begin lessons at once," he said gaily, "if you don't mind giving them. Do you?"

She smiled non-committally, and looked around her at the departing vehicles.

"We have a limousine waiting for us behind the station," he said. "It's five muddy miles."

"I had been wondering all the way up in the train just how I was to get to Silverwood——"

"You didn't suppose I'd leave you to find your way, did you?"

"Business people don't expect limousines," she said, with an unmistakable accent that sounded priggish even to herself—so prim, indeed, that he laughed outright; and she finally laughed, too.

"This is very jolly, isn't it?" he remarked, as they sped away through the rain.

She conceded that it was.

"It's going to be a most delightful day," he predicted.

She thought it was likely to be a busy day.

"And delightful, too," he insisted politely.

"Why particularly delightful, Mr. Desboro?"

"I thought you were looking forward with keen pleasure to your work in the Desboro collection!"

She caught a latent glimmer of mischief in his eye, and remained silent, not yet quite certain that she liked this constant running fire of words that always seemed to conceal a hint of laughter at her expense.

Had they been longer acquainted, and on a different footing, she knew that whatever he said would have provoked a response in kind from her. But friendship is not usually born from a single business interview; nor is it born perfect, like a fairy ring, over night. And it was only last night, she made herself remember, that she first laid eyes on Desboro. Yet it seemed curious that whatever he said seemed to awaken in her its echo; and, though she knew it was an absurd idea, the idea persisted that she already began to understand this young man better than she had ever understood any other of his sex.

He was talking now at random, idly but agreeably, about nothing in particular. She, muffled in the fur robe, looked out through the limousine windows into the rain, and saw brown fields set with pools in every furrow, and squares of winter wheat, intensely green.

And now the silver birch woods, which had given the house its name, began to appear as outlying clumps across the hills; and in a few moments the car swung into a gateway under groves of solemnly-dripping Norway spruces, then up a wide avenue, lined with ranks of leafless, hardwood trees and thickets of laurel and rhododendron, and finally stopped before a house made of grayish-brown stone, in the rather inoffensive architecture of early eighteen hundred.

Mrs. Quant, in best bib and tucker, received them in the hallway, having been instructed by Desboro concerning her attitude toward the expected guest. But when she became aware of the slender youth of the girl, she forgot her sniffs and misgivings, and she waddled, and bobbed, and curtsied, overflowing with a desire to fondle, and cherish, and instruct, which only fear of Desboro choked off.

But as soon as Jacqueline had followed her to the room assigned, and had been divested of wet outer-clothing, and served with hot tea, Mrs. Quant became loquacious and confidential concerning her own personal ailments and sorrows, and the history and misfortunes of the Desboro family.

Jacqueline wished to decline the cup of tea, but Mrs. Quant insisted; and the girl yielded.

"Air you sure you feel well, Miss Nevers?" she asked anxiously.

"Why, of course."

"Don't be too sure," said Mrs. Quant ominously. "Sometimes them that feels bestest is sickest. I've seen a sight of sickness in my day, dearie—typod, mostly. You ain't never had typod, now, hev you?"

"Typhoid?"

"Yes'm, typod!"

"No, I never did."

"Then you take an old woman's advice, Miss Nevers, and don't you go and git it!"

Jacqueline promised gravely; but Mrs. Quant was now fairly launched on her favourite topic.

"I've been forty-two years in this place—and Quant—my man—he was head farmer here when he was took. Typod, it was, dearie—and you won't never git it if you'll listen to me—and Quant, a man that never quarreled with his vittles, but he was for going off without 'em that morning. Sez he, 'Cassie, I don't feel good this mornin'!'—and a piece of pie and a pork chop layin' there onto his plate. 'My vittles don't set right,' sez he; 'I ain't a mite peckish.' Sez I, 'Quant, you lay right down, and don't you stir a inch! You've gone and got a mild form of typod,' sez I, knowing about sickness as I allus had a gift, my father bein' a natural bone-setter. And those was my very words, dearie, 'a mild form of typod.' And I was right and he was took. And when folks ain't well, it's mostly that they've got a mild form of typod which some call malairy——"

There was no stopping her; Jacqueline tasted her hot tea and listened sympathetically to that woman of many sorrows. And, sipping her tea, she was obliged to assist at the obsequies of Quant, the nativity of young Desboro, the dissolution of his grandparents and parents, and many, many minor details, such as the freezing of water-pipes in , the menace of the chestnut blight, mysterious maladies which had affected cattle and chickens on the farm— every variety of death, destruction, dissolution, and despondency that had been Mrs. Quant's portion to witness.

And how she gloried in detailing her dismal career; and presently pessimistic prophecies for the future became plainer as her undammed eloquence flowed on:

"And Mr. James, he ain't well, neither," she said in a hoarse whisper. "He don't know it, and he won't listen to me, dearie, but I know he's got a mild form of typod—he's that unwell the mornings when he's been out late in the city. Say what you're a mind to, typod is typod! And if you h'ain't got it you're likely to git it most any minute; but he won't swaller the teas and broths and suffusions I bring him, and he'll be took like everybody else one of these days, dearie— which he wouldn't if he'd listen to me——"

"Mrs. Quant," came Desboro's voice from the landing.

"Y—yes, sir," stammered that guilty and agitated Cassandra.

Jacqueline set aside her teacup and came to the stairs; their glances met in the suppressed amusement of mutual comprehension, and he conducted her to the hallway below, where a big log fire was blazing.

"What was it—death, destruction, and general woe, as usual?" he asked.

"And typod," she whispered. "It appears that you have it!"

"Poor old soul! She means all right; but imagine me here with her all day, dodging infusions and broths and red flannel! Warm your hands at the blaze, Miss Nevers, and I'll find the armoury keys. It will be a little colder in there."

She spread her hands to the flames, conscious of his subtle change of manner toward her, now that she was actually under his roof—and liked him for it— not in the least surprised that she was comprehending still another phase of this young man's most interesting personality.

For, without reasoning, her slight misgivings concerning him were vanishing; instinct told her she might even permit herself a friendlier manner, and she looked up smilingly when he came back swinging a bunch of keys.

"These belong to the Quant," he explained, "—honest old soul! Every gem and ivory and lump of jade in the collection is at her mercy, for here are the keys to every case. Now, Miss Nevers, what do you require? Pencil and pad?"

"I have my note-book, thanks—a new one in your honour."

He said he was flattered and led the way through a wide corridor to the eastern wing; unlocked a pair of massive doors, and swung them wide. And, beside him, she walked into the armoury of the famous Desboro collection.

Straight ahead of her, paved with black marble, lay a lane through a double rank of armed and mounted men in complete armour; and she could scarcely suppress a little cry of surprise and admiration.

"This is magnificent!" she exclaimed; and he saw her cheeks brighten, and her breath coming faster.

"It is fine," he said soberly.

"It is, indeed, Mr. Desboro! That is a noble array of armour. I feel like some legendary princess of long ago, passing her chivalry in review as I move between these double ranks. What a wonderful collection! All Spanish and Milanese mail, isn't it? Your grandfather specialised?"

"I believe he did. I don't know very much about the collection, technically."

"Don't you care for it?"

"Why, yes—more, perhaps, than I realised—now that you are actually here to take it away."

"But I'm not going to put it into a magic pocket and flee to New York with it!"

She spoke gaily, and his face, which had become a little grave, relaxed into its habitual expression of careless good humour.

They had slowly traversed the long lane, and now, turning, came back through groups of men-at-arms, pikemen, billmen, arquebussiers, crossbowmen, archers, halbardiers, slingers—all the multitudinous arms of a polyglot service, each apparently equipped with his proper weapon and properly accoutred for trouble.

Once or twice she glanced at the trophies aloft on the walls, every group bunched behind its shield and radiating from it under the drooping remnants of banners emblazoned with arms, crests, insignia, devices, and quarterings long since forgotten, except by such people as herself.

"Now and then she ... halted on tip-toe to lift some slitted visor"

She moved gracefully, leisurely, pausing now and then before some panoplied manikin, Desboro sauntering beside her. Now and then she stopped to inspect an ancient piece of ordnance, wonderfully wrought and chased, now and then halted on tip-toe to lift some slitted visor and peer into the dusky cavern of the helmet, where a painted face stared back at her out of painted eyes.

"Who scours all this mail?" she asked.

"Our old armourer. My grandfather trained him. But he's very old and rheumatic now, and I don't let him exert himself. I think he sleeps all winter, like a woodchuck, and fishes all summer."

"You ought to have another armourer."

"I can't turn Michael out to starve, can I?"

She swung around swiftly: "I didn't mean that!" and saw he was laughing at her.

"I know you didn't," he said. "But I can't afford two armourers. That's the reason I'm disposing of these tin-clothed tenants of mine—to economise and cut expenses."

She moved on, evidently desiring to obtain a general impression of the task before her, now and then examining the glass-encased labels at the feet of the figures, and occasionally shaking her head. Already the errant lock curled across her cheek.

"What's the trouble?" he inquired. "Aren't these gentlemen correctly ticketed?"

"Some are not. That suit of gilded mail is not Spanish; it's German. It is not very difficult to make such a mistake sometimes."

Steam heat had been put in, but the vast hall was chilly except close to the long ranks of oxidised pipes lining the walls. They stood a moment, leaning against them and looking out across the place, all glittering with the mail-clad figures.

"I've easily three weeks' work before me among these mounted figures alone, to say nothing of the men on foot and the trophies and artillery," she said. "Do you know it is going to be rather expensive for you, Mr. Desboro?"

This did not appear to disturb him.

"Because," she went on, "a great many mistakes have been made in labelling, and some mistakes in assembling the complete suits of mail and in assigning weapons. For example, that mounted man in front of you is wearing tilting armour and a helmet that doesn't belong to it. That's a childish mistake."

"We'll put the proper lid on him," said Desboro. "Show it to me and I'll put it all over him now."

"It's up there aloft with the trophies, I think—the fifth group."

"There's a ladder on wheels for a closer view of the weapons. Shall I trundle it in?"

He went out into the hallway and presently came back pushing a clanking extension ladder with a railed top to it. Then he affixed the crank and began to grind until it rose to the desired height.

"All I ask of you is not to tumble off it," he said. "Do you promise?"

She promised with mock seriousness: "Because I need all my brains, you see."

"You've a lot of 'em, haven't you, Miss Nevers?"

"No, not many."

He shrugged: "I wonder, then, what a quantitative analysis of mine might produce."

She said: "You are as clever as you take the trouble to be—" and stopped herself short, unwilling to drift into personalities.

"It's the interest that is lacking in me," he said, "—or perhaps the incentive."

She made no comment.

"Don't you think so?"

"I don't know."

"—And don't care," he added.

She flushed, half turned in protest, but remained silent.

"I beg your pardon," he said, "I didn't mean to force your interest in myself. Tell me, is there anything I can do for your comfort before I go? And shall I go and leave you to abstruse and intellectual meditation, or do I disturb you by tagging about at your heels?"

His easy, light tone relieved her. She looked around her at the armed figures:

"You don't disturb me. I was trying to think where to begin. To-morrow I'll bring up some reference books——"

"Perhaps you can find what you want in my grandfather's library. I'll show you where it is when you are ready."

"I wonder if he has Grenville's monograph on Spanish and Milanese mail?"

"I'll see."

He went away and remained for ten minutes. She was minutely examining the sword belonging to a rather battered suit of armour when he returned with the book.

"You see," she said, "you are useful. I did well to suggest that you remain here. Now, look, Mr. Desboro. This is German armour, and here is a Spanish sword of a different century along with it! That's all wrong, you know. Antonius was the sword-maker; here is his name on the hexagonal, gilded iron hilt —'Antonius Me Fecit'."

"You'll put that all right," he said confidently. "Won't you?"

"That's why you asked me here, isn't it?"

He may have been on the point of an indiscreet rejoinder, for he closed his lips suddenly and began to examine another sword. It belonged to the only female equestrian figure in the collection—a beautifully shaped suit of woman's armour, astride a painted war-horse, the cuirass of Milan plates.

"The Countess of Oroposa," he said. "It was her peculiar privilege, after the Count's death, to ride in full armour and carry a naked sword across her knees when the Spanish Court made a solemn entry into cities. Which will be about all from me," he added with a laugh. "Are you ready for luncheon?"

"Quite, thank you. But you said that you didn't know much about this collection. Let me see that sword, please."

"She took it ... then read aloud the device in verse"

He drew it from its scabbard and presented the hilt. She took it, studied it, then read aloud the device in verse:

"'Paz Comigo Nunca Veo Y Siempre Guera Dese.'" ("There is never peace with me; my desire is always war!")

Her clear young voice repeating the old sword's motto seemed to ring a little through the silence—as though it were the clean-cut voice of the blade itself.

"What a fine motto," he said guilelessly. "And you interpret it as though it were your own."

"I like the sound of it. There is no compromise in it."

"Why not assume it for your own? 'There is never peace with me; my desire is always war!' Why not adopt it?"

"Do you mean that such a militant motto suits me?" she asked, amused, and caught the half-laughing, half malicious glimmer in his eyes, and knew in an instant he had divined her attitude toward himself, and toward to her own self, too—war on them both, lest they succumb to the friendship that threatened. Silent, preoccupied, she went back with him through the armoury, through the hallway, into a rather commonplace dining-room, where a table had already been laid for two.

Desboro jingled a small silver bell, and presently luncheon was announced. She ate with the healthy appetite of the young, and he pretended to. Several cats and dogs of unaristocratic degree came purring and wagging about the table, and he indulged them with an impartiality that interested her, playing no favourites, but allotting to each its portion, and serenely chastising the greedy.

"What wonderful impartiality!" she ventured.

"I couldn't do it; I'd be sure to prefer one of them."

"Why entertain preference for anything or anybody?"

"That's nonsense."

"No; it's sense. Because, if anything happens to one, there are the others to console you. It's pleasanter to like impartially."

She was occupied with her fruit cup; presently she glanced up at him:

"Is that your policy?"

"Isn't it a safe one?"

"Yes. Is it yours?"

"Wisdom suggests it to me—has always urged it. I'm not sure that it always works. For example, I prefer champagne to milk, but I try not to."

"You always contrive to twist sense into nonsense."

"You don't mind, do you?"

"No; but don't you ever take anything seriously?"

"Myself."

"I'm afraid you don't."

"Indeed, I do! See how my financial mishaps sent me flying to you for help!"

She said: "You don't even take seriously what you call your financial mishaps."

"But I take the remedy for them most reverently and most thankfully."

"The remedy?"

"You."

A slight colour stained her cheeks; for she did not see just how to avoid the footing they had almost reached—the understanding which, somehow, had been impending from the moment they met. Intuition had warned her against it. And now here it was.

How could she have avoided it, when it was perfectly evident from the first that he found her interesting—that his voice and intonation and bearing were always subtly offering friendship, no matter what he said to her, whether in jest or earnest, in light-hearted idleness or in all the decorum of the perfunctory and commonplace.

To have made more out of it than was in it would have been no sillier than to priggishly discountenance his harmless good humour. To be prim would have been ridiculous. Besides, everything innocent in her found an instinctive pleasure, even in her own misgivings concerning this man and the unsettled problem of her personal relations with him—unsolved with her, at least; but he appeared to have settled it for himself.

As they walked back to the armoury together, she was trying to think it out; and she concluded that she might dare be toward him as unconcernedly friendly as he would ever think of being toward her. And it gave her a little thrill of pride to feel that she was equipped to carry through her part in a light, gay, ephemeral friendship with one belonging to a world about which she knew nothing at all.

That ought to be her attitude—friendly, spirited, pretending to a savoir faire only surmised by her own good taste—lest he find her stupid and narrow, ignorant and dull. And it occurred to her very forcibly that she would not like that.

So—let him admire her.

His motives, perhaps, were as innocent as hers. Let him say the unexpected and disconcerting things it amused him to say. She knew well enough how to parry them, once her mind was made up not to entirely ignore them; and that would be much better. That, no doubt, was the manner in which women of his own world met the easy badinage of men; and she determined to let him discover that she was interesting if she chose to be.

She had produced her note-book and pencil when they entered the armoury. He carried Grenville's celebrated monograph, and she consulted it from time to time, bending her dainty head beside his shoulder, and turning the pages of the volume with a smooth and narrow hand that fascinated him.

From time to time, too, she made entries in her note-book, such as: "Armet, Spanish, late XV century. Tilting harness probably made by Helmschmid; espaliers, manteau d'armes, coude, left cuisse and colleret missing. War armour, Milanese, XIV century; probably made by the Negrolis; rere-brace, gorget, rondel missing; sword made probably by Martinez, Toledo. Armour made in Germany, middle of XVI century, probably designed by Diego de Arroyo; cuisses laminated."

They stopped before a horseman, clad from head to spurs in superb mail. On a ground of blackened steel the pieces were embossed with gold grotesqueries; the cuirass was formed by overlapping horizontal plates, the three upper ones composing a gorget of solid gold. Nymphs, satyrs, gods, goddesses and cupids in exquisite design and composition framed the "lorica"; cuisses and tassettes carried out the lorica pattern; coudes, arm-guards, and genouillères were dolphin masks, gilded.

"Parade armour," she said under her breath, "not war armour, as it has been labelled. It is armour de luxe, and probably royal, too. Do you see the collar of the Golden Fleece on the gorget? And there hangs the fleece itself, borne by two cupids as a canopy for Venus rising from the sea. That is probably Sigman's XVI century work. Is it not royally magnificent!"

"Lord! What a lot of lore you seem to have acquired!" he said.

"But I was trained to this profession by the ablest teacher in America—" her voice fell charmingly, "—by my father. Do you wonder that I know a little about it?"

They moved on in silence to where a man-at-arms stood leaning both clasped hands over the gilded pommel of a sword.

She said quickly: "That sword belongs to parade armour! How stupid to give it to this pikeman! Don't you see? The blade is diamond sectioned; Horn of Solingen's mark is on the ricasse. And, oh, what a wonderful hilt! It is a miracle!"

The hilt was really a miracle; carved in gold relief, Italian renaissance style, the guard centre was decorated with black arabesques on a gold ground; quillons curved down, ending in cupid's heads of exquisite beauty.

The guard was engraved with a cartouche enclosing the Three Graces; and from it sprang a beautiful counter-guard formed out of two lovely Caryatids united. The grip was made of heliotrope amethyst inset with gold; the pommel constructed by two volutes which encompassed a tiny naked nymph with emeralds for her eyes.

"What a masterpiece!" she breathed. "It can be matched only in the Royal Armoury of Madrid."

"Have you been abroad, Miss Nevers?"

"Yes, several times with my father. It was part of my education in business."

He said: "Yours is a French name?"

"Father was French."

"He must have been a very cultivated man."

"Self-cultivated."

"Perhaps," he said, "there once was a de written before 'Nevers.'"

She laughed: "No. Father's family were always bourgeois shopkeepers—as I am."

He looked at the dainty girl beside him, with her features and slender limbs and bearing of an aristocrat.

"Too bad," he said, pretending disillusion. "I expected you'd tell me how your ancestors died on the scaffold, remarking in laudable chorus, 'Vive le Roi!'"

She laughed and sparkled deliciously: "Alas, no, monsieur. But, ma foi! Some among them may have worked the guillotine for Sanson or drummed for Santerre.

"You seem to me to symbolise all the grace and charm that perished on the Place de Grève."

She laughed: "Look again, and see if it is not their Nemesis I more closely resemble."

And as she said it so gaily, an odd idea struck him that she did embody something less obvious, something more vital, than the symbol of an aristocratic régime perishing en masse against the blood-red sky of Paris.

He did not know what it was about her that seemed to symbolise all that is forever young and fresh and imperishable. Perhaps it was only the evolution of the real world he saw in her opening into blossom and disclosing such as she to justify the darkness and woe of the long travail.

She had left him standing alone with Grenville's book open in his hands, and was now examining a figure wearing a coat of fine steel mail, with a black corselet protecting back and breast decorated with horizontal bands.

"Do you notice the difference?" she asked. "In German armour the bands are vertical. This is Milanese, and I think the Negrolis made it. See how exquisitely the morion is decorated with these lions' heads in gold for cheek pieces, and these bands of gold damascene over the skull-piece, that meet to form Minerva's face above the brow! I'm sure it's the Negrolis work. Wait! Ah, here is the inscription! 'P. Iacobi et Fratr Negroli Faciebant MDXXXIX.' Bring me Grenville's book, please."

She took it, ran over the pages rapidly, found what she wanted, and then stepped forward and laid her white hand on the shoulder of another grim, mailed figure.

"This is foot-armour," she said, "and does not belong with that morion. It's neither Milanese nor yet of Augsburg make; it's Italian, but who made it I don't know. You see it's a superb combination of parade armour and war mail, with all the gorgeous design of the former and the smoothness and toughness of the latter. Really, Mr. Desboro, this investigation is becoming exciting. I never before saw such a suit of foot-armour."

"Perhaps it belonged to the catcher of some ancient baseball club," he suggested.

She turned, laughing, but exasperated: "I'm not going to let you remain near me," she said. "You annihilate every atom of romance; you are an anachronism here, anyway."

"I know it; but you fit in delightfully with tournaments and pageants and things——"

"Go up on that ladder and sit!" resolutely pointing.

He went. Perched aloft, he lighted a cigarette and surveyed the prospect.

"Mark Twain killed all this sort of thing for me," he observed.

She said indignantly: "It's the only thing I never have forgiven him."

"He told the truth."

"I know it—I know it. But, oh, how could he write what he did about King Arthur's Court! And what is the use of truth, anyway, unless it leaves us ennobling illusions?"

Ennobling illusions! She did not know it; but except for them she never would have existed, nor others like her that are yet to come in myriads.

Desboro waved his cigarette gracefully and declaimed:

"The knights are dust,

Their good swords bust;

Their souls are up the spout we trust—"

"Mr. Desboro!"

"Mademoiselle?"

"That silly parody on a noble verse is not humorous."

"Truth seldom is. The men who wore those suits of mail were everything that nobody now admires—brutal, selfish, ruthless——"

"Mr. Desboro!"

"Mademoiselle?"

"Are there not a number of such gentlemen still existing on earth?"

"New York's full of them," he admitted cheerfully, "but they conceal what they really are on account of the police."

"Is that all that five hundred years has taught men—concealment?"

"Yes, and five thousand," he muttered; but said aloud: "It hasn't anything to do with admiring the iron hats and clothes they wore. If you'll let me come down I'll admire 'em——"

"No."

"I want to carry your book for you."

"No."

"—And listen to everything you say about the vertical stripes on their Dutch trousers——"

"Very well," she consented, laughing; "you may descend and examine these gold inlaid and checkered trousers. They were probably made for a fashionable dandy by Alonso Garcia, five hundred years ago; and you will observe that they are still beautifully creased."

So they passed on, side by side, while she sketched out her preliminary work. And sometimes he was idly flippant and irresponsible, and sometimes she thrilled unexpectedly at his quick, warm response to some impulsive appeal that he share her admiration.

Under the careless surface, she divined a sort of perverse intelligence; she was certain that what appealed to her he, also, understood when he chose to; because he understood so much—much that she had not even imagined—much of life, and of the world, and of the men and women in it. But, having lived a life so full, so different from her own, perhaps his interest was less easily aroused; perhaps it might be even a little fatigued by the endless pageant moving with him amid scenes of brightness and happiness which seemed to her as far away from herself and as unreal as scenes in the painted arras hanging on the walls.

They had been speaking of operas in which armour, incorrectly designed and worn, was tolerated by public ignorance; and, thinking of the "horseshoe," where all that is wealthy, and intelligent, and wonderful, and aristocratic in New York is supposed to congregate, she had mentally placed him there among those elegant and distant young men who are to be seen sauntering from one gilded box to another, or, gracefully posed, decorating and further embellishing boxes already replete with jeweled and feminine beauty; or in the curtained depths, mysterious silhouettes motionless against the dull red glow.

And, if those gold-encrusted boxes had been celestial balconies, full of blessed damosels leaning over heaven's edge, they would have seemed no farther away, no more accessible to her, than they seemed from where she sometimes sat or stood, all alone, to listen to Farrar and Caruso.

The light in the armoury was growing a little dim. She bent more closely over her note-book, the printed pages of Mr. Grenville, and the shimmering, inlaid, and embossed armour.

"Shall we have tea?" he suggested.

"Tea? Oh, thank you, Mr. Desboro; but when the light fails, I'll have to go."

It was failing fast. She used the delicate tips of her fingers more often in examining engraved, inlaid, and embossed surfaces.

"I never had electricity put into the armoury," he said. "I'm sorry now—for your sake."

"I'm sorry, too. I could have worked until six."

"There!" he said, laughing. "You have admitted it! What are you going to do for nearly two hours if you don't take tea? Your train doesn't leave until six. Did you propose to go to the station and sit there?"

Her confused laughter was very sweet, and she admitted that she had nothing to do after the light failed except to fold her hands and wait for the train.

"Then won't you have tea?"

"I'd—rather not!"

He said: "You could take it alone in your room if you liked—and rest a little. Mrs. Quant will call you."

She looked up at him after a moment, and her cheeks were very pink and her eyes brilliant.

"I'd rather take it with you, Mr. Desboro. Why shouldn't I say so?"

No words came to him, and not much breath, so totally unexpected was her reply.

Still looking at him, the faint smile fading into seriousness, she repeated:

"Why shouldn't I say so? Is there any reason? You know better than I what a girl alone may do. And I really would like to have some tea—and have it with you."

He didn't smile; he was too clever—perhaps too decent.

"It's quite all right," he said. "We'll have it served in the library where there's a fine fire."

So they slowly crossed the armoury and traversed the hallway, where she left him for a moment and ran up stairs to her room. When she rejoined him in the library, he noticed that the insurgent lock of hair had been deftly tucked in among its lustrous comrades; but the first shake of her head dislodged it again, and there it was, threatening him, as usual, from its soft, warm ambush against her cheek.

"Can't you do anything with it?" he asked, sympathetically, as she seated herself and poured the tea.

"Do anything with what?"

"That lock of hair. It's loose again, and it will do murder some day."

She laughed with scarcely a trace of confusion, and handed him his cup.

"That's the first thing I noticed about you," he added.

"That lock of hair? I can't do anything with it. Isn't it horribly messy?"

"It's dangerous."

"How absurd!"

"Are you ever known as 'Stray Lock' among your intimates?"

"I should think not," she said scornfully. "It sounds like a children's picture-book story."

"But you look like one."

"Mr. Desboro!" she protested. "Haven't you any common sense?"

"You look," he said reflectively, "as though you came from the same bookshelf as 'Gold Locks,' 'The Robber Kitten,' and 'A Princess Far Away,' and all those immortal volumes of the 'days that are no more.' Would you mind if I label you 'Stray Lock,' and put you on the shelf among the other immortals?"

Her frank laughter rang out sweetly:

"I very much object to being labeled and shelved—particularly shelved."

"I'll promise to read you every day——"

"No, thank you!"

"I'll promise to take you everywhere with me——"

"In your pocket? No, thank you. I object to being either shelved or pocketed—to be consulted at pleasure—or when you're bored."

They both had been laughing a good deal, and were slightly excited by their game of harmless double entendre. But now, perhaps it was becoming a trifle too obvious, and Jacqueline checked herself to glance back mentally and see how far she had gone along the path of friendship.

She could not determine; for the path has many twists and turnings, and she had sped forward lightly and swiftly, and was still conscious of the exhilaration of the pace in his gay and irresponsible company.

Her smile changed and died out; she leaned back in her leather chair, gazing absently at the fiery reflections crimsoning the andirons on the hearth, and hearing afar, on some distant roof, the steady downpour of the winter rain.

Subtly the quiet and warmth of the room invaded her with a sense of content, not due, perhaps, to them alone. And dreamily conscious that this might be so, she lifted her eyes and looked across the table at him.

"I wonder," she said, "if this is all right?"

"What?"

"Our—situation—here."

"Situations are what we make them."

"But," she asked candidly, "could you call this a business situation?"

He laughed unrestrainedly, and finally she ventured to smile, secretly reassured.

"'Are business and friendship incompatible?'"

"Are business and friendship incompatible?" he inquired.

"I don't know. Are they? I have to be careful in the shop, with younger customers and clerks. To treat them with more than pleasant civility would spoil them for business. My father taught me that. He served in the French Army."

"Do you think," he said gravely, "that you are spoiling me for business purposes?"

She smiled: "I was thinking—wondering whether you did not more accurately represent the corps of officers and I the line. I am only a temporary employee of yours, Mr. Desboro, and some day you may be angry at what I do and you may say, 'Tonnerre de Dieu!' to me—which I wouldn't like if we were friends, but which I'd otherwise endure."

"We're friends already; what are you going to do about it?"

She knew it was so now, for better or worse, and she looked at him shyly, a little troubled by what the end of this day had brought her.

Silent, absent-eyed, she began to wonder what such men as he really thought of a girl of her sort. It could happen that his attitude toward her might become like that of the only men of his kind she had ever encountered—wealthy clients of her father, young and old, and all of them inclined to offer her attentions which instinct warned her to ignore.

As for Desboro, even from the beginning she felt that his attitude toward her depended upon herself; and, warranted or not, this sense of security with him now, left her leisure to study him. And she concluded that probably he was like the other men of his class whom she had known—a receptive opportunist, inevitably her antagonist at heart, but not to be feared except under deliberate provocation from her. And that excuse he would never have.

Aware of his admiration almost from the very first, perplexed, curious, uncertain, and disturbed by turns, she was finally convinced that the matter lay entirely with her; that she might accept a little, venture a little in safety; and, perfectly certain of herself, enjoy as much of what his friendship offered as her own clear wits and common sense permitted. For she had found, so far, no metal in any man unalloyed. Two years' experience alone with men had educated her; and whatever the alloy in Desboro might be that lowered his value, she thought it less objectionable than the similar amalgam out of which were fashioned the harmless youths in whose noisy company she danced, and dined, and bathed, and witnessed Broadway "shows"; the Eddies and Joes of the metropolis, replicas in mind and body of clothing advertisements in street cars.

Her blue eyes, wandering from the ruddy andirons, were arrested by the clock. What had happened? Was the clock still going? She listened, and heard it ticking.

"Is that the right time?" she demanded incredulously.

He said, so low she could scarcely hear him: "Yes, Stray Lock. Must I close the story book and lay it away until another day?"

She rose, brushing the bright strand from her cheek; he stood up, pulled the tassel of an old-time bell rope, and, when the butler came, ordered the car.

She went away to her room, where Mrs. Quant swathed her in rain garments and veils, and secretly pressed into her hand a bottle containing "a suffusion" warranted to discourage any insidious advances of typod.

"A spoonful before meals, dearie," she whispered hoarsely; "and don't tell Mr. James—he'd be that disgusted with me for doin' of a Christian duty. I'll have some of my magic drops ready when you come to-morrow, and you can just lock the door and set and rock and enj'y them onto a lump of sugar."

A little dismayed, but contriving to look serious, Jacqueline thanked her and fled. Desboro put her into the car and climbed in beside her.

"You needn't, you know," she protested. "There are no highwaymen, are there?"

"None more to be dreaded than myself."

"Then why do you go to the station with me?"

He did not answer. She presently settled into her corner, and he wrapped her in the fur robe. Neither spoke; the lamplight flashed ahead through the falling rain; all else was darkness—the widest world of darkness, it seemed to her fancy, that she ever looked out upon, for it seemed to leave this man and herself alone in the centre of things.

Conscious of him beside her, she was curiously content not to look at him or to disturb the silence encompassing them. The sense of speed, the rush through obscurity, seemed part of it—part of a confused and pleasurable irresponsibility.

Later, standing under the dripping eaves of the station platform with him, watching the approaching headlight of the distant locomotive, she said:

"You have made it a very delightful day for me. I wanted to thank you."

He was silent; the distant locomotive whistled, and the vista of wet rails began to glisten red in the swift approach.

"I don't want you to go to town alone on that train," he said abruptly.

"What?" in utter surprise.

"Will you let me go with you, Miss Nevers?"

"Nonsense! I wander about everywhere alone. Please don't spoil it all. Don't even go aboard to find a seat for me."

The long train thundered by, brakes gripping, slowed, stopped. She sprang aboard, turned on the steps and offered her hand:

"Good-bye, Mr. Desboro."

"To-morrow?" he asked.

"Yes."

They exchanged no further words; she stood a moment on the platform, as the cars glided slowly past him and on into the rainy night. All the way to New York she remained motionless in the corner of the seat, her cheek resting against her gloved palm, thinking of what had happened—closing her blue eyes, sometimes, to bring it nearer and make more real a day of life already ended.

CHAPTER IV

When the doorbell rang the maid of all work pushed the button and stood waiting at the top of the stairs. There was a pause, a moment's whispering, then light footsteps flying through the corridor, and:

"Where on earth have you been for a week?" asked Cynthia Lessler, coming into Jacqueline's little parlour, where the latter sat knitting a white wool skating jacket for herself.

Jacqueline laid aside the knitting and greeted her visitor with a warm, quick embrace.

"Oh, I've been everywhere," she said. "Out in Westchester, mostly. To-day being Sunday, I'm at home."

"What were you doing in the country, sweetness?"

"Business."

"What kind?"

"Oh, cataloguing a collection. Take the armchair and sit near the stove, dear. And here are the chocolates. Put your feet on the fender as I do. It was frightfully cold in Westchester yesterday—everything frozen solid—and we— I skated all over the flooded fields and swamps. It was simply glorious, Cynthia———"

"I thought you were out there on business," remarked Cynthia dryly.

"I was. I merely took an hour at noon for luncheon."

"Did you?"

"Certainly. Even a bricklayer has an hour at noon to himself."

"Whose collection are you cataloguing?"

"It belongs to a Mr. Desboro," said Jacqueline carelessly.

"Where is it?"

"In his house—a big, old house about five miles from the station———"

"How do you get there?"

"They send a car for me———"

"Who?"

"They—Mr. Desboro."

"They? Is he plural?"

"Don't be foolish," said Jacqueline. "It is his car and his collection, and I'm having a perfectly good time with both."

"And with him, too? Yes?"

"If you knew him you wouldn't talk that way."

"I know who he is."

"Do you?" said Jacqueline calmly.

"Yes, I do. He's the 'Jim' Desboro whose name you see in the fashionable columns. I know something about that young man," she added emphatically.

Jacqueline looked up at her with dawning displeasure. Cynthia, undisturbed, bit into a chocolate and waved one pretty hand:

"Read the Tattler, as I do, and you'll see what sort of a man your young man is."

"I don't care to read such a——"

"I do. It tells you funny things about society. Every week or two there's something about him. You can't exactly understand it—they put it in a funny way—but you can guess. Besides, he's always going around town with Reggie Ledyard, and Stuyve Van Alstyne, and—Jack Cairns——"

"Don't speak that way—as though you usually lunched with them. I hate it."

"How do you know I don't lunch with some of them? Besides everybody calls them Reggie, and Stuyve, and Jack——"

"Everybody except their mothers, probably. I don't want to hear about them, anyway."

"Why not, darling?"

"Because you and I don't know them and never will——"

Cynthia said maliciously: "You may meet them through your friend, Jimmy Desboro——"

"That is the limit!" exclaimed Jacqueline, flushing; and her pretty companion leaned back in her armchair and laughed until Jacqueline's unwilling smile began to glimmer in her wrath-darkened eyes.

"Don't torment me, Cynthia," she said. "You know quite well that it's a business matter with me entirely."

"Was it a business matter with that Dawley man? You had to get me to go with you into that den of his whenever you went at all."

Jacqueline shrugged and resumed her knitting: "What a horrid thing he was," she murmured.

Cynthia assented philosophically: "But most men bother a girl sooner or later," she concluded. "You don't read about it in novels, but it's true. Go down town and take dictation for a living. It's an education in how to look out for yourself."

"It's a rotten state of things," said Jacqueline under her breath.

"Yes. It's funny, too. So many men are that way. What do they care? Do you suppose we'd be that way, too, if we were men?"

"'There are nice men, too'"

"No. There are nice men, too."

"Yes—dead ones."

"Nonsense!"

"With very few exceptions, Jacqueline. There are horrid, horrid ones, and nice, horrid ones, and dead ones and dead ones—but only a few nice, nice ones. I've known some. You think your Mr. Desboro is one, don't you?"

"I haven't thought about him———"

"Honestly, Jacqueline?"

"I tell you I haven't! He's nice to me. That's all I know."

"Is he too nice?"

"No. Besides, he's under his own roof. And it depends on a girl, anyway."

"Not always. If we behave ourselves we're dead ones; if we don't we'd better be. Isn't it a rotten deal, Jacqueline! Just one fresh man after another dropped into the discards because he gets too gay. And being employed by the kind who'd never marry us spoils us for the others. You could marry one of your clients, I suppose, but I never could in a million years."

"You and I will never marry such men," said Jacqueline coolly. "Perhaps we wouldn't if they asked us."

"You might. You're educated and bright, and—you look the part, with all the things you know—and your trips to Europe—and the kind of beauty yours is. Why not? If I were you," she added, "I'd kill a man who thought me good enough to hold hands with, but not good enough to marry."

"I don't hold hands," observed Jacqueline scornfully.

"I do. I've done it when it was all right; and I've done it when I had no business to; and the chances are I'll do it again without getting hurt. And then I'll finally marry the sort of man you call Ed," she added disgustedly.

Jacqueline laughed, and looked intently at her: "You're so pretty, Cynthia— and so silly sometimes."

Cynthia stretched her young figure full length in the chair, yawning and crooking both arms back under her curly brown head. Her eyes, too, were brown, and had in them always a half-veiled languor that few men could encounter undisturbed.

"A week ago," she said, "you told me over the telephone that you would be at the dance. I never laid eyes on you."

"I came home too tired. It was my first day at Silverwood. I overdid it, I suppose."

"Silverwood?"

"Where I go to business in Westchester," she explained patiently.

"Oh, Mr. Desboro's place!" with laughing malice.

"Yes, Mr. Desboro's place."

The hint of latent impatience in Jacqueline's voice was not lost on Cynthia; and she resumed her tormenting inquisition:

"How long is it going to take you to catalogue Mr. Desboro's collection?"

"I have several weeks' work, I think—I don't know exactly."

"All winter, perhaps?"

"Possibly."

"Is he always there, darling?"

Jacqueline was visibly annoyed: "He has happened to be, so far. I believe he is going South very soon—if that interests you."

"'Phone me when he goes," retorted Cynthia, unbelievingly.

"What makes you say such things!" exclaimed Jacqueline. "I tell you he isn't that kind of a man."

"Read the Tattler, dearest!"

"I won't."

"Don't you ever read it?"

"No. Why should I?"

"Curiosity."

"I haven't any."

Cynthia laughed incredulously:

"People who have no curiosity are either idiots or they have already found out. Now, you are not an idiot."

Jacqueline smiled: "And I haven't found out, either."

"Then you're just as full of curiosity as the rest of us."

"Not of unworthy curiosity——"

"I never knew a good person who wasn't. I'm good, am I not, Jacqueline?"

"Of course."

"Well, then, I'm full of all kinds of curiosities—worthy and unworthy. I want to know about everything!"

"Everything good."

"Good and bad. God lets both exist. I want to know about them."

"Why be curious about what is bad? It doesn't concern us."

"If you know what concerns you only, you'll never know anything. Now, when I read a newspaper I read about fashionable weddings, millionaires, shows, murders—I read everything—not because I'm going to be fashionably married, or become a millionaire or a murderer, but because all these things exist and happen, and I want to know all about them because I'm not an idiot, and I haven't already found out. And so that's why I buy the Tattler whenever I have five cents to spend on it!"

"It's a pity you're not more curious about things worth while," commented Jacqueline serenely.

Cynthia reddened: "Dear, I haven't the education or brain to be interested in the things that occupy you."

"I didn't mean that," protested Jacqueline, embarrassed. "I only——"

"I know, dear. You are too sweet to say it; but it's true. The bunch you play with knows it. We all realise that you are way ahead of us—that you're different——"

"Please don't say that—or think it."

"But it's true. You really belong with the others—" she made a gay little gesture—"over there in the Fifth Avenue district, where art gets gay with fashion; where lady highbrows wear tiaras; where the Jims and Jacks and Reggies float about and hand each other new ones between quarts; where you belong, darling—wherever you finally land!"

Jacqueline was laughing: "But I don't wish to land there! I never wanted to."

"All girls do! We all dream about it!"

"Here is one girl who really doesn't. Of course, I'd like to have a few friends of that kind. I'd rather like to visit houses where nobody has to think of money, and where young people are jolly, and educated, and dress well, and talk about interesting things——"

"Dear, we all would like it. That's what I'm saying. Only there's a chance for you because you know something—but none for us. We understand that perfectly well—and we dream on all the same. We'd miss a lot if we didn't dream."

Jacqueline said mockingly: "I'll invite you to my Fifth Avenue residence the minute I marry what you call a Reggie."

"I'll come if you'll stand for me. I'm not afraid of any Reggie in the bench show!"

They laughed; Cynthia stretched out a lazy hand for another chocolate; Jacqueline knitted, the smile still hovering on her scarlet lips.

Bending over her work, she said: "You won't misunderstand when I tell you how much I enjoy being at Silverwood, and how nice Mr. Desboro has been."

"Has been."

"Is, and surely will continue to be," insisted Jacqueline tranquilly. "Shall I tell you about Silverwood?"

Cynthia nodded.

"Well, then, Mr. Desboro has such a funny old housekeeper there, who gives me 'magic drops' on lumps of sugar. The drops are aromatic and harmless, so I take them to please her. And he has an old, old butler, who is too feeble to be very useful; and an old, old armourer, who comes once a week and potters about with a bit of chamois; and a parlour maid who is sixty and wears glasses; and a laundress still older. And a whole troop of dogs and cats come to luncheon with us. Sometimes the butler goes to sleep in the pantry, and Mr. Desboro and I sit and talk. And if he doesn't wake up, Mr. Desboro hunts about for somebody to wait on us. Of course there are other servants there, and farmers and gardeners, too. Mr. Desboro has a great deal of land. And so," she chattered on quite happily and irrelevantly, "we go skating for half an hour after lunch before I resume my cataloguing. He skates very well; we are learning to waltz on skates———"

"Who does the teaching?"

"He does. I don't skate very well; and unless it were for him I'd have such tumbles! And once we went sleighing—that is, he drove me to the station—in rather a roundabout way. And the country was so beautiful! And the stars—oh, millions and millions, Cynthia! It was as cold as the North Pole, but I loved it —and I had on his other fur coat and gloves. He is very nice to me. I wanted you to understand the sort of man he is."

"Perhaps he is the original hundredth man," remarked Cynthia skeptically.

"Most men are hundredth men when the nine and ninety girls behave themselves. It's the hundredth girl who makes the nine and ninety men horrid."

"That's what you believe, is it?"

"I do."

"Dream on, dear." She went to a glass, pinned her pretty hat, slipped into the smart fur coat that Jacqueline held for her, and began to draw on her gloves.

"Can't you stay to dinner," asked Jacqueline.

"Thank you, sweetness, but I'm dining at the Beaux Arts."

"With any people I know?"

"You don't know that particular 'people'," said Cynthia, smiling, "but you know a friend of his."

"Who?"

"Mr. Desboro."

"Really!" she said, colouring.

Cynthia frowned at her: "Don't become sentimental over that young man!"

"No, of course not."

"Because I don't think he's very much good."

"He is—but I won't," explained Jacqueline laughing. "I know quite well how to take care of myself."

"Do you?"

"Yes; don't you?"

"I—don't—know."

"Cynthia! Of course you know!"

"Do I? Well, perhaps I do. Perhaps all girls know how to take care of themselves. But sometimes—especially when their home life is the limit——" She hesitated, slowly twisting a hairpin through the buttonhole of one glove. Then she buttoned it decisively. "When things got so bad at home two years ago, and I went with that show—you didn't see it—you were in mourning— but it ran on Broadway all winter. And I met one or two Reggies at suppers, and another man—the same sort—only his name happened to be Jack—and I want to tell you it was hard work not to like him."

Jacqueline stood, slim and straight, and silent, listening unsmilingly.

Cynthia went on leisurely:

"He was a friend of Mr. Desboro—the same kind of man, I suppose. That's why I read the Tattler—to see what they say about him."

"Wh-what do they say?"

"Oh, things—funny sorts of things, about his being attentive to this girl, and being seen frequently with that girl. I don't know what they mean exactly—they always make it sound queer—as though all the men and women in society are fast. And this man, too—perhaps he is."

"But what do you care, dear?"

"Nothing. It was hard work not to like him. You don't understand how it was; you've always lived at home. But home was hell for me; and I was getting fifteen per; and it grew horribly cold that winter. I had no fire. Besides—it was so hard not to like him. I used to come to see you. Do you remember how I used to come here and cry?"

"I—I thought it was because you had been so unhappy at home."

"Partly. The rest was—the other thing."

"You did like him, then!"

"Not—too much."

"I understand that. But it's over now, isn't it?"

Cynthia stood idly turning her muff between her white-gloved hands.

"Oh, yes," she said, after a moment, "it's over. But I'm thinking how nearly over it was with me, once or twice that winter. I thought I knew how to take care of myself. But a girl never knows, Jacqueline. Cold, hunger, debt, shabby clothes are bad enough; loneliness is worse. Yet, these are not enough, by themselves. But if we like a man, with all that to worry over—then it's pretty hard on us."

"How could you care for a bad man?"

"Bad? Did I say he was? I meant he was like other men. A girl becomes accustomed to men."

"And likes them, notwithstanding?"

"Some of them. It depends. If you like a man you seem to like him anyhow. You may get angry, too, and still like him. There's so much of the child in them. I've learned that. They're bad; but when you like one of them, he seems to belong to you, somehow—badness and all. I must be going, dear."

Still, neither moved; Cynthia idly twirled her muff; Jacqueline, her slender hands clasped behind her, stood gazing silently at the floor.

Cynthia said: "That's the trouble with us all. I'm afraid you like this man,

Desboro. I tell you that he isn't much good; but if you already like him, you'll go on liking him, no matter what I say or what he does. For it's that way with us, Jacqueline. And where in the world would men find a living soul to excuse them if it were not for us? That seems to be about all we're for—to forgive men what they are—and what they do."

"I don't forgive them," said Jacqueline fiercely; "—or women, either."

"Oh, nobody forgives women! But you will find excuses for some man some day—if you like him. I guess even the best of them require it. But the general run of them have got to have excuses made for them, or no woman would stand for her own honeymoon, and marriages would last about a week. Good-bye, dear."

They kissed.

At the head of the stairs outside, Jacqueline kissed her again.

"How is the play going?" she inquired.

"Oh, it's going."

"Is there any chance for you to get a better part?"

"No chance I care to take. Max Schindler is like all the rest of them."

Jacqueline's features betrayed her wonder and disgust, but she said nothing; and presently Cynthia turned and started down the stairs.

"Good-night, dear," she called back, with a gay little flourish of her muff. "They're all alike—only we always forgive the one we care for!"

CHAPTER V

On Monday, Desboro waited all the morning for her, meeting every train. At noon, she had not arrived. Finally, he called up her office and was informed that Miss Nevers had been detained in town on business, and that their Mr. Kirk had telephoned him that morning to that effect.

He asked to speak to Miss Nevers personally; she had gone out, it appeared, and might not return until the middle of the afternoon.

So Desboro went home in his car and summoned Farris, the aged butler, who was pottering about in the greenhouses, which he much preferred to attending to his own business.

"Did anybody telephone this morning?" asked the master.

Farris had forgotten to mention it—was very sorry—and stood like an aged hound, head partly lowered and averted, already blinking under the awaited reprimand. But all Desboro said was:

"Don't do it again, Farris; there are some things I won't overlook."

He sat for a while in the library where a sheaf of her notes lay on the table beside a pile of books—Grenville, Vanderdyne, Herrara's splendid folios—just as she had left them on Saturday afternoon for the long, happy sleigh-ride that ended just in time for him to swing her aboard her train.

He had plenty to do beside sitting there with keen, gray eyes fixed on the pile of manuscript she had left unfinished; he always had plenty to do, and seldom did it.

His first impulse had been to go to town. Her absence was making the place irksome. He went to the long windows and stood there, hands in his pockets, smoking and looking out over the familiar landscape—a rolling country, white with snow, naked branches glittering with ice under the gilded blue of a cloudless sky, and to the north and west, low, wooded mountains—really nothing more than hills, but impressively steep and blue in the distance.

A woodpecker, one of the few feathered winter residents, flickered through the trees, flashed past, and clung to an oak, sticking motionless to the bark for a minute or two, bright eyes inspecting Desboro, before beginning a rapid, jerky exploration for sustenance.

The master of Silverwood watched him, then, hands driven deeper into his pockets, strolled away, glancing aimlessly at familiar objects—the stiff and rather picturesque portraits of his grandparents in the dress of ; the atrocious portraits of his parents in the awful costume of ; his own portrait, life size, mounted on a pony.

He stood looking at the funny little boy, with the half contemptuous, half curious interest which a man in the pride of his strength and youth sometimes feels for the absurdly clothed innocence of what he was. And, as usual when noticing the picture, he made a slight, involuntary effort to comprehend that he had been once like that; and could not.

At the end of the library, better portraits hung—his great-grandmother, by Gilbert Stuart, still fresh-coloured and clear under the dim yellow varnish which veiled but could not wither the delicate complexion and ardent mouth, and the pink rosebud set where the folds of her white kerchief crossed on her breast.

And there was her husband, too, by an unknown or forgotten painter—the sturdy member of the Provincial Assembly, and major in Colonel Thomas's Westchester Regiment—a fine old fellow in his queue-ribbon and powdered hair standing in the conventional fortress port-hole, framed by it, and looking straight out of the picture with eyes so much like Desboro's that it amused people. His easy attitude, too, the idle grace of the posture, irresistibly recalled Desboro, and at the moment more than ever. But he had been a man of vigour and of wit and action; and he was lying out there in the snow, under an old brown headstone embellished with cherubim; and the last of his name lounged here, in sight, from the windows, of the spot where the first house of Desboro in America had stood, and had collapsed amid the flames started by Tarleton's blood-maddened troopers.

To and fro sauntered Desboro, passing, unnoticed, old-time framed engravings of the Desboros in Charles the Second's time, elegant, idle, handsome men in periwigs and half-armour, and all looking out at the world through port-holes with a hint of the race's bodily grace in their half insolent attitudes.

But office and preferment, peace and war, intrigue and plot, vigour and idleness, had narrowed down through the generations into a last inheritance for this young man; and the very last of all the Desboros now idled aimlessly among the phantoms of a race that perhaps had better be extinguished.

He could not make up his mind to go to town or to remain in the vague hope that she might come in the afternoon.

He had plenty to do—if he could make up his mind to begin—accounts to go over, household expenses, farm expenses, stable reports, agents' memoranda concerning tenants and leases, endless lists of necessary repairs. And there was business concerning the estate neglected, taxes, loans, improvements to attend to—the thousand and one details which irritated him to consider; but which, although he maintained an agent in town, must ultimately come to himself for the final verdict.

What he wanted was to be rid of it all—sell everything, pension his father's servants, and be rid of the entire complex business which, he pretended to himself, was slowly ruining him. But he knew in his heart where the trouble lay, and that the carelessness, extravagance, the disinclination for self-denial, the impatient and good-humoured aversion to economy, the profound distaste for financial detail, were steadily wrecking one of the best and one of the last of the old-time Westchester estates.

In his heart he knew, too, that all he wanted was to concentrate sufficient capital to give him the income he thought he needed.

No man ever had the income he thought he needed. And why Desboro required it, he himself didn't know exactly; but he wanted sufficient to keep him comfortable—enough so that he could feel he might do anything he chose, when, how, and where he chose, without fear or care for the future. And no man ever lived to enjoy such a state of mind, or to do these things with impunity.

But Desboro's mind was bent on it; he seated himself at the library table and began to figure it out. Land in Westchester brought high prices—not exactly in that section, but near enough to make his acreage valuable. Then, the house, stable, garage, greenhouses, the three farms, barns, cattle houses, water supply, the timber, power sites, meadow, pasture—all these ought to make a pretty figure. And he jotted it down for the hundredth time in the last two years.

Then there was the Desboro collection. That ought to bring——

"And he sat thinking of Jacqueline Nevers"

He hesitated, his pencil finally fell on the table, rolled to the edge and dropped; and he sat thinking of Jacqueline Nevers, and of the week that had ended as the lights of her train faded far away into the winter night.

He sat so still and so long that old Farris came twice to announce luncheon. After a silent meal in company with the dogs and cats of low degree, he lighted a cigarette and went back into the library to resume his meditations.

Whatever they were, they ceased abruptly whenever the distant telephone rang, and he waited almost breathlessly for somebody to come and say that he was wanted on the wire. But the messages must have been to the cook or butler, from butcher, baker, and gentlemen of similar professions, for nobody disturbed him, and he was left free to sink back into the leather corner of the lounge and continue his meditations. Once the furtive apparition of Mrs. Quant disturbed him, hovering ominously at the library door, bearing tumbler and spoon.

"I won't take it," he said decisively.

There was a silence, then:

"Isn't the young lady coming, Mr. James?"

"I don't know. No, probably not to-day."

"Is—is the child sick?" she stammered.

"No, of course not. I expect she'll be here in the morning."

She was not there in the morning. Mr. Mirk, the little old salesman in the silk skull-cap, telephoned to Farris that Miss Nevers was again detained in town on business at Mr. Clydesdale's, and that she might employ a Mr. Sissly to continue her work at Silverwood, if Mr. Desboro did not object. Mr. Desboro was to call her up at three o'clock if he desired further information.

Desboro went into the library and sat down. For a while his idle reflections, uncontrolled, wandered around the main issue, errant satellites circling a central thought which was slowly emerging from chaos and taking definite weight and shape. And the thought was of Jacqueline Nevers.

Why was he waiting here until noon to talk to this girl? Why was he here at all? Why had he not gone South with the others? A passing fancy might be enough to arouse his curiosity; but why did not the fancy pass? What did he want to say to her? What did he want of her? Why was he spending time thinking about her—disarranging his routine and habits to be here when she came? What did he want of her? She was agreeable to talk to, interesting to watch, pretty, attractive. Did he want her friendship? To what end? He'd never see her anywhere unless he sought her out; he would never meet her in any circle to which he had been accustomed, respectable or otherwise. Besides, for conversation he preferred men to women.

What did he want with her or her friendship—or her blue eyes and bright hair —or the slim, girlish grace of her? What was there to do? How many more weeks did he intend to idle about at her heels, follow her, look at her, converse with her, make a habit of her until, now, he found that to suddenly break the habit of only a week's indulgence was annoying him!

And suppose the habit were to grow. Into what would it grow? And how unpleasant would it be to break when, in the natural course of events, circumstances made the habit inconvenient?

And, always, the main, central thought was growing, persisting. What did he want of her? He was not in love with her any more than he was always lightly in love with feminine beauty. Besides, if he were, what would it mean? Another affair, with all its initial charm and gaiety, its moments of frivolity, its moments of seriousness, its sudden crisis, its combats, perplexities, irresolution, the faint thrill of its deeper significance startling both to clearer vision; and then the end, whatever it might be, light or solemn, irresponsible or care-ridden, gay or sombre, for one or the other.

What did he want? Did he wish to disturb her tranquility? Was he trying to awaken her to some response? And what did he offer her to respond to? The flattery of his meaningless attentions, or the honour of falling in love with a Desboro, whose left hand only would be offered to support both slim white hands of hers?

He ought to have gone South, and he knew it, now. Last week he had told himself—and her occasionally—that he was going South in a week. And here he was, his head on his hands and his elbows on the table, looking vacantly at the pile of manuscript she had left there, and thinking of the things that should not happen to them both.

And who the devil was this fellow Sissly? Why had she suddenly changed her mind and suggested a creature named Sissly? Why didn't she finish the cataloguing herself? She had been enthusiastic about it. Besides, she had enjoyed the skating and sleighing, and the luncheons and teas, and the cats and dogs—and even Mrs. Quant. She had said so, too. And now she was too busy to come any more.

Had he done anything? Had he been remiss, or had he ventured too many attentions? He couldn't recall having done anything except to show her plainly enough that he enjoyed being with her. Nor had she concealed her bright pleasure in his companionship. And they had become such good comrades, understanding each other's moods so instinctively now—and they had really found such unfeigned amusement in each other that it seemed a pity—a pity

"Damn it," he said, "if she cares no more about it than that, she can send Sissly, and I'll go South!"

But the impatience of hurt vanity died away; the desire to see her grew; the habit of a single week was already unpleasant to break. And it would be unpleasant to try to forget her, even among his own friends, even in the South, or in drawing-rooms, or at the opera, or at dances, or in any of his haunts and in any sort of company.

He might forget her if he had only known her better, discovered more of her real self, unveiled a little of her deeper nature. There was so much unexplored —so much that interested him, mainly, perhaps, because he had not discovered it. For theirs had been the lightest and gayest of friendships, with nothing visible to threaten a deeper entente; merely, on her part, a happy enjoyment and a laughing parrying in the eternal combat that never entirely ends, even when it means nothing. And on his side it had been the effortless attentions of a man aware of her young and unspoiled charm—conscious of an unusual situation which always fascinates all men.

He had had no intention, no idea, no policy except to drift as far as the tides of destiny carried him in her company. The situation was agreeable; if it became less so, he could take to the oars and row where he liked.

But the tides had carried him to the edge of waters less clear; he was vaguely aware of it now, aware, too, that troubled seas lay somewhere behind the veil.

The library clock struck three times. He got up and went to the telephone booth. Miss Nevers was there; would speak to him if he could wait a moment. He waited. Finally, a far voice called, greeting him pleasantly, and explaining that matters which antedated her business at Silverwood had demanded her personal attention in town. To his request for particulars, she said that she had work to do among the jades and Chinese porcelains belonging to a Mr. Clydesdale.

"I know him," said Desboro curtly. "When do you finish?"

"I have finished for the present. Later there is further work to be done at Mr. Clydesdale's. I had to make certain arrangements before I went to you—being already under contract to Mr. Clydesdale, and at his service when he wanted me."

There was a silence. Then he asked her when she was coming to Silverwood.

"Did you not receive my message?" she asked.

"About—what's his name? Sissly? Yes, I did, but I don't want him. I want you or nobody!"

"You are unreasonable, Mr. Desboro. Lionel Sissly is a very celebrated connoisseur."

"Don't you want to come?"

"I have so many matters here——"

"Don't you want to?" he persisted.

"Why, of course, I'd like to. It is most interesting work. But Mr. Sissly——"

"Oh, hang Mr. Sissly! Do you suppose he interests me? You said that this work might take you weeks. You said you loved it. You apparently expected to be busy with it until it was finished. Now, you propose to send a man called Sissly! Why?"

"Don't you know that I have other things——"

"What have I done, Miss Nevers?"

"I don't understand you."

"What have I done to drive you away?"

"How absurd! Nothing! And you've been so kind to me——"

"You've been kind to me. Why are you no longer?"

"I—it's a question—of business—matters which demand——"

"Will you come once more?"

No reply.

"Will you?" he repeated.

"Is there any reason——"

"Yes."

Another pause, then:

"Yes, I'll come—if there's a reason——"

"When?"

"To-morrow?"

"Do you promise?"

"Yes."

"Then I'll meet you as usual."

"Thank you."

He said: "How is your skating jacket coming along?"

"I have—stopped work on it."

"Why?"

"I do not expect to—have time—for skating."

"Didn't you ever expect to come up here again?" he asked with a slight shiver.

"I thought that Mr. Sissly could do what was necessary."

"Didn't it occur to you that you were ending a friendship rather abruptly?"

She was silent.

"Don't you think it was a trifle brusque, Miss Nevers?"

"Does the acquaintanceship of a week count so much with you, Mr. Desboro?"

"You know it does."

"No. I did not know it. If I had supposed so, I would have written a polite letter regretting that I could no longer personally attend to the business in hand."

"Doesn't it count at all with you?" he asked.

"What?"

"Our friendship."

"Our acquaintanceship of a single week? Why, yes. I remember it with pleasure—your kindness, and Mrs. Quant's——"

"How on earth can you talk to me that way?"

"I don't understand you."

"Then I'll say, bluntly, that it meant a lot to me, and that the place is intolerable when you're not here. That is specific, isn't it?"

"Very. You mean that, being accustomed to having somebody to amuse you, your own resources are insufficient."

"Are you serious?"

"Perfectly. That is why you are kind enough to miss my coming and going— because I amuse you."

"Do you think that way about me?"

"I do when I think of you. You know sometimes I'm thinking of other things, too, Mr. Desboro."

He bit his lip, waited for a moment, then:

"If you feel that way, you'll scarcely care to come up to-morrow. Whatever arrangement you make about cataloguing the collection will be all right. If I am not here, communications addressed to the Olympian Club will be forwarded——"

"Mr. Desboro!"

"Yes?"

"Forgive me—won't you?"

There was a moment's interval, fraught heavily with the possibilities of Chance, then the silent currents of Fate flowed on toward her appointed destiny and his—whatever it was to be, wherever it lay, behind the unstirring, inviolable veil.

"Have you forgiven me?"

"And you me?" he asked.

"I have nothing to forgive; truly, I haven't. Why did you think I had? Because I have been talking flippantly? You have been so uniformly considerate and kind to me—you must know that it was nothing you said or did that made me think—wonder—whether—perhaps——"

"What?" he insisted. But she declined further explanation in a voice so different, so much gayer and happier than it had sounded before, that he was content to let matters rest—perhaps dimly surmising something approaching the truth.

She, too, noticed the difference in his voice as he said:

"Then may I have the car there as usual to-morrow morning?"

"Please."

He drew an unconscious sigh of relief. She said something more that he could scarcely hear, so low and distant sounded her voice, and he asked her to repeat it.

"I only said that I would be happy to go back," came the far voice.

Quick, unconsidered words trembled on his lips for utterance; perhaps fear of undoing what had been done restrained him.

"Not as happy as I will be to see you," he said, with an effort.

"Thank you. Good-bye, Mr. Desboro."

"Good-bye."

The sudden accession of high spirits filled him with delightful impatience. He ranged the house restlessly, traversing the hallway and silent rooms. A happy inclination for miscellaneous conversation impelled him to long-deferred interviews with people on the place. He talked business to Mrs. Quant, to Michael, the armourer; he put on snow-shoes and went cross lots to talk to his deaf head-farmer, Vail. Then he came back and set himself resolutely to his accounts; and after dinner he wrote letters, a yellow pup dozing on his lap, a cat purring on his desk, and occasionally patting with tentative paw the letter-paper when it rustled.

A mania for cleaning up matters which had accumulated took possession of him—and it all seemed to concern, in some occult fashion, the coming of Jacqueline on the morrow—as though he wished to begin again with a clean slate and a conscience undisturbed. But what he was to begin he did not specify to himself.

Bills—heavy ones—he paid lightly, drawing check after check to cover necessities or extravagances, going straight through the long list of liabilities incurred from top to bottom.

Later, the total troubled him, and he made himself do a thing to which he was averse—balance his check-book. The result dismayed him, and he sat for a while eyeing the sheets of carelessly scratched figures, and stroking the yellow pup on his knees.

"What do I want with all these clubs and things?" he said impatiently. "I never use 'em."

On the spur of impulse, he began to write resignations, wholesale, ridding himself of all kinds of incumbrances—shooting clubs in Virginia and Georgia and North Carolina, to which he had paid dues and assessments for years, and to which he had never been; fishing clubs in Maine and Canada and Nova Scotia and California; New York clubs, including the Cataract, the Old Fort, the Palisades, the Cap and Bells, keeping only the three clubs to which men of his sort are supposed to belong—the Patroons, the Olympian, and his college club. But everything else went—yacht clubs, riding clubs, golf clubs, country clubs of every sort—everything except his membership in those civic, educational, artistic, and charitable associations to which such New York families as his owed a moral and perpetual tribute.

It was nearly midnight when the last envelope was sealed and stamped, and he leaned back with a long, deep breath of relief. To-morrow he would apply the axe again and lop off such extravagances as saddle-horses in town, and the two cars he kept there. They should go to the auction rooms; he'd sell his Long Island bungalow, too, and the schooner and the power boats, and his hunters down at Cedar Valley; and with them would go groom and chauffeur, captain and mechanic, and the thousand maddening expenses that were adding daily to a total debt that had begun secretly to appal him.

In his desk he knew there was an accumulated mass of unpaid bills. He remembered them now and decided he didn't want to think about them. Besides, he'd clear them away pretty soon—settle accounts with tailor, bootmaker, haberdasher—with furrier, modiste and jeweler—and a dull red settled under his cheek bones as he remembered these latter bills, which he would scarcely care to exhibit to the world at large.

"Ass that I've been," he muttered, absently stroking the yellow pup. Which reflection started another train of thought, and he went to a desk, unlocked it, pulled out the large drawer, and carried it with its contents to the fireplace.

The ashes were still alive and the first packet of letters presently caught fire. On them he laid a silken slipper of Mrs. Clydesdale's and watched it shrivel and burn. Next, he tossed handfuls of unassorted trifles, letters, fans, one or two other slippers, gloves of different sizes, dried remnants of flowers, programmes scribbled over; and when the rubbish burned hotly, he added photographs and more letters without even glancing at them, except where, amid the flames, he caught a momentary glimpse of some familiar signature, or saw some pretty, laughing phantom of the past glow, whiten to ashes, and evaporate.

Fire is a great purifier; he felt as though the flames had washed his hands. Much edified by the moral toilet, and not concerned that all such ablutions are entirely superficial, he watched with satisfaction the last bit of ribbon shrivel, the last envelope flash into flame. Then he replaced the desk drawer, leaving the key in it—because there was now no reason why all the world and its relatives should not rummage if they liked.

He remembered some letters and photographs and odds and ends scattered about his rooms in town, and made a mental note to clear them out of his life, too.

Mentally detached, he stood aloof in spirit and viewed with interest the spectacle of his own regeneration, and calmly admired it.

"I'll cut out all kinds of things," he said to himself. "A devout girl in Lent will have nothing on me. Nix for the bowl! Nix for the fat pat hand! Throw up the sponge! Drop the asbestos curtain!" He made pretence to open an imaginary door: "Ladies, pass out quietly, please; the show is over."

The cat woke up and regarded him gravely; he said to her:

"You don't even need a pocket-book, do you? And you are quite right; having things is a nuisance. The less one owns the happier one is. Do you think I'll have sense enough to remember this to-morrow, and not be ass enough to acquire more—a responsibility, for example? Do you think I can be trusted to mind my business when she comes to-morrow? And not say something that I'll be surely sorry for some day—or something she'll be sorry for? Because she's so pretty, pussy—so disturbingly pretty—and so sweet. And I ought to know by this time that intelligence and beauty are a deadly combination I had better let alone until I find them in the other sort of girl. That's the trouble, pussy." He lifted the sleepy cat and held it at arm's length, where it dangled, purring all the while. "That's the trouble, kitty. I haven't the slightest intentions; and as for friends, men prefer men. And that's the truth, between you and me. It's rather rotten, isn't it, pussy? But I'll be careful, and if I see that she is capable of caring for me, I'll go South before it hurts either of us. That will be the square thing to do, I suppose—and neither of us the worse for another week together."

He placed the cat on the floor, where it marched to and fro with tail erect, inviting further attentions. But Desboro walked about, turning out the electric lights, and presently took himself off to bed, fixed in a resolution that the coming week should be his last with this unusual girl. For, after all, he concluded she had not moved his facile imagination very much more than had other girls of various sorts, whose souvenirs lay now in cinders on his hearth, and long since had turned to ashes in his heart.

What was the use? Such affairs ended one way or another—but they always ended. All he wanted to find out, all he was curious about, was whether such an unusual girl could be moved to response—he merely wanted to know, and then he would let her alone, and no harm done—nothing to disturb the faint fragrance of a pretty souvenir that he and she might carry for a while—a week or two—perhaps a month—before they both forgot.

And, conscious of his good intentions, feeling tranquil, complacent, and slightly noble, he composed himself to slumber, thinking how much happier this world would be if men invariably behaved with the self-control that occasionally characterised himself.

In the city, Jacqueline lay awake on her pillow, unable to find a refuge in sleep from the doubts, questions, misgivings assailing her.

Wearied, impatient, vexed, by turns, that her impulse and decision should keep her sleepless—that the thought of going back to Silverwood should so excite her, she turned restlessly in her bed, unwilling to understand, humiliated in heart, ashamed, vaguely afraid.

Why should she have responded to an appeal from such a man as Desboro? Her own calm judgment had been that they had seen enough of each other—for the present, anyway. Because she knew, in her scared soul, that she had not meant it to be final—that some obscure idea remained of seeing him again, somewhere.

Yet, something in his voice over the wire—and something more disturbing still when he spoke so coolly about going South—had swayed her in her purpose to remain aloof for a while. But there was no reason, after all, for her to take it so absurdly. She would go once more, and then permit a long interval to elapse before she saw him again. If she actually had, as she began to believe, an inclination for his society, she would show herself that she could control that inclination perfectly.

Why should any man venture to summon her—for it was a virtual summons over the wire—and there had been arrogance in it, too. His curt acquiescence in her decision, and his own arbitrary decision to go South had startled her out of her calmly prepared rôle of business woman. She was trying to recall exactly what she had said to him afterward to make his voice change once more, and her own respond so happily.

Why should seeing him be any unusual happiness to her—knowing who and what he had been and was—a man of the out-world with which she had not one thing in common—a man who could mean nothing to her—could not even remain a friend because their two lives would never even run within sight of each other.

She would never know anybody he knew. They would never meet anywhere except at Silverwood. How could they, once the business between them was transacted? She couldn't go to Silverwood except on business; he would never think of coming here to see her. Could she ask him—venture, perhaps, to invite him to dinner with some of her friends? Which friends? Cynthia and—who else? The girls she knew would bore him; he'd have only contempt for the men.

Then what did all this perplexity mean that was keeping her awake? And why was she going back to Silverwood? Why! Why! Was it to see with her own eyes the admiration for herself in his? She had seen it more than once. Was it to learn more about this man and his liking for her—to venture a guess, perhaps, as to how far that liking might carry him with a little encouragement —which she would not offer, of course?

She began to wonder how much he really did like her—how greatly he might care if she never were to see him again. Her mind answered her, but her heart appealed wistfully from the clear decision.

Lying there, blue eyes open in the darkness, head cradled on her crossed arms, she ventured to recall his features, summoning them shyly out of space; and she smiled, feeling the tension subtly relaxing.

Then she drifted for a while, watching his expression, a little dreading lest even his phantom laugh at her out of those eyes too wise.

Visions came to her awake to reassure her; he and she in a sleigh together under the winter stars—he and she in the sunlight, their skates flashing over the frozen meadows—he and she in the armoury, heads together over some wonder of ancient craftsmanship—he and she at luncheon—in the library— always he and she together in happy companionship. Her eyelids fluttered and drooped; and sleep came, and dreams—wonderful, exquisite, past belief—and still of him and of herself together, always together in a magic world that could not be except for such as they.

CHAPTER VI

When the sombre morning broke at last, Jacqueline awoke, sprang from her bed, and fluttered away about her dressing as blithely as an April linnet in a hurry.

She had just time to breakfast and catch her train, with the help of heaven and a taxicab, and she managed to do it about the same moment that Desboro, half a hundred miles away, glanced out of his dressing-room window and saw the tall trees standing like spectres in the winter fog, and the gravel on the drive shining wet and muddy through melting snow. But he turned to the mirror again, whistling a gay air, and twisted his necktie into a smarter knot. Then he went out to the greenhouses and snipped off enough carnations to make a great sheaf of clove-scented blossoms for Jacqueline's room; and after that he proceeded through the other sections of the fragrant glass galleries, cutting, right and left, whatever he considered beautiful enough to do her fresh, young beauty honour.

At the station, he saw her standing on the platform of the drawing-room car as the train thundered in, veil and raincoat blowing, just as he had seen her there the first time she arrived at Silverwood station.

The car steps were sheathed in ice; she had already ventured down a little way when he reached her and offered aid; and she permitted him to swing her to the cinder-strewn ground.

"Are you really here!" he exclaimed, oblivious of interested glances from trainmen and passengers.

They exchanged an impulsive hand-clasp. Both were unusually animated.

"Are you well?" she asked, as though she had been away for months.

"Yes. Are you? It's perfectly fine of you to come"—still retaining her hand—"I wonder if you know how glad I am to see you! I wonder if you really do!"

She started to say something, hesitated, blushed, then their hands parted, and she answered lightly:

"What a very cordial welcome for a business girl on a horrid day! You mustn't spoil me, Mr. Desboro."

"I was afraid you might not come," he said; and indiscreet impulse prompted her to answer, as she had first answered him there on the platform two weeks ago:

"Do you suppose that mere weather could have kept me away from the famous Desboro collection?"

The charming malice in her voice, the delightful impertinence of her reply, so obviously at variance with fact, enchanted him. She was conscious of its effect on him, and, already slightly excited, ventured to laugh at her own thrust as though challenging his self-conceit to believe that she had even grazed herself with the two-edged weapon.

"Do I count for absolutely nothing?" he said.

"Do you flatter yourself that I returned to see you?"

"Let me believe it for just one second."

"I don't doubt that you will secretly and triumphantly believe it all the time."

"If I dared——"

"Is that sort of courage lacking in you, Mr. Desboro? I have heard otherwise. And how long are we going to remain here on this foggy platform?"

Here was an entirely new footing; but in the delightful glow of youthful indiscretion she still maintained her balance lightly, mockingly.

"Please tell me," she said, as they entered the car, and he drew the big fur robe around her, "just how easily you believe in your own overpowering attractions. Do women encourage you in such modest faith in yourself? Or are you merely created that way?"

"The house has been a howling wilderness without you," he said. "I admit my loneliness, anyway."

"I admit nothing. Besides, I wasn't."

"Is that true?"

She laughed tormentingly, eyes and cheeks brilliant, now undisguisedly on guard—her first acknowledgment that in this man she condescended to divine the hereditary adversary.

"I mean to punish," said her eyes.

"What an attack from a clear sky on a harmless young man," he said, at last.

"No, an attack from the fog on an insufferable egoist—an ambush, Mr. Desboro. And I thought a little sword-play might do your complacent wits a service. Has it?"

"But you begin by a dozen thrusts, then beat down my guard, and cuff me about with blade and pommel——"

"I had to. Now, does your vanity believe that my return to Silverwood was influenced by your piteous appeal over the wire—and your bad temper, too?"

"No," he said solemnly.

"Well, then! I came here partly to put my notes in better shape for Mr. Sissly, partly to clear up odds and ends and leave him a clear field to plow—in your persistent company," she added, with such engaging malice that even the name of Sissly, which he hated, made him laugh.

"You won't do that," he said confidently.

"Do what, Mr. Desboro?"

"Turn me over to anything named Sissly."

"Indeed, I will—you and your celebrated collection! Of course you could go South, but, judging from your devotion to the study of ancient armour——"

"You don't mean it, do you?"

"What? About your devotion?"

"No, about Sissly."

"Yes, I do. Listen to me, Mr. Desboro. I made up my mind that sleighing, and skating, and luncheon and tea, and—you, are not good for a busy girl's business career. I'm going to be very practical and very frank with you. I don't belong here except on business, and you make it so pleasant and unbusinesslike for me that my conscience protests. You see, if the time I now take to lunch with you, tea with you, skate, sleigh, talk, listen, in your very engaging company is properly employed, I can attend to yards and yards of business in town. And I'm going to. I mean it, please," as he began to smile.

His smile died out. He said, quietly:

"Doesn't our friendship count for anything?"

She looked at him; shrugged her shoulders:

"Oh, Mr. Desboro," she said pleasantly, "does it, really?"

The blue eyes were clear and beautiful, and a little grave; only the upcurled corners of her mouth promised anything.

The car drew up at the house; she sprang out and ran upstairs to her room. He heard her in animated confab with Mrs. Quant for a few minutes, then she came down in her black business gown, with narrow edges of lawn at collar and cuffs, and the bright lock already astray on her cheek. A white carnation was tucked into her waist; the severe black of her dress, as always, made her cheeks and lips and golden hair more brilliant by contrast.

"Now," she said, "for my notes. And what are you going to do while I'm busy?"

"Watch you, if I may. You've heard about the proverbial cat?"

"Care killed it, didn't it?"

"Yes; but it had a good look at the Queen first."

A smile touched her eyes and lips—a little wistfully.

"You know, Mr. Desboro, that I like to waste time with you. Flatter your vanity with that confession. And even if things were—different—but they couldn't ever be—and I must work very hard if I'm ever going to have any leisure in my old age. But come to the library for this last day, and smoke as usual. And you may talk to amuse me, if you wish. Don't mind if I'm too busy to answer your folly in kind."

They went together to the library; she placed the mass of notes in front of her and began to sort them—turned for a second and looked around at him with adorable malice, then bent again to the task before her.

"Miss Nevers!"

"Yes?"

"You will come to Silverwood again, won't you?"

She wrote busily with a pencil.

"Won't you?"

She made some marginal notes and he looked at the charming profile in troubled silence.

"She turned leisurely.... 'Did you say anything recently, Mr. Desboro?'"

About ten minutes later she turned leisurely, tucking up the errant strand of hair with her pencil:

"Did you say anything recently, Mr. Desboro?"

"Out of the depths, yes. The voice in the wilderness as usual went unheeded. I wished to explain to you how we might give up our skating and sleighing and everything except the bare necessities—and you could still come to Silverwood on business——"

"What are the 'bare necessities'?"

"Your being here is one——"

"Answer me seriously, please."

"Food, then. We must eat."

She conceded that much.

"We've got to motor to and from the station!"

She admitted that, too.

"Those," he pointed out, "are the bare necessities. We can give up everything else."

She sat looking at him, playing absently with her pencil. After a while, she turned to her desk again, and, bending over it, began to make meaningless marks with her pencil on the yellow pad.

"What is the object," she said, "of trying to make me forget that I wouldn't be here at all except on business?"

"Do you think of that every minute?"

"I—must."

"It isn't necessary."

"It is imperative, Mr. Desboro—and you know it."

She wrote steadily for a while, strapped a bundle of notes with an elastic band, laid it aside, and turned around, resting her arm on the back of the chair. Blue eyes level with his, she inspected him curiously. And, if the tension of excitement still remained, all her high spirits and the indiscreet impulses of a gay self-confidence had vanished. But curiosity remained—the eternal, insatiable curiosity of the young.

How much did this man really mean of what he said to her? What did his liking for her signify other than the natural instinct of an idle young man for any pretty girl? What was he going to do about it? For she seemed to be conscious that, sooner or later, somewhere, sometime, he would do something further about it.

Did he mean to make love to her sometime? Was he doing it now? It resembled the preliminaries; she recognised them—had been aware of them almost from the very first.

Men had made love to her before—men in her own world, men in his world. She had learned something since her father died—not a great deal; perhaps more from hearsay than from experience. But some unpleasant knowledge had been acquired at first hand; two clients of her father's had contributed, and a student, named Harroun, and an amateur of soft paste statuettes, the Rev. Bertie Dawley.

Innocently and wholesomely equipped to encounter evil, cool and clear eyed mistress of herself so far, she had felt, with happy contempt, that her fate was her own to control, and had wondered what the word "temptation" could mean to any woman.

What Cynthia had admitted made her a little wiser, but still incredulous. Cold, hunger, debts, loneliness—these were not enough, as Cynthia herself had said.

Nor, after all, was Cynthia's liking for Cairns. Which proved conclusively that woman is the arbiter of her own destiny.

Desboro, one knee crossed over the other, sat looking into the fire, which burned in the same fireplace where he had recently immolated the frivolous souvenirs of the past.

Perhaps some gay ghost of that scented sacrifice took shape for a moment in the curling smoke, for he suddenly frowned and passed his hand over his eyes in boyish impatience.

Something—the turn of his head and shoulders—the shape of them—she did not know what—seemed to set her heart beating loudly, ridiculously, without any apparent reason on earth. Too much surprised to be disturbed, she laid her slim hand on her breast, then against her throat, till her pulses grew calmer.

Resting her chin on her arm, she gazed over her shoulder into the fire. He had laid another log across the flames; she watched the bark catch fire, dully conscious, now, that her ideas were becoming as irresponsible and as reasonless as the sudden stirring of her heart had been.

For she was thinking how odd it would be if, like Cynthia, she too, ever came to care about a man of Desboro's sort. She'd see to it that she didn't; that was all. There were other men. Better still, there were to be no men; for her mind fastidiously refused to consider the only sort with whom she felt secure—her intellectual inferiors whose moral worthiness bored her to extinction.

Musing there, half turned on her chair, she saw Desboro rise, still looking intently into the fire, and stand so, his well-made, graceful figure, in silhouette, edged with the crimson glow.

"What do you see in it, Mr. Desboro?"

He turned instantly and came over to her:

"A bath of flames would be very popular," he said, "if burning didn't hurt. I was just thinking about it—how to invent——"

She quoted: "'But I was thinking of a plan to dye one's whiskers green.'"

He said: "I suppose you think me as futile as that old man 'a-settin' on a gate.'"

"Your pursuits seem to be about as useful as his."

"Why should I pursue things? I don't want 'em."

"You are hopeless. There is pleasure even in pursuit of anything, no matter whether you ever attain it or not. I will never attain wisdom, but it's a pleasure to pursue it."

"It's a pleasure even to pursue pleasure—and it's the only pleasure in pleasure," he said, so gravely that for a moment she thought with horror that he was trying to be precious. Then the latent glimmer in his eyes set them laughing, and she rose and went over to the sofa and curled up in one corner, abandoning all pretense of industry.

"Once," she said, "I knew a poet who emitted such precious thoughts. He was the funniest thing; he had the round, pale, ancient eyes of an African parrot, a pasty countenance, and a derby hat resting on top of a great bunch of colourless curly hair. And that's the way he talked, Mr. Desboro!"

He seated himself on the other arm of the sofa:

"Did you adore him?"

"At first. He was a celebrity. He did write some pretty things."

"What woke you up?"

She blushed.

"I thought so," observed Desboro.

"Thought what?"

"That he came out of his trance and made love to you."

"How did you know? Wasn't it dreadful! And he'd always told me that he had never experienced an emotion except when adoring the moon. He was a very dreadful young man—perfectly horrid in his ideas—and I sent him about his business very quickly; and I remember being a little frightened and watching him from the window as he walked off down the street in his soiled drab overcoat and the derby hat on his frizzly hair, and his trousers too high on his ankles——"

Desboro was so immensely amused at the picture she drew that her pretty brows unbent and she smiled, too.

"What did he want of you?" he asked.

"I didn't fully understand at the time——" she hesitated, then, with an angry blush: "He asked me to go to Italy with him. And he said he couldn't marry me because he had already espoused the moon!"

Desboro's laughter rang through the old library; and Jacqueline was not quite certain whether she liked the way he took the matter or not.

"I know him," said Desboro. "I've seen him about town kissing women's hands, in company with a larger and fatter one. Isn't his name Munger?"

"Yes," she said.

"Certainly. And the fat one's name is Waudle. They were a hot team at fashionable literary stunts—the Back Alley Club, you know."

"No, I don't know."

"Oh, it's just silly; a number of fashionable and wealthy young men and women pin on aprons, now and then, and paint and model lumps of wet clay in several severely bare studios over some unfragrant stables. They proudly call it The Back Alley Club."

"Why do you sneer at it?"

"Because it isn't the real thing. It's a strutting ground for things like Munger and Waudle, and all the rag-tag that is always sniffing and snuffling at the back doors of the fine arts."

"At least," she said, "they sniff."

He said, good-humouredly: "Yes, and I don't even do that. Is that what you mean?"

She considered him: "Haven't you any profession?"

"I'm a farmer."

"Why aren't you busy with it, then?"

"I have been, disastrously. There was a sickening deficit this autumn."

She said, with pretty scorn: "I'll wager I could make your farm pay."

He smiled lazily, and indulgently. After a moment he said:

"So the spouse of the moon wanted you to go to Italy with him?"

She nodded absently: "A girl meets queer men in the world."

"Did you ever meet any others?"

She looked up listlessly: "Yes, several."

"As funny as the poet?"

"If you call him funny."

"I wonder who they were," he mused.

"Did you ever hear of the Reverend Bertie Dawley?"

"No."

"He was one."

"That kind?"

"Oh, yes. He collects soft paste figurines; he was a client of father's; but I found very soon that I couldn't go near him. He has a wife and children, too, and he keeps sending his wife to call on me. You know he's a good-looking young man, too, and I liked him; but I never dreamed——"

"Sure," he said, disgusted at his own sex—with the exception of himself.

"That seems to be the way of it," she said thoughtfully. "You can't be friends with men; they all annoy you sooner or later in one way or another!"

"Annoy you? Do you mean make love to you?"

"Yes."

"I don't; do I?"

She bent her head and sat playing with the petals of the white carnation drooping on her breast.

"No," she said calmly. "You don't annoy me."

"Would it seriously annoy you if I did make love to you some day?" he asked, lightly.

Instinct was whispering hurriedly to her: "Here it is at last. Do something about it, and do it quick!" She waited until her heart beat more regularly, then:

"You couldn't annoy—make love—to a girl you really don't care for. That is very simple, isn't it?"

"Suppose I did care for you."

She looked up at him with troubled eyes, then lowered them to the blossom from which her fingers were detaching petal after petal.

"If you did really care, you wouldn't tell me, Mr. Desboro."

"Why not?"

"Because it would not be fair to me." A flush of anger—or she thought it was, brightened her cheeks. "This is nonsense," she said abruptly. "And I'll tell you another thing; I can't come here again. You know I can't. We talk foolishness —don't you know it? And there's another reason, anyway."

"What reason?"

"The real reason," she said, clenching both hands. "You know what it is and so do I—and—and I'm tired of pretending that the truth isn't true."

"What is the truth?"

She had turned her back on him and was staring out of the windows into the mist.

"The truth is," she answered deliberately, "that you and I can not be friends."

"Why?"

"Because we can't be! Because—men are always men. There isn't any way for men and women to be friends. Forgive me for saying it. But it is quite true. A business woman in your employment—can't forget that a real friendship with you is impossible. That is why, from the very beginning, I wanted it to be purely a matter of business between us. I didn't really wish to skate with you, or do anything of that kind with you. I'd rather not lunch with you; I—I had rather you drew the line—and let me draw it clearly, cleanly, and without mistake—as I draw it between myself and my employees. If you wish, I can continue to come here on that basis until my work is finished. Otherwise, I shall not come again."

Her back was still toward him.

"Very well," he said, bluntly.

She heard him rise and walk toward the door; sat listening without turning her head, already regretting what she had said. And now she became conscious that her honesty with herself and with him had been a mistake, entailing humiliation for her—the humiliation of letting him understand that she couldn't afford to care for him, and that she did already. She had thought of him first, and of herself last—had conceded a hopeless situation in order that her decision might not hurt his vanity.

It had been a bad mistake. And now he might be thinking that she had tried to force him into an attitude toward herself which she could not expect, or—God knew what he might be thinking.

Dismayed and uncertain, she stood up nervously as he reëntered the room and came toward her, holding out his hand.

"I'm going to town," he said pleasantly. "I won't bother you any more. Remain; come and go as you like without further fear of my annoying you. The servants are properly instructed. They will be at your orders. I'm sorry—I meant to be more agreeable. Good-bye, Miss Nevers."

She laid her hand in his, lifelessly, then withdrew it. Dumb, dreadfully confused, she looked up at him; then, as he turned coolly away, an inarticulate sound of protest escaped her lips. He halted and turned around.

"It isn't fair—what you are doing—Mr. Desboro."

"What else is there to do?"

"Why do you ask me? Why must the burden of decision always rest with me?"

"But my decision is that I had better go. I can't remain here without—annoying you."

"Why can't you remain here as my employer? Why can't we enjoy matter-of-fact business relations? I ask no more than that—I want no more. I am afraid you think I do expect more—that I expect friendship. It is impossible, unsuitable—and I don't even wish for it——"

"I do," he said.

"How can we be friends, from a social standpoint? There is nothing to build on, no foundation—nothing for friendship to subsist on——"

"Could you and I meet anywhere in the world and become less than friends?" he asked. "Tell me honestly. It is impossible, and you and I both know it."

And, as she made no reply: "Friends—more than friends, possibly; never less. And you know it, and so do I," he said under his breath.

She turned sharply toward the window and looked out across the foggy hills.

"If that is what you believe, Mr. Desboro, perhaps you had better go."

"Do you send me?"

"Always the decision seems to lie with me. Why do you not decide for yourself?"

"I will; and for you, too, if you will let me relieve you of the burden."

"I can carry my own burdens."

Her back was still toward him. After a moment she rested her head against the curtained embrasure, as though tired.

He hesitated; there were good impulses in him, but he went over to her, and scarcely meaning to, put one arm lightly around her waist.

She laid her hands over her face, standing so, golden head lowered and her heart so violent that she could scarcely breathe.

"Jacqueline."

A scarcely perceptible movement of her head, in sign that she listened.

"Are we going to let anything frighten us?" He had not meant to say that, either. He was adrift, knew it, and meant to drop anchor in a moment. "Tell me honestly," he added, "don't you want us to be friends?"

She said, her hands still over her face:

"I didn't know how much I wanted it. I don't see, even now, how it can be. Your own friends are different. But I'll try—if you wish it."

"I do wish it. Why do you think my friends are so different from you? Because some happen to be fashionable and wealthy and idle? Besides, a man has many different kinds of friends——"

She thought to herself: "But he never forgets to distinguish between them. And here it is at last—almost. And I—I do care for him! And here I am—like Cynthia—asking myself to pardon him."

She looked up at him out of her hands, a little pale, then down at his arm, resting loosely around her waist.

"Don't hold me so, please," she said, in a low voice.

"Of course not." But instead he merely took her slender hands between his own, which were not very steady, and looked her straight in the eyes. Such men can do it, somehow. Besides, he really meant to control himself and cast anchor in a moment or two.

"Will you trust me with your friendship?" he said.

"I—seem to be doing it. I don't exactly understand what I am doing. Would you answer me one question?"

"If I can, Jacqueline."

"Then, friendship is possible between a man and a woman, isn't it?" she insisted wistfully.

"I don't know."

"What! Why don't you know? It's merely a matter of mutual interest and respect, isn't it?"

"I've heard so."

"Then isn't a friendship between us possible without anything threatening to spoil it? Isn't it to be just a matter of enjoying together what interests each? Isn't it? Because I don't mind waiving social conditions that can't be helped, and conventions that we simply can't observe."

"Yes, you wonderful girl," he said under his breath, meaning to anchor at once. But he drifted on.

"You know," she said, forcing a little laugh, "I am rather wonderful, to be so honest with a man like you. There's so much about you that I don't care for."

He laughed, enchanted, still retaining her hands between his own, the palms joined together, flat.

"You're so wonderful," he said, "that you make the most wonderful masterpiece in the Desboro collection look like a forgery."

She strove to speak lightly again: "Even the gilding on my hair is real. You didn't think so once, did you?"

"You're all real. You are the most real thing I've ever seen in the world!"

She tried to laugh: "You mustn't believe that I've never before been real when I've been with you. And I may not be real again, for a long time. Make the most of this moment of expansive honesty, Mr. Desboro. I'll remember presently that you are an hereditary enemy."

"Have I ever acted that part?"

"Not toward me."

He reddened: "Toward whom?"

"Oh," she said, with sudden impatience, "do you suppose I have any illusions concerning the sort of man you are? But what do I care, as long as you are nice to me?" she laughed, more confidently. "Men!" she repeated. "I know something about them! And, knowing them, also, I nevertheless mean to make a friend of one of them. Do you think I'll succeed?"

He smiled, then bent lightly and kissed her joined hands.

"Luncheon is served," came the emotionless voice of Farris from the doorway. Their hands fell apart; Jacqueline blushed to her hair and gave Desboro a lovely, abashed look.

She need not have been disturbed. Farris had seen such things before.

That evening, Desboro went back to New York with her and took her to her own door in a taxicab.

"Are you quite sure you can't dine with me?" he asked again, as they lingered on her doorstep.

"I could—but——"

"But you won't!"

One of her hands lay lightly on the knob of the partly open door, and she stood so, resting and looking down the dark street toward the distant glare of electricity where Broadway crossed at right angles.

"We have been together all day, Mr. Desboro. I'd rather not dine with you—yet."

"Are you going to dine all alone up there?" glancing aloft at the lighted windows above the dusky old shop.

"Yes. Besides, you and I have wasted so much time to-day that I shall go down stairs to the office and do a little work after dinner. You see a girl always has to pay for her transgressions."

"I'm terribly sorry," he said contritely. "Don't work to-night!"

"Don't be sorry. I've really enjoyed to-day's laziness. Only it mustn't be like this to-morrow. And anyway, I knew I'd have to make it up to-night."

"I'm terribly sorry," he said again, almost tenderly.

"But you mustn't be, Mr. Desboro. It was worth it——"

He looked up, surprised, flushing with emotion; and the quick colour in her cheeks responded. They remained very still, and confused, and silent, as fire answered fire; suddenly aware how fast they had been drifting.

She turned, nervously, pushed open the door, and entered the vestibule; he held the door ajar for her while she fitted her key with unsteady fingers.

"So—thank you," she said, half turning around, "but I won't dine with you—to-night."

"Then, perhaps, to-morrow——"

"Don't come into town with me to-morrow, Mr. Desboro."

"I'm coming in anyway."

"Why?"

"There's an affair—a kind of a dance. There are always plenty of things to take me into town in the evenings."

"Is that why you came in to-night?" She knew she should not have said it.

He hesitated, then, with a laugh: "I came in to town because it gave me an hour longer with you. Are you going to send me away now?" And her folly was answered in kind.

She said, confused and trying to smile: "You say things that you don't mean. Evening, for us, must always mean 'good-night.'"

"Why, Jacqueline?"

"Because. Also, it is my hour of freedom. You wouldn't take that away from me, would you?"

"What do you do in the evenings?"

"Sew, read, study, attend to the thousand wretched little details which concern my small household. And, sometimes, when I have wasted the day, I make it up at night. Because, whether I have enjoyed it or not, this day has been wasted."

"But sometimes you dine out and go to the theatre and to dances and things?"

"Yes," she said gravely. "But you know there is no meeting ground there for us, don't you?"

"Couldn't you ask me to something?"

"Yes—I could. But you wouldn't care for the people. You know it. They are not like the people to whom you are accustomed. They would only bore you."

"So do many people I know."

"Not in the same way. Why do you ask me? You know it is better not." She added smilingly: "There is neither wealth nor fashion nor intellectual nor social distinction to be expected among my friends——"

She hesitated, and added quietly: "You understand that I am not criticising them. I am merely explaining them to you. Otherwise, I'd ask you to dinner with a few people—I can only have four at a time, my dining room is so small ——"

"Ask me, Jacqueline!" he insisted.

She shook her head; but he continued to coax and argue until she had half promised. And now she stood, facing him irresolutely, conscious of the steady drift that was forcing her into uncharted channels with this persuasive pilot who seemed to know no more of what lay ahead of them than did she.

But there was to be no common destination; she understood that. Sooner or later she must turn back toward the harbour they had left so irresponsibly together, her brief voyage over, her last adventure with this man ended for all time.

And now, as the burden of decision still seemed to rest upon her, she offered him her hand, saying good-night; and he took it once more and held it between both of his. Instantly the impending constraint closed in upon them; his face became grave, hers serious, almost apprehensive.

"You have—have made me very happy," he said. "Do you know it, Jacqueline?"

"Yes."

A curious lassitude was invading her; she leaned sideways against the door frame, as though tired, and stood so, one hand abandoned to him, gazing into the lamp-lit street.

"Good-night, dear," he whispered.

"Good-night."

She still gazed into the lamp-lit darkness beyond him, her hand limp in his; and he saw her blue eyes, heavy lidded and dreamy, and the strand of hair curling gold against her cheek.

When he kissed her, she dropped her head, covering her face with her forearm, not otherwise stirring—as though the magic pageant of her fate which had been gathering for two weeks had begun to move at last, passing vision-like through her mind with a muffled uproar—sweeping on, on, brilliant, disarrayed, timed by the deafening beating of her heart.

Dully she realised that it was here at last—all that she had dreaded—if dread be partly made of hope!

"Are you crying?" he said, unsteadily.

She lifted her face from her arm, like a dazed child awaking.

"You darling," he whispered.

Eyes remote, she stood watching unseen things in the darkness beyond him.

"Must I go, Jacqueline?"

"Yes."

"You are very tired, aren't you?"

"Yes."

"You won't sit up and work, will you?"

"No."

"Will you go straight to bed?"

She nodded slowly, yielding to him as he drew her into his arms.

"To-morrow, then?" he asked under his breath.

"Yes."

"And the next day, and the next, and next, and—always, Jacqueline?" he demanded, almost fiercely.

After a moment she slowly turned her head and looked at him. There was no answer, and no question in her gaze, only the still, expressionless clairvoyance of a soul that sees but does not heed.

There was no misunderstanding in her eyes, nothing wistful, nothing afraid or hurt—nothing of doubt. What had happened to others in the world was happening now to her. She understood it; that was all—as though the millions of her sisters who had passed that way had left to her the dread legacy of familiarity with the smooth, wide path they had trodden since time began on earth. And here it was, at last! Her own calmness surprised her.

He detained her for another moment in a swift embrace; inert, unresponsive, she stood looking down at the crushed gardenia in his buttonhole, dully conscious of being bruised. Then he let her go; her hand fell from his arm; she turned and faced the familiar stairs and mounted them.

Dinner waited for her; whether she ate or not, she could not afterward remember. About eleven o'clock, she rose wearily from the bed where she had been lying, and began to undress.

As for Desboro, he had gone straight to his rooms very much excited and unbalanced by the emotions of the moment.

He was a man not easily moved to genuine expression. Having acquired certain sorts of worldly wisdom in a career more or less erratic, experience had left him unconvinced and even cynical—or he thought it had.

But now, for the moment, all that lay latent in him of that impetuous and heedless vigour which may become strength, if properly directed, was awakening. Every recurring memory of her had already begun to tamper with his self-control; for the emotions of the moments just ended had been confusingly real; and, whatever they were arousing in him, now clamoured for some sort of expression.

The very thought of her, now, began to act on him like some freshening perfume alternately stimulating and enervating. He made the effort again and again, and could not put her from his mind, could not forget the lowered head and the slender, yielding grace of her, and her fragrance, and her silence.

Dressing in his rooms, growing more restless every moment, he began to walk the floor like some tormented thing that seeks alleviation in purposeless activity.

He said, half aloud, to himself:

"I can't go on this way. This is damn foolish! I've got to find out where it's landing me. It will land her, too—somewhere. I'd better keep away from her, go off somewhere, get out, stop seeing her, stop remembering her!—if she's what I think she is."

Scowling, he went to the window and jerked aside the curtain. Across the street, the Olympian Club sparkled with electricity.

"Good Lord!" he muttered. "What a tempest in a teapot! What the devil's the matter with me? Can't I kiss a girl now and then and keep my senses?"

It seemed that he couldn't, in the present instance, for after he had bitten the amber stem of his pipe clean through, he threw the bowl into the fireplace. It had taken him two years to colour it.

"Idiot!" he said aloud. "What are you sorry about? You know damn well there are only two kinds of women, and it's up to them what sort they are—not up to any man who ever lived! What are you sorry for? For her?"

He stared across the street at the Olympian Club. He was expected there.

"If she only wasn't so—so expressionless and—silent about it. It's like killing something that lets you do it. That's a crazy thing to think of!"

Suddenly he found he had a fight on his hands. He had never had one like it; didn't know exactly what to do, except to repeat over and over:

"It isn't square—it isn't square. She knows it, too. She's frightened. She knows it isn't square. There's nothing ahead but hell to pay! She knows it. And she doesn't defend herself. There are only two kinds of women. It is up to them, too. But it's like killing something that lets you kill it. Good God! What a damn fool I am!"

Later he repeated it. Later still he found himself leaning over his desk, groping blindly about for a pen, and cursing breathlessly as though he had not a moment to lose.

He wrote:

"Dear Little Jacqueline: I'm not going to see you again. Where the fool courage to write this comes from I don't know. But you will now learn that there is nothing to me after all—not even enough of positive and negative to make me worth forgiveness. And so I let it go at that. Good-bye.

"Desboro."

In the same half blind, half dazed way, cursing something all the while, he managed to seal, stamp, and direct the letter, and get himself out of the house with it.

A club servant at the Olympian mailed it; he continued on his way to the dining room, and stumbled into a chair between Cairns and Reggie Ledyard, who were feasting noisily and unwisely with Stuyvesant Van Alstyne; and the racket and confusion seemed to help him. He was conscious of laughing and talking and drinking a great deal—conscious, too, of the annoyance of other men at other tables. Finally, one of the governors came over and very pleasantly told him to shut up or go elsewhere.

They all went, with cheerfulness unimpaired by gubernatorial admonition. There was a large dinner dance for debutantes at the Barkley's. This function they deigned to decorate with their presence for a while, Cairns and Van Alstyne behaving well enough, considering the manners of the times; Desboro, a dull fire smouldering in his veins, wandered about, haunted by a ghost whose soft breath touched his cheek.

His manners were good when he chose; they were always faultless when he was drunk. Perfectly steady on his legs, very pale, and a trifle over polite, the drunker he was the more courtly he invariably became, measuredly graceful, in speech reticent. Only his pallor and the lines about his mouth betrayed the tension.

Later, one or two men familiar with the house strolled into the distant billiard room and discovered him standing there looking blankly into space.

Ledyard, bad tempered when he had dined too well, announced that he had had enough of that debutante party:

"Look at 'em," he said to Desboro. "Horrible little fluffs just out of the incubator—with their silly brains and rotten manners, and their 'Bunny Hugs' and 'Turkey Trots' and 'Dying Chickens,' and the champagne flaming in their baby cheeks! Why, their mothers are letting 'em dance like filles de Brasserie! Men used to know where to go for that sort of thing——"

Cairns, balancing gravely on heels and toes, waved one hand comprehensively.

"Problem was," he said, "how to keep the young at home. Bunny Hug solves it. See? All the comforts of the Tenderloin at home. Tha's 'splaination."

"Come on to supper," said Ledyard. "Your Blue Girl will be there, Jim."

"By all means," said Desboro courteously. "My car is entirely at your disposal." But he made no movement.

"Come to supper," insisted Ledyard.

"Commer supper," echoed Cairns gravely. "Whazzer mazzer? Commer supper!"

"Nothing," said Desboro, "could give me greater pleasure." He rose, bowed courteously to Ledyard, included Cairns in a graceful salute, and reseated himself.

Ledyard lost his temper and began to shout at him.

"I beg your pardon for my inexcusable absent-mindedness," said Desboro, getting slowly onto his feet once more. With graceful precision, he made his way to his hostess and took faultless leave of her, Cairns and Ledyard attempting vainly to imitate his poise, urbanity and self-possession.

The icy air of the street did Cairns good and aided Ledyard. So they got themselves out across the sidewalk and ultimately into Desboro's town car, which was waiting, as usual.

"Little bunny-hugging, bread-and-butter beasts," muttered Ledyard to himself. "Lord! Don't they want us to draw the line between them and the sort we're to meet at supper?"

"They're jus' fools," said Cairns. "No harm in 'em! And I'm not going to supper. I'll take you there an' go'me!"

"What's the matter with you?" demanded Ledyard.

"No—I'm through, that's all. You 'sult nice li'l debutantes. Rotten bad taste. Nice li'l debbys."

"Come on, you jinx!"

"That girl in blue. Will she be there—the one who does the lute solo in 'The Maid of Shiraz'?"

"Yes, but she's crazy about Desboro."

"I waive all pretension to the charming condescension of that very lovely young lady, and cheerfully concede your claims," said Desboro, raising his hat and wrecking it against the roof of the automobile.

"As you wish, dear friend. But why so suddenly the solitary recluse?"

"A personal reason, I assure you."

"I see," remarked Ledyard. "And what may be the name and quality of this personal reason? And is she a blonde?"

Desboro shrugged his polite impatience. But when the others got out at the Santa Regina he followed. Cairns was inclined to shed a few tears over

Ledyard's insults to the "debbys."

"Sure," said the latter, soothingly. "The brimming beaker for you, dear friend, and it will pass away. Hark! I hear the fairy feetsteps of a houri!" as they landed from the elevator and encountered a group of laughing, bright-eyed young girls in the hallway, seeking the private supper room.

One of them was certainly the girl in blue. The others appeared to Desboro as merely numerous and, later, exceedingly noisy. But noise and movement seemed to make endurable the dull pain thudding ceaselessly in his heart. Music and roses, flushed faces, the ringing harmony of crystal and silver, and the gaiety à diable of the girl beside him would ease it—must ease it, somehow. For it had to be first eased, then killed. There was no sense, no reason, no excuse for going on this way—enduring such a hurt. And just at present the remedy seemed to lie in a gay uproar and many brilliant lights, and in the tinted lips of the girl beside him, babbling nonsense while her dark eyes laughed, promising all they laughed at—if he cared to ask an answer to the riddle.

But he never asked it.

Later somebody offered a toast to Desboro, but when they looked around for him in the uproar, glasses aloft, he had disappeared.

CHAPTER VII

There was no acknowledgment of his note to Jacqueline the day following; none the next day, or the next. It was only when telephoning to Silverwood he learned by chance from Mrs. Quant that Jacqueline had been at the house every day as usual, busy in the armoury with the work that took her there.

He had fully expected that she would send a substitute; had assumed that she would not wish to return and take the chance of his being there.

What she had thought of his note to her, what she might be thinking of him, had made him so miserable that even the unwisdom of excess could not dull the pain of it or subdue the restless passion ever menacing him with a shameful repudiation of the words he had written her. He had fought one weakness with another, and there was no strength in him now. He knew it, but stood on guard.

For he knew, too, in his heart that he had nothing to offer her except a sentiment which, in the history of man, has never been anything except temporary. With it, of course, and part of it, was a gentler inclination—love, probably, of one sort or another—with it went also genuine admiration and intellectual interest, and sympathy, and tenderness of some unanalysed kind.

But he knew that he had no intention of marrying anybody—never, at least, of marrying out of his own social environment. That he understood fully; had wit and honesty enough to admit to himself. And so there was no way—nothing, now, anyway. He had settled that definitely—settled it for her and for himself, unrequested; settled, in fact, everything except how to escape the aftermath of restless pain for which there seemed to be no remedy so far—not even the professional services of old Doctor Time. However, it had been only three days—three sedative pills from the old gentleman's inexhaustible supply. It is the regularity of taking it, more than the medicine itself which cures.

On the fourth day, he emerged from the unhappy seclusion of his rooms and ventured into the Olympian Club, where he deliberately attempted to anæsthetise his badly battered senses. But he couldn't. Cairns found him there, sitting alone in the library—it was not an intellectual club—and saw what Desboro had been doing to himself by the white tensity of his features.

"Look here," he said. "If there's really anything the matter with you, why don't you go into business and forget it? You can't fool real trouble with what you buy in bottles!"

"What business shall I go into?" asked Desboro, unoffended.

"Stocks or literature. All the ginks who can't do anything else go into stocks or literature."

Desboro waved away the alternatives with amiable urbanity.

"Then run for your farms and grow things for market. You could do that, couldn't you? Even a Dutchess County millionaire can run a milk-route."

"I don't desire to grow milk," explained Desboro pleasantly.

Cairns regarded him with a grin of anxiety.

"You're jingled," he concluded. "That is, you are as jingled as you ever get. Why?"

"No reason, thanks."

"It isn't some girl, is it? You never take them seriously. All the same, is it?"

Desboro smiled: "Do you think it's likely, dear friend?"

"No, I don't. But whatever you're worrying about isn't improving your personal beauty. Since you hit this hamlet you've been on one continuous tootlebat. Why don't you go back to Westchester and hoe potatoes?"

"One doesn't hoe them in January, you know," said Desboro, always deprecatingly polite. "Please cease to trouble yourself about me. I'm quite all right, thanks."

"You've resigned from a lot of clubs and things, I hear."

"Admirably reported, dear friend, and perfectly true."

"Why?"

"Motives of economy; nothing more serious, John."

"You're not in any financial trouble, are you?"

"I—ah—possibly have been a trifle indiscreet in my expenditures—a little unfortunate in my investments, perhaps. You are very kind to ask me. It may afford you some gratification to learn that eventually I anticipate an agreeable return to affluence."

Cairns laughed: "You are jingled all right," he said. "I recognise the urbane symptoms of your Desboro ancestors."

"You flatter them and me," said Desboro, bowing. "They were the limit, and I'm nearing it."

"Pardon! You have arrived, sir," said Cairns, returning the salute with exaggerated gravity.

They parted with pomp and circumstance, Desboro to saunter back to his rooms and lie limply in his arm chair beside an empty fireplace until sleep overcame him where he sat. And he looked very young, and white, and somewhat battered as he lay there in the fading winter daylight.

The ringing racket of his telephone bell aroused him in total darkness. Still confused by sleep, he groped for the electric light switch, could not find it; but presently his unsteady hand encountered the telephone, and he unhooked the receiver and set it to his ear.

At first his imagination lied to him, and he thought it was Jacqueline's distant voice, though he knew in his heart it could not be.

"Jim," repeated the voice, "what are you doing this evening?"

"Nothing. I was asleep. It's you, Elena, isn't it?"

"Of course. To whom are you in the habit of talking every evening at seven by special request?"

"I didn't know it was seven."

"That's flattering to me. Listen, Jim, I'm coming to see you."

"I've told you a thousand times it can't be done——"

"Do you mean that no woman has ever been in your apartments?"

"You can't come," he repeated obstinately. "If you do, it ends my interest in your various sorrows. I mean it, Elena."

She laughed: "I only wanted to be sure that you are still afraid of caring too much for me. Somebody told me a very horrid thing about you. It was probably a lie—as long as you are still afraid of me."

He closed his eyes patiently and leaned his elbow on the desk, waiting for her to go on or to ring off.

"Was it a lie, Jim?"

"Was what a lie?"

"That you are entertaining a very pretty girl at Silverwood House—unchaperoned?"

"Do you think it likely?"

"Why not? They say you've done it before."

"Nobody has been there except on business. And, after all, you know, it doesn't——"

"Yes, it does concern me! Oh, Jim, are you being horrid—when I'm so unhappy and helpless——"

"Be careful what you say over the wire!"

"I don't care who hears me. If you mean anybody in your apartment house, they know my voice already. I want to see you, Jim——"

"No!"

"You said you'd be friendly to me!"

"I am—by keeping away from you."

"Do you mean that I am never to see you at all?"

"You know well enough that it isn't best, under the circumstances."

"You could come here if you only would. He is not in town to-night——"

"Confound it, do you think I'm that sort?"

"I think you are very absurd and not very consistent, considering the things that they say you are not too fastidious to do——"

"Will you please be a little more reticent over the telephone!"

"Then take me out to dinner somewhere, where we can talk!"

"I'm sorry, but it won't do."

"I thought you'd say that. Very well, then, listen: they are singing Ariane to-night; it's an : curtain. I'll be in the Barkley's box very early; nobody else will arrive before nine. Will you come to me at eight?"

"Yes, I'll do that for a moment."

"Thank you, dear. I just want to be happy for a few minutes. You don't mind, do you?"

"It will be very jolly," he said vaguely.

The galleries were already filling, but there were very few people in the orchestra and nobody at all to be seen in the boxes when Desboro paused before a door marked with the Barkleys' name. After a second's hesitation, he turned the knob, stepped in, and found Mrs. Clydesdale already seated in the tiny foyer, under the hanging shadow of her ermine coat—a charming and youthful figure, eyes and cheeks bright with trepidation and excitement.

"What the dickens do you suppose prompted Mrs. Hammerton to arrive at such an hour?" she said, extending her hand to Desboro. "That very wicked old cat got out of somebody's car just as I did, and I could feel her beady eyes boring into my back all the way up the staircase."

"Do you mean Aunt Hannah?"

"Yes, I do! What does she mean by coming here at such an unearthly hour? Don't go out into the box, Jim. She can see you from the orchestra. I'll wager that her opera glasses have been sweeping the house every second since she saw me!"

"If she sees me she won't talk," he said, coolly. "I'm one of her exempts——"

"Wait, Jim! What are you going to do?"

"Let her see us both. I tell you she never talks about me, or anybody with whom I happen to be. It's the best way to avoid gossip, Elena——"

"I don't want to risk it, Jim! Please don't! I'm in abject terror of that woman ——"

But Desboro had already stepped out to the box, and his keen, amused eyes very soon discovered the levelled glasses of Mrs. Hammerton.

"Come here, Elena!"

"Had I better?"

"Certainly. I want her to see you. That's it! That's enough. She won't say a word about you now."

Mrs. Clydesdale shrank back into the dim, rosy half-light of the box; Desboro looked down at Mrs. Hammerton and smiled; then rejoined his flushed companion.

"Don't worry; Aunt Hannah's fangs are extracted for this evening. Elena, you are looking pretty enough to endanger the record of an aged saint! There goes that meaningless overture! What is it you have to say to me?"

"Why are you so brusque with me, Jim?"

"I'm not. But I don't want the Barkleys and their guests to find us here together."

"Betty knows I care for you——"

"Oh, Lord!" he said impatiently. "You always did care for anything that is just out of reach when you stand on tip-toe. You always were that way, Elena. When we were free to see each other you would have none of me."

She was looking down while he spoke, smoothing one silken knee with her white-gloved hand. After a moment, she lifted her head. To his surprise, her eyes were brilliant with unshed tears.

"You don't love me any more, do you, Jim?"

"I—I have—it is about as it always will be with me. Circumstances have altered things."

"Is that all?"

He thought for a moment, and his eyes grew sombre.

"Jim! Are you going to marry somebody?" she said suddenly.

He looked up with a startled laugh, not entirely agreeable.

"Marry? No."

"Is there any girl you want to marry?"

"No. God forbid!"

"Why do you say that? Is it because of what you know about marriages—like mine?"

"Probably. And then some."

"There are happy ones."

"Yes, I've read about them."

"But there really are, Jim."

"Mention one."

She mentioned several among people both knew. He smiled. Then she said, wearily:

"There are plenty of decent people and decent marriages in the world. The people we play with are no good. It's only restlessness, idleness, and discontent that kills everything among people of our sort. I know I'm that way, too. But I don't believe I would be if I had married you."

"You are mistaken."

"Why? Don't you believe any marriage can be happy?"

"Elena, have you ever heard of a honeymoon that lasts? Do you know how long any two people can endure each other without merciful assistance from a third? Don't you know that, sooner or later, any two people ever born are certain to talk each other out—pump each other dry—love each other to satiation—and ultimately recoil, each into the mysterious seclusion of its own individuality, from whence it emerged temporarily in order that the human race might not perish from the earth!"

"What miserable lesson have you learned to teach you such a creed?" she asked. "I tell you the world is full of happy marriages—full of honoured husbands and beloved wives, and children worshipped and adored——"

"Children, yes, they come the nearest to making the conventional contract endurable. I wish to God you had some!"

"Jim!"

He said, almost savagely: "If you can, and don't, you'll make a hell for yourself with any man, sooner or later—mark my words! And it isn't worth while to enact the hypocrisy of marriage with nothing more than legal license in view! Why bother with priest or clergyman? That contract won't last. And it's less trouble not to make one at all than to go West and break one."

"Do you know you are talking very horridly to me?" she said.

"Yes—I suppose I am. I've got to be going now, anyway——"

As he spoke, the glittering house became dark; the curtain opened upon a dim scene of shadowy splendour, into which, exquisite and bewitchingly immortal as any goddess in the heavenly galaxy, glided Farrar, in the shimmering panoply of Ariane.

"Desboro stood staring down at the magic picture. Mrs. Clydesdale, too, had risen"

Desboro stood staring down at the magic picture. Mrs. Clydesdale, too, had risen. Below them the beauty of Farrar's matchless voice possessed the vast obscurity, searching the darkness like a ray of crystal light. One by one the stone crypts opened, disclosing their tinted waterfalls of jewels.

"I've got to go," he whispered. "Your people will be arriving."

They moved silently to the door.

"Jim?"

"Yes."

"There is no other woman; is there?"

"Not now."

"Oh! Was there?"

"There might have been."

"You mean—to—to marry?"

"No."

"Then—I suppose I can't help that sort. Men are—that way. Was it that girl at Silverwood?"

"No," he said, lying.

"Oh! Who was that girl at Silverwood?"

"A business acquaintance."

"I hear she is unusually pretty."

"Yes, very."

"You found it necessary to be at Silverwood when she was there?"

"Once or twice."

"It is no longer necessary?"

"No longer necessary."

"So you won't see her again?"

"No."

"I'm glad. It hurt, Jim. Some people I know at Willow Lake saw her. They said she was unusually beautiful."

"Elena," he said, "will you kindly come to your senses? I'm not going to marry anybody; but that doesn't concern you. I advise you to attend to your own life's business—which is to have children and bring them up more decently than the present generation are being brought up in this fool of a town! If nothing else will make your husband endurable, children will come nearest to it——"

"Jim—please——"

"For heaven's sake, don't cry!" he whispered.

"I—won't. Dear, don't you realise that you are all I have in the world——"

"We haven't got each other, I tell you, and we're not going to have each other ——"

"Yes—but don't take anybody else—marry anyone——"

"I won't. Control yourself!"

"Promise me!"

"Yes, I do. Go forward into the box; those people will be arriving——"

"Do you promise?"

"Yes, if you want me to. Go forward; nobody can see you in the dark. Good-bye——"

"Good-bye, dear. And thank you——"

He coolly ignored the upturned face; she caught his hand in a flash of impatient passion, then, with a whispered word, turned and went forward, mistress of herself again, to sit there for an hour or two and witness a mystery that has haunted the human heart for aeons, unexpressed.

On the fifth day, Desboro remained indoors and wrote business letters until late in the afternoon.

Toward evening he telephoned to Mrs. Quant to find out whether everything was being done to render Miss Nevers's daily sojourn at Silverwood House agreeable.

He learned that everything was being done, that the young lady in question had just departed for New York, and, furthermore, that she had inquired of Mrs. Quant whether Mr. Desboro was not coming soon to Silverwood, desiring to be informed because she had one or two business matters on which to consult him.

"Hold the wire," he said, and left it for a few moments' swift pacing to and fro. Then he came again to the telephone.

"Ask Miss Nevers to be kind enough to write me about the matters she has in mind, because I can not leave town at present."

"Yes, Mr. James. Are you well, sir?"

"Perfectly."

"Thank you, sir. If you feel chilly like at night——"

"But I don't. Good-night!"

He dressed, dined at the club, and remained there reading the papers until he had enough of their complacent ignorance. Then he went home, still doggedly refusing to attempt to analyse the indirect message from Jacqueline.

If it had any significance other than its apparent purport, he grimly refused to consider even such a possibility. And, deadly weary at last, he fell asleep and slept until late in the morning.

It was snowing hard when he awoke. His ablutions ended, he rang for breakfast. On his tray was a note from the girl in blue; he read it and dropped it into his pocket, remembering the fireplace sacrifice of a few days ago at Silverwood, and realising that such frivolous souvenirs were beginning to accumulate again.

He breakfasted without interest, unfolded the morning paper, glanced over the headlines, and saw that there was a little more murder, divorce, and boot-licking than he cared for, laid it aside, and lighted a cigarette. As he dropped the burnt match on the tray, he noticed under it another letter which he had overlooked among the bills and advertisements composing the bulk of the morning mail.

For a little while he held the envelope in his hand, not looking at it; then, with careless deliberation, he cut it open, using a paper knife, and drew out the letter. As he slowly opened it his hands shook in spite of him.

"My Dear Mr. Desboro: I telephoned Mrs. Quant last night and learned that she had given you my message over the wire only a few minutes before; and that you had sent word you could not come to Silverwood, but that I might communicate with you by letter.

"This is what I had to say to you: There is a suit of armour here which is in a very bad condition. It will be expensive to have it repaired by a good armourer. Did you wish to include it in the sale as it is, or have it repaired? It is No. in the old list; No. in my catalogue, now almost completed and ready for the printer. It is that rather unusual suit of black plate-mail, called 'Brigandine Armour,' a XV century suit from Aragon; and the quilted under-jacket has been ruined by moths and has gone completely to pieces. It is a very valuable suit.

"Would you tell me what to do?

"Very sincerely yours,

"Jacqueline Nevers."

An hour later he still sat there with the letter in his hand, gazing at nothing. And until the telephone beside him rang twice he had not stirred.

"Who is it?" he asked finally.

At the reply his face altered subtly, and he bowed his head to listen.

The distant voice spoke again, and:

"Silverwood?" he asked.

"Yes, here's your party."

An interval filled with a vague whirring, then:

"Mr. Desboro?"

"Yes. Good-morning, Miss Nevers."

"Good-morning. Have you a note from me?"

"Yes, thank you. It came this morning. I was just reading it—again."

"I thought I ought to consult you in such a matter."

"Certainly."

"Then—what are your wishes?"

"My wishes are yours."

"I cannot decide such a matter. It will be very expensive——"

"If it is worth the cost to you, it is worth it to me."

"I don't know what you mean. The burden of decision lies with you this time, doesn't it?"

"With us both. Unless you wish me to assume it."

"But it is yours to assume!"

"If you wish, then. But I may ask your opinion, may I not?"

There was a silence, then:

"Whatever you do I approve. I have no—opinion."

"You do not approve all I do."

The rejoinder came faintly: "How do you know?"

"I—wrote to you. Do you approve my writing to you?"

"Yes. If you do."

"And do you approve of what I wrote?"

"Not of all that you wrote."

"I wrote that I would not see you again."

"Yes."

"Do you think that is best?"

"I—do not think about it."

He said: "That, also, is best. Don't think of it at all. And about the armour, do exactly what you would do if you were in my place. Good-bye."

"Mr. Desboro——"

"Yes."

"Could you wait a moment? I am trying to think——"

"Don't try, Jacqueline!"

"Please wait—for me!"

There was a silence; a tiny spot of blood reddened his bitten lip before she spoke again; then:

"I wished to tell you something. I knew why you wrote. Is it right for me to tell you that I understood you? I wanted to write and say so, and—say something else—about how I felt—but it seems I can't. Only—we could be friends more easily now—if you wish."

"You have not understood!" he said.

"Yes, I have, Mr. Desboro. But we can be friends?"

"Could you be mine, after what I have written?"

"I thought I couldn't, at first. But that day was a—long one. And when a girl is much alone she becomes very honest with herself. And it all was entirely new to me. I didn't know what I ought to have done about it—only what I wished to do."

"And—what is that, Jacqueline?"

"Make things as they were—before———"

"Before I wrote?"

"Yes."

"All up to that time you wish might be again as it was? All?"

No answer.

"All?" he repeated.

"Don't ask me. I don't know—I don't know what I think any more."

"How deeply do you suppose I feel about it?"

"I did not know you felt anything very deeply."

There was a long pause, then her voice again:

"You know—you need not be afraid. I did not know enough to be until you wrote. But I understand, now."

He said: "It will be all right, then. It will be quite all right, Jacqueline. I'll come up on the noon train."

His car met him at the station. The snow had melted and the wet macadam road glittered under a declining winter sun, as the car rolled smoothly away through the still valleys of Westchester.

Mrs. Quant, in best bib and tucker and lilac ribbons, welcomed him, and almost wept at his pallor; but he shrugged impatiently and sprang up the low steps. Here the necessity for self-control stopped him short on his way to the armoury. He turned to Mrs. Quant with an effort:

"Is everything all right?"

"No, Mr. James. Phibby broke a cup and saucer Saturday, and there is new kittens in the laundry—which makes nine cats———"

"Oh, all right! Miss Nevers is here?"

"Yes, sir—in the liberry—which ain't been dusted right by that Phibby minx
———"

"Tell Phoebe to dust it!" he said sternly. "Do you suppose Miss Nevers cares to
handle dirty books!" His restless glance fell on the clock: "Tell Farris I'm here
and that Miss Nevers and I will lunch as soon as it's served. And say to Miss
Nevers that I'll be down in a few minutes." He turned and mounted the stairs
to his room, and found it full of white, clove-scented carnations.

Mrs. Quant came panting after him:

"Miss Nevers, she cut them in the greenhouse, and told me to put 'em in your
room, sayin' as how clove pinks is sanitary. Would you—would you try a few
m-m-magic drops, Mr. James, sir? Miss Nevers takes 'em regular."

"Oh, Lord!" he exclaimed, laughing in sheer exuberance of spirits. "I'll
swallow anything you like, only hurry!"

She dosed him with great content, he, both hands in soap-suds, turning his
head to receive the potion. And at last, ablutions finished, he ran down the
stairs, checked himself, and managed to stroll leisurely through the hall and
into the library.

She was writing; looked up, suddenly pale under her golden crown of hair; and
the red lips quivered, but her eyes were steady.

She bent her head again, both hands abandoned to him, sitting in silence while
his lips rested against her fingers.

"Is all well with you, Jacqueline?"

"Yes. And with you?"

"All is well with me. I missed you—if you know what that really means."

"Did you?"

"Yes. Won't you even look at me?"

"In a moment. Do you see all these piles of manuscript? All that is your new
catalogue—and mine," she added, with a faint smile; but her head remained
averted.

"You wonderful girl!" he said softly. "You wonderful girl!"

"Thank you. It was a labor of—pleasure." Colour stole to the tips of her ears.
"I have worked—worked—every minute since———"

"Yes."

"Really, I have—every minute. But somehow, it didn't seem to tire me. To-day —now—I begin to feel a little tired." She rested her cheek on one hand, still looking away from him.

"I took a peep into the porcelain and jade rooms," she said, "just a glance over what lies before me. Mrs. Quant very kindly gave me the keys. Did you mind?"

"Do I mind anything that it pleases you to do? What did you find in the jade room?"

She smiled: "Jadeite, of course; and lapis and crystals—the usual."

"Any good ones?"

"Some are miracles. I don't really know, yet; I gave just one swift glance and fled—because you see I haven't finished in the armoury, and I ought not to permit myself the pleasures of curiosity."

"The pleasures of curiosity and of anticipation are the only real ones. Sages have said it."

She shook her head.

"Isn't it true?" he insisted.

She looked up at him at last, frank-eyed but flushed:

"'Which is the real pleasure?' she asked"

"Which is the real pleasure," she asked, "seeing each other, or anticipating the —the resumption of the entente cordial?"

"You've smashed the sages and their philosophy," he nodded, studying the exquisite, upturned features unsmilingly. "To be with you is the greater— content. It's been a long time, hasn't it?"

She nodded thoughtfully: "Five days and a half."

"You—counted them, too?"

"Yes."

This wouldn't do. He rose and walked over to the fire, which needed a log or two; she turned and looked after him with little expression in her face except that the blue of her eyes had deepened to a lilac tint, and the flush on her cheeks still remained.

"You know," she said, "I didn't mean to take you from any business in New York—or pleasures——"

He shuddered slightly.

"Did I?" she asked.

"No."

"I only wished you to come—when you had time——"

"I know, Jacqueline. Don't show me your soul in every word you utter."

"What?"

He turned on his heel and came back to her, and she shrank a little, not knowing why; but he came no nearer than her desk.

"'The thing to do,' he said ... 'is for us both to keep very busy'"

"The thing to do," he said, speaking with forced animation and at random, "is for us both to keep very busy. I think I'll go into farming—raise some dinky thing or other—that's what I'll do. I'll go in for the country squire business—that's what I'll do. And I'll have my neighbours in. I'm never here long enough to ask 'em. They're a funny lot; they're all right, though—deadly respectable. I'll give a few parties—ask some people from town, too. Betty Barkley could run the conventional end of it. And you'd come floating in with other unattached girls——"

"You want me!"

He said, astonished: "Well, why on earth do you suppose I'm taking the trouble to ask the others?"

"You want me—to come—where your friends——"

"Don't you care to?"

"I—don't know." The surprise of it still widened her eyes and parted her lips a little. She looked up at him, perplexed, encountered something in his eyes which made her cheeks redden again.

"What would they think?" she asked.

"Is there anything to think?"

"N-no. But they don't know who I am. And I have nobody to vouch for me."

"You ought to have a companion."

"I don't want any——"

"Of course; but you ought to have one. Can you afford one?"

"I don't know. I don't know what they—they cost——"

"Let me fix that up," he said, with animation. "Let me think it out. I know a lot of people—I know some indigent and respectable old terrors who ought to fill the bill and hold their tongues as long as their salary is paid——"

"Oh, please don't, Mr. Desboro!"

He seated himself on the arm of her chair:

"Jacqueline, dear, it's only for your sake——"

"But I did understand your letter!"

"I know—I know. I just want to see you with other people. I just want to have them see you——"

"But I don't need a chaperon. Business women are understood, aren't they? Even women whom you know go in for house decoration, and cigarette manufacturing, and tea rooms, and hats and gowns."

"But they were socially known before they went in for these things. It's the way of the world, Jacqueline—nothing but suspicion when intelligence and beauty step forward from the ranks. And what do you suppose would happen if a man of my sort attempts to vouch for any woman?"

"Then don't—please don't try! I don't care for it—truly I don't. It was nice of you to wish it, Mr. Desboro, but—I'd rather be just what I am and—your friend."

"It can't be," he said, under his breath. But she heard him, looked up dismayed, and remained mute, crimsoning to the temples.

"This oughtn't to go on," he said, doggedly.

She said: "You have not understood me. I am different from you. You are not to blame for thinking that we are alike at heart; but, nevertheless, it is a mistake. I can be what I will—not what I once seemed to be—for a moment— with you—" Her head sank lower and remained bowed; and he saw her slender hands tightening on the arm of the chair.

"I—I've got to be honest," she said under her breath. "I've got to be—in every way. I know it perfectly well, Mr. Desboro. Men seem to be different—I don't know why. But they seem to be, usually. And all I want is to remain friends with you—and to remember that we are friends when I am at work somewhere. I just want to be what I am, a business woman with sufficient character and intelligence to be your friend quietly—not even for one evening in competition with women belonging to a different life—women with wit and beauty and charm and savoir faire——"

"Jacqueline!" he broke out impulsively. "I want you to be my guest here. Won't you let me arrange with some old gorgon to chaperon you? I can do it! And with the gorgon's head on your moral shield you can silence anybody!"

He began to laugh; she sat twisting her fingers on her lap and looking up at him in a lovely, distressed sort of way, so adorably perplexed and yet so pliable, so soft and so apprehensive, that his laughter died on his lips, and he sat looking down at her in silence.

After a while he spoke again, almost mechanically:

"I'm trying to think how we can best be on equal terms, Jacqueline. That is all. After your work is done here, I want to see you here and elsewhere—I want you to come back at intervals, as my guest. Other people will ask you. Other people must be here, too, when you are. I know some who will accept you on your merits—if you are properly chaperoned. That is all I am thinking about. It's fairer to you."

But even to himself his motive was not clear—only the rather confused idea persisted that women in his own world knew how to take care of themselves, whatever they chose to do about it—that Jacqueline would stand a fairer chance with herself, and with him, whatever his intentions might really be. It would be a squarer deal, that was all.

She sat thinking, one slim forefinger crook'd under her chin; and he saw her blue eyes deep in thought, and the errant lock curling against her cheek. Then she raised her head and looked at him:

"Do you think it best?"

"Yes—you adorable little thing!"

She managed to sustain his gaze:

"Could you find a lady gorgon?"

"I'm sure I can. Shall I?"

"Yes."

A moment later Farris announced luncheon. A swarm of cats greeted them at the door, purring and waiving multi-coloured tails, and escorted them to the table, from whence they knew came the delectable things calculated to satisfy the inner cat.

CHAPTER VIII

The countryside adjacent to Silverwood was eminently and self-consciously respectable. The fat, substantial estates still belonged to families whose forefathers had first taken title to them. There were, of course, a number of "colonial" houses, also a "colonial" inn, The Desboro Arms, built to look as genuine as possible, although only two years old, steam heated, and electric lighted.

But things "colonial" were the traditional capital of Silverwood, and its thrifty and respectable inhabitants meant to maintain the "atmosphere." To that end they had solemnly subscribed a very small sum for an inn sign to swing in front of The Desboro Arms; the wheelwright painted it; somebody fired a shotgunful of antiquity into it, and American weather was rapidly doing the rest, with a gratifying result which no degenerate European weather could have accomplished in half a century of rain and sunshine.

The majority of the mansions in Silverwood township were as inoffensively commonplace as the Desboro house. Few pre-Revolutionary structures survived; the British had burned the countryside from Major Lockwood's mansion at Pound Ridge all the way to Bedford Village and across to the Connecticut line. With few exceptions, Silverwood houses had shared the common fate when Tarleton and DeLancy galloped amuck among the Westchester hills; but here and there some sad old mansion still remained and was reverently cherished, as was also the graveyard, straggling up the hill, set with odd old headstones, upon which most remarkable cherubim smirked under a gladly permitted accumulation of lichen.

Age, thrift, substance, respectability—these were the ideals of Silverwood; and Desboro and his doings would never have been tolerated there had it not been that a forbear of his, a certain dissolute half-pay captain, had founded the community in . This sacred colonial fact had been Desboro's social salvation, for which, however, he did not seem to care very much. Good women continued to be acidly civil to him on this account, and also because Silverwood House and its estates could no more be dropped from the revered galaxy of the county than could a star be cast out of their country's flag for frivolous behavior.

So worthy men endured him, and irreproachable women grieved for him, although it was rumoured that he gave parties now and then which real actresses had actually attended. Also, though he always maintained the Desboro pew in church, he never decorated it with his person. Nor could the countryside count on him socially, except at eccentric intervals when his careless, graceful presence made the Westchester gaiety seem rather stiff and pallid, and gave the thin, sour claret an unwonted edge. And another and radical incompatibility; the Desboros were the only family of Cavalier descent in the township. And deep in the hearts of Silverwood folk the Desboros had ever seemed a godless race.

Now, there had been already some gossip among the Westchester hills concerning recent doings at Silverwood House. Even when it became known that the pretty girl who sped to and fro in Desboro's limousine, between house and station, was a celebrated art expert, and was engaged in cataloguing the famous Desboro collection, God-fearing people asked each other why Desboro should find it necessary to meet her at the station in the morning, and escort her back in the evening; and whether it were actually obligatory for him to be present while the cataloguing was in progress.

Westchester womanhood was beginning to look wan and worried; substantial gentlemen gazed inquiringly at each other over the evening chess-board; several flippant young men almost winked at each other. But these latter had been accustomed to New York, and were always under suspicion in their own families.

Therefore, it was with relief and surprise that Silverwood began to observe Desboro in furs, driving a rakish runabout, and careering about Westchester with Vail, his head farmer, seated beside him, evidently intent on committing future agriculture—palpably planning for two grass-blades where only one, or a mullein, had hitherto flourished within the memory of living man.

Fertiliser in large loads was driven into the fallow fields of the Desboros; brush and hedges and fences were being put in order. People beheld these radical preliminaries during afternoon drives in their automobiles; local tradesmen reported purchases of chemicals for soil enriching, and the sale of all sorts of farm utensils to Desboro's agent.

At the Country Club all this was gravely discussed; patriarchs mentioned it over their checkers; maidens at bowls or squash or billiards listened to the exciting tale, wide-eyed; hockey, ski, or skating parties gossiped recklessly about it. The conclusion was that Desboro had already sowed his wilder oats; and the worthy community stood watching for the prodigal's return, intending to meet him while yet he was far off.

He dropped in at the Country Club one day, causing a little less flutter than a hawk in a hen-yard. Within a week he had drifted casually into the drawing-rooms of almost all his father's old friends for a cup of tea or an informal chat—or for nothing in particular except to saunter into his proper place among them with all of the Desboro grace and amiable insouciance which they had learned to tolerate but never entirely to approve or understand.

It was not quite so casually that he stopped at the Hammerton's. And he was given tea and buns by Mrs. Hammerton, perfectly unsuspicious of his motives. Her husband came rambling in from the hothouses, presently, where he spent most of his serious life in pinching back roses and chrysanthemums; and he extended to Desboro a large, flat and placid hand.

"Aunt Hannah and Daisy are out—somewhere—" he explained vaguely. "You must have passed them on the way."

"Yes, I saw Daisy in the distance, exercising an old lady," said Desboro carelessly. He did not add that the sight of Aunt Hannah marching across the Westchester horizon had inspired him with an idea.

From her lair in town, she had come hither, for no love of her nephew and his family, nor yet for Westchester, but solely for economy's bitter sake. She made such pilgrimages at intervals every year, upsetting the Hammerton household with her sarcasms, her harsh, high-keyed laughter, her hardened ways of defining the word "spade"—for Aunt Hannah was a terror that Westchester dreaded but never dreamed of ignoring, she being a wayward daughter of the sacred soil, strangely and weirdly warped from long transplanting among the gay and godless of Gotham town. And though her means, after her husband's scared soul had taken flight, were painfully attenuated, the high priests and captains among the gay and godless feared her, and she bullied them; and she and they continued to foregather from sheer tradition, but with mutual and sincere dislike. For Aunt Hannah's name would always figure among the names of certain metropolitan dowagers, dragons, gorgons, and holy harridans; always be connected with certain traditional social events as long as the old lady lived. And she meant to survive indefinitely, if she had anything to say about it.

She came in presently with Daisy Hammerton. The latter gave her hand frankly to her childhood's comrade; the former said:

"Hah! James Desboro!" very disagreeably, and started to nourish herself at once with tea and muffins.

"James Desboro," she repeated scornfully, darting a wicked glance at him where he stood smiling at her, "James Desboro, turning plow-boy in Westchester! What's the real motive? That's what interests me. I'm a bad old woman—I know it! All over paint and powder, and with too small a foot and too trim a figger to be anything except wicked. Lindley knows it; it makes his fingers tremble when he pinches crysanthemums; Susan knows it; so does Daisy. And I admit it. And that's why I'm suspicious of you, James; I'm so wicked myself. Come, now; why play the honest yokel? Eh? You good-looking good-for-nothing!"

"My motive," he said amiably, "is to make a living and learn what it feels like."

"Been stock-gambling again?"

"Yes, dear lady."

"Lose much?" she sniffed.

"Not a very great deal."

"Hah! And now you've got to raise the wind, somehow?"

He repeated, good-humouredly: "I want to make a living."

The trim little old lady darted another glance at him.

"Ha—ha!" she laughed, without giving any reason for the disagreeable burst of mirth; and started in on another muffin.

"I think," said Mr. Hammerton, vaguely, "that James will make an excellent agriculturist——"

"Excellent fiddlesticks!" observed Aunt Hannah. "He'd make a good three-card man."

Daisy Hammerton said aside to Desboro:

"Isn't she a terror!"

"Oh, she likes me!" he said, amused.

"I know she does, immensely. She makes me take her for an hour's walk every day—and I'm so tired of exercising her and listening to her—unconventional stories—about you."

"She's a bad old thing," said Desboro affectionately, and, in his natural voice: "Aren't you, Aunt Hannah? But there isn't a smarter foot, or a prettier hand, or a trimmer waist in all Gotham, is there?"

"Philanderer!" she retorted, in a high-pitched voice. "What about that Van Alstyne supper at the Santa Regina?"

"Which one?" he asked coolly. "Stuyve is always giving 'em."

"Read the Tattler!" said the old lady, seizing more muffins.

Mrs. Hammerton closed her tight lips and glanced uneasily at her daughter. Daisy sipped her tea demurely. She had read all about it, and burned the paper in her bedroom grate.

Desboro gracefully ignored the subject; the old lady laughed shrilly once or twice, and the conversation drifted toward the more decorous themes of pinching back roses and mixing plant-food, and preparing nourishment for various precocious horticultural prodigies now developing in Lindley Hammerton's hothouses.

Daisy Hammerton, a dark young girl, with superb eyes and figure, chatted unconcernedly with Desboro, making a charming winter picture in her scarlet felt hat and jacket, from which the black furs had fallen back. She went in for things violent and vigorous, and no nonsense; rode as hard as she could in such a country, played every game that demanded quick eye and flexible muscle—and, in secret, alas, wrote verses and short stories unanimously rejected by even the stodgier periodicals. But nobody suspected her of such weakness—not even her own mother.

Desboro swallowed his tea and took leave of his rose-pinching host and hostess, and their sole and lovely progeny, also, perhaps, the result of scientific concentration. Aunt Hannah retained his hand:

"Where are you going now, James?"

"Nowhere—home," he said, pretending embarrassment, which was enough to interest Aunt Hannah in the trap.

"Oh! Nowhere—home!" she mimicked him. "Where is 'nowhere home'? Somewhere out? I've a mind to go with you. What do you say to that, young man?"

"Come along," he said, a shade too promptly; and the little, bright, mink-like eyes sparkled with malice. The trap was sprung, and Aunt Hannah was in it. But she didn't yet suspect it.

"Slip on my fur coat for me," she said. "I'll take a spin with you in your runabout."

"You overwhelm me," he protested, holding up the fur coat.

"I may do that yet, my clever friend! Come on! No shilly-shallying! Susan! Tell your maid to lay out that Paquin gown which broke my financial backbone last month! I'll bring James back to dinner—or know the reason why!"

"I'll tell you why not, now," said Desboro. "I'm going to town early this evening."

"Home, nowhere, and then to town," commented Aunt Hannah loudly. "A multi-nefarious destination. James, if you run into the Ewigkeit by way of a wire fence or a tree, I'll come every night and haunt you! But don't poke along as Lindley pokes, or I'll take the wheel myself."

The deaf head-farmer, Vail, who had kept the engine going for fear of freezing, left the wheel and crawled resignedly into the tonneau.

Aunt Hannah and Desboro stowed themselves aboard; the swift car went off like a firecracker, then sped away into the darkness at such a pace that presently Aunt Hannah put her marmot-like face close to Desboro's ear and swore at him.

"Didn't you want speed?" he asked, slowing down.

"Where are you going, James—home, or nowhere?"

"Nowhere."

"Well, we arrived there long ago. Now, go home—your home."

"Sure, but I've got to catch that train——"

"Oh, you'll catch it—or something else. James?"

"Madame?"

"Some day I want to take a look at that young woman who is cataloguing your collection."

"That's just what I want you to do now," he said cheerfully. "I'm taking her to New York this evening."

Aunt Hannah, astonished and out of countenance, remained mute, her sharp nose buried in her furs. She had been trapped, and she knew it. Then her eyes glittered:

"You're being talked about," she said with satisfaction. "So is she! Ha!"

"Much?" he asked coolly.

"No. The good folk are only asking each other why you meet her at the station with your car. They think she carries antique gems in her satchel. Later they'll suspect who the real jewel is. Ha!"

"I like her; that's why I meet her," he said coolly.

"You like her?"

"I sure do. She is some girl, dear lady."

"Do you think your pretense of guileless candour is disarming me, young man?"

"I haven't the slightest hope of disarming you or of concealing anything from you."

"Follows," she rejoined ironically, "that there's nothing to conceal. Bah!"

"Quite right; there is nothing to conceal."

"What do you want with her, then?"

"Initially, I want her to catalogue my collection; subsequently, I wish to remain friends with her. The latter wish is becoming a problem. I've an idea that you might solve it."

"Friends with her," repeated Aunt Hannah. "Oh, my!

"'And angels whisper

Lo! the pretty pair!'

"I suppose! Is that the hymn-tune, James?"

"Precisely."

"What does she resemble—Venus, or Rosa Bonheur?"

"Look at her and make up your mind."

"Is she very pretty?"

"I think so. She's thin."

"Then what do you see unusual about her?"

"Everything, I think."

"Everything—he thinks! Oh, my sense of humour!"

"That," said Desboro, "is partly what I count on."

"Have you any remote and asinine notions of educating her and marrying her, and foisting her on your friends? There are a few fools still alive on earth, you know."

"So I've heard. I haven't the remotest idea of marrying her; she is better fitted to educate me than I am her. Not guilty on these two counts. But I had thought of foisting some of my friends on her. You, for example."

Aunt Hannah glared at him—that is, her tiny eyes became almost luminous, like the eyes of small animals at night, surprised by a sudden light.

"I know what you're meditating!" she snapped.

"I suppose you do, by this time."

"You're very impudent. Do you know it?"

"Lord, Aunt Hannah, so are you!" he drawled. "But it takes genius to get away with it."

The old lady was highly delighted, but she concealed it and began such a rapid-fire tirade against him that he was almost afraid it might bewilder him enough to affect his steering.

"Talk to me of disinterested friendship between you and a girl of that sort!" she ended. "Not that I'd care, if I found material in her to amuse me, and a monthly insult drawn to my order against a solvent bank balance! What is she, James; a pretty blue-stocking whom nobody 'understands' except you?"

"Make up your own mind," he repeated, as he brought around the car and stopped before his own doorstep. "I'm not trying to tell you anything. She is here. Look at her. If you like her, be her friend—and mine."

Jacqueline had waited tea for him; the table was in the library, kettle simmering over the silver lamp; and the girl was standing before the fire, one foot on the fender, her hands loosely linked behind her back.

She glanced up with unfeigned pleasure as his step sounded outside along the stone hallway; and the smile still remained, curving her lips, but died out in her eyes, as Mrs. Hammerton marched in, halted, and stared at her unwinkingly.

Desboro presented them; Jacqueline came forward, offering a shy hand to Aunt Hannah, and, bending her superb young head, looked down into the beady eyes which were now fairly electric with intelligence.

Desboro began, easily:

"I asked Mrs. Hammerton to have tea with——"

"I asked myself," remarked Aunt Hannah, laying her other hand over Jacqueline's—she did not know just why—perhaps because she was vain of her hands, as well as of her feet and "figger."

She seated herself on the sofa and drew Jacqueline down beside her.

"This young man tells me that you are cataloguing his grandfather's accumulation of ancient tin-ware."

"Yes," said Jacqueline, already afraid of her. And the old lady divined it, too, with not quite as much pleasure as it usually gave her to inspire trepidation in others.

Her shrill voice was a little modified when she said:

"Where did you learn to do such things? It's not usual, you know."

"You have heard of Jean Louis Nevers," suggested Desboro.

"Yes—" Mrs. Hammerton turned and looked at the girl again. "Oh!" she said. "I've heard Cary Clydesdale speak of you, haven't I?"

Jacqueline made a slight, very slight, but instinctive movement away from the old lady, on whom nothing that happened was lost.

"Mr. Clydesdale," said Mrs. Hammerton, "told several people where I was present that you knew more about antiquities in art than anybody else in New York since your father died. That's what he said about you."

Jacqueline said: "Mr. Clydesdale has been very kind to me."

"Kindness to people is also a Clydesdale tradition—isn't it, James?" said the old lady. "How kind Elena has always been to you!"

The covert impudence of Aunt Hannah, and her innocent countenance, had no significance for Jacqueline—would have had no meaning at all except for the dark flush of anger that mounted so suddenly to Desboro's forehead.

He said steadily: "The Clydesdales are very old friends, and are naturally kind. Why you don't like them I never understood."

"Perhaps you can understand why one of them doesn't like me, James."

"Oh! I can understand why many people are not crazy about you, Aunt Hannah," he said, composedly.

"Which is going some," said the old lady, with a brisk and unabashed employment of the vernacular. Then, turning to Jacqueline: "Are you going to give this young man some tea, my child? He requires a tonic."

Jacqueline rose and seated herself at the table, thankful to escape. Tea was soon ready; Aunt Hannah, whose capacity for browsing was infinite, began on jam and biscuits without apology. And Jacqueline and Desboro exchanged their first furtive glances—dismayed and questioning on the girl's part, smilingly reassuring on Desboro's. Aunt Hannah, looking intently into her teacup, missed nothing.

"Come to see me!" she said so abruptly that even Desboro started.

"'I—I beg your pardon,' said Jacqueline"

"I—I beg your pardon," said Jacqueline, not understanding.

"Come to see me in town. I've a rotten little place in a fashionable apartment house—one of the Park Avenue kind, which they number instead of calling it the 'Buena Vista' or the 'Hiawatha.' Will you come?"

"Thank you."

The old lady looked at her grimly:

"What does 'thank you' mean? Yes or no? Because I really want you. Don't you wish to come?"

"I would be very glad to come—only, you know, I am in business—and go out very little——"

"Except on business," added Desboro, looking Aunt Hannah unblushingly in the eye until she wanted to pinch him. Instead, she seized another biscuit, which Farris presented on a tray, smoking hot, and applied jam to it vigorously. After she had consumed it, she rose and marched around the room, passing the portraits and book shelves in review. Half turning toward Jacqueline:

"I haven't been in the musty old mansion for years; that young man never asks me. But I used to know the house. It was this sort of house that drove me out of Westchester, and I vowed I'd marry a New York man or nobody. Do you know, child, that there is a sort of simpering smugness about a house like this that makes me inclined to kick dents in the furniture?"

Jacqueline ventured to smile; Desboro's smile responded in sympathy.

"I'm going home," announced Aunt Hannah. "Good-bye, Miss Nevers. I don't want you to drive me, James; I'd rather have your man take me back. Besides, you've a train to catch, I understand——" She turned and looked at Jacqueline, who had risen, and they stood silently inspecting each other. Then, with a grim nod, as though partly of comprehension, partly in adieu, Aunt Hannah sailed out. Desboro tucked her in beside Vail. The latter being quite deaf, they talked freely under his very nose.

"James!"

"Yes, dear lady."

"You gave yourself away about Elena Clydesdale. Haven't you any control over your countenance?"

"Sometimes. But don't do that again before her! The story is a lie, anyway."

"So I've heard—from you. Tell me, James, do you think this little Nevers girl dislikes me?"

"Do you want her to?"

"No. You're a very clever young one, aren't you? Really quite an expert! Do you know, I don't think that girl would care for what I might have to offer her. There's more to her than to most people."

"How do you know? She scarcely spoke a word."

The old lady laughed scornfully:

"I know people by what they don't say. That's why I know you so much better than you think I do—you and Elena Clydesdale. And I don't think you're much good, James—or some of your married friends, either."

She settled down among the robes, with a bright, impertinent glance at him. He shrugged, standing bareheaded by the mud-guard, a lithe, handsome young fellow. "—A Desboro all over," she thought, with a mental sniff of admiration.

"Are you going to speak to Miss Nevers?" she asked, abruptly.

"About what!"

"About employing me, you idiot!"

"Yes, if you like. If she comes up here as my guest, she'll need a gorgon."

"I'll gorgon you," she retorted, wrathfully.

"Thanks. So you'll accept the—er—job?"

"Of course, if she wishes. I need the money. It's purely mercenary on my part."

"That's understood."

"Are you going to tell her I'm mercenary?"

"Naturally."

"Well, then—don't—if you don't mind. Do you think I want every living creature to detest me?"

"I don't detest you. And you have an unterrified tabby-cat at home, haven't you?"

She could have boxed his ears as he leaned over and deliberately kissed her cheek.

"I love you because you're so bad," he whispered; and, stepping lightly aside, nodded to Vail to go ahead.

The limousine, acetylenes shining, rolled up as the other car departed. He went back to the library and found Jacqueline pinning on her hat.

"Well?" he inquired gaily.

"Why did you bring her, Mr. Desboro?"

"Didn't you like her?"

"Who is she?"

"A Mrs. Hannah Hammerton. She knows everybody. Most people are afraid of her. She's poor as a guinea-pig."

"She was beautifully gowned."

"She always is. Poor Aunt Hannah!"

"Is she your aunt?"

"No, she's Lindley Hammerton's aunt—a neighbour of mine. I call her that; it made her very mad in the beginning, but she rather likes it now. You'll go to call on her, won't you?"

Jacqueline turned to him, drawing on her gloves:

"Mr. Desboro, I don't wish to be rude; and, anyway, she will forget that she asked me in another half-hour. Why should I go to see her?"

"Because she's one species of gorgon. Now, do you understand?"

"What!"

"Of course. It isn't a case of pin-money with her; it's a case of clothing, rent, and nourishment. A microscopic income, supplemented by gifts, commissions, and odd social jobs, keeps her going. What you and I want of her is for her to be seen at various times with you. She'll do the rest in talking about you—'my unusually talented young friend, Miss Nevers,' and that sort of thing. It will deceive nobody; but you'll eventually meet some people—she knows all kinds. The main point is that when I ask you here she'll bring you. People will understand that you are another of her social enterprises, for which she's paid. But it won't count against you. It will depend on yourself entirely how you are received. And not a soul will be able to say a word—" he laughed, "—except that I am very devoted to the beautiful Miss Nevers—as everybody else will be."

Jacqueline remained motionless for a few moments, an incomprehensible expression on her face; then she went over to him and took one of his hands in her gloved ones, and stood looking down at it in silence.

"Well," he asked, smiling.

She said, still looking down at his hand lying between her own:

"You have behaved in the sweetest way to me—" Her voice grew unsteady, and she turned her head sharply away.

"Jacqueline!" he exclaimed under his breath. "It's a broken reed you're trusting. Don't, dear. I'm like all the others."

She shook her head slightly, still looking away from him. After a short silence, her voice returned to her control again.

"You are very kind to me, Mr. Desboro. When a man sees that a girl likes him—and is kind to her—it is wonderful to her."

He tried to take a lighter tone.

"It's the case of the beast born in captivity, Jacqueline. I'm only going through the tricks convention has taught me. But every instinct remains unaltered."

"That is civilisation, isn't it?"

"Oh, I don't know what it is—you wonderful little thing!"

He caught her hand, then encircled her waist, drawing her close. After a moment, she dropped her big, fluffy muff on his shoulder and hid her flushed face in the fur.

"Don't trust me, will you?" he said, bluntly.

"No."

"Because I—I'm an unaccountable beast."

"We—both have to account—sometime—to somebody. Don't we?" she said in a muffled voice.

"That would never check me."

"It would—me."

"Spiritual responsibility?"

"Yes."

"Is that all?"

"What else is there to remember—when a girl—cares for a man."

"Do you really care very much?"

Perhaps she considered the question superfluous, for she remained silent until his nerveless arm released her. Then she lifted her face from the muff. It was pale but smiling when he met her eyes.

"I'll go to see Mrs. Hammerton, some day," she said, "because it would hurt too much not to be able to come here when you ask me—and other people—like the—the Clydesdales. You were thinking of me when you thought of this, weren't you?"

"In a way. A girl has got to reckon with what people say."

She nodded, pale and expressionless, slowly brushing up the violets fastened to her muff.

Farris appeared, announced the time, and held Desboro's coat. They had just margin enough to make their train.

CHAPTER IX

The following morning, Aunt Hannah returned to her tiny apartment on Park Avenue, financially benefitted by her Westchester sojourn, having extracted a bolt of Chinese loot-silk for a gown from her nephew's dismayed wife, and the usual check from her nephew.

Lindley, a slow, pallid, and thrifty soul, had always viewed Aunt Hannah's event with unfeigned alarm, because, somehow or other, at the close of every visit he found himself presenting her with a check. And it almost killed him.

Years ago he had done it for the first time. He had never intended to; certainly never meant to continue. Every time she appeared he vowed to himself that he wouldn't. But before her visit ended, the pressure of custom became too much for him; a deadly sense of obligation toward this dreadful woman—of personal responsibility for her indigence—possessed him, became gradually an obsession, until he exorcised it by the present of a check.

She never spoke of it—never seemed to hint at it—always seemed surprised and doubtful of accepting; but some devilish spell certainly permeated the atmosphere in her immediate vicinity, drawing perfectly good money out of his innermost and tightly buttoned breast-pockets and leaving it certified and carelessly crumpled in her velvet reticule.

It happened with a sickening regularity which now he had come to view with the modified internal fury of resignation. It had simply become a terrible custom, and, with all his respectable inertia and thrifty caution, adherence to custom ruled Lindley Hammerton. For years he had pinched roses; for years he had drawn checks for Aunt Hannah. Nothing but corporeal dissolution could terminate these customs.

As for Aunt Hannah, she banked her check and had her bolt of silk made into a gown, and trotted briskly about her business with perennial self-confidence in her own ability to get on.

Once or twice during the following fortnight she remembered Jacqueline, and mentally tabulated her case as a possible source of future income; but social duties were many and acridly agreeable, and pecuniary pickings plenty. Up to her small, thin ears in intrigue, harmless and not quite so harmless, she made hay busily while the social sun shone; and it was near the end of February before a stagnation in pleasure and business brought Jacqueline's existence into her mind again.

She called up Silverwood, and eventually got Desboro on the wire.

"Do you know," she said, "that your golden-headed and rather attenuated inamorata has never had the civility to call on me!"

"She has been too busy."

"Too busy gadding about Silverwood with you!"

"She hasn't been here since you saw her."

"What!"

"It's quite true. An important collection is to be sold under the hammer on the premises; she had the contract to engineer that matter before she undertook to catalogue my stuff."

"Oh! Haven't you seen her since?"

"Yes."

"Not at Silverwood?"

"No, only at her office."

He could hear her sniff and mutter something, then:

"I thought you were going to give some parties at Silverwood, and ask me to bring your pretty friend," she said.

"I am. She has the jades and crystals to catalogue. What I want, as soon as she gets rid of Clydesdale, is for her to resume work here—come up and remain as my guest until the cataloguing is finished. So you see I'll have to have you, too."

"That's a cordial and disinterested invitation, James!"

"Will you come? I'll ask half a dozen people. You can kill a few at cards, too."

"When?"

"The first Thursday in March. It's a business proposition, but it's between you and me, and she is not to suspect it."

"Very well," said Aunt Hannah cheerfully. "I'll arrange my engagements accordingly. And do try to have a gay party, James; and don't ask the Clydesdales. You know how Westchester gets on my nerves. And I always hated her."

"You are very unjust to her and to him——"

"You can't tell me anything about Cary Clydesdale, or about his wife, either," she interrupted tartly, and rang off in a temper. And Desboro went back to his interrupted business with Vail.

Since Jacqueline had been compelled to suspend temporarily her inventory at Silverwood in favor of prior engagements, Desboro had been to the city only twice, and both times to see her.

He had seen her in her office, remained on both occasions for an hour only, and had then taken the evening train back to Silverwood. But every evening he had written her of the day just ended—told her about the plans for farming, now maturing, of the quiet life at Silverwood, how gradually he was reëstablishing neighbourly relations with the countryside, how much of a country squire he was becoming.

"—And the whole thing with malice aforethought," he wrote. "—Every blessed move only a strategy in order that, to do you honour, I may stand soberly and well before the community when you are among my guests.

"In tow of Aunt Hannah; engaged for part of the day in your business among the jades, crystals, and porcelains of a celebrated collection; one of a house party; and the guest of a young man who has returned very seriously to till the soil of his forefathers; all that anybody can possibly think of it will be that your host is quite as captivated by your grace, wisdom, and beauty as everybody else will be.

"And what do you think of that, Jacqueline?"

"I think," she wrote, "that no other man has ever been as nice to me. I do not really care about the other people, but I quite understand that you and I could not see each other as freely as we have been doing, without detriment to me. I like you—superfluous admission! And I should miss seeing you—humble confession! And so I suppose it is best that everybody should know who and what I am—a business woman well-bred enough to sit at table with your friends, with sufficient self-confidence to enter and leave a room properly, to maintain my grasp on the conversational ball, and to toss it lightly to my vis-à-vis when the time comes.

"All this is worth doing and enduring for the sake of being your guest. Without conscientious scruples, apprehensions, perplexities, and fears I could never again come to Silverwood and be there alone with you as I have been. Always I have been secretly unhappy and afraid after a day with you at Silverwood. Sooner or later it would have had to end. It can not go on—as it has been going. I know it. The plea of business is soon worn threadbare if carelessly used.

"And so—caring for your friendship as I do—and it having become such a factor in my life—I find it easy to do what you ask me; and I have arranged to go with Mrs. Hammerton to Silverwood on the first Thursday in March, to practice my profession, enjoy the guests at your house party, and cultivate our friendship with a clear conscience and a tranquil and happy mind.

"It was just that little element of protection I needed to make me more happy than I have ever been. Somehow, I couldn't care for you as frankly and freely as I wanted to. And some things have happened—you know what I mean. I didn't reproach you, or pretend surprise or anger. I felt neither—only a confused sense of unhappiness. But—I cared for you enough to submit.

"Now I go to you with a sense of security that is delightful. You don't understand how a girl situated as I am feels when she knows that she is in a position where any woman has the right to regard her with suspicion. Skating, motoring, with you, I could not bear to pass people you knew and to whom you bowed—women—even farmers' wives.

"But now it will be different; I feel so warmly confident at heart, so secure, that I shall perhaps dare to say and do and be much that you never suspected was in me. The warm sun of approval makes a very different person of me. A girl, who, in her heart, does not approve of what she is doing, and who is always expecting to encounter other women who would not approve, is never at her best—isn't even herself—and isn't really happy, even with a man she likes exceedingly. You will, I think, see a somewhat different girl on Thursday."

"If your words are sometimes a little misty," he wrote, "your soul shines through everything you say, with a directness entirely heavenly. Life, for us, begins on Thursday, under cover no longer, but in the open. And the field will be as fair for you as for me. That is as it should be; that is as far as I care to look. But somehow, after all is done and said that ever will be said and done between you and me, I am conscious that when we two emerge from the dream called 'living,' you will lead and direct us both—even if you never do so here on earth.

"I am not given to this sort of stuff.

"Jacqueline, dear, I'd like to amuse my guests with something unusual. Could you help me out?"

She answered: "I'll do anything in the world I can to make your house party pleasant for you and your guests. So I've asked Mr. Sissly to give a recital. It is quite the oddest thing; you don't listen to a symphony which he plays on the organ; you see it. He will send the organ, electrical attachments, lights, portable stage and screen, to Silverwood; and his men will install everything in the armoury.

"Then, if it would amuse your guests, I could tell them a little about your jades and crystals, and do it in a rather unusual way. I think you'd rather like it. Shall I?"

He wrote some days later: "What a darling you are! Anything you do will be charming. Sissly's men have arrived and are raising a racket in the armoury with hammer and saw.

"The stage will look quite wonderful between the wide double rank of equestrian figures in armour.

"Aunt Hannah writes that you called on her and that you and she are coming up on the train together, which is delightfully sensible, and exactly as it should be. Heaven alone knows how long you are going to be able to endure her. It's rather odd, you know, but I like her and always have, though she's made things disagreeable for me more than once in my life.

"Your room is ready; Aunt Hannah's adjoins. Quarters for other guests are ready also. Have you any idea how I look forward to your coming?"

Three days later his guests arrived on the first three morning trains—a jolly crowd of young people—nineteen of them—who filled his automobiles and horse-drawn vehicles. Their luggage followed in vans, from which protruded skis and hockey sticks. There being no porter, the butler of Silverwood House received them in front of the lodge at the outer gates, offering the "guest cup," a Desboro custom of many generations, originating in England, although the lodge had stood empty and the gates open since his grandfather's time.

"There was, for a moment, an unconscious and unwonted grace in his manner"

Desboro welcomed them on his own doorstep; and there was, for a moment, an unconscious and unwonted grace in his manner and bearing—an undefined echo in his voice of other and more courtly times, as he gave his arm to Aunt Hannah and led her inside the hall.

There it exhaled and vanished as Mrs. Quant and the maids smilingly conducted the guests to their various quarters—vanished with the smiling formality of his greeting to Jacqueline.

The men returned first, clad in their knickerbockers and skating jackets. Cocktails awaited them in the billiard-room, and they gathered there in noisy curiosity over this celebrated house not often opened to anybody except its owner.

"Who is the dream, Jim?" demanded Reginald Ledyard. "I mean the wonder with the gold hair, that Mrs. Hammerton has in tow?"

"A friend of Aunt Hannah's—an expert in antique art—and as clever and charming as she is pretty," said Desboro pleasantly.

"High-brow! Oh, help!" muttered Ledyard. "Where's your library? I want to read up."

"She can talk like other people," remarked Van Alstyne. "I got next on the train—old lady Hammerton stood for me. She can flirt some, I'll tell you those."

Bertie Barkley extracted the olive from a Bronx and considered it seriously.

"The old lady is on a salary, of course. Nobody ever heard of anybody named Neve

rs," he remarked.

"They'll hear of somebody named Nevers now," observed Captain Herrendene with emphasis, "or," he added in modest self-depreciation, "I am all kinds of a liar."

"Where did you know her, Jim?" inquired Ledyard curiously.

"Oh, Miss Nevers's firm has charge of cataloguing my armour and jades. They're at it still. That's how I first met her—in a business way. And when I found her to be a friend of Aunt Hannah's, I asked them both up here as my guests."

"You always had an eye for beauty," said Cairns. "What do you suppose Mrs. Hammerton's game is?"

"Why, to make Miss Nevers known where she really ought to belong," replied Desboro frankly.

"How high does she plan to climb?" asked Barkley. "Above the vegetating line?"

"Probably not as far as the line of perpetual stupidity," said Desboro. "Miss Nevers appears to be a very busy, and very intelligent, and self-sufficient young lady, and I imagine she would have neither time nor inclination to decorate any of the restless, gilt-encrusted sets."

Van Alstyne said: "She's got the goods to deliver almost anywhere Mrs. Hammerton chooses—F. O. B. what?"

"She's some dream," admitted Ledyard as they all moved toward the library.

There were a lot of gay young girls there in skating costumes; Ledyard's sister Marie, with her large figure and pretty but slightly stupid face; Helsa Steyr, blonde, athletic, and red-haired; Athalie Vannis, with her handsome, dark face, so often shadowed by discontent; Barkley's animated little wife, Elizabeth, grey-eyed and freckled and brimming with mischief of the schoolboy quality; the stately Katharine Frere; Aunt Hannah; and Jacqueline.

All except the latter two had been doing something to cocktails of various species; Jacqueline took nothing; Aunt Hannah, Scotch whiskey with relish.

"It's about the last of the skating," said Desboro, "so we'd better take what we can get as soon as luncheon is over. Pick your partners and don't squabble. Me for Mrs. Hammerton!" and he led her out.

At table he noticed that Captain Herrendene had secured Jacqueline, and that Reggie Ledyard, on the other side, was already neglecting his own partner in his eager, good-looking and slightly loutish fashion of paying court to the newest and prettiest girl.

Aunt Hannah's glance continually flickered sideways at Desboro, but when she discovered that he was aware of her covert scrutiny, she said under her breath:

"I've been shopping with her; the little thing didn't know how to clothe herself luxuriously in the more intimate details. I'd like to see anybody's maid patronise her now! Yours don't know enough—but she'll go where there are those who do know, sooner or later. What do you think of her?"

"What I always think," he said coolly. "She is the most interesting girl I ever met."

"She's too clever to care very much for what I can offer her," said Mrs. Hammerton drily. "Glitter and tinsel would never dazzle her, James; pretense, complacency, bluff, bragg, she'd devilish soon see through it all with those clear, intelligent eyes—see at the bottom what lies squirming there—anxiety, self-distrust, eternal dread, undying envy, the secret insecurity of those who imitate the real—which does not exist in America—and who know in their hopeless hearts that they are only shams, like that two-year-old antique tavern yonder, made quaint to order."

He said smilingly: "She'll soon have enough of your particular familiars. But, little by little, she'll find herself in accord with people who seek her as frankly as she seeks them. Natural selection, you know. Your only usefulness is to give her the opportunity, and you've begun to do it, bless your heart."

She flashed a malicious glance at him; under cover of the gay hubbub she said:

"I may do more than that, James."

"Really."

"Yes; I may open her eyes to men of your sort."

"Her eyes are open already, I suppose."

"Not very wide. For example—you'd never marry her. Would you?"

"Don't talk that way," he said coldly.

"No, I don't have to talk at all. I know. If you ever marry, I know what deadly species of female it will be. You're probably right; you're that kind, too—no real substance to you, James. And so I think I'll have to look after my intellectual protégée, and be very sure that her pretty eyes are wide open."

He turned toward her; their glances met level and hard:

"Let matters alone," he said. "I have myself in hand."

"You have in hand a horse with a runaway record, James."

Cairns, on her left, spoke to her; she turned and answered, then presented her well-shaped back to that young gentleman and again crossed glances with Desboro, who was waiting, cool as steel.

"Come, James," she said in a low voice, "what do you mean to do? A man always means something or nothing; and the latter is the more dangerous."

As that was exactly what Desboro told himself he had always meant, he winced and remained silent.

"Oh, you—the lot of you!" she said with smiling contempt. "I'll equip that girl to take care of herself before I'm through with her. Watch me."

"It is part of your business. Equip her to take care of herself as thoroughly as anybody you know. Then it will be up to her—as it is up to all women, after all—and to all men."

"Oh, is it? You've all the irresponsibility and moral rottenness of your Cavalier ancestors in you; do you know it, James? The Puritan, at least, never doubted that he was his brother's keeper."

Desboro said doggedly: "With the individual alone rests what that individual will be."

"Is that your mature belief?" she asked ironically.

"It is, dear lady."

"Lord! To think of a world full of loosened creatures like you! A civilised society swarming with callow and irresponsible opportunists, amateur Jesuits, idle intelligences reinfected with the toxins of their own philosophy! But," she shrugged, "I am indicting man himself—nations and nations of him. Besides, we women have always known this. And hybrids are hybrids. If there's any claret in the house, tell Farris to fetch some. Don't be angry, James. Man and woman once were different species, and the world has teemed with their hybrids since the first mating."

Mrs. Barkley leaned across the table toward him:

"What's the matter, James? You look dangerous."

His face cleared and he smiled:

"Nobody is really dangerous except to themselves, Betty."

She quoted saucily: "Il n'y a personne qui ne soit dangereux pour quelqu'un!"

Mrs. Hammerton added: "Il faut tout attendre et tout craindre du temps et des hommes."

Reggie Ledyard, much flattered, admitted the wholesale indictment against his sex:

"How can we help it? Man, possessing always dual personality, is naturally inclined toward a double life."

"Man's chief study has been man for so long," observed Mrs. Hammerton, "that the world has passed by, leaving him behind, still engrossed in counting his thumbs. Name your French philosopher who can beat that reflection," she added to Desboro, who smiled absently.

"All the men there had yielded to the delicate attraction of her"

From moment to moment he had been watching Jacqueline and the men always leaning toward her—Reggie Ledyard persistently bringing to bear on her the full splendour of his straw-blond and slightly coarse beauty; Cairns, receptive and débonnaire as usual; Herrendene, with his keen smile and sallow visage lined with the memory of things that had left their marks—all the men there had yielded to the delicate attraction of her.

Desboro said to Mrs. Hammerton: "Now you realise where she really belongs."

"Better than you do," she retorted drily.

After luncheon there were vehicles to convey them to the pond, a small sheet of water down in the Desboro woods. And while a declining sun glittered through the trees, the wooded shores echoed with the clatter and scrape of skates and the rattle of hockey-sticks crossed in lively combat.

But inshore the ice had rotted; the end of such sport was already in sight. Along the gravelly inlet, where water rippled, a dozen fingerling trout lay half hidden among the pebbles; over a bank of soft, sun-warmed snow, gnats danced in the sunset light; a few tree-buds had turned sticky.

Later, Vail came and built a bonfire; Farris arrived with tea baskets full of old-fashioned things, such as turnovers and flip in stone jugs of a century ago.

Except for a word or two at intervals, Desboro had found no chance to talk to Jacqueline. Now and then their glances encountered, lingered, shifted, with scarcely a ghost of a smile in forced response to importunities. So he had played an impartial game of hockey, skated with any girl who seemed to be receptive, cut intricate figures with Mrs. Hammerton in a cove covered with velvet-smooth black ice, superintended the bonfire construction, directed Farris with the tea.

Now, absently executing a "grape-vine," he was gliding along the outer ranks of his guests with the mechanical patrolling instinct of a collie, when Jacqueline detached herself from a fire-lit group and made him a gay little sign to halt.

Picking her way through the soft snow on the points of her skates, she took to the ice and joined him. They linked hands and swung out into the starlight.

"Are you enjoying it?" he asked.

"That's why I signalled you. I never have had such a good time. I wanted you to know it."

"You like my friends?"

She looked up: "They are all so charming to me! I didn't expect people to be cordial."

"You need expect nothing else wherever you go and whomever you meet— barring the inevitable which no attractive girl can avoid arousing. Do you get on with Aunt Hannah?"

She laughed: "Isn't it odd? I call her that, too. She asked me to. And do you know, she has been a perfect dear about everything. We shopped together; I never had quite ventured to buy certain fascinating things to wear. And we had such a good time lunching at the Ritz, where I had never dared go. Such beautiful women! Such gowns! Such jewels!"

They halted and looked back across the ice at the distant fire and the dark forms moving about it.

"You've bowled over every man here, as a matter of course," he said lightly. "If you'll tell me how you like the women I'll know whether they like you."

"Oh, I like them; they are as nice to me as they are to each other!" she exclaimed, "—except, perhaps, one or two——"

"Marie Ledyard is hopelessly spoiled; Athalie Vannis is usually discontented," he said philosophically. "Don't expect either of them to give three cheers for another girl's popularity."

They crossed hands and swept toward the centre of the pond on the "outer edge." Jacqueline's skating skirt was short enough for her to manage a "Dutch roll," steadied and guided by Desboro; then they exchanged it for other figures, not intricate.

"Your friend, Mr. Sissly, is dining with us," he observed.

"He's really very nice," she said. "Just a little too—artistic—for you, perhaps, and for the men here—except Captain Herrendene——"

"Herrendene is a fine fellow," he said.

"I like him so much," she admitted.

He was silent for a moment, turned toward her as though to speak, but evidently reconsidered the impulse.

"He is not very young, is he?" she asked.

"Herrendene? No."

"I thought not. Sometimes in repose his face seems sad. But what kind eyes he has!"

"He's a fine fellow," said Desboro without emphasis.

Before they came within the firelight, he asked her whether she had really decided to give them a little lecture on jades and crystals; and she said that she had.

"It won't be too technical or too dry, I hope," she added laughingly. "I told Captain Herrendene what I was going to say and do, and he liked the idea."

"Won't you tell me, too, Jacqueline?"

"No, I want you to be surprised. Besides, I haven't time; we've been together too long already. Doesn't one's host have to be impartially attentive? And I think that pretty little Miss Steyr is signalling you."

Herrendene came out on the ice toward them:

"The cars are here," he said, "and Mrs. Hammerton is cold."

Dinner was an uproariously lively function, served amid a perfect eruption of bewildering gowns and jewels and flowers. Desbo

ro had never before seen Jacqueline in a dinner gown, or even attempted to visualise her beauty amid such surroundings in contrast with other women.

She fitted exquisitely into the charming mosaic; from crown to toe she was part of it, an essential factor that, once realised, became indispensable to the harmony.

Perhaps, he told himself, she did not really dominate with the fresh delicacy of her beauty; perhaps it was only what he saw in her and what he knew of her that made the others shadowy and commonplace to him.

"In all the curious eyes turned toward her, he saw admiration, willing or conceded."

Yet, in all the curious eyes repeatedly turned toward her, he saw admiration, willing or conceded, recognised every unspoken tribute of her own sex as well as the less reserved surrender of his; saw her suddenly developed into a blossom of unabashed and youthful loveliness under what she had once called "the warm sun of approval"; and sat in vague and uneasy wonder, witnessing the transfiguration.

Sissly was there, allotted to Katharine Frere; and that stately girl, usually credited among her friends with artistic aspirations, apparently found him interesting.

So all went well enough, whether gaily or seriously, even with Aunt Hannah, who had discovered under Desboro's smiling composure all kinds of food for reflection and malicious diversion.

For such a small party it was certainly a gay one—at least people were beginning to think so half way through dinner—which merely meant that everybody was being properly appreciated by everybody's neighbours, and that made everybody feel unusually witty, and irrepressible, and a little inclined to be silly toward the end.

But then the after-dinner guests began to arrive—calm, perfectly poised and substantial Westchester propositions who had been bidden to assist at an unusual programme, and to dance afterward.

The stodgy old house rang with chatter and laughter; hall, stairs, library, and billiard-room resounded delightfully; you could scare up a pretty girl from almost any cover—if you were gunning for that variety of girl.

Reggie Ledyard had managed to corner Jacqueline on the stairs, but couldn't monopolise her nor protect himself against the shameless intrusion of Cairns, who spoiled the game until Herrendene raided the trio and carried her off to the billiard-room on a most flimsy pretext.

Here, very properly, a Westchester youth of sterling worth got her away and was making toward the library with her when Desboro unhooked a hunting horn from the wall and filled the house with deafening blasts as signal that the show was about to begin in the armoury.

The armoury had been strung with incandescent lights, which played over the huge mounted figures in mail, and glanced in a million reflections from the weapons on the wall. A curtained and raised stage faced seats for a hundred people, which filled the long, wide aisle between the equestrian shapes; and into these the audience was pouring, excited and mystified by the odd-looking and elaborate electrical attachments flanking the stage in front of the curtained dressing-rooms.

Jacqueline, passing Desboro, whispered:

"I'm so thrilled and excited. I know people will find Mr. Sissly's lecture interesting, but do you think they'll like mine?"

"How do I know, you little villain? You've told Herrendene what you are going to do, but you haven't given me even a hint!"

"I know it; I wanted to—to please you—" Her light hand fell for a moment on his sleeve, and he saw the blue eyes a little wistful.

"You darling," he whispered.

"Thank you. It isn't the proper thing to say to me—but I've quite recovered my courage."

"Have you quite recovered all the scattered fragments of your heart? I am afraid some of these men may carry portions of it away with them."

"I don't think so, monsieur. Really, I must hurry and dress——"

"Dress?"

"Certainly; also make up!"

"But I thought you were to give us a little talk on Chinese jades."

"But I must do it in my own way, Mr. Des——"

"Wait!" They were in the rear of the dressing-room and he took her hand.

"I call you Jacqueline, unreproved. Is my name more difficult for you?"

"Do you wish me to? In cold blood?"

"Not in cold blood."

He took her into his arms; she bent her head gravely, but he felt her restless fingers worrying his sleeve.

"Jacqueline?"

"Yes—Jim."

The swift fire in his face answered the flush in hers; he drew her nearer, but she averted her dainty head in silence and stood so, her hand always restless on his arm.

"You haven't changed toward me in these few weeks, have you, Jacqueline?"

"Do you think I have?"

He was silent. After a moment she glanced up at him with adorable shyness. He kissed her, but her lips were cold and unresponsive, and she bent her head, still picking nervously at the cloth of his sleeve.

"I must go," she said.

"I know it." He released her waist.

She drew a quick, short breath and looked up smiling; then sighed again, and once more her blue eyes became aloof and thoughtful.

He stood leaning against the side of the dressing-room, watching her.

Finally she said with composure: "I must go. Please like what I shall do. It will be done to please you—Jim."

He opened the dressing-room door for her; she entered, turned to look back at him for an instant, then closed the door.

He went back to his place among the audience.

A moment later a temple gong struck three times; the green curtains parted, revealing a white screen, and Mr. Lionel Sissly advancing with a skip to the footlights. The audience looked again at its programme cards and again read:

"No. : A Soundless Symphony ... Lionel Sissly."

"Colour," lisped Mr. Sissly, "is not only precious for its own sake, but also because it is the blessed transmogrification of sound. And sound is sacred because all vibrations, audible or inaudible, are in miraculous harmony with that holiest of all phenomena, silence!"

"Help!" whispered Ledyard to Cairns, with resignation.

"Any audible rate of regular air vibrations is a musical note," continued Mr. Sissly. "If you double that vibratory speed, you have the first note of the octave above it. Now, the spectrum band is the colour counterpart of the musical octave; the ether vibrates with double the speed at the violet end of the spectrum band that it does at the opposite extremity, or red end. Let me show you the chromatic scales in colour and music—the latter the equivalent of the former, revealing how the intervals correspond when C represents red." And he flashed upon the screen a series of brilliant colours.

"Remember," he said, "that it is with colour as it is with sound—there is a long range of vibrations below and above the first and last visible colour and the first and last audible note—a long, long range beyond compass of the human eye and ear. Probably the music of the spheres is composed of such harmonies," he simpered.

"Modern occidental music is evolved in conformity with an arbitrary scale," he resumed earnestly. "An octave consists of seven whole tones and five half-tones. Combinations and sequences of notes or tints affect us emotionally—pleasurably when harmonious, painfully when discordant. But," and his voice shook with soulful emotion, "the holiest and the most precious alliance ever dreamed of beyond the Gates of Heaven lies in the sacred intermingling of harmonious colour and harmonious silence. Let me play for you, upon my colour organ, my soundless symphony which I call 'Weather.' Always in the world there will be weather. We have it constantly; there is so much of it that nobody knows how much there is; and I do not see very clearly how there ever could be any less than there is. Weather, then, being the only earthly condition which is eternal, becomes precious beyond human comprehension; and I have tried to interpret it as a symphony of silence and of colour divinely intermingled."

Ledyard whispered to Betty Barkley: "I'll go mad and bite if he says another word!"

She cautioned him with a light touch of her gloved hand, and strove very hard to remain serious as Mr. Sissly minced over to his "organ," seated himself, and gazed upward.

All at once every light in the house went out.

For a while the great screen remained invisible, then a faint sheen possessed its surface, blotted out at eccentric intervals by a deep and thunderous tint which finally absorbed it and slowly became a coldly profound and depthless blue.

The blue was not permanent; almost imperceptible pulsations were stirring and modifying it toward a warmer and less decisive hue, and through it throbbed and ebbed elusive sensations of palest turquoise, primrose and shell-pink. This waned and deepened into a yellow which threatened to become orange.

Suddenly all was washed out in unaccented grey; the grey gradually became instinct with rose and gold; the gold was split by a violet streak; then virile scarlet tumbled through crashing scales of green, amethyst, crimson, into a chaos of chromatic dissonance, and vanished engulfed in shimmering darkness.

The lights flashed up, disclosing Mr. Sissly, very pale and damp of features, facing the footlights again.

"That," he faltered, amid a stillness so profound that it seemed to fill the ear like a hollow roar,—"that is weather. If you approve it, the most precious expression of your sympathy will be absolute silence."

Fortunately, not even Reggie Ledyard dropped.

Mr. Sissly passed a lank and lily hand across his large pale eyes.

"Like the Japanese," he lisped, "I bring to you my most precious thought-treasures one at a time—and never more than two between the rising of the orb of day and the veiling of it at eventide. I offer you, on the altar of my colour organ, a transposition of Von Schwiggle's symphony in A minor; and I can only say that it is replete with a meaning so exquisitely precious that no human intelligence has yet penetrated it."

Out went the lights. Presently the screen became visible. Upon it there seemed to be no colour, no hint of any tint, no quality, no value. It was merely visible, and remained so for three mortal minutes. Then the lights broke out, revealing Mr. Sissly half fainting at his organ, and two young women in Greek robes waving bunches of violets at him. And the curtain fell.

"There only remains," whispered Ledyard, "the funny-house for me."

"If you make me laugh I'll never forgive you," Mrs. Barkley warned him under her breath. "But—oh, do look at Mrs. Hammerton!"

Aunt Hannah's visage resembled that of a cornered and enraged mink surrounded by enemies.

"If that man comes near me," she said to Desboro, "I shall destroy him with hatpins. You'd better keep him away. I'm morally and nervously disorganised."

Sissly had come off the stage and now stood in the wide aisle, surrounded by the earnest and intellectual womanhood of Westchester, eagerly seeking more light.

But there was little in Mr. Sissly's large and washed-out eyes; even less, perhaps, than illuminated his intellect. He gazed wanly upon adoration, edging his way toward Miss Frere, who, at dinner, had rashly admitted that she understood him.

"Was it satisfying?" he lisped, when he had attained to her vicinity.

"It was most—remarkable," she said, bewildered. "So absolutely new to me that I can find nothing as yet to say to you, except thank you."

"Why say it? Why not merely look it? Your silence would be very, very precious to me," he said in a low voice. And the stately Miss Frere blushed.

The audience, under the stimulus of the lights, recovered very quickly from its semi-stupor, and everybody was now discussing with animation the unique experience of the past half-hour. New York chattered; Westchester discussed; that was the difference. Both had expected a new kind of cabaret show; neither had found the weird performance disappointing. Flippant and unintellectual young men felt safe in the certainty that neither their pretty partners nor the more serious representatives of the substantial county knew one whit more about soundless symphonies than did they.

"She lost herself in a dreamy Bavarian folk-song"

So laughter and noise filled the armoury with a gaily subdued uproar, silenced only when Katharine Frere's harp was brought in, and the tall, handsome girl, without any preliminaries, went forward and seated herself, drew the gilded instrument back against her

right shoulder, set her feet to the pedals, her fingers to the strings, and wandered capriciously from Le Donne Curiose and the far, brief echoes of its barcarolle, into Koenigskinder, and on through Versiegelt, till she lost herself in a dreamy Bavarian folk-song which died out as sunset dies on the far alms of the Red Valepp.

Great applause; no cabaret yet. The audience looked at the programme and read:

"A Thousand Years B.C. ... Miss Nevers."

And Reggie Ledyard was becoming restless, thinking perhaps that a little ragtime of the spheres might melt the rapidly forming intellectual ice, and was saying so to anybody who'd listen, when ding-dong-dang! ding-dong! echoed the oriental gong. Out went the lights, the curtain split open and was gathered at the wings; a shimmering radiance grew upon the stage disclosing a huge gold and green dragon of porcelain on its faïence pedestal. And there, high cradled between the forepaws of the ancient Mongolian monster, sat a slim figure in silken robes of turquoise, rose, and scarlet, a Chinese lute across her knees, slim feet pendant below the rainbow skirt.

Her head-dress was wrought fantastically of open-work gold, inlaid with a thousand tiny metallic blue feathers, accented by fiery gems; across the silky folds of her slitted tunic were embroidered in iris tints the single-winged birds whirling around each other between floating clouds; little clog-like shoes of silk and gold, embroidered with moss-green arabesques inset with orange and scarlet, shod the feet.

Ancient Cathay, exquisitely, immortally young, sat in jewelled silks and flowers under the huge and snarling dragon. And presently, string by string, her idle lute awoke, picked with the plectrum, note after note in strange and unfamiliar intervals; and, looking straight in front of her, she sang at random, to "the sorrows of her lute," verses from "The Maker of Moons," sung by Chinese lovers a thousand years ago:

"Like to a Dragon in the Sky

The fierce Sun flames from East to West;

The flower of Love within my breast

Blooms only when the Moon is high

And Thou art nigh."

The dropping notes of her lute answered her, rippled on, and were lost like a little rill trickling into darkness.

"The Day burns like a Dragon's flight

Until Thou comest in the night

With thy cool Moon of gold—

Then I unfold."

A faint stirring of the strings, silence; then she struck with her plectrum the weird opening chord of that sixth century song called "The Night Revel"; and sang to the end the ancient verses set to modern music by an unknown composer:

"Along the River scarlet Lanterns glimmer,

Where gilded Boats and darkling Waters shimmer;

Laughter with Singing blends;

But Love begins and ends

Forever with a sigh—

A whispered sigh.

"In fire-lit pools the crimson Carp are swirling;

The painted peacocks shining plumes are furling;

Now in the torch-light by the Gate

A thousand Lutes begin the Fête

With one triumphant Cry!

Why should Love sigh?"

The curtain slowly closed on the echoes of her lute; there came an interval of absolute silence, then an uproar of cries and of people getting to their feet, calling out: "Go on! Go on! Don't stop!" No applause except this excited clamour for more, and the racket of moving chairs.

"Good Lord!" muttered Captain Herrendene. "Did you ever see anything as beautiful as that girl?"

And: "Where did she learn such things?" demanded people excitedly of one another. "It must be the real business! How does she know?"

The noise became louder and more emphatic; calls for her reappearance redoubled and persisted until the gong again sounded, the lights went out, and the curtains twitched once more and parted.

She slid down from her cradled perch between the forelegs of the shadowy dragon and came to the edge of the footlights.

"I was going to show you one or two jades from the Desboro collection, and tell you a little about them," she began, "but my lute and I will say for you another song of ancient China, if you like. It was made by Kao-Shih about seven hundred years after the birth of Christ. He was one of the T'ang poets— and not a very cheerful one. This is his song."

And she recited for them: "There was a king of Liang."

After that she stepped back; but they would not have it, to the point of enthusiastic rudeness.

She recited for them Mêng Hao-Jan's "A Friend Expected," from "The Maker of Moons," and the quatrains of the lovely, naïve little "Spring Dream," written by Ts'en-Ts'an in the eighth century.

But they demanded still more. She laid aside her lute and intoned for them the noble lines of China's most famous writer:

"Thou that hast seen six kingdoms pass away———"

Then, warming to her audience, and herself thrilled with the spirit of the ancient splendour, she moved forward in her whispering silks, and, slightly bending, her finger lifted like one who hushes children with a magic tale, she spoke to them of Fei-yen, mistress of the Emperor; and told them how T'ai-Chên became an empress; sang for them the song of Yu Lao, the "Song of the Moon Moth":

"The great Night Moth that bears her name

Is winged in green,

Pale as the June moon's silver flame

Her silken sheen:

No other flame they know, these twain

Where dark dews rain—

This great Night Moth that bears her name

And my sweet Queen;

So let me light my Lantern flame

And breathe Her name."

She held her audience in the palm of her smooth little hand; she knew it, and tasted power. She told them of the Blue Mongol's song, reciting:

"From the Gray Plains I ride,

Where the gray hawks wheel,

In armour of lacquered hide,

Sabre and shield of steel;

The lance in my stirrup rattles,

And the quiver and bow at my back

Clatter! I sing of Battles,

Of Cities put to the sack!

Where is the Lord of the West,

The Golden Emperor's son?

I swung my Mongol sabre;—

He and the Dead are one.

For the tawny Lion of the Iort

And the Sun of the World are One!"

Then she told them the old Chinese tale called "The Never-Ending Wrong"—the immortal tragedy of that immortal maid, "a reed in motion and a rose in flame," from where she alights "in the white hibiscus bower" to where "death is drumming at the door" and "ten thousand battle-chariots on the wing" come clashing to a halt; and the trapped King, her lover, sends her forth

"Lily pale,

Between tall avenues of spears, to die."

And so, amid "the sullen soldiery," white as a flower, and all alone in soul, she "shines through tall avenues of spears, to die."

"The King has sought the darkness of his hands," standing in stricken grief, then turns and gazes at what lies there at his feet amid its scattered

"—Ornaments of gold,

One with the dust; and none to gather them;—

Hair-pins of jade and many a costly gem,

Kingfishers' wings and golden beads scarce cold."

Lingering a moment in the faint reflection of the low-turned footlights, she stood looking out over the silent audience; and perhaps her eyes found what they had been seeking, for she smiled and stepped back as the curtain closed. And no uproar of applause could lure her forth again until the lights had been long blazing and the dancers were whirling over the armoury floor, and she had washed the paint from lid and lip and cheek, and put off her rustling antique silken splendour to bewitch another century scarce begun.

Desboro, waiting at her dressing-room door for her, led her forth.

"You have done so much for me," he whispered. "Is there anything in all the world I can do for you, Jacqueline?"

She was laughing, flushed by the flattery and compliments from every side, but she heard him; and after a moment her face altered subtly. But she answered lightly:

"Can I ask for more than a dance or two with you? Is not that honour enough?" Her voice was gay and mocking, but the smile had faded from eye and lip; only the curved sweetness of the mouth remained.

They caught the music's beat and swung away together among the other dancers, he piloting her with great adroitness between the avenues of armoured figures.

When he had the opportunity, he said: "What may I send you that you would care for?"

"Send me?" She laughed lightly again. "Let me see! Well, then, perhaps you may one day send me—send me forth 'between tall avenues of spears, to die.'"

"What!" he said sharply.

"The song is still ringing in my head—that's all. Send me any inexpensive thing you wish—a white carnation—I don't really care—" she looked away from him—"as long as it comes from you."

CHAPTER X

Desboro's guests were determined to turn the house out of the windows; its stodgy respectability incited them; every smug, smooth portrait goaded them to unusual effort, and they racked their brains to invent novelties.

On one day they opened all the windows in the disused west wing, flooded the ground floor, hung the great stone room with paper lanterns, and held an ice carnival. As masks and costumes had been made entirely out of paper, there were several startling effects and abrupt retirements to repair damages; but the dancing on skates in the lantern light was very pretty, and even the youth and pride of Westchester found the pace not unsuitably rapid.

On another day, Desboro's feminine guests sent to town for enough green flannel to construct caricatures of hunting coats for everybody.

The remains of a stagnant pack of harriers vegetated on a neighbouring estate; Desboro managed to mount his guests on his own live-stock, including mules, farm horses, polo ponies, and a yoke of oxen; and the county saw a hunting that they were not likely to forget.

Reggie Ledyard was magnificent astride an ox, with a paper megaphone for a hunting horn, rubber boots, and his hastily basted coat split from skirt to collar. The harriers ran wherever they pleased, and the astonished farm mules wouldn't run at all. There was hysterical excitement when one cotton-tail rabbit was started behind a barn and instantly lost under it.

The hunt dinner was a weird and deafening affair, and the Weber-Field ball costumes unbelievable.

Owing to reaction and exhaustion, repentant girls came to Jacqueline requesting an interim of intellectual recuperation; so she obligingly announced a lecture in the jade room, and talked to them very prettily about jades and porcelains, suiting her words to their intellectual capacity, which could grasp Kang-he porcelains and Celedon and Sang-de-bœuf, but balked at the "three religions," and found blanc de Chine uninspiring. So she told them about the famille vert and the famille rose; about the K'ang Hsi period, which they liked, and how the imperial kilns at Kiangsi developed the wonderful clair de lune "turquoise blue" and "peach bloom," for which some of their friends or relatives had paid through their various and assorted noses.

All of this her audience found interesting because they recognised in the exquisite examples from Desboro's collection, with which Jacqueline illustrated her impromptu lecture, objects both fashionable and expensive; and what is both fashionable and expensive appeals very forcibly to mediocrity.

"I saw a jar like that one at the Clydesdales'," said Reggie Ledyard, a trifle excited at his own unexpected intelligence. "How much is it worth, Miss Nevers?"

She laughed and looked at the vase between her slender fingers.

"Really," she said, "it isn't worth very much. But wealthy people have established fictitious values for many rather crude and commonplace things. If people had the courage to buy only what appealed to them personally, there would be a mighty crash in tumbling values."

"We'd all wake up and find ourselves stuck," remarked Van Alstyne, who possessed some pictures which he had come to loathe, but for which he had paid terrific prices. "Jim, do you want to buy any primitives, guaranteed genuine?"

"There's the thrifty Dutch trader for you," said Reggie. "I'm loaded with rickety old furniture, too. They got me to furnish my place with antiques! But you don't see me trying to sell 'em to my host at a house party!"

"Stop your disputing," said Desboro pleasantly, "and ask Miss Nevers for her professional opinion later. The chances are that you both have been properly stuck, and I never had any sympathy for wealthy ignorance, anyway."

But Ledyard and Van Alstyne, being very wealthy, became frightfully depressed over the unfeeling jibes of Desboro; and Jacqueline seemed to be by way of acquiring a pair of new clients.

In fact, both young men at various moments approached her on the subject, but Desboro informed them that they might with equal propriety ask a physician to prescribe for them at a dance, and that Miss Nevers' office was open from nine until five.

"Gad," remarked Ledyard to Van Alstyne, with increasing respect, "she is some girl, believe me, Stuyve. Only if she ever married up with a man of our kind—good-night! She'd quit him in a week."

Van Alstyne touched his forehead significantly.

"Sure," he said. "Nothing doing inside our conks. But why the Lord made her such a peach outside as well as inside is driving me to Jersey! Most of 'em are so awful to look at, don't y'know. Come on, anyway. I can't keep away from her."

"She's somewhere with the others playing baseball golf," said Reggie, gloomily, following his friend. "Isn't it terrible to see a girl in the world like that—apparently created to make some good gink happy—and suddenly find out that she has even more brains than beauty! My God, Stuyve, it's hard on a man like me."

"Are you really hard hit?"

"Am I? And how about you?"

"It's the real thing here," admitted Van Alstyne. "But what's the use?"

They agreed that there was no use; but during the dance that evening both young men managed to make their intentions clear to Jacqueline.

Reggie Ledyard had persuaded her to a few minutes' promenade in the greenhouse; and there, standing amid thickets of spicy carnations, the girl listened to her first proposal from a man of that outer world about which, until a few days ago, she had known nothing.

The boy was not eloquent; he made a clumsy attempt to kiss her and was defeated. He seemed to her very big, and blond, and handsome as he stood there; and she felt a little pity for him, too, partly because his ideas were so few and his vocabulary so limited.

Perplexed, silent, sorry for him, yet still conscious of a little thrill of wonder and content that a man of the outer world had found her eligible, she debated within herself how best to spare him. And, as usual, the truth presented itself to her as the only explanation.

"You see," she said, lifting her troubled eyes, "I am in love with some one else."

"Good God!" he muttered. After a silence he said humbly: "Would it be unpardonable if I—would you tell me whether you are engaged?"

She blushed with surprise at the idea.

"Oh, no," she said, startled. "I—don't expect to be."

"What?" he exclaimed incredulously. "Is there a man on earth ass enough not to fall in love with you if you ever condescended to smile at him twice?"

But the ideas which he was evoking seemed to distress her, and she averted her face and stood twisting a long-stemmed carnation with nervous fingers.

Not even to herself, either before or since Desboro's letter which had revealed him so unmistakably, had the girl ventured in her inmost thoughts to think the things which this big, blond, loutish boy had babbled.

What Desboro was, she understood. She had had the choice of dismissing him from her mind, with scorn and outraged pride as aids to help the sacrifice, or of accepting him as he was—as she knew him to be—for the sake of something about him as yet inexplicable even to herself.

And she had chosen.

But now a man of Desboro's world had asked her to be his wife. More than that; he had assumed that she was fitted to be the wife of anybody.

They walked back together. She was adorable with him, kind, timidly sympathetic and smilingly silent by turns, venturing even to rally him a little, console him a little, moved by an impulse toward friendship wholly unfeigned.

"All I have to say is," he muttered, "that you're a peach and a corker; and I'm going to invent some way of marrying you, even if it lands me in an East Side night-school."

Even he joined in her gay laughter; and presently Van Alstyne, who had been glowering at them, managed to get her away. But she would have nothing further to do with greenhouses, or dark landings, or libraries; so he asked her bluntly while they were dancing; and she shook her head, and very soon dropped his arm.

There was a bay-window near them; she made a slight gesture of irritation; and there, in the partly curtained seclusion, he learned that she was grateful and happy that he liked her so much; that she liked him very much, but that she loved somebody else.

He took it rather badly at first; she began to understand that few girls would have lightly declined a Van Alstyne; and he was inclined to be patronising, sulky and dignified—an impossible combination—for it ditched him finally, and left him kissing her hands and declaring constancy eternal.

That night, at parting, Desboro retained her offered hand a trifle longer than convention required, and looked at her more curiously than usual.

"Are you enjoying the party, Jacqueline?"

"Every minute of it. I have never been as happy."

"I suppose you realise that everybody is quite mad about you."

"Everybody is nice to me! People are so much kinder than I imagined."

"Are they? How do you get on with the gorgon?"

"Mrs. Hammerton? Do you know she is perfectly sweet? I never dreamed she could be so gentle and thoughtful and considerate. Why—and it seems almost ridiculous to say it—she seems to have the ideas of a mother about whatever concerns me. She actually fusses over me sometimes—and—it is—agreeable."

An inexplicable shyness suddenly overcame her, and she said good-night hastily, and mounted the stairs to her room.

Later, when she was prepared for bed, Mrs. Hammerton knocked and came in.

"Jacqueline," she said bluntly, "what was Reggie Ledyard saying to you this evening? I'll box his ears if he proposed to you. Did he?"

"I—I am afraid he did."

"You didn't take him?"

"No."

"I should think not! I'd as soon expect you to marry a stable groom. He has all the beauty and healthy colour of one. Also the distinguished mental capacity. You don't want that kind."

"I don't want any kind."

"I'm glad of it. Did any other fool hint anything more of that sort?"

"Mr. Van Alstyne."

"Oho! Stuyvesant, too? Well, what did you say to him?" asked the old lady, with animation.

"I said no."

"What?"

"Of course, I said no. I am not in love with Mr. Van Alstyne."

"Child! Do you realise that you had the opportunity of your life!"

Jacqueline's smile was confused and deprecating.

"But when a girl doesn't care for a man——"

"Do you mean to marry for love?"

The girl sat silent a moment, then shook her head.

"I shall not marry," she said.

"Nonsense! And if you feel that way, what am I good for? What earthly use am I to you? Will you kindly inform me?"

She had seated herself on the bed's edge, leaning over the girl where she lay on her pillows.

"Answer me," she insisted. "Of what use am I to you?"

For a full minute the girl lay there looking up at her without stirring. Then a smile glimmered in her eyes; she lifted both arms and laid them on the older woman's shoulders.

"You are useful—this way," she said; and kissed her lightly on the forehead.

The effect on Aunt Hannah was abrupt; she caught the girl to her breast and held her there fiercely and in silence for a moment; then, releasing her, tucked her in with mute violence, turned off the light and marched out without a word.

Day after day Desboro's guests continued to turn the house inside out, ransacking it from garret to cellar.

"We don't intend to do anything in this house that anybody has ever done here, or at any house party," explained Reggie Ledyard to Jacqueline. "So if any lady cares to walk down stairs on her head the incident will be quite in order."

"Can she slide down the banisters instead?" asked Helsa Steyr.

"Oh, you'll have to slide up to be original," said Betty Barkley.

"How can anybody slide up the banisters?" demanded Reggie hotly.

"You've the intellect of a terrapin," said Betty scornfully. "It's because nobody has ever done it that it ought to be done here."

Desboro, seated on the pool table, told her she could do whatever she desired, including arson, as long as she didn't disturb the Aqueduct Police.

Katharine Frere said to Jacqueline: "Everything you do is so original. Can't you invent something new for us to do?"

"She might suggest that you all try to think," said Mrs. Hammerton tartly. "That would be novelty enough."

Cairns seized the megaphone and shouted: "Help! Help! Aunt Hannah is after us!"

Captain Herrendene, seated beside Desboro with a half smile on his face, glanced across at Jacqueline who stood in the embrasure of a window, a billiard cue resting across her shoulders.

"Please invent something for us, Miss Nevers," he said.

"Why don't you play hide and seek?" sneered Mrs. Hammerton, busily knitting a tie. "It's suited to your intellects."

"Let Miss Nevers suggest a new way of playing the oldest game ever invented," added Betty Barkley. "There is no possibility of inventing anything new; everything was first done in the year one. Even protoplasmic cells played hide-and-seek together."

"What rot!" said Reggie. "You can't play that in a new way."

"You could play it in a sporting way," said Cairns.

"How's that, old top?"

"Well, for example, you conceal yourself, and whatever girl finds you has got to marry you. How's that for a reckless suggestion?"

But it had given Reggie something resembling an idea.

"Let us be hot sports," he said, with animation; "draw lots to see which girl will hide somewhere in the house; make a time-limit of one hour; and if any man finds her she'll marry him. There isn't a girl here," he added, jeeringly, "who has the sporting nerve to try it!"

A chorus of protests greeted the challenge. Athalie Vannis declared that she was crazy to marry somebody; but she insisted that the men would only pretend to search, and were really too cowardly to hunt in earnest. Cairns retorted that the girl in concealment would never permit a real live man to miss her hiding place while she possessed lungs to reveal it.

"There isn't," repeated Reggie, "a girl who has the nerve! Not one!" He inspected them scornfully through the wrong end of the megaphone. "Phony sports," he added. "No nerves and all fidgets. Look at me; I don't want to get married; but I'm game for an hour. There isn't a girl here to call my bluff!" And he ventured to glance at Jacqueline.

"They've had a chance to look at you by daylight, Reggie, and that is fatal," said Cairns. "Now, if they were only sure that I'd discover 'em, or the god-like captain yonder, or the beautiful Mr. Desboro——"

"I've half a mind to do it," said Helsa Steyr. "Marie, will you draw lots to see who hides?"

"Why doesn't a man hide?" drawled Miss Ledyard. "I'm very sure I could drag him to the altar in ten minutes."

Cairns had found a sheet of paper, torn it into slips, and written down every woman's name, including Aunt Hannah's.

"She's retired to her room in disgust," said Jacqueline, laughing.

"Is she included?" faltered Reggie.

"You've brought it on yourself," said Cairns. "Are you going to renig just because Aunt Hannah is a possible prize? Are you really a tin sport?"

"No, by heck! Come on, Katharine!" to Miss Frere. "But Betty Barkley can't figure in this, or there may be bigamy done."

"That makes it a better sporting proposition," said Betty coolly. "I insist on figuring; Bertie can take his chances."

"Then I'm jingled if I don't play, too," said Barkley. "And I'm not sure I'll hunt very hard if it's Betty who hides."

The pretty little woman turned up her nose at her husband and sent a dazzling smile at Desboro.

"I'll whistle three times, like the daughter in the poem," she said. "Please beat my husband to it."

Cairns waved the pool basket aloft: "Come ladies!" he cried. "Somebody reach up and draw; and may heaven smile upon your wedding day!"

Betty Barkley, standing on tip-toe, reached up, stirred the folded ballots with tentative fingers, grasped one, drew it forth, and flourished it.

"Goodness! How my heart really beats!" she said. "I don't know whether I want to open it or not. I hadn't contemplated bigamy."

"If it's my name, I'm done for," said Katharine Frere calmly. "I'm nearly six feet, and I can't conceal them all."

"Open it," said Athalie Vannis, with a shiver. "After all there's the divorce court!" And she looked defiantly at Cairns.

Betty turned over the ballot between forefinger and thumb and regarded it with dainty aversion.

"Well," she said, "if I'm in for a scandal, I might as well know it. Will you be kind to me, Jim, and not flirt with my maid?"

She opened the ballot, examined the name written there, turned and passed it to Jacqueline, who flushed brightly as a delighted shout greeted her.

"The question is," said Reggie Ledyard excitedly, "are you a sport, Miss Nevers, or are you not? Kindly answer with appropriate gestures."

The girl stood with her golden head drooping, staring at the bit of paper in her hand; then, as Desboro watched her, she glanced up with that sudden, reckless smile which he had seen once before—the first day he met her—and made a gay little gesture of acceptance.

"You're not really going to do it, are you?" said Betty, incredulously. "You don't have to; they're every one of them short sports themselves!"

"I am not," said Jacqueline, smiling.

"But," argued Katharine Frere, "suppose Reggie should find you. You'd never marry him, would you?"

"Great Heavens!" shouted Ledyard. "She might have a worse fate. There's Desboro!"

"You don't really mean it, do you, Miss Nevers?" asked Captain Herrendene.

"Yes, I do," said Jacqueline. "I always was a gambler by nature."

The tint of excitement was bright on her cheeks; she shot a daring glance at Ledyard, looked at Van Alstyne and laughed, but her back remained turned toward Desboro.

He said: "If the papers ever get wind of this they'll print it as a serious item."

"I am perfectly serious," she said, looking coolly at him over her shoulder. "If there is a man here clever enough to find me, I'll marry him in a minute. But"—and she laughed in Desboro's face—"there isn't. So nobody need really lose one moment in anxiety. And if a girl finds me it's all off, of course. May I have twenty minutes? And will you time me, Mr. Ledyard? And will you all remain in this room with the door closed?"

"If nobody finds you," cried Cairns, as she crossed the threshold, "we each forfeit whatever you ask of us?"

She paused at the door, looking back: "Is that understood?"

Everybody cried: "Yes! Certainly!"

She nodded and disappeared.

For twenty minutes they waited; then, as Reggie closed his watch, a general stampede ensued. Amazed servants shrank aside as Cairns, blowing fearful blasts on the megaphone, cheered on the excited human pack; everywhere Desboro's cats and dogs fled before the invasion; room after room was ransacked, maids routed, butler and valet defied. Even Aunt Hannah's sanctuary was menaced until that lady sat up on her bed and swore steadily at Ledyard, who had scaled the transom.

Desboro, hunting by himself, entered the armoury, looked suspiciously at the armoured figures, shook a few, opened the vizors of others, and peered at the painted faces inside the helmets.

Others joined him, prying curiously, gathering in groups amid the motionless army of mailed men. Then, as more than half of the allotted hour had already expired, Ledyard suggested an attic party, where trunks full of early XIXth century clothing might be rifled with pleasing results.

"We may find her up there in a chest, like the celebrated bride," remarked Aunt Hannah, who had reappeared from her retreat. "It's the lesser of several tragedies that might happen," she added insolently, to Desboro.

"To the attic!" thundered Cairns through his megaphone; and they started.

But Desboro still lingered at the armoury door, looking back. The noise of the chase died away in the interior of the main house; the armoury became very still under the flood of pale winter sunshine.

He glanced along the steel ranks of men-at-arms; he looked up at the stately mounted figures; dazzling sunlight glittered over helmet and cuirass and across the armoured flanks of horses.

Could it be possible that she was seated up there, hidden inside some suit of blazing mail, astride a battle-horse?

Cautiously he came back, skirting the magnificent and motionless ranks, hesitated and halted.

Of course the whole thing had been proposed and accepted in jest; he told himself that. And yet—if some other man did discover her—the foundation of the jest might serve for a more permanent understanding. He didn't want her to have any intimate understanding with anybody until he and she understood each other, and he understood himself.

He didn't want another man to find and claim the forfeit, even in jest, because he didn't know what might happen. No man was ever qualified to foretell what another man might do; and men already were behaving toward her with a persistency and seriousness unmistakable—men like Herrendene, who meant what he looked and said; and young Hammerton, Daisy's brother, eager, inexperienced and susceptible; and Bertie Barkley, a little, hard-faced snob, with an unerring instinct for anybody who promised to be popular among desirable people, was beginning to test her metal with the acid of his experience.

Desboro stood quite still, looking almost warily about him and thinking faster and faster, trying to recollect who it was who had dragged in the silly subject of marriage. That blond and hulking ass Ledyard, wasn't it?

He began to walk, slowly passing the horsemen in review.

Suppose a blond animal like Reggie Ledyard offered himself in earnest. Was she the kind of girl who would nail the worldly opportunity? And Herrendene —that quiet, self-contained, keen-eyed man of forty-five. You could never tell what Herrendene was thinking about anything, or what he was capable of doing. And his admiration for Jacqueline was undisguised, and his attentions frankly persistent. Last night, too, when they were coasting under the new moon, there was half an hour's disappearance for which neither Herrendene nor Jacqueline had even pretended to account, though bantered and challenged —to Desboro's vague discomfort. And the incident had left Desboro a trifle cool toward her that morning; and she had pretended not to be aware of the slight constraint between them, which made him sulky.

He had reached the end of the double lane of horsemen. Now he pivoted and retraced his steps, hands clasped behind his back, absently scanning the men-at-arms, preoccupied with his own reflections.

How seriously had she taken the rôle she was playing somewhere at that moment? Only fools accepted actual hazards when dared. He himself was apt to be that kind of a fool. Was she? Would she really have abided by the terms if discovered by Herrendene, for example, or Dicky Hammerton—if they were mad enough to take it seriously?

He thought of that sudden and delicious flash of recklessness in her eyes. He had seen it twice now.

"By God!" he thought. "I believe she would! She is the sort that sees a thing through to the bitter end."

He glanced up, startled, as though something, somewhere in the vast, silent place, had moved. But he heard nothing, and there was no movement anywhere among the armoured effigies.

Suppose she were here hidden somewhere within a hollow suit of steel. She must be! Else why was he lingering? Why was he not hunting her with the pack? And still, if she actually were here, why was he not searching for her under every suit of sunlit mail? Could it be because he did not really want to find her—with this silly jest of marriage dragged in—a thing not to be mentioned between her and him even in jest?

Was it that he had become convinced in his heart that she must be here, and was he merely standing guard like a jealous, sullen dog, watching lest some other fool come blundering back from a false trail to discover the right one— and perhaps her?

Suddenly, without reason, he became certain that she and he were there in the armoury alone together. He knew it somehow, felt it, divined it in every quickening pulse beat.

He heard the preliminary click of the armoury clock, indicating five minutes' grace before the hour struck. He looked up at the old dial, where it was set against the wall—an ancient piece in azure and gold under a foliated crest borne by some long dead dignitary.

Four more minutes now. And suppose she should stir in her place, setting her harness clashing? Had the thought of marrying him ever entered her head? Was it in such a girl to challenge the possibility, make it as near a serious question as it ever could be? It had never existed for them, even as a question. It was not a dead issue, because it had never lived. If she made one movement now, if she so much as lifted her finger, this occult thing would be alive. He knew it—knew that it lay with her; and stood silent, unstirring, listening for the slightest sound. There was no sound.

It lacked now only a minute to the hour. He looked at the face of the lofty clock; and, looking, all in a moment it flashed upon him where she was concealed.

Wheeling in his tracks, on the impulse of the moment he walked straight back to the great painted wooden charger, sheathed in steel and cloth of gold, bearing on high a slender, mounted figure in full armour—the dainty Milanese mail Of the Countess of Oroposa.

The superb young figure sat its saddle, hollow backed, graceful, both delicate gauntlets resting easily over the war-bridle on the gem-set pommel. Sunbeams turned the long spurs to two golden flames, and splintered into fire across the helmet's splendid crest. He could not pierce the dusk behind the closed vizor; but in every heart-beat, every nerve, he felt her living presence within that hollow shell of inlaid steel and gold.

For a moment he stood staring up at her, then glanced mechanically toward the high clock. Thirty seconds! Time to speak if he would; time for her to move, if in her heart there ever had been the thought which he had never uttered, never meant to voice. Twenty seconds! Through that slitted vizor, also, the clock was in full view. She could read the flight of time as well as he. Now she must move—if ever she meant to challenge in him that to which he never would respond.

He waited now, looking at the clock, now at the still figure above him. Ten seconds! Five!

"Jacqueline!" he cried impulsively.

There was no movement, no answer from the slitted helmet.

"Jacqueline! Are you there?"

No sound.

Then the lofty gold and azure clock struck. And when the last of the twelve resounding strokes rang echoing through the sunlit armoury, the mailed figure stirred in its saddle, stretched both stirrups, raised its arms and flexed them.

"You nearly caught me," she said calmly. "I was afraid you'd see my eyes through the helmet slits. Was it your lack of enterprise that saved me—or your prudence?"

"I spoke to you before the hour was up. It seems to me that I have won."

"Not at all. You might just as well have stood in the cellar and howled my name. That isn't discovering me, you know."

"I felt in my heart that you were there," he said, in a low voice.

She laughed. "What a man feels in his heart doesn't count. Do you realise that I'm nearly dead sitting for an hour here? This helmet is abominably hot! How in the world could that poor countess have stood it?"

"Shall I climb up beside you and unlace your helmet?" he asked.

"No, thank you. Mrs. Quant will get me out of it." She rose in the stirrups, swung one steel-shod leg over, and leaped to the floor beside him, clashing from crest to spur.

"What a silly game it was, anyway!" she commented, lifting her vizor and lowering the beaver. Her face was deliciously flushed, and the gold hair straggled across her cheeks.

"It's quite wonderful how the armour of the countess fits me," she said. "I wonder what she looked like. I'll wager, anyway, that she never played as risky a game in her armour as I have played this morning."

"You didn't really mean to abide by the decision, did you?" he asked.

"Do you think I did?"

"No, of course not."

She smiled. "Perhaps you are correct. But I've always been afraid I'd do something radical and irrevocable, and live out life in misery to pay for it. Probably I wouldn't. I must take off these gauntlets, anyway. Thank you"—as he relieved her of them and tossed them under the feet of the wooden horse.

"Last Thursday," he said, "you fascinated everybody with your lute and your Chinese robes. Heaven help the men when they see you in armour! I'll perform my act of fealty now." And he lifted her hands and kissed them lightly where the gauntlets had left pink imprints on the smooth white skin.

As always when he touched her, she became silent; and, as always, he seemed to divine the instant change in her to unresponsiveness under physical contact. It was not resistance, it was a sort of inertia—an endurance which seemed to stir in him a subtle brutality, awaking depths which must not be troubled— unless he meant to cut his cables once for all and drift headlong toward the rocks of chance.

"You and Herrendene behaved shockingly last night," he said lightly. "Where on earth did you go?"

"Is it to you that I must whisper 'je m'accuse'?" she asked smilingly.

"To whom if not to me, Jacqueline?"

"Please—and what exactly then may be your status? Don't answer," she added, flushing scarlet. "I didn't mean to say that. Because I know what is your status with me."

"How do you know?"

"You once made it clear to me, and I decided that your friendship was worth everything to me—whatever you yourself might be."

"Whatever I might be?" he repeated, reddening.

"Yes. You are what you are—what you wrote me you were. I understood you. But—do you notice that it has made any difference in my friendship? Because it has not."

The dull colour deepened over his face. They were standing near the closed door now; she laid one hand on the knob, then ventured to raise her eyes.

"It has made no difference," she repeated. "Please don't think it has."

His arms had imprisoned her waist; she dropped her head and her hand slipped from the knob of the great oak door as he drew her toward him.

"In armour!" she protested, trying to speak lightly, but avoiding his eyes.

"Is that anything new?" he said. "You are always instantly in armour when my lightest touch falls on you. Why?"

He lifted her drooping head until it rested against his arm.

"Isn't it anything at all to you when I kiss you?" he asked unsteadily.

She did not answer.

"Isn't it, Jacqueline?"

But she only closed her eyes, and her lips remained coldly unresponsive to his.

After a moment he said: "Can't you care for me at all—in this way? Answer me!"

"I—care for you."

"This way?"

Over her closed lids a tremor passed, scarcely perceptible.

"Don't you know how—how deeply I—care for you?" he managed to say, feeling prudence and discretion violently tugging at their cables. "Don't you know it, Jacqueline?"

"Yes. I know you—care for me."

"Good God!" he said, trying to choke back the very words he uttered. "Can't you respond—when you know I find you so adorable! When—when you must know that I love you! Isn't there anything in you to respond?"

"I—care for you. If I did not, could I endure—what you do?"

A sort of blind passion seized and possessed him; he kissed again and again the fragrant, unresponsive lips. Presently she lifted her head, loosened his clasp at her waist, stepped clear of the circle of his arms.

"You see," she managed to say calmly, "that I do care for you. So—may I go now?"

He opened the door for her and they moved slowly out into the hall.

"You do not show that you care very much, Jacqueline."

"How can a girl show it more honestly? Could you tell me?"

"I have never stirred you to any tenderness—never!"

She moved beside him with head lowered, hands resting on her plated hips, the bright hair in disorder across her cheeks. Presently she said in a low voice:

"I wish you could see into my heart."

"I wish I could! And I wish you could see into mine. That would settle it one way or another!"

"No," she said, "because I can see into your heart. And it settles nothing for me—except that I would like to—remain."

"Remain? Where?"

"There—in your heart."

He strove to speak coolly: "Then you can see into it?"

"Yes."

"And you know that you are there alone?"

"Yes—I think so."

"And now that you have looked into it and know what is there, do you care to remain in the heart of—of such a man as I am?"

"Yes. What you are I—forgive."

An outburst of merriment came from the library, and several figures clad in the finery of the early nineteenth century came bustling out into the hall.

"Cheer after cheer rang through the hallway"

Evidently his guests had rifled the chests and trunks in the attic and had attired themselves to their heart's content. At sight of Desboro approaching accompanied by a slim figure in complete armour, they set up a shout of apprehension and then cheer after cheer rang through the hallway.

"Do you know," cried Betty Barkley, "you are the most darling thing in armour that ever happened! I want to get into some steel trousers like yours immediately! Are there any in the armoury that will fit me, Jim?"

"Did you discover her?" demanded Reggie Ledyard, aghast.

"Not within the time limit, old chap," said Desboro, pretending deep chagrin.

"Then you don't have to marry him, do you, Miss Nevers?" exclaimed Cairns, gleefully.

"I don't have to marry anybody, Mr. Cairns. And isn't it humiliating?" she returned, laughingly, edging her way toward the stairs amid the noisy and admiring group surrounding her.

"No! No!" cried Katharine Frere. "You can't escape! You are too lovely that way, and you certainly must come to lunch in your armour!"

"I'd perish!" protested Jacqueline. "No Christian martyr was ever more absolutely cooked than am I in this suit of mail."

Helsa Steyr started for her, but Jacqueline sprang to the stairs and ran up, pursued by Helsa and Betty.

"Isn't she the cunningest, sweetest thing!" sighed Athalie Vannis, looking after her. "I'm simply and sentimentally mad over her. Why didn't you have brains enough to discover her, Jim, and make her marry you?"

"I'd have knocked 'em out if he had had enough brains for that," muttered Ledyard. "But the horrible thing is that I haven't any brains, either, and Miss Nevers has nothing but!"

"A girl like that marries diplomats and dukes, and discoverers and artists and things," commented Betty. "You're just a good-looking simp, Reggie. So is Jim."

Ledyard retorted wrathfully; Desboro, who had been summoned to the telephone, glanced at Aunt Hannah as he walked away, and was rather disturbed at the malice in the old lady's menacing smile.

But what Daisy Hammerton said to him over the telephone disturbed him still more.

"Jim! Elena and Cary Clydesdale are stopping with us. May I bring them to dinner this evening?"

For a moment he was at a loss, then he said, with forced cordiality:

"Why, of course, Daisy. But have you spoken to them about it? I've an idea that they might find my party a bore."

"Oh, no! Elena wished me to ask you to invite them. And Cary was listening."

"Did he care to come?"

"I suppose so."

"What did he say?"

"He grinned. He always does what Elena asks him to do."

"Oh! Then bring them by all means."

"Thank you, Jim."

And that was all; and Desboro, astonished and troubled for a few moments, began to see in the incident not only the dawn of an understanding between Clydesdale and his wife, but something resembling a vindication for himself in this offer to renew a friendship so abruptly terminated. More than that, he saw in it a return of Elena to her senses, and it pleased him so much that when he passed Aunt Hannah in the hall he was almost smiling.

"What pleases you so thoroughly, James—yourself?" she asked grimly.

But he only smiled at her and sauntered on, exchanging friendly body-blows with Reggie Ledyard as he passed.

"Reggie," said Mrs. Hammerton, with misleading mildness, "come and exercise me for a few moments—there's a dear." And she linked arms with him and began to march up and down the hall vigorously.

"She's very charming, isn't she?" observed Aunt Hannah blandly.

"Who?"

"Miss Nevers."

"She's a dream," said Reggie, with emphasis.

"Such a thoroughbred air," commented the old lady.

"Rather!"

"And yet—she's only a shop-keeper."

"Eh?"

"Didn't you know that Miss Nevers keeps an antique shop?"

"What of it?" he said, turning red. "I peddle stocks. My grandfather made snuff. What do I care what Miss Nevers does?"

"Of course. Only—would you marry her?"

"Huh! Like a shot! But I see her letting me! Once I was even ass enough to think I could kiss her, but it seems she won't even stand for that! And Herrendene makes me sick—the old owl—sneaking off with her whenever he can get the chance! They all make me sick!" he added, lighting a cigarette. "I wish to goodness I had a teaspoonful of intellect, and I'd give 'em a run for her. Because I have the looks, if I do say it," he added, modestly.

"Looks never counted seriously with a woman yet," said Mrs. Hammerton maliciously. "Also, I've seen better looking coachmen than you."

"Thanks. What are you going to do with her anyway?"

"I don't have to do anything. She'll do whatever is necessary."

"That's right, too. Lord, but she'll cut a swathe! Even that dissipated creature Cairns sits up and takes notice. I should think Desboro would, too—more than he does."

"I understand there's a girl in blue, somewhere," observed Mrs. Hammerton.

"That's a different kind of girl," said the young man, with contempt, and quite oblivious to his own naïve self-revelation. Mrs. Hammerton shrugged her trim shoulders.

"Also," he said, "there is Elena Clydesdale—speaking of scandal and James Desboro in the same breath."

"Do you believe that story?"

"Yes. But that sort of affair never counts seriously with a man who wants to marry."

"Really? How charming! But perhaps it might count against him with the girl he wants to marry. Young girls are sometimes fastidious, you know."

"They never hear about such things until somebody tells 'em, after they're married. Then it's rather too late to throw any pre-nuptial fits," he added, with a grin.

"Reginald," said Mrs. Hammerton, "day by day I am humbly learning how to appreciate the innate delicacy, chivalry, and honourable sentiments of your sex. You yourself are a wonderful example. For instance, when rumour couples Elena Clydesdale's name with James Desboro's, does it occur to you to question the scandal? No; you take it for granted, and very kindly explain to me how easily Mrs. Clydesdale can be thrown over if her alleged lover decides he'd like to marry somebody."

"That's what's done," he said sulkily. "When a man——"

"You don't have to tell me!" she fairly hissed, turning on him so suddenly that he almost fell backward. "Don't you think I know what is the code among your sort—among the species of men you find sympathetic? You and Jack Cairns and James Desboro—and Cary Clydesdale, too? Let him reproach himself if his wife misbehaves! And I don't blame her if she does, and I don't believe she does! Do you hear me, you yellow-haired, blue-eyed little beast?"

Ledyard stood open-mouthed, red to the roots of his blond hair, and the tiny, baleful black eyes of Mrs. Hammerton seemed to hypnotise him.

"You're all alike," she said with withering contempt. "Real men are out in the world, doing things, not crawling around over the carpet under foot, or sitting in clubs, or dancing with a pack of women, or idling from polo field to tennis court, from stable to steam-yacht. You've no real blood in you; it's only Scotch and soda gone flat. You've the passions of overfed lap dogs with atrophied appetites. There's not a real man here—except Captain Herrendene—and he's going back to his post in a week. You others have no posts. And do you think that men of your sort are fitted to talk about marrying such a girl as Miss Nevers? Let me catch one of you trying it! She's in my charge. But that doesn't count. She'll recognise a real man when she sees one, and glittering counterfeits won't attract her."

"Great heavens!" faltered Reggie. "What a horrible lambasting! I—I've heard you could do it; but this is going some—really, you know, it's going some! And I'm not all those things that you say, either!" he added, in naïve resentment. "I may be no good, but I'm not as rotten as all that."

He stood with lips pursed up into a half-angry, half-injured pout, like a big, blond, blue-eyed yokel facing school-room punishment.

Mrs. Hammerton's harsh face relaxed; and finally a smile wrinkled her eyes.

"I suppose men can't help being what they are—a mixture of precocious child and trained beast. The best of 'em have both of these in 'em. And you are far from the best. Reggie, come here to me!"

He came, after a moment's hesitation, doubtfully.

"Lord!" she said. "How we cherish the worst of you! I sometimes think we don't know enough to appreciate the best. Otherwise, perhaps they'd give us more of their society. But, generally, all we draw is your sort; and we cast our nets in vain into the real world—where Captain Herrendene is going on Monday. Reggie, dear?"

"What?" he said suspiciously.

"Was I severe with you and your friends?"

"Great heavens! There isn't another woman I'd take such a drubbing from!"

"But you do take it," she said, with one of her rare and generous smiles which few people ever saw, and of which few could believe her facially capable.

And she slipped her arm through his and led him slowly toward the library where already Farris was announcing luncheon.

"By heck!" he repeated later, in the billiard room, to a group of interested listeners. "Aunt Hannah is all that they say she is. She suddenly let out into me, and I give y'm'word she had me over the ropes in one punch—tellin' me what beasts men are—and how we're not fit to associate with nice girls—no b'jinks—nor fit to marry 'em, either."

Cairns laughed unfeelingly.

"Oh, you can laugh!" muttered Ledyard. "But to be lit into that way hurts a man's self-respect. You'd better be careful or you'll be in for a dose of Aunt Hannah, too. She evidently has no use for any of us—barrin' the Captain, perhaps."

That gentleman smiled and picked up his hockey stick.

"There's enough ice left—if you don't mind a wetting," he said. "Shall we start?"

Desboro rose, saying carelessly: "The Hammertons and Clydesdales are coming over. I'll have to wait for them."

Bertie Barkley turned his hard little smooth-shaven face toward him.

"Where are the Clydesdales?"

"I believe they're stopping with the Hammertons for a week or two—I really don't know. You can ask them, as they'll be here to dinner."

Cairns laid aside a cue with which he had been punching pool-balls; Van Alstyne unhooked his skate-bag, and the others followed his example in silence. Nobody said anything further about the Clydesdales to Desboro.

Out in the hall a gay group of young girls in their skating skirts were gathering, among them Jacqueline, now under the spell of happiness in their companionship.

Truly, even in these few days, the "warm sunlight of approval" had done wonders for her. She had blossomed out deliriously and exquisitely in her half-shy friendships with these young girls, responding diffidently at first to their overtures, then frankly and with a charming self-possession based on the confidence that she was really quite all right if everybody only thought so.

Everybody seemed to think so; Athalie Vannis's friendship for her verged on the sentimental, for the young girl was enraptured at the idea that Jacqueline actually earned her own living. Marie Ledyard lazily admired and envied her slight but exceedingly fashionable figure; Helsa Steyr passionately adored her; Katharine Frere was profoundly impressed by her intellectual attainments; Betty Barkley saw in her a social success, with Aunt Hannah to pilot her—that is, every opportunity for wealth or position, or even both, through the marriage to which, Betty cheerfully conceded, her beauty entitled her.

So everybody of her own sex was exceedingly nice to her; and the men already were only too anxious to be. And what more could a young girl want?

As the jolly party started out across the snow, in random and chattering groups made up by hazard, Jacqueline turned from Captain Herrendene, with whom she found herself walking, and looked back at Desboro, who had remained standing bareheaded on the steps.

"Aren't you coming?" she called out to him, in her clear young voice.

He shook his head, smiling.

"Please excuse me a moment," she murmured to Herrendene, and ran back along the middle drive. Desboro started forward to meet her at the same moment, and they met under the dripping spruces.

"Why aren't you coming with us?" she asked.

"I can't very well. I have to wait here for some people who might arrive early."

"You are going to remain here all alone?"

"Yes, until they come. You see they are dining here, and I can't let them arrive and find the house empty."

"Do you want me to stay with you? Mrs. Hammerton is in her room, and it would be perfectly proper."

He said, reddening with surprise and pleasure: "It's very sweet of you. I—had no idea you'd offer to do such a thing——"

"Why shouldn't I? Besides, I'd rather be where you are than anywhere else."

"With me, Jacqueline?"

"Are you really surprised to hear me admit it?"

"A little."

"Why, if you please?"

"Because you never before have been demonstrative, even in speech."

She blushed: "Not as demonstrative as you are. But you know that I might learn to be."

He looked at her curiously, but with more or less self-control.

"Do you really care for me that way, Jacqueline?"

"I know of no way in which I don't care for you," she said quickly.

"Does your caring for me amount to—love?" he asked deliberately.

"I—think so—yes."

The emotion in his face was now palely reflected in hers; their voices were no longer quite steady under the sudden strain of self-repression.

"Say it, Jacqueline, if it is true," he whispered. His face was tense and white, but not as pale as hers. "Say it!" he whispered again.

"I can't—in words. But it is true—what you asked me."

"That you love me?"

"Yes. I thought you knew it long ago."

They stood very still, facing each other, breathing more rapidly. Her fate was upon her, and she knew it.

Captain Herrendene, who had waited, watched them for a moment more, then, lighting a cigarette, sauntered on carelessly, swinging his hockey-stick in circles.

Desboro said in a low, distinct voice, and without a tremor: "I am more in love with you than ever, Jacqueline. But that is as much as I shall ever say to you—nothing more than that."

"I know it."

"Yes, I know you do. Shall I leave you in peace? It can still be done. Or—shall I tell you again that I love you?"

"Yes—if you wish, tell me—that."

"Is love enough for you, Jacqueline?"

"Ask yourself, Jim. With what you give I must be content—or starve."

"Do you realise—what it means for us?" He could scarcely speak now.

"Yes—I know." She turned and looked back. Herrendene was now a long way off, walking slowly and alone. Then she turned once more to Desboro, absently, as though absorbed in her own reflections. Herrendene had asked her to marry him that morning. She was thinking of it now.

Then, in her remote gaze the brief dream faded, her eyes cleared, and she looked up at the silent man beside her.

"Shall I remain here with you?" she asked.

He made an effort to speak, but his voice was no longer under command. She waited, watching him; then they both turned and slowly entered the house together. Her hand had fallen into his, and when they reached the library he lifted it to his lips and noticed that her fingers were trembling. He laid his other hand over them, as though to quiet the tremor; and looked into her face and saw how colourless it had become.

"My darling!" But the time had not yet come when he could tolerate his own words; contempt for them choked him for a moment, and he only took her into his arms in silence.

She strove to think, to speak, to master her emotion; but for a moment his mounting passion subdued her and she remained silent, quivering in his embrace.

Then, with an effort, she found her voice and loosened his arms.

"Listen," she whispered. "You must listen. I know what you are—how you love me. But you are wrong! If I could only make you see it! If you would not think me selfish, self-seeking—believe unworthy motives of me———"

"What do you mean?" he asked, suddenly chilled.

"I mean that I am worth more to you than—than to be—what you wish me to be to you. You won't misunderstand, will you? I am not bargaining, not begging, not trading. I love you! I couldn't bargain; I could only take your terms—or leave them. And I have not decided. But—may I say something— for your sake more than for my own?"

"Yes," he said, coolly.

"Then—for your sake—far more than for mine—if you do really love me— make more of me than you have thought of doing! I know I shall be worth it to you. Could you consider it?"

After a terrible silence, he said: "I can—get out of your life—dog that I am! I can leave you in peace. And that is all."

"If that is all you can do—don't leave me—in peace. I—I will take the chances of remaining—honest———"

The hint of fear in her eyes and in her voice startled him.

"There is a martyrdom," she said, "which I might not be able to endure forever. I don't know. I shall never love another man. And all my life I have wanted love. It is here; and I may not be brave enough to deny it and live my life out in ignorance of it. But, Jim, if you only could understand—if you only knew what I can be to you—to the world for your sake—what I can become merely because I love you—what I am capable of for the sake of your pride in —in me—and———" She turned very white. "Because it is better for your sake, Jim. I am not thinking of myself, and how wonderful it would be for me— truly I am not. Don't you believe me? Only—there is so much to me—I am really so much of a woman—that it would begin to trouble you if ever I became anything—anything less than your—wife. And you would feel sorry for me—and I couldn't truthfully console you because all the while I'd know in my heart what you had thrown away that might have belonged to us both."

"Your life?" he said, with dry lips.

"Oh, Jim! I mean more than your life and mine! For our lives—yours and mine—would not be all you would throw away and deny. Before we die we would want children. Ought I not to say it?" She turned away, blind with tears, and dropped onto the sofa. "I'm wondering if I'm in my right mind," she sobbed, "for yesterday I did not even dare think of these things I am saying to you now! But—somehow—even while Captain Herrendene was speaking—it all flashed into my mind. I don't know how I knew it, but I suddenly understood that you belonged to me—just as you are, Jim—all the good, all the evil in you—everything—even your intentions toward me—how you may deal with me—all, all belonged to me! And so I went back to you, to help you. And now I have said this thing—for your sake alone, not for my own—only so that in years to come you may not have me on your conscience. For if you do not marry me—and I let myself really love you—you will wish that the beginning was to be begun again, and that we had loved each other—otherwise."

He came over and stood looking down at her for a moment. His lips were twitching.

"Would you marry me now," he managed to say, "now, after you know what a contemptible cad I am?"

"You are only a man. I love you, Jim. I will marry you—if you'll let me——"

Suddenly she covered her eyes with her hands. He seated himself beside her, sick with self-contempt, dumb, not daring to touch her where she crouched, trembling in every limb.

For a long while they remained so, in utter silence; then the doorbell startled them. Jacqueline fled to her room; Desboro composed himself with a desperate effort and went out into the hall.

He welcomed his guests on the steps when Farris opened the door, outwardly master of himself once more.

"We came over early, Jim," explained Daisy, "because Uncle John is giving a dinner and father and mother need the car. Do you mind?"

He laughed and shook hands with her and Elena, who looked intently and unsmilingly into his face, and then let her expressionless glance linger for a moment on her husband, who was holding out a huge hand to Desboro.

"I'm glad to see you, Clydesdale," said Desboro pleasantly, and took that bulky gentleman's outstretched hand, who mumbled something incoherent; but the fixed grin remained. And that was the discomforting—yes, the dismaying—characteristic of the man—his grin never seemed to be affected by his emotions.

Mrs. Quant bobbed away upstairs, piloting Daisy and Elena. Clydesdale followed Desboro to the library—the same room where he had discovered his wife that evening, and had learned in what esteem she held the law that bound her to him. Both men thought of it now—could not avoid remembering it. Also, by accident, they were seated very nearly as they had been seated that night, Clydesdale filling the armchair with his massive figure, Desboro sitting on the edge of the table, one foot resting on the floor.

Farris brought whiskey; both men shook their heads.

"Will you have a cigar, Clydesdale?" asked the younger man.

"Thanks."

They smoked in silence for a few moments, then:

"I'm glad you came," said Desboro simply.

"Yes. Men don't usually raise that sort of hell with each other unless a woman starts it."

"Don't talk that way about your wife," said Desboro sharply.

"See here, young man, I have no illusions concerning my wife. What happened here was her doing, not yours. I knew it at the time—if I didn't admit it. You behaved well—and you've behaved well ever since—only it hurt me too much to tell you so before to-day."

"That's all right, Clydesdale——"

"Yes, it is going to be all right now, I guess." A curious expression flitted across his red features, softening the grin for a moment. "I always liked you, Desboro; and Elena and I were staying with the Hammertons, so she told that Daisy girl to ask you to invite us. That's all there is to it."

"Good business!" said Desboro, smiling. "I'm glad it's all clear between us."

"Yes, it's clear sailing now, I guess." Again the curiously softening expression made his heavy red features almost attractive, and he remained silent for a while, occupied with thoughts that seemed to be pleasant ones.

Then, abruptly emerging from his revery, he grinned at Desboro:

"So Mrs. Hammerton has our pretty friend Miss Nevers in tow," he said. "Fine girl, Desboro. She's been at my collection, you know, fixing it up for the hammer."

"So you are really going to sell?" inquired Desboro.

"I don't know. I was going to. But I'm taking a new interest in my hobby since ——" he reddened, then added very simply, "since Elena and I have been getting on better together."

"Sure," nodded Desboro, gravely understanding him.

"Yes—it's about like that, Desboro. Things were rotten bad up to that night. And afterward, too, for a while. They're clearing up a little better, I think. We're going to get on together, I believe. I don't know much about women; never liked 'em much—except Elena. It's funny about Miss Nevers, isn't it?"

"What do you mean?"

"Mrs. Hammerton's being so crazy about her. She's a good girl, and a pretty one. Elena is wild to meet her."

"Didn't your wife ever meet her at your house?" asked Desboro dryly.

"When she was there appraising my jim-cracks? No. Elena has no use for my gallery or anybody who goes into it. Besides, until this morning she didn't even know that Miss Nevers was the same expert you employed. Now she wants to meet her."

Desboro slowly raised his eyes and looked at Clydesdale. The unvaried grin baffled him, and presently he glanced elsewhere.

Clydesdale, smoking, slowly crossed one ponderous leg over the other. Desboro continued to gaze out of the window. Neither spoke again until Daisy Hammerton came in with Elena. If the young wife remembered the somewhat lurid circumstances of her last appearance in that room, her animated and smiling face betrayed no indication of embarrassment.

"When is that gay company of yours going to return, Jim?" she demanded. "I am devoured by curiosity to meet this beautiful Miss Nevers. Fancy her coming to my house half a dozen times this winter and I never suspecting that my husband's porcelain gallery concealed such a combination of genius and beauty! I could have bitten somebody's head off in vexation," she rattled on, "when I found out who she was. So I made Daisy ask you to invite us to meet her. Is she so unusually wonderful, Jim?"

"I believe so," he said drily.

"They say every man who meets her falls in love with her immediately—and that most of the women do, too," appealing to Daisy, who nodded smiling corroboration.

"She is very lovely and very clever, Elena. I think I never saw anything more charming than that rainbow dance she did for us last night in Chinese costume," turning to Desboro, "'The Rainbow Skirt,' I think it is called?"

"A dance some centuries old," said Desboro, and let his careless glance rest on Elena for a moment.

"She looked," said Daisy, "like some exquisite Chinese figure made of rose-quartz, crystal and green jade."

"Jade?" said Clydesdale, immediately interested. "That girl knows jades, I can tell you. By gad! The first thing she did when she walked into my gallery was to saw into a few glass ones with a file; and good-night to about a thousand dollars in Japanese phony!"

"That was pleasant," said Desboro, laughing.

"Wasn't it! And my rose-quartz Fêng-huang! The Chia-Ching period of the Ming dynasty! Do you get me, Desboro? It was Jap!"

"Really?"

Clydesdale brought down his huge fist with a thump on the table:

"I wouldn't believe it! I told Miss Nevers she didn't know her business! I asked her to consider the fact that the crystallisation was rhombohedral, the prisms six-sided, hardness , specific gravity ., no trace of cleavage, immune to the three acids or the blow-pipe alone, and reacted with soda in the flame. I thought I knew it all, you see. First she called my attention to the colour. 'Sure,' I said, 'it's a little faded; but rose-quartz fades when exposed to light!' 'Yes,' said she, 'but moisture restores it.' So we tried it. Nix doing! Only a faint rusty stain becoming visible and infecting that delicious rose colour. 'Help!' said I. 'What the devil is it?' 'Jap funny business,' said she. 'Your rose-quartz phoenix of the Ming dynasty is common yellow crystal carved in Japan and dyed that beautiful rose tint with something, the composition of which my chemist is investigating!' Wasn't it horrible, Desboro?"

Daisy's brown eyes were very wide open, and she exclaimed softly:

"What a beautiful knowledge she has of a beautiful profession!" And to Desboro: "Can you imagine anything in the world more fascinating than to use such knowledge? And how in the world did she acquire it? She is so very young to know so much!"

"Her father began her training as a child," said Desboro. There was a slight burning sensation in his face, and a hotter pride within him. After a second or two he felt Elena's gaze; but did not choose to encounter it at the moment, and was turning to speak to Daisy Hammerton when Jacqueline entered the library.

Clydesdale lumbered to his feet and tramped over to shake hands with her; Daisy greeted her cordially; she and Elena were presented, and stood smiling at each other for a second's silence. Then Mrs. Clydesdale moved a single step forward, and Jacqueline crossed to her and offered her hand, looking straight into her eyes so frankly and intently that Elena's colour rose and for once in her life her tongue remained silent.

"Your husband and I are already business acquaintances," said Jacqueline. "I know your very beautiful gallery, too, and have had the privilege of identifying and classifying many of the jades and porcelains."

Elena's eyes were level and cool as she said: "If I had known who you were I would have received you myself. You must not think me rude. Mr. Desboro's unnecessary reticence concerning you is to blame; not I."

Jacqueline's smile became mechanical: "Mr. Desboro's reticence concerning a business acquaintance was very natural. A busy woman neither expects nor even thinks about social amenities under business circumstances."

"'Business is kinder to men than women sometimes believe'"

Elena's flush deepened: "Business is kinder to men than women sometimes believe—if it permits acquaintance with such delightful people as yourself."

Jacqueline said calmly: "All business has its compensations,"—she smiled and made a friendly little salute with her head to Clydesdale and Desboro,—"as you will witness for me. And I am employed by other clients who also are considerate and kind. So you see the woman who works has scarcely any time to suffer from social isolation."

Daisy said lightly: "Nobody who is happily employed worries over social matters. Intelligence and sweet temper bring more friends than a busy girl knows what to do with. Isn't that so, Miss Nevers?"

Jacqueline turned to Elena with a little laugh: "It's an axiom that nobody can have too many friends. I want all I can have, Mrs. Clydesdale, and am most grateful when people like me."

"And when they don't," asked Elena, smiling, "what do you do then, Miss Nevers?"

"What is there to do, Mrs. Clydesdale?" she said gaily. "What would you do about it?"

But Elena seemed not to have heard her, for she was already turning to Desboro, flushed, almost feverish in her animation:

"So many things have happened since I saw you, Jim——" she hesitated, then added daringly, "at the opera. Do you remember Ariane?"

"I think you were in the Barkley's box," he said coolly.

"Your memory is marvellous! In point of fact, I was there. And since then so many, many things have happened that I'd like to compare notes with you—sometime."

"I'm quite ready now," he said.

"Do you think your daily record fit for public scrutiny, Jim?" she laughed.

"I don't mind sharing it with anybody here," he retorted gaily, "if you have no objection."

His voice and hers, and their laughter seemed so perfectly frank that thrust and parry pa

ssed as without significance. She and Desboro were still lightly rallying each other; Clydesdale was explaining to Daisy that lapis lazuli was the sapphire of the ancients, while Jacqueline was showing her a bit under a magnifying glass, when the noise of sleighs and motors outside signalled the return of the skating party.

As Desboro passed her, Elena said under her breath: "I want a moment alone with you this evening."

"It's impossible," he motioned with his lips; and passed on with a smile of welcome for his returning guests.

Later, in the billiard room, where they all had gathered before the impromptu dance which usually terminated the evening, Elena found another chance for a word aside: "Jim, I must speak to you alone, please."

"It can't be done. You see that for yourself, don't you?"

"It can be done. Go to your room and I'll come——"

"Are you mad?"

"Almost. I tell you you'd better find some way——"

"What has happened?"

"I mean to have you tell me, Jim."

A dull flush came into his face: "Oh! Well, I'll tell you now, if you like."

Her heart seemed to stop for a second, then almost suffocated her, and she instinctively put her hand to her throat.

He was leaning over the pool table, idly spinning the ivory balls; she, seated on the edge, one pretty, bare arm propping her body, appeared to be watching him as idly. All around them rang the laughter and animated chatter of his guests, sipping their after-dinner coffee and cordial around the huge fireplace.

"Don't say—that you are going to—Jim——" she breathed. "It isn't true—it mustn't be——"

He interrupted deliberately: "What are you trying to do to me? Make a servant out of me? Chain me up while you pass your life deciding at leisure whether to live with your husband or involve yourself and me in scandal?"

"Are you in love with that girl—after what you have promised me?"

"Are you sane or crazy?"

"You once told me you would never marry. I have rested secure in the knowledge that when the inevitable crash came you would be free to stand by me!"

"You have a perfectly good husband. You and he are on better terms—you are getting on all right together. Do you expect to keep me tied to the table-leg in case of eventualities?" he said, in a savage whisper. "How many men do you wish to control?"

"One! I thought a Desboro never lied."

"Have I lied to you?"

"If you marry Miss Nevers you will have lied to me, Jim."

"Very well. Then you'll release me from that fool of a promise. I remember I did say that I would never marry. I've changed my mind, that's all. I've changed otherwise, too—please God! The cad you knew as James Desboro is not exactly what you're looking at now. It's in me to be something remotely resembling a man. I learned how to try from her, if you want to know. What I was can't be helped. What I'm to make of the débris of what I am concerns myself. If you ever had a shred of real liking for me you'll show it now."

"Jim! Is this how you betray me—after persuading me to continue a shameful and ghastly farce with Cary Clydesdale! You have betrayed me—for your own ends! You have made my life a living lie again—so that you could evade responsibility——"

"Was I ever responsible for you?"

"You asked me to marry you——"

"Before you married Cary. Good God! Does that entail hard labour for life?"

"You promised not to marry——"

"What is it to you what I do—if you treat your husband decently?"

"I have tried——" She crimsoned. "I—I endured degradation to which I will never again submit—whatever the law may be—whatever marriage is supposed to include! Do you think you can force me to—to that—for your own selfish ends—with your silly and unsolicited advice on domesticity and—and children—when my heart is elsewhere—when you have it, and you know you possess it—and all that I am—every bit of me. Jim! Don't be cruel to me who have been trying to live as you wished, merely to satisfy a moral notion of your own! Don't betray me now—at such a time—when it's a matter of days, hours, before I tell Cary that the farce is ended. Are you going to leave me to face things alone? You can't! I won't let you! I am——"

"'Be careful,' he said.... 'People are watching us'"

"Be careful," he said, spinning the ball into a pocket. "People are watching us. Toss that cue-ball back to me, please. Laugh a little when you do it."

For a second she balanced the white ivory ball in a hand which matched it; then the mad impulse to dash it into his smiling face passed with a shudder, and she laughed and sent it caroming swiftly from cushion to cushion, until it darted into his hand.

"Jim," she said, "you are not really serious. I know it, too; and because I do know it, I have been able to endure the things you have done—your idle fancies for a pretty face and figure—your indiscretions, ephemeral courtships, passing inclinations. But this is different——"

"Yes, it is different," he said. "And so am I, Elena. Let us be about the honest business of life, in God's name, and clear our hearts and souls of the morbid and unwholesome mess that lately entangled us."

"Is that how you speak of what we have been to each other?" she asked, very pale.

He was silent.

"Jim, dear," she said timidly, "won't you give me ten minutes alone with you?"

He scarcely heard her. He spun the last parti-coloured ball into a corner pocket, straightened his shoulders, and looked at Jacqueline where she sat in the corner of the fireplace. Herrendene, cross-legged on the rug at her feet, was doing Malay card tricks to amuse her; but from moment to moment her blue eyes stole across the room toward Desboro and Mrs. Clydesdale where they leaned together over the distant pool table. Suddenly she caught his eye and smiled a pale response to the message in his gaze.

After a moment he said quietly to Elena: "I am deeply and reverently in love —for the first and only time in my life. It is proper that you should know it. And now you do know it. There is absolutely nothing further to be said between us."

"There is—more than you think," she whispered, white to the lips.

CHAPTER XI

Nobody, apparently, was yet astir; not a breakfast tray had yet tinkled along the dusky corridors when Desboro, descending the stairs in the dim morning light, encountered Jacqueline coming from the general direction of the east wing, her arms loaded with freshly cut white carnations.

"Good morning," he whispered, in smiling surprise, taking her and her carnations into his arms very reverently, almost timidly.

She endured the contact shyly and seriously, as usual, bending her head aside to avoid his lips.

"Do you suppose," he said laughingly, "that you could ever bring yourself to kiss me, Jacqueline?"

She did not answer, and presently he released her, saying: "You never have yet; and now that we're engaged——"

"Engaged!"

"You know we are!"

"Is that what you think, Jim?"

"Certainly! I asked you to marry me——"

"No, dear, I asked you. But I wasn't certain you had quite accepted me——"

"Are you laughing at me?"

"I don't know—I don't know what I am doing any more; laughter and tears seem so close to each other—sometimes—and I can never be certain which it is going to be any more."

Her eyes remained grave, but her lips were sweet and humourous as she stood there on the stairs, her chin resting on the sheaf of carnations clasped to her breast.

"What is troubling you, Jacqueline?" he asked, after a moment's silence.

"Nothing. If you will hold these flowers a moment I'll decorate you."

He took the fragrant sheaf from her; she selected a magnificent white blossom, drew the stem through the lapel of his coat, patted the flower into a position which suited her, regarded the effect critically, then glanced up out of her winning blue eyes and found him watching her dreamily.

"I try to realise it, and I can't," he said vaguely. "Can you, dear?"

"Realise what?" she asked, in a low voice.

"That we are engaged."

"Are you so sure of me, Jim?"

"Do you suppose I could live life through without you now?"

"I don't know. Try it for two minutes anyway; these flowers must stand in water. Will you wait here for me?"

He stepped forward to aid her, but she passed him lightly, avoiding his touch, and sped across the corridor. In a few minutes she returned and they descended the stairs together, and entered the empty library. She leaned back against the table, both slender hands resting on the edge behind her, and gazed out at the sparrows in the snow. And she did not even appear to notice his arm, which ventured around her waist, or his lips resting against the lock of bright hair curling on her cheek, so absorbed she seemed to be in her silent reflections.

After a few moments she said, still looking out of the window: "I must tell you something now."

"Are you going to tell me that you love me?"

"Yes—perhaps I had better begin that way."

"Then begin, dearest."

"I—I love you."

His arm tightened around her, but she gently released herself.

"There is a—a little more to say, Jim. I love you enough to give you back your promise."

"My promise!"

"To marry me," she said steadily. "I scarcely knew what I was saying yesterday—I was so excited, so much in love with you—so fearful that you might sometime be unhappy if things continued with us as they threatened to continue. I'm afraid I overvalued myself—made you suspect that I am more than I really am—or can ever be. Besides, I frightened you—and myself— unnecessarily. I never could be in any danger of—of loving you—unwisely. It was not perfectly fair to you to hint such a thing—because, after all, there is a third choice for you. A worthy one. For you could let me go my way out of your life, which is already so full, and which would fill again very easily, even if my absence left a little void for a while. And if it was any kind of pity you felt for me—for what I said to you—that stirred you to—ask of me what I begged you to ask—then I give you back your promise. I have not slept for thinking over it. I must give it back."

He remained silent for a while, then his arms slipped down around her body and he dropped on one knee beside her and laid his face close against her. She had to bend over to hear what he was saying, he spoke so low and with such difficulty.

"How can you care for me?" he said. "How can you? Don't you understand what a beast I was—what lesser impulse possessed me———"

"Hush, Jim! Am I different?"

"Good God! Yes!"

"No, dear."

"You don't know what you're saying!"

"You don't know. Do you suppose I am immune to—to the—lesser love—at moments———"

He lifted his head and looked up at her, dismayed.

"You!"

"I. How else could I understand you?"

"Because you are so far above everything unworthy."

"No, dear. If I were, you would only have angered and frightened me—not made me sorry for us both. Because women and men are something alike at moments; only, somehow, women seem to realise that—somehow—they are guardians of—of something—of civilisation, perhaps. And it is their instinct to curb and silence and ignore whatever unworthy threatens it or them. It is that way with us, Jim."

She looked out of the window at the sky and the trees, and stood thinking for a while. Then: "Did you suppose it is always easy for a girl in love—whose instinct is to love—and to give? Especially such a girl as I am, especially when she is so dreadfully afraid that her lover may think her cold-blooded—self-seeking—perhaps a—a schemer———"

She covered her face with her hand—the quick, adorable gesture he knew so well.

"I—did ask you to marry me," she said, in a stifled voice, "but I am not a schemer; my motive was not self-interest. It was for you I asked it, Jim, far more than for myself—or I never could have found the courage—perhaps not even the wish. Because, somehow, I am too proud to wish for anything that is not offered."

As he said nothing, she broke out suddenly with a little sob of protest in her voice: "I am not a self-seeking, calculating woman! I am not naturally cold and unresponsive! I am—inclined to be—otherwise. And you had better know it. But you won't believe it, I am afraid, because I—I have never responded to —to you."

Tears fell between her fingers over the flushed cheeks. She spoke with increasing effort: "You don't understand; and I can't explain—except to say that to be demonstrative seemed unworthy in me."

He put his arms around her shoulders very gently; she rested her forehead against his shoulder.

"Don't think me calculating and cold-blooded—or a fool," she whispered. "Probably everybody kisses or is kissed. I know it as well as you do. But I haven't the—effrontery—to permit myself—such emotions. I couldn't, Jim. I'd hate myself. And I thought of that, too, when I asked you to marry me. Because if you had refused—and—matters had gone on—you would have been sorry for me sooner or later—or perhaps hated me. Because I would have been—been too much ashamed of myself to have—loved you—unwisely."

He stood with head bent, listening; and, as he listened, the comparison between this young girl and himself forced itself into his unwilling mind— how that all she believed and desired ennobled her, and how what had always governed him had made of him nothing more admirable than what he was born, a human animal. For what he began as he still was—only cleverer.

What else was he—except a trained animal, sufficiently educated to keep out of jail? What had he done with his inheritance? His body was sane and healthy; he had been at pains to cultivate that. How was it with his mind? How was it with his spiritual beliefs? Had he cultivated and added to either? He had been endowed with a brain. Had he made of it anything except an instrument for idle caprice and indolent passions to play upon?

"Do you understand me now?" she whispered, touching wet lashes with her handkerchief.

He replied impetuously, hotly; her hands dropped from her face and she looked up at him with sweet, confused eyes, blushing vividly under his praise of her.

He spoke of himself, too, with all the quick, impassioned impulse of youthful emotion, not sparing himself, promising better things, vowing them before the shrine of her innocence. Yet, a stronger character might have registered such vows in silence. And his fervour and incoherence left her mute; and after he had ceased to protest too much she stood quiet for a while, striving to search herself so that nothing unworthy should remain—so that heart and soul should be clean under the magic veil of happiness descending before her enraptured eyes.

Gently his arms encircled her; her clasped hands rested on his shoulder, and she gazed out at the blue sky and sun-warmed snow as at a corner of paradise revealed.

Later, when the household was astir, she went out with him into the greenhouse, where the enchanted stillness of growing things thrilled her, and the fragrance and sunlight made the mystery of love and its miracle even more exquisitely unreal to her.

At first they did not speak; her hand lay loosely in his, her blue eyes remained remote; and together they slowly paced the long, glass-sheeted galleries between misty, scented mounds of bloom, to and fro, under the flood of pallid winter sunshine, pale as the yellow jasmine flowers overhead.

After a while a fat gardener came into one of the further wings. Presently the sound of shovelled coal from the furnace-pit aroused them from their dream; and they looked at each other gravely.

After a moment, he said: "Does it make a difference to you, Jacqueline, what I was before I knew you?"

"No."

"I was only wondering what you really think of me."

"You know already, Jim."

He shook his head slowly.

"Jim! Of course you know!" she insisted hotly. "What you may have been before I knew you I refuse to consider. Anyway, it was you—part of you—and belongs to me now! Because I choose to make it mine—all that you were and are—good and evil! For I won't give up one atom of you—even to the devil himself!"

He tried to laugh: "What a fierce little partisan you are," he said.

"Very—where it concerns you," she said, unsmiling.

"Dear—I had better tell you now; you may hear things about me——"

"I won't listen to them!"

"No; but one sometimes hears without listening. People may say things. They will say things. I wish I could spare you. If I had known—if I had only known

—that you were in the world———"

"Don't, Jim! It—it isn't best for me to hear. It doesn't concern me," she insisted excitedly. "And if anybody dares say one word to me———"

"Wait, dear. All I want to be sure of is that you do love me enough to—to go on loving me. I want to be certain, and I want you to be certain before you are a bride———"

She was growing very much excited, and suddenly near to tears, for the one thing that endangered her self-control seemed to be his doubt of her.

"There is nothing that I haven't forgiven you," she said. "Nothing! There is nothing I won't forgive—except—one thing———"

"What?"

"I can't say it. I can't even think it. All I know is that now I couldn't forgive it." Suddenly she became perfectly quiet.

"I know what you mean," he said.

"Yes. It is what no wife can forgive." She looked at him, clear eyed, intelligent, calm; for the moment without any illusion; and he seemed to feel that, in the light of what she knew of him, she was coolly weighing the danger of the experiment. Never had he seen so cold and lustrous a brow, such limpid clarity of eye, searching, fearless, direct. Then, in an instant, it all seemed to melt into flushed and winsome loveliness; and she was murmuring that she loved him, and asking pardon for even one second's hesitation.

"It never could be; it is unthinkable," she whispered. "And it is too late anyway for me—I would love you now, whatever you killed in me. Because I must go on loving you, Jim; for that is the way it is with me, and I know it now. As long as there is life in me I'll strive for you in my own fashion—even against yourself—to keep you for mine, to please you, to be to you and to the world what you wish me to be—for your honour and your happiness—which also must be my own—the only happiness, now, that I can ever understand."

He held her in his arms, smoothing the bright hair, touching the white brow with his lips at moments, happy because he was so deeply in love, fearful because of it—and, deep in his soul, miserable, afraid lest aught out of his past life return again to mock her—lest some echo of folly offend her ears—some shadow fall—some phantom of dead days rise from their future hearth to stand between them.

It is that way with a man who has lived idly and irresponsibly, and who has gone lightly about the pleasure of life and not its business. For sometimes there arrives an hour of unbidden clairvoyance—not necessarily a spiritual awakening—but a moment of balanced intelligence and sanity and clear vision. And when it arrives, the road to yesterday suddenly becomes visible for its entire length; and when a man looks back he sees it stretching away behind him, peopled with every shape that has ever traversed it, and every spectre that ever has haunted it.

Sorrow for what need not have been, regret and shame for what had been—and the bitterness of the folly—the knowledge, too late, of what he could have been to the girl he held now in his arms—how he could have met her on more equal terms had he saved his youth and strength and innocence and pride for her alone—how he could have given it unsullied into her keeping. All this Desboro was beginning to realise now. And many men have realised it when the tardy understanding came too late. For what has been is still and will be always; and shall appear here or hereafter, or after that—somewhere, sometime, inevitably, inexorably. There is no such thing as expunging what has been, or of erasing what is to be. All records stand; hope lies only in lengthening the endless chapters—chapters which will not be finished when the sun dies, and the moon fails, and the stars go out forever.

Walking slowly back together, they passed Herrendene in the wing hall, and his fine and somewhat melancholy face lighted up at the encounter.

"I'm so sorry you are going to-day," said Jacqueline, with all her impulsive and sweet sincerity. "Everybody will miss you and wish you here again."

"To be regretted is one of the few real pleasures in life," he said, smiling. His quick eye had rested on Desboro and then reverted to her, and his intuition was warning him with all the brutality and finality of reason that his last hope of her must end.

Desboro said: "I hate to have you go, Herrendene, but I suppose you must."

"Must you?" echoed Jacqueline, wistful for the moment. But the irresistible radiance of happiness had subtly transfigured her, and Herrendene looked into her eyes and saw the new-born beauty in them, shyly apparent.

"Yes," he said, "I must be about the business of life—the business of life, Miss Nevers. Everybody is engaged in it; it has many names, but it's all the same business. You, for example, pass judgment on beautiful things; Desboro, here, is a farmer, and I play soldier with sword and drum. But it's all the same business—the business of life; and one can work at it or idle through it, but never escape it, because, at the last, every soul in the world must die in harness. And the idlest are the heaviest laden." He laughed. "That's quite a sermon, isn't it, Miss Nevers? And shall I make my adieux now? Were you going anywhere? You see I am leaving Silverwood directly after breakfast ——"

"As though Mr. Desboro and I would go off anywhere and not say good-bye to you!" she exclaimed indignantly, quite unconscious of being too obvious.

So they all three returned to the breakfast room together, where Clydesdale, who had come over from the Hammertons' for breakfast, was already tramping hungrily around the covered dishes on the sideboard, hot plate in hand, evidently meditating a wholesale assault. He grinned affably as Jacqueline and Desboro came in, and they all helped themselves from the warmers, returning laden to the table with whatever suited their fancy. Other guests, to whom no trays had been sent, arrived one after another to prowl around the browse and join in the conversation if they chose, or sulk, as is the fashion with some perfectly worthy souls at breakfast-tide.

"This thaw settles the skating for good and all," remarked Reggie Ledyard. "Will you go fishing with me, Miss Nevers? It's our last day, you know."

Cairns growled over his grape-fruit: "You can't make dates with Miss Nevers at the breakfast table. It isn't done. I was going to ask her to do something with me, anyway."

"I hate breakfast," said Van Alstyne. "When I see it I always wish I were dead or that everybody else was. Zooks! This cocktail helps some! Try one, Miss Nevers."

"There's reason in your grouch," remarked Bertie Barkley, with his hard-eyed smile, "considering what Aunt Hannah and I did to you and Helsa at auction last night."

"Aunt Hannah will live in luxury for a year on it," added Cairns maliciously. "Doesn't it make you happy, Stuyve?"

"Oh—blub!" muttered Van Alstyne, hating everybody and himself—and most of all hating to think of his losses and of the lady who caused them. Only the really rich know how card losses rankle.

Cairns glanced banteringly across at Jacqueline. It was his form of wit to quiz her because she neither indulged in cocktails nor cigarettes, nor played cards for stakes. He lifted his eyebrows and tapped the frosted shaker beside him significantly.

"I've a new kind of mountain dew, warranted to wake the dead, Miss Nevers. I call it the 'Aunt Hannah,' in her honour—honour to whom honour is dew," he added impudently. "Won't you let me make you a cocktail?"

"Wait until Aunt Hannah hears how you have honoured her and tempted me," laughed Jacqueline.

"I never tempted maid or wife

Or suffragette in all my life——"

sang Ledyard, beating time on Van Alstyne, who silently scowled his displeasure.

Presently Ledyard selected a grape-fruit, with a sour smile at one of Desboro's cats which had confidently leaped into his lap.

"Is this a zoo den in the Bronx, or a breakfast room, Desboro? I only ask because I'm all over cats."

Bertie Barkley snapped his napkin at an intrusive yellow pup who was sniffing and wagging at his elbow.

Jacqueline comforted the retreating animal, bending over and crooning in his floppy ear:

"They gotta stop kickin' my dawg aroun'."

"What do you care what they do to Jim's live stock, Miss Nevers?" demanded Ledyard suspiciously.

She laughed, but to her annoyance a warmer colour brightened her cheeks.

"Heaven help us!" exclaimed Reggie. "Miss Nevers is blushing at the breakfast table. Gentlemen, are we done for without even suspecting it? And by that—that"—pointing a furious finger at Desboro—"that!"

"Certainly," said Desboro, smiling. "Did you imagine I'd ever let Miss Nevers escape from Silverwood?"

Ledyard heaved a sigh of relief: "Gad," he muttered, "I suspected you both for a moment. Anyway, it doesn't matter. Every man here would have murdered you in turn. Come on, Miss Nevers; you've made a big splash with me, and I'll play you a game of rabbit—or anything on earth, if you'll let me run along beside you."

"No, I'm driving with Captain Herrendene to the station," she said; and that melancholy soldier looked up in grateful surprise.

And she did go with him; and everybody came out on the front steps to wish him bon voyage.

"Are you coming back, Miss Nevers?" asked Ledyard, in pretended alarm.

"I don't know. Is Manila worth seeing, Captain Herrendene?" she asked, laughingly.

"If you sail for Manila with that tin soldier I'll go after you in a hydroplane!" called Reggie after them, as the car rolled away. He added frankly, for everybody's benefit: "I hate any man who even looks at her, and I don't care who knows it. But what's the use? Going to night-school might help me, but I doubt it. No; she's for a better line of goods than the samples at Silverwood. She shines too far above us. Mark that, James Desboro! And take what comfort you can in your reflected glory. For had she not been the spotlight, you'd look exactly like the rest of us. And that isn't flattering anybody, I'm thinking."

It was to be the last day of the party. Everybody was leaving directly after luncheon, and now everybody seemed inclined to do nothing in particular. Mrs. Clydesdale came over from the Hammerton's. The air was soft and springlike; the snow in the fields was melting and full of golden pools. People seemed to be inclined to stroll about outdoors without their hats; a lively snowball battle began between Cary Clydesdale on one side and Cairns and Reggie Ledyard on the other—and gradually was participated in by everybody except Aunt Hannah, who grimly watched it from the library window. But her weather eye never left Mrs. Clydesdale.

She was still standing at the window when somebody entered the library behind her, and somebody else followed. She knew who they were; the curtains screened her. For one second the temptation to listen beset her, but she put it away with a sniff, and had already turned to disclose herself when she heard Mrs. Clydesdale say something that stiffened her into a rigid silence.

What followed stiffened her still more—and there were only a few words, too —only:

"For God's sake, what are you thinking of?" from Desboro; and from Elena Clydesdale:

"This has got to end—I can't stand it, Jim——"

"Stand what?"

"Him! And what you are doing!"

"Be careful! Do you want people to overhear us?" he said, in a low voice of concentrated anger.

"Then where——"

"I don't know. Wait until these people leave——"

"To-night?"

"How can we see each other to-night!"

"Cary is going to New York——"

Voices approaching through the hall warned him:

"All right, to-night," he said, desperately. "Go out into the hall."

"To-night, Jim?"

"Yes."

She turned and walked out into the hall. He heard her voice calmly joining in the chatter now approaching, and, without any reason, he walked to the window. And found Mrs. Hammerton there.

Astonishment and anger left him dumb and scarlet to the roots of his hair.

"It isn't my fault," she hissed. "You and that other fool had already committed yourselves before I could stir to warn you. What do I care for your vile little intrigues, anyway! I don't have to listen behind curtains to learn what anybody could have seen at the Metropolitan Opera——"

"You are absolutely mistaken——"

"No doubt, James. But whether I am or not makes absolutely no difference to me—or to Jacqueline Nevers——"

"What do you mean by that?"

"What I say, exactly. It will make no difference to Jacqueline, because you are going to keep your distance."

"Do you think so?"

"If you don't keep away from her I'll tell her a few things. Listen to me very carefully, James. You think I'm fond of you, don't you? Well, I am. But I've taken a fancy to Jacqueline Nevers that—well, if I were not childless I might feel it less deeply. I've put my arms around her once and for all. Now do you understand?"

"I tell you," he said steadily, "you are mistaken in believing——"

"Very well. Granted. What of it? One dirty little intrigue more or less doesn't alter what you are and have been. The plain point of the matter is this, James: you are not fit to aspire seriously to Jacqueline Nevers. Are you? I ask you, now, honestly; are you?"

"Does that concern you?"

She fairly snapped her teeth and her eyes sparkled:

"Yes; it concerns me! Keep away! I warn you—you and the rest of the Jacks and Reggies and similar assorted pups. Your hunting ground is elsewhere."

A sort of cold fury possessed him: "You had better not say anything to Miss Nevers about what you overheard in this room," he said in a colourless voice.

"I'll use my own judgment," she retorted tartly.

"Use mine. It is perhaps better. Don't interfere."

"Don't be a fool, James."

"Will you listen to me——"

"About Elena Clydesdale?" she asked maliciously.

"There is nothing to tell about her."

"Naturally. I never heard the Desboros were blackguards—only a trifle airy, James—a trifle gallant! Dear child, don't anger me. You know it wouldn't be well for you."

"I ask you merely to mind your business."

"That I shall do. My life's business is Jacqueline. You yourself made her so ——" Malice indescribable snapped in her tiny black eyes, and she laughed harshly. "You made that motherless girl my business. Ask yourself if you've ever, inadvertently, done as decent a thing?"

"Do you understand that I wish to marry her?" he asked, white with passion.

"You! What do I care what your patronising intentions may be? And, James, if you drive me to it——" she fairly glared at him, "—I'll destroy even your acquaintanceship with her. And I possess the means to do it!"

"Try it!" he motioned with dry lips.

A moment later the animated chatter of young people filled the room, and among them sounded Jacqueline's voice.

"Oh!" she said, laughing, when she saw Mrs. Hammerton and Desboro coming from the embrasure of the window. "Have you been flirting again, Aunt Hannah!"

"Yes," said the old lady grimly, "and I think I've taken him into camp."

"Then it's my turn," said Jacqueline. "Come on, Mr. Desboro, you can't escape me. I'm going to beat you a game of rabbit!"

Everybody drifted into the billiard-room at their heels, and found them already at their stations on either side of the pool table, each one covering the side pocket with left hand spread wide. Jacqueline had the cue-ball; it lay on the cloth in front of her, and her slim right hand covered it.

"Ready?" she asked of Desboro.

"Ready," he said, watching her.

She made a feint; he sprang to the left; she shot the ball toward the right corner pocket, missed, carromed, and tried to recover it; but Desboro's arm shot out across the cloth and he seized it and shot it at her left corner pocket. It went in with a plunk!

"One for Jim!" said Reggie gravely, and, picking up a cue, scored with a button overhead.

"Plunk!" went the ball again into the same pocket; and Jacqueline gave a little cry of dismay as Desboro leaned far over the table, threatening, feinting, moving the ball so fast she could scarcely follow his hand. Then she thought she saw the crisis coming, sprang toward the left corner pocket, gave a cry of terror, and plunk! went the ball into her side pocket.

Flushed, golden hair in pretty disorder, she sprang back on guard again, and the onlookers watched the movement of her hands, fascinated by their grace and beauty as she defended her side of the table and, finally, snatched the ball from the very jaws of the right corner.

It was a breathless, exciting game, even for rabbit, and was fought to a furious finish; but she went down to defeat, and Desboro came around the table to condole with her, and together they stepped aside to leave the arena free for Katharine Frere and Reggie.

"I'm so sorry, dear," he said under his breath.

"It's what I want, Jim. Never let me take the lead again—in anything."

His laugh was not genuine. He glanced across the room and saw Aunt Hannah pretending not to watch him. Near her stood Elena Clydesdale beside her husband, making no such pretence.

He said in a low voice: "Jacqueline, would you marry me as soon as I can get a license—if I asked you to do it?"

She blushed furiously; then walked over to the window and gazed out, dismayed and astounded. He followed.

"Will you, dear? I have the very best of reasons for asking you."

"Could you tell me the reasons, Jim?" she asked, still dazed.

"I had rather not—if you don't mind. Will you trust me when I say it is better for us to marry quietly and at once?"

She looked up at him dumbly, the scarlet slowly fading from brow and cheek.

"Do you trust me?" he repeated.

"Yes—I trust you."

"Will you marry me, then, as soon as I can arrange for it?"

She was silent.

"Will you?" he urged.

"Jim—darling—I wanted to be equipped—I wanted to have some pretty things, in order to—to be at my very best—for you. A girl is a bride only once in her life; a man remembers her as she came to him first."

"Dearest, as I saw you first, so I will always think of you."

"Oh, Jim! In that black gown and cuffs and collar!"

"You don't understand men, dear. No coronation robe ever could compete with that dress in my affections. You always are perfect; I never saw you when you weren't bewitching——"

"But, dear, there are other things——"

"We'll buy them together!"

"Jim, must we do it this way? I don't mean that I wished for any ostentation ——"

"I did! I would have wished for a ceremony suited to your beauty and——"

"No, no! I didn't expect——"

"But I did—damn it!" he said between his teeth. "I wished it; I expected it. Don't you think I know what a girl ought to have? Indeed I do, Jacqueline. And in New York town another century will never see a bride to compare with you! But, my darling, I cannot risk it!"

"Risk it?"

"Don't ask me any more."

"No."

"And—will you do it—for my sake?"

"Yes."

There was a silence between them; he lighted a cigarette, turned coolly around, and glanced across the room. Elena instantly averted her gaze. Mrs. Hammerton sustained his pleasant inspection with an unchanging stare almost insolent.

After a moment he smiled at her. It was a mistake to do it.

After luncheon, Elena Clydesdale found an opportunity for a word with him.

"Will you remember that you have an engagement to-night?" she said in a guarded voice.

"I shall break it," he replied.

"What!"

"This is going to end here and now! Your business is with your husband. He's a decent fellow; he's devoted to you. I won't even discuss it with you. Break with him if you want to, but don't count on me!"

"I can't break with him unless I can count on you. Are you going to lie to me, Jim?"

"You can call it what you like. But if you break with him it will end our friendship."

"I tell you I've got to break with him. I've got to do it now—at once!"

"Why?"

"Because—because I've got to. I can't go on fencing with him."

"Oh!"

She crimsoned and set her little white teeth.

"I've got to leave him or be what—I won't be!"

"Then break with him," he said contemptuously, "and give a decent man another chance in life!"

"I can't—unless you———"

"Good God! I'd sooner cut my throat. My sympathy is for your husband. You're convicting yourself, I tell you! I've always had a dim idea that he was all right. Now I know it—and my obligations to you are ended."

"Then—you leave me—to him? Answer me, Jim. You refuse to stand between me and my—my degradation? Is that what you mean to do? Knowing I have no other means of escaping it except through you—except by defying the world with you!"

She broke off with a sob.

"Elena," he said, "your one salvation in this world is to have children! It will mean happiness and honour for you both—mutual respect, and, if not romantic love, at least a cordial understanding and mutual toleration. If you have such a chance, don't throw it away. Your husband is a slow, intelligent, kind, and patient man, who has borne much from you because he is honestly in love with you. Don't mistake his consideration for weakness, his patience for acquiescence. What kindness you have pretended to show him recently has given him courage. He is trying to make good because he believes that he can win you. This is clear reason; it is logic, Elena."

She turned on him in a flash of tears and exasperation.

"Logic! Do you think a woman wants that?" she stammered. "Do you think a woman arrives at any conclusion through the kind of reasoning that satisfies men? What difference does what you say make to me, when I hate him and I love you? How does your logic help me to escape what is—is abhorrent to me! Do you suppose your reasoning makes it more endurable? Oh, Jim! For heaven's sake don't leave me to that—that man! Let me come here this evening after he has gone, and try to explain to you how I———"

"No."

"You won't!"

"No. I am going to town with Mrs. Hammerton and Miss Nevers on the evening train. And some day I am going to marry Miss Nevers."

CHAPTER XII

During her week's absence from town Jacqueline's mail had accumulated; a number of business matters had come into the office, the disposal of which now awaited her decision—requests from wealthy connoisseurs for expert opinion, offers to dispose of collections entire or in part, invitations to dealers' secret conferences, urgent demands for appraisers, questions concerning origin or authenticity, commissions to buy, sell, advertise, or send searchers throughout the markets at home or abroad for anything from a tiny shrine of Limoges enamel to a complete suit of equestrian armour to fill a gap in a series belonging to some rich man's museum.

On the evening of her arrival at the office, she was beset by her clerks and salesmen, bringing to her hundreds of petty routine details requiring her personal examination. Also, it appeared that one of her clients had been outrageously swindled by a precious pair of fly-by-nights; and the matter required immediate investigation. So she was obliged to telephone to Mrs. Hammerton that she could not dine with her at the Ritz, and to Desboro that she could not see him for a day or two. In Desboro's case, a postscript added: "Except for a minute, dearest, whenever you come."

She did not even take the time to dine that evening, but settled down at her office desk as soon as the retail shop below was closed; and, with the tea urn and a rack of toast at her elbow, plunged straight into the delightfully interesting chaos confronting her.

As far as the shop was concerned, the New Year, as usual, had brought to that part of the business a lull in activity. It always happened so after New Years; and the stagnation steadily increased as spring approached, until by summer time the retail business was practically dead.

But a quiet market did not mean that there was nothing for her to do. Warehouse sales must be watched, auctions, public and private, in town and country, must be attended by one or more of her representatives; private clients inclined to sell always required tactful handling and careful consideration; her confidential agents must always be alert.

Also, always her people were continually searching for various objects ardently desired by all species of acquisitive clients; she must keep in constant touch with everything that was happening in her business abroad; she must keep abreast of her times at home, which required much cleverness, intuition, and current reading, and much study in the Museum and among private collections to which she had access. She was a very, very busy girl, almost too busy at moments to remember that she had fallen in love.

That night she worked alone in her office until long after midnight; and all the next day until noon she was busy listening to or instructing salesmen, clerks, dealers, experts, auctioneers, and clients. Also, the swindle and the swindlers were worrying her extremely.

Luncheon had been served on a tray beside her desk, and she was still absent-mindedly going over the carbon files of business letters, which she had dictated and dispatched that morning, when Desboro's card was brought to her. She sent word that she would receive him.

"Will you lunch with me, Jim?" she asked demurely, when he had appeared and shaken hands vigorously. "I've a fruit salad and some perfectly delicious sherbet! Please sit on the desk top and help me consume the banquet."

"Do you call that a banquet, darling?" he demanded. "Come out to the Ritz with me this instant——"

"Dearest! I can't! Oh, you don't know what an exciting and interesting mess my business affairs are in! A girl always has to pay for her pleasure. But in this case it's a pleasure to pay. Bring up that chair and share my luncheon like a good fellow, so we can chat together for a few minutes. It's all the time I can give you to-day, dearest."

He pulled up a chair and seated himself, experiencing somewhat mixed emotions in the presence of such bewildering business capability.

"You make me feel embarrassed and ashamed," he said. "Rotten loafer that I am! And you so energetic and industrious—you darling thing!"

"But, dear, your farmer can't plow frozen ground, you know; all your men can do just now is to mend fences and dump fertiliser and lime and gypsum over everything. And I believe they were doing that when I left."

"If," he said, "I were a real instead of a phony farmer, I'd read catalogues about wire fences; I'd find plenty to do if I were not a wretched sham. It's only, I hope, because you're in town that I can't drive myself back where I belong. I ought to be sitting in a wood-shed, in overalls, whittling sticks and yelling bucolic wisdom at Ezra Vail—— Oh, you needn't laugh, darling, but that's where I ought to be, and what I ought to be doing if I'm ever going to support a wife!"

"Jim! You're not going to support a wife! You absurd boy!"

"What!" he demanded, losing countenance.

"Did you think you were obliged to support me? How ridiculous! I'd be perfectly miserable——"

"Jacqueline! What on earth do you mean? We are going to live on my income."

"Indeed we are not! What use would I be to you if I brought you nothing except an idle, useless, lazy girl to support! It's unthinkable!"

"Do you expect to remain in business?" he asked, incredulously.

"Certainly I expect it!"

"But—darling——"

"Jim! I love my business. It was father's business; it represents my childhood, my girlhood, my maturity. Every detail of it is inextricably linked with memories of him—the dearest memories, the tenderest associations of my life! Do you wish me to give them up?"

"How can you be my wife, Jacqueline, and still remain a business woman?"

"Dear, I am certainly going to marry you. Permit me to arrange the rest. It will not interfere with my being your devoted and happy wife. It wouldn't ever interfere with—with my being a—a perfectly good mother—if that's what you fear. If it did, do you suppose I'd hesitate to choose?"

"No," he said, adoring her.

"Indeed, I wouldn't! But remaining in business will give me what every girl should have as a right—an object in life apart from her love for her husband—and children—apart from her proper domestic duties. It is her right to engage in the business of life; it makes the contract between you and me fairer. I love you more than anything in the world, but I simply couldn't keep my self-respect and depend on you for everything I have."

"But, my darling, everything I have is already yours."

"Yes, I know. We can pretend it is. I know I could have it—just as you could have this rather complicated business of mine—if you want it."

"Oh, Lord!" he exclaimed. "Imagine the fury of a connoisseur who engaged me to identify his priceless penates!"

He was laughing, too, now. They had finished their fruit salad and sherbet; she lighted a cigarette for him, taking a dainty puff and handing it to him with an adorable shudder.

"I don't like it! I don't like any vices! How women can enjoy what men enjoy is a mystery to me. Smoke slowly, darling, because when that cigarette is finished you must make a very graceful bow and say good-bye to me until to-morrow."

"This is simply devilish, Jacqueline! I never see you any more."

"Nonsense! You have plenty to do to amuse you—haven't you, dear?"

But the things that once occupied his leisure so casually and so agreeably no longer attracted him.

"I don't want to read seed catalogues," he protested. "Couldn't I be of use to you, Jacqueline? I'll do anything you say—take off my coat and sweep out your office, or go behind the counter in the shop and sell gilded gods——"

"Imagine the elegant Mr. Desboro selling antiquities to the dangerous monomaniacs who haunt such shops as mine! Dear, they'd either drive you crazy or have you arrested for fraud inside of ten minutes. No; you will make a perfectly good husband, Jim, but you were never created to decorate an antique shop."

He tried to smile, but only flushed rather painfully. A sudden and wholly inexplicable sense of inferiority possessed him.

"You know," he said, "I'm not going to stand around idle while you run a prosperous business concern. And anyway, I can't see it, Jacqueline. You and I are going to have a lot of social obligations to——"

"We are likely to have all kinds of obligations," she interrupted serenely, "and our lives are certain to be very full, and you and I are going to be equal to every opportunity, every demand, every responsibility—and still have leisure to love each other, and to be to each other everything that either could desire."

"After all," he said, serious and unconvinced, "there are only twenty-four hours in a day for us to be together."

"Yes, darling, but there will be no wasted time in those twenty-four hours.

That is where we save a sufficient number of minutes to attend to the business of life."

"Do you mean that you intend to come into this office every day?"

"For a while, yes. Less frequently when I have trained my people a little longer. What do you suppose my father was doing all his life? What do you suppose I have been doing these last three years? Why, Jim, except that hitherto I have loved to fuss over details, this office and this business could almost run itself for six months at a time. Some day, except for special clients here and there, Lionel Sissly will do what expert work I now am doing; and this desk will be his; and his present position will be filled by Mr. Mirk. That is how it is planned. And if you had given me two or three months, I might have been able to go on a bridal trip with you!"

"We are going, aren't we?" he asked, appalled.

"If I've got to marry you offhand," she said seriously, "our wedding trip will have to wait. Don't you know, dear, that it always costs heavily to do anything in a hurry? At this time of year, and under the present conditions of business, and considering my contracts and obligations, it would be utterly impossible for me to go away again until summer."

He sprang up irritated, yet feeling utterly helpless under her friendly but level gaze. Already he began to realise the true significance of her position and his own in the world; how utterly at a moral disadvantage he stood before this young girl—moral, intellectual, spiritual—he was beginning to comprehend it all now.

A dull flush of anger made his face hot and altered his expression to sullenness. Where was all this leading them, anyway—this reversal of rôles, this self-dependent attitude of hers—this calm self-reliance—this freedom of decision?

Once he had supposed there was something in her to protect, to guide, advise, make allowance for—perhaps to persuade, possibly, even, to instruct. Such has been the immemorial attitude of man; it had been instinctively, and more or less unconsciously, his.

And now, in spite of her youth, her soft pliability, her almost childish grace and beauty, he was experiencing a half-dazed sensation as though, in full and confident career, he had come, slap! into collision with an occult barrier. And the impact was confusing him and even beginning to hurt him.

He looked around him uneasily. Everything in the office, somehow, seemed to be in subtle league with her to irritate him—her desk, her loaded letter-files, her stacks of ledgers—all these accused and offended him. But most of all his own helpless inferiority made him angry and ashamed—the inferiority of idleness confronted by industry; of aimlessness face to face with purpose; of irresolution and degeneracy scrutinised by fearlessness, confidence, and happy and innocent aspiration. And the combination silenced him.

And every mute second that he stood there, he felt as though something imperceptible, intangible, was slipping away from him—perhaps his man's immemorial right to lead, to decide, to direct the common destiny of this slim, sweet-lipped young girl and himself.

For it was she who was serenely deciding—who had already laid out the business of life for herself without hesitation, without resort to him, to his man's wisdom, experience, prejudices, wishes, desires. Moreover, she was leaving him absolutely free to decide his own business in life for himself; and that made her position unassailable. For if she had presumed to advise him, to suggest, even hint at anything interfering with his own personal liberty to decide for himself, he might have found some foothold, some niche, something to sustain him, to justify him, in assuming man's immemorial right to leadership.

"Dear," she said wistfully, "you look at me with such very troubled eyes. Is there anything I have said that you disapprove?"

"I had not expected you to remain in business," was all he found to say.

"If my remaining in business ever interferes with your happiness or with my duty to you, I will give it up. You know that, don't you?"

He reddened again.

"It looks queer," he muttered, "—your being in business and I—playing farmer —like one of those loafing husbands of celebrated actresses."

"Jim!" she exclaimed, scarlet to the ears. "What a horrid simile!"

"It's myself I'm cursing out," he said, almost angrily. "I can't cut such a figure. Don't you understand, Jacqueline? I haven't anything to occupy me! Do you expect me to hang around somewhere while you work? I tell you, I've got to find something to do as soon as we're married—or I couldn't look you in the face."

"That is for you to decide. Isn't it?" she asked sweetly.

"Yes, but on what am I to decide?"

"Whatever you decide, don't do it in a hurry, dear," she said, smiling.

The sullen sense of resentment returned, reddening his face again:

"I wouldn't have to hurry if you'd give up this business and live on our income and be free to travel and knock about with me——"

"Can't you understand that I will be free to be with you—free in mind, in conscience, in body, to travel with you, be with you, be to you whatever you desire—but only if I keep my self-respect! And I can't keep that if I neglect the business of life, which, in my case, lies partly here in this office."

She rose and laid one slim, pretty hand on his shoulder. She rarely permitted herself to touch him voluntarily.

"Don't you wish me to be happy?" she asked gently.

"It's all I wish in the world, Jacqueline."

"But I couldn't be happy and remain idle; remain dependent on you for anything—except love. Life to the full—every moment filled—that is what living means to me. And only one single thing never can fill one's life—not intellectual research alone; not spiritual remoteness; nor yet the pursuit of pleasure; nor the swift and endless hunt for happiness; nor even love, dearest among men! Only the business of life can quite fill life to the brimming for me; and that business is made up of everything worthy—of the pleasures of effort, duty, aspiration, and noble repose, but never of the pleasures of idleness. Jim, have I bored you with a sermon? Forgive me; I am preaching only to instruct myself."

He took her hand from his shoulder and stood holding it and looking at her with a strange expression. So dazed, yet so terribly intent he seemed at moments that she laid her other hand over his, pressing it in smiling anxiety.

"What is it, dearest?" she murmured. "Don't you approve of me as much as you thought you did? Am I disappointing you already?"

"Good God!" he muttered to himself. "If there is a heaven, and your sort inhabit it, hell was reformed long ago."

"What are you muttering all to yourself, Jim?" she insisted. "What troubles you?"

"I'll tell you. You've picked the wrong man. I'm absolutely unfit for you. I know about all those decent things you believe in—all the things you are! But I don't know about them from personal experience; I never did anything decent because it was my duty to do it—except by accident. I never took a spiritual interest in anything or anybody, including myself! I never made a worthy effort; I never earned one second's worth of noble repose. And now—if there's anything in me to begin on—it's probably my duty to release you until I have made something of myself, before I come whining around asking you to marry a man not fit to marry——"

"My darling!" she protested, half laughing, half in tears, and closing his angry lips with both her hands. "I want you, not a saint or a holy man, or an archangel fresh from paradise! I want you as you are—as you have been—as you are going to be dear! Did any girl who ever lived find pleasure in perfection? Even in art it is undesirable. That's the beauty of aspiration; the pleasures of effort never pall. I don't know whether I'm laughing or crying, Jim! You look so solemn and miserable, and—and funny! But if you try to look dignified now, I'll certainly laugh! You dear, blessed, overgrown boy—just as bad as you possibly can be! Just as funny and unreasonable and perverse as are all boys! But Jacqueline loves you dearly—oh, dearly—and she trusts you with her heart and her happiness and with every beauty yet undreamed and unrevealed that a girl could learn to desire on earth! Are you contented? Oh, Jim! Jim! If you knew how I adore you! You must go, dear. It will mean a long night's work for me if you don't. But it's so hard to let you go —when I—love you so! When I love you so! Good-bye. Yes, to-morrow. Don't call at noon; Mrs. Hammerton is coming for a five-minute chat. And I do want you to myself for the few moments we may have together. Come about five and we can have tea here beside my desk."

He came next day at five. The day after that he arrived at the same hour, bringing with him her ring; and, as he slipped it over her finger, for the first time her self-control slipped, too, and she bent swiftly and kissed the jewel that he was holding.

Then, flushed and abashed, she shrank away, an exquisite picture of confusion, and stood turning and turning the ring around, her head obstinately lowered, absolutely unresponsive again to his arm around her and his cheek resting close against hers.

"What a beauty of a ring, Jim!" she managed to say at last. "No other engagement ring ever existed half as lovely and splendid as my betrothal ring. I am sorry for all the empresses and queens and princesses who can never hope to possess a ring to equal the ring of Jacqueline Nevers, dealer in antiquities."

"Nor can they hope to possess such a hand to adorn it," he said, "—the most beautiful, the purest, whitest, softest, most innocent hand in the world! The magic hand of Jacqueline!"

"Do you like it?" she asked, shyly conscious of its beauty.

"It is matchless, darling. Let empresses shriek with envy."

"I'm listening very intently, but I don't hear them. Jim. Also, I've seen a shop-girl with far lovelier hands. But please go on thinking so and hearing crowned heads shriek. I rather like your imagination."

He laughed from sheer happiness:

"I've got something to whisper to you. Shall I?"

"What?"

"Shall I whisper it?"

She inclined her small head daintily, then:

"Oh!" she exclaimed, startled and blushing to the tips of her ears.

"Will you be ready?"

"I—yes. Yes—I'll be ready——"

"Does it make you happy?"

"I can't realise—I didn't know it was to be so soon—so immediate——"

"We'll go to Silverwood. We can catch the evening express——"

"Dearest!"

"You can go away with me for one week, can't you?"

"I can't go now!" she faltered.

"For how long can you go, Jacqueline?"

"I—I've got to be back on Tuesday morning."

"Tuesday!"

"Isn't it dreadful, Jim. But I can't avoid it if we are to be married on Monday next. I must deal honourably by my clients who trust me. I warned you that our wedding trip would have to be postponed if you married me this way—didn't I, dear?"

"Yes."

She stood looking at him timidly, almost fearfully, as he took two or three quick, nervous steps across the floor, turned and came back to her.

"All right," he said. "Our wedding trip will have to wait, then; but our wedding won't. We'll be married Monday, go to Silverwood, and come back Tuesday— if it's a matter of honour. I never again mean to interfere with your life's business, Jacqueline. You know what is best; you are free and entitled to the right of decision."

"Yes. But because I must decide about things that concern myself alone, you don't think I adore you any the less, do you, Jim?"

"Nor do I love you the less, Jacqueline, because I can decide nothing for you, do nothing for you."

"Jim! You can decide everything for me—do everything! And you have done everything for me—by giving me my freedom to decide for myself!"

"I gave it to you, Jacqueline?"

"Did you think I would have taken it if you had refused it?"

"But you said your happiness depended on it."

"Which is why you gave it to me, isn't it?" she asked seriously.

He laughed. "You wonderful girl, to make me believe that any generosity of mine is responsible for your freedom!"

"But it is! Otherwise, I would have obeyed you and been disgraced in my own estimation."

"Do you mean that mine is to be the final decision always?"

"Why, of course, Jim."

He laughed again. "Empty authority, dear—a shadowy symbol of traditional but obsolete prerogative."

"You are wrong. Your decision is final. But—as I know it will always be for my happiness, I can always appeal from your prejudice to your intelligence," she added naïvely. And for a moment was surprised at his unrestrained laughter.

"What does it matter?" she admitted, laughing, too. "Between you and me the right thing always will be done sooner or later."

His laughter died out; he said soberly: "Always, God willing. It may be a little hard for me to learn—as it's hard, now, for example, to say good-bye."

"Jim!"

"You know I must, darling."

"But I don't mind sitting up a few minutes later to-night——"

"I know you don't. But here's where I exercise my harmlessly arbitrary authority for your happiness and for the sake of your good digestion."

"What a brute you are!"

"I know it. Back to your desk, darling! And go to bed early."

"I wanted you to stay——"

"Ha! So you begin to feel the tyranny of man! I'm going! I've got a job, too, if you want to know."

"What!"

"Certainly! How long did you suppose I could stand it to see you at that desk and then go and sit in a silly club?"

"What do you mean, darling?" she asked, radiant.

"I mean that Jack Cairns, who is a broker, has offered me a job at a small but perfectly proper salary, with the usual commission on all business I bring in to the office. And I've taken it!"

"But, dear——"

"Oh, Vail can run my farm without any advice from me. I'm going to give him more authority and hold him responsible. If the place can pay for itself and let us keep the armour and jades, that's all I ask of it. But I am asking more of myself—since I have begun to really know you. And I'm going to work for our bread and butter, and earn enough to support us both and lay something aside. You know we've got to think of that, because——" He looked very serious, hesitated, bent and whispered something that sent the bright colour flying in her cheeks; then he caught her hand and kissed the ring-finger.

"Good-bye," she murmured, clinging for an instant to his hand.

The next moment he was gone; and she stood alone for a while by her desk, his ring resting against her lips, her eyes closed.

Sunday she spent with him. They went together to St. John's Cathedral in the morning—the first time he had been inside a church in years. And he was in considerable awe of the place and of her until they finally emerged into the sunshine of Morningside Park.

Under a magnificent and cloudless sky, they walked together, silent or loquacious by turns, bold and shy, confident and timid. And she was a little surprised to find that, in the imminence of marriage, her trepidation was composure itself compared to the anxiety which seemed to assail him. All he had thought of was the license and the clergyman; and they had attended to those matters together. But she had wished him to have Jack Cairns present, and had told him that she desired to ask some friend of her girlhood to be her bridesmaid.

"Have you done so?" he inquired, as they descended the heights of Morningside, the beautiful weather tempting them to a long homeward stroll through Central Park.

"Yes, Jim, I must tell you about her. She, like myself, is not a girl that men of your sort might expect to meet——"

"The loss is ours, Jacqueline."

"That is very sweet of you. Only I had better tell you about Cynthia Lessler ——"

"Who?" he asked, astonished.

"Cynthia Lessler, my girlhood friend."

"She is an actress, isn't she?"

"Yes. Her home life was very unhappy. But I think she has much talent, too."

"She has."

"I am glad you think so. Anyway, she is my oldest friend, and I have asked her to be my bridesmaid to-morrow."

He continued silent beside her so long that she said timidly:

"Do you mind, Jim?"

"I was only thinking—how it might look in the papers—and there are other girls you already know whose names would mean a lot——"

"Yes, I know. But I don't want to pretend to be what I am not, even in the papers. I suppose I do need all the social corroboration I can have. I know what you mean, dear. But there were reasons. I thought it all over. Cynthia is an old friend, not very happy, not the fortunate and blessed girl that your love is making of me. But she is good and sweet and loyal to me, and I can't abandon old friends, especially one who is not very fortunate—and I—I thought perhaps it might help her a little—in various ways—to be my bridesmaid."

"That is like you," he said, reddening. "You never say or do anything but there lies in it some primary lesson in decency to me."

"You goose! Isn't it natural for a girl to wish for her oldest friend at such a time? That's really all there is to the matter. And I do hope you will like Cynthia."

He nodded, preoccupied. After a few moments he said:

"Did you know that Jack Cairns had met her?"

"Yes."

"Oh!" His troubled eyes sought hers, then shifted.

"That was another reason I wish to ask her," she said in a low voice.

"What reason?"

"Because Mr. Cairns knew her only as a very young, very lonely, very unhappy girl, inexperienced, friendless, poor, almost shelterless; and engaged in a profession upon which it is almost traditional for men to prey. And I wish him to know her again as a girl who is slowly advancing in an honest profession—as a modest, sweet, self-respecting woman—and as my friend."

"And mine," he said.

"You—darling!" she whispered.

CHAPTER XIII

They were married in the morning at St. George's in Stuyvesant Square.

Gay little flurries of snow, like wind-blown petals from an apple bough, were turning golden in the warm outbreak of brilliant sunshine; and there was blue sky overhead and shining wet pavements under foot as Jacqueline and

Desboro came out of the shadows of the old-time church into the fresh splendour of the early morning.

The solemn beauty of the service still possessed and enthralled them. Except for a low word or two, they were inclined to silence.

But the mating sparrows were not; everywhere the little things, brown wings a-quiver, chattered and chirped in the throes of courtship; now and then, from some high façade rang out the clear, sweet whistle of a starling; and along the warm, wet streets ragged children were selling violets and narcissus, and yellow tulips tinted as delicately as the pale spring sunshine.

A ragged little girl came to stare at Jacqueline, the last unsold bunch of wilted violets lying on her tray; and Jacqueline laid the cluster over the prayer-book which she was carrying, while Desboro slipped a golden coin into the child's soiled hand.

Down the street his chauffeur was cranking the car; and while they waited for it to draw up along the curb, Jacqueline separated a few violets from the faintly fragrant cluster and placed them between the leaves of her prayer-book.

After a few moments he said, under his breath:

"Do you realise that we are married, Jacqueline?"

"No. Do you?"

"I'm trying to comprehend it, but I can't seem to. How soft the breeze blows! It is already spring in Stuyvesant Square."

"The Square is lovely! They will be setting out hyacinths soon, I think." She shivered. "It's strange," she said, "but I feel rather cold. Am I horridly pale, Jim?"

"You are a trifle colourless—but even prettier than I ever saw you," he whispered, turning up the collar of her fur coat around her throat. "You haven't taken cold, have you?"

"No; it is—natural—I suppose. Miracles frighten one at first."

Their eyes met; she tried to smile. After a moment he said nervously:

"I sent out the announcements. The evening papers will have them."

"I want to see them, Jim."

"You shall. I have ordered all this evening's and to-morrow morning's papers.

They will be sent to Silverwood."

The car rolled up along the curb and stopped.

"Can't I take you to your office?" he whispered.

"No, dear."

She laid one slim hand on his arm and stood for a moment looking at him.

"How pale you are!" he said again, under his breath.

"Brides are apt to be. It's only a swift and confused dream to me yet—all that has happened to us to-day; and even this sunshine seems unreal—like the first day of spring in paradise!"

She bent her proud little head and stood in silence as though unseen hands still hovered above her, and unseen lips were still pronouncing her his wife. Then, lifting her eyes, winningly and divinely beautiful, she looked again on this man whom the world was to call her husband.

"Will you be ready at five?" he whispered.

"Yes."

They lingered a moment longer; he said:

"I don't know how I am going to endure life without you until five o'clock."

She said seriously: "I can't bear to leave you, Jim. But you know you have almost as many things to do as I have."

"As though a man could attend to things on his wedding day!"

"This girl has to. I don't know how I am ever going to go through the last odds and ends of business—but it's got to be managed somehow. Do you really think we had better go up to Silverwood in the car? Won't this snow make the roads bad? It may not have melted in the country."

"Oh, it's all right! And I'll have you to myself in the car———"

"Suppose we are ditched?" She shivered again, then forced a little laugh. "Do you know, it doesn't seem possible to me that I am going to be your wife to-morrow, too, and the next day, and the next, and always, year after year. Somehow, it seems as though our dream were already ending—that I shall not see you at five o'clock—that it is all unreal———"

The smile faded, and into her blue eyes came something resembling fear—gone instantly—but the hint of it had been there, whatever it was; and the ghost of it still lingered in her white, flower-like face.

She whispered, forcing the smile again: "Happiness sometimes frightens; and it is making me a little afraid, I think. Come for me at five, Jim, and try to make me comprehend that nothing in the world can ever harm us. Tell your man where to take me—but only to the corner of my street, please."

He opened the limousine door; she stepped in, and he wrapped the robe around her. A cloud over the sun had turned the world grey for a moment. Again she seemed to feel the sudden chill in the air, and tried to shake it off.

"Look at Mr. Cairns and Cynthia," she whispered, leaning forward from her seat and looking toward the church.

He turned. Cairns and Miss Lessler had emerged from the portico and were lingering there in earnest consultation, quite oblivious of them.

"Do you like her, Jim?" she asked.

He smiled.

"I didn't notice her very much—or Jack either. A man isn't likely to notice anybody at such a time—except the girl he is marrying——"

"Look at her now. Don't you think her expression is very sweet?"

"It's all right. Dear, do you suppose I can fix my attention on——"

"You absurd boy! Are you really as much in love with me as that? Please be nice to her. Would you mind going back and speaking to her when I drive away?"

"All right," he said.

Their glances lingered for a moment more; then he drew a quick, sharp breath, closed the limousine door, and spoke briefly to the chauffeur.

As long as the car remained in sight across the square, he watched it; then, when it had disappeared, he turned toward the church. But Cairns and Cynthia were already far down the street, walking side by side, very leisurely, apparently absorbed in conversation. They must have seen him. Perhaps they had something more interesting to say to each other than to him.

He followed them irresolutely for a few steps, then, as the idea persisted that they might not desire his company, he turned and started west across the sunny, wet pavement.

It was quite true that Cairns and Cynthia had seen him; also it was a fact that neither had particularly wanted him to join them at that exact moment.

Meeting at St. George's for the first time in two years, and although prepared for the encounter, these two, who had once known each other so well, experienced a slight shock when they met. The momentary contact of her outstretched hand and his hand left them both very silent; even the formal commonplaces had failed them after the first swift, curious glance had been exchanged.

Cairns noticed that she had grown taller and slenderer. And though there seemed to be no more of maturity to her than to the young girl he had once known, her poise and self-control were now in marked contrast to the impulsive and slightly nervous Cynthia he had found so amusing in callower days.

Once or twice during the ceremony he had ventured to glance sideways at her. In the golden half-light of the altar there seemed to be an unfamiliar dignity and sweetness about the girl that became her. And in the delicate oval of her face he thought he discerned those finer, nobler contours made by endurance, by self-denial, and by sorrow.

Later, when he saw her kiss Jacqueline, something in the sweet sincerity of the salute suddenly set a hidden chord vibrating within him; and, to his surprise, he found speech difficult for a moment, checked by emotions for which there seemed no reason.

And at last Jacqueline and Desboro went away, and Cynthia slowly turned to him, offering her hand in adieu.

"Mr. Cairns," she said quietly, "this is the last place on earth that you and I ever thought to meet. Perhaps it is to be our last meeting place. So—I will say good-bye——"

"May I not walk home with you? Or, if you prefer to drive, my car is here ——" he began.

"Thank you; it's only to the theatre—if you care to walk with me——"

"Are you rehearsing?"

"There is a rehearsal called for eleven."

"Shall we drive or walk, Cynthia?"

"I prefer to walk. Please don't feel that you ought to go back with me."

He said, reddening: "I do not remember that my sense of duty toward you has ever been persistent enough to embarrass either of us."

"Of course not. Why should you ever have felt that you owed any duty to me?"

"I did not say that I ever felt it."

"Of course not. You owed me none."

"That is a different matter. Obligations once sat very lightly on my shoulders."

"You owe me none," she repeated smilingly, as they emerged from the church into the warm March sunshine.

He was saying: "But isn't friendship an obligation, Cynthia?"

She laughed: "Friendship is merely an imaginary creation, and exists only until the imagination wearies. That is not original," she added. "It is in the new Barrie comedy we are rehearsing."

She turned her pretty head and glanced down the street where Jacqueline and Desboro still stood beside the car. Cairn's car was also waiting, and its owner made a signal to the chauffeur that he did not need him.

Looking at Jacqueline, Cynthia said:

"Long ago I knew that she was fitted for a marriage such as this—or a better one," she added in a lower voice.

"A better one?" he repeated, surprised.

"Yes," she nodded calmly. "Can you not imagine a more desirable marriage for a girl?"

"Don't you like Desboro?" he demanded.

"I like him—considering the fact that I scarcely know him. He has very handsome and very reckless eyes, but a good mouth. To look at him for the first time a woman would be inclined to like him—but he might hesitate to trust him. I had hoped Jacqueline might marry a professional man— considerably older than Mr. Desboro. That is all I meant."

He said, looking at her smilingly but curiously: "Have you any idea, Cynthia, how entirely you have changed in two years?"

She shook her head: "I haven't changed."

"Indeed you have——"

"Only superficially. What I was born I shall always be. Years teach endurance and self-control—if they teach anything. All one can learn is how to control and direct what one already is."

"The years have taught you a lot," he murmured, astonished.

"I have been to school to many masters, Mr. Cairns; I have studied under Sorrow; graduated under Poverty and Loneliness; and I am now taking a finishing course with Experience. Truly enough, I should have learned something, as you say, by this time. Besides, you, also, once were kind enough to be interested in my education. Why should I not have learned something?"

He winced and bit his lip, watching Desboro and Jacqueline below. And, after a moment:

"Shall we walk?" she suggested, smilingly.

He fell into step beside her. Half way down the block she glanced back. Desboro was already crossing the square; the limousine had disappeared.

"I wonder sometimes," she remarked, "what has become of all those amusing people we once knew so well—Marianne Valdez, Jessie Dain, Reggie Ledyard, Van Alstyne. Do you ever see them any more?"

"Yes."

"And are they quite as gay and crazy as ever?"

"They're a bit wild—sometimes."

"Do they ever speak of me? I—wonder," she mused, aloud.

"Yes. They know, of course, what a clever girl you have turned into. It isn't usual, you know, to graduate from a girlie show into the legit. And I was talking to Schindler the other evening; and he had to admit that he had seen nothing extraordinary in you when you were with his noisy shows. It's funny, isn't it?"

"Slightly."

"Besides, you were such a wild little thing—don't you remember what crazy things we used to do, you and I——"

"Did I? Yes, I remember. In those days a good dinner acted on me like champagne. You see I was very often hungry, and when I wasn't starved it went to my head."

"You need not have wanted for anything!" he said sharply.

"Oh, no! But I preferred the pangs of hunger to the pangs of conscience," she retorted gaily.

"I didn't mean that. There was no string to what I offered you, and you know it! And you know it now!"

"Certainly I do," she said calmly. "You mean to be very kind, Jack."

"Then why the devil didn't——"

"Why didn't I accept food and warmth and raiment and lodging from a generous and harebrained young man? I'll tell you now, if you wish. It was because my conscience forbade me to accept all and offer nothing in return."

"Nonsense! I didn't ask——"

"I know you didn't. But I couldn't give, so I wouldn't take. Besides, we were together too much. I knew it. I think even you began to realise it, too. The situation was impossible. So I went on the road."

"You never answered any of those letters of mine."

"Mentally I answered every one."

"A lot of good that did me!"

"It did us both a lot of good. I meant to write to you some day—when my life had become busy enough to make it difficult for me to find time to write."

He looked up at her sharply, and she laughed and swung her muff.

"I suppose," he said, "now that the town talks about you a little, you will have no time to waste on mere Johnnies."

"Well, I don't know. When a mere Johnnie is also a Jack, it makes a difference —doesn't it? Do you think that you would care to see me again?"

"Of course I do."

"The tickets," she said demurely, "are three dollars—two weeks in advance
——"

"I know that by experience."

"Oh! Then you have seen 'The Better Way'?"

"Certainly."

"Do you like—the show?"

"You are the best of it. Yes, I like it."

"It's my first chance. Did you know that? If poor little Graham hadn't been so
ill, I'd never have had a look in. They wouldn't give me anything—except in a
way I couldn't accept it. I tell you, Jack, I was desperate. There seemed to be
absolutely no chance unless I—paid."

"Why didn't you write me and let me——"

"You know why."

"It would have been reward enough to see you make good—and put it all over
that bald-headed, dog-faced——"

"My employer, please remember," she said, pretending to reprove him. "And,
Jack, he's amusingly decent to me now. Men are really beginning to be kind.
Walbaum's people have written to me, and O'Rourke sent for me, and I'm just
beginning to make professional enemies, too, which is the surest sign that I'm
almost out of the ranks. If I could only study! Now is the time! I know it; I feel
it keenly—I realise how much I lack in education! You see I only went to
high-school. It's a mercy that my English isn't hopeless——"

"It's good! It's better than I ever supposed it would be——"

"I know. I used to be careless. But what can you expect? After I left home you
know the sort of girls I was thrown among. Fortunately, father was educated—
if he was nothing else. My degeneracy wasn't permanent. Also, I had been
thrown with Jacqueline, and with you——"

"Fine educational model I am!"

"And," she continued, not heeding him, "when I met you, and men like you, I
was determined that whatever else happened to me my English should not
degenerate. Jacqueline helped me so much. I tried to study, too, when I was
not on the road with the show. But if only I could study now—study seriously
for a year or two!"

"What do you wish to study, Cynthia?" he asked carelessly.

"English! Also French and German and Italian. I would like to study what girls in college study. Then I'd like to learn stage dancing thoroughly. And, of course, I'm simply crazy to take a course in dramatic art——"

"But you already know a lot! Every paper spoke well of you——"

"Oh, Jack! Does that mean anything—when I know that I don't know anything!"

"Rot! Can you beat professional experience as an educator?"

"I'm not quite ready for it——"

"Very well. If you feel that way, will you be a good sort, Cynthia, and let me ——"

"No!"

"I ask you merely to let me take a flyer!"

"No, Jack."

"Why can't I take a flyer? Why can't I have the pleasure of speculating on a perfectly sure thing? It's a million to nothing that you'll make good. For the love of Mike, Cynthia, borrow the needful and——"

"From you?"

"Naturally."

"No, Jack!"

"Why not? Why cut off your nose to spite your face? What difference does it make where you get it as long as it's a decent deal? You can't afford to take two or three years off to complete your education——"

"Begin it, you mean."

"I mean finish it! You can't afford to; but if you'll borrow the money you'll make good in exactly one-tenth of the time you'd otherwise take to arrive ——"

"Jack, I won't discuss it with you. I know you are generous and kind——"

"I'm not! I'm anything but! For heaven's sake let a man indulge his vanity, Cynthia. Imagine my pride when you are famous! Picture my bursting vanity as I sit in front and tell everybody near me that the credit is all mine; that if it were not for me you would be nowhere!"

"It's so like you," she said sweetly. "You always were an inordinate boaster, so I am not going to encourage you."

"Can't you let me make you a business loan at exorbitant interest without expiring of mortification?"

They had reached the theatre; a few loafers sunning themselves by the stage entrance leered at them.

"Hush, Jack! I can't discuss it with you. But you know how grateful I am, don't you?"

"No, I don't——" he said sulkily.

"You are cross now, but you'll see it as I do half an hour hence."

"No, I won't!" he insisted.

She laughed: "You haven't changed, at all events, have you? It takes me back years to see that rather becoming scowl gather over the bridge of your ornamental nose. But it is very nice to know that you haven't entirely forgotten me; that we are still friends."

"Where are you living, Cynthia?"

She told him, adding: "Do you really mean to come?"

"Watch me!" he said, almost savagely, took off his hat, shook her hand until her fingers ached, and marched off still scowling.

The stage loafers shifted quids and looked after him with sneers.

"Trun out!" observed one.

"All off!" nodded another.

The third merely spat and slowly closed his disillusioned and leisure-weary eyes.

Cairns' energetic pace soon brought him to the Olympian Club, where he was accustomed to lunch, it being convenient to his office, which was on Forty-sixth Street.

Desboro, who, at Jacqueline's request, had gone back to business, appeared presently and joined Cairns at a small table.

"Anything doing at the office?" inquired the latter. "I suppose you were too nervous and upset to notice the market though."

"Well, ask yourself how much you'd feel like business after marrying the most glorious and wonderful——"

"Ring off! I concede everything. It is going to make some splash in the papers. Yes? Lord! I wish you could have had a ripping big wedding though! Wouldn't she have looked the part? Oh, no!"

"It couldn't be helped," said Desboro in a low, chagrined voice. "I'd have given the head off my shoulders to have had the sort of a wedding to which she was entitled. But—I couldn't."

Cairns nodded, not, however, understanding; and as Desboro offered no explanation, he remained unenlightened.

"Rather odd," he remarked, "that she didn't wish to have Aunt Hannah with her at the fatal moment. They're such desperate chums these days."

"She did want her. I wouldn't have her."

"Is that so?"

"It is. I'll tell you why some day. In fact, I don't mind telling you now. Aunt Hannah has it in for me. She's a devil sometimes. You know it and I do. She has it in for me just now. She's wrong; she's made a mistake; but I couldn't tell her anything. You can't tell that sort of a woman anything, once she's made up her mind. And the fact is, Jack, she's already made up her mind that I was not to marry Jacqueline. And I was afraid of her. And that's why I married Jacqueline this way."

Cairns stared.

"So now," added Desboro, "you know how it happened."

"Quite so. Rotten of her, wasn't it?"

"She didn't mean it that way. She got a fool idea into her head, that's all. Only I was afraid she'd tell it to Jacqueline."

"I see."

"That's what scared me. I didn't know what she might tell Jacqueline. She threatened to tell her—things. And it would have involved a perfectly innocent woman and myself—put me in a corner where I couldn't decently explain the real facts to Jacqueline. Now, thank God, it's too late for Aunt Hannah to make mischief."

Cairns nodded, thinking of Mrs. Clydesdale. And whatever he personally was inclined to believe, he knew that gossip was not dealing very leniently with that young wife and the man who sat on the other side of the table, nervously pulling to pieces his unlighted cigarette.

But it needed no rumour, no hearsay evidence, no lifted eyebrows, no shrugs, no dubious smiles, no half-hearted defence of Elena Clydesdale, to thoroughly convince Mrs. Hammerton of Desboro's utter unfitness as a husband for the motherless girl she had begun to love with a devotion so fierce that at present it could brook no rival at all of either sex.

For Mrs. Hammerton had never before loved. She had once supposed that she loved her late husband, but soon came to regard him as a poor sort of thing. She had been extremely fond of Desboro, too, in her own way, but in the vivid fire of this new devotion to Jacqueline, any tenderness she ever might have cherished for that young man was already consumed and sacrificed to a cinder in the fiercer flame.

Into her loneliness, into her childless solitude, into the hardness, cynicism, and barren emptiness of her latter years, a young girl had stepped from nowhere, and she had suddenly filled her whole life with the swift enchantment of love.

A word or two, a smile, the magic of two arms upon her bony shoulders, the shy touch of youthful lips—these were the very simple ingredients which apparently had transmuted the brass and tinsel and moral squalor of Aunt Hannah's life into charming reality.

From sudden tenderness to grim love, to jealous, watchful, passionate adoration—these were the steps Mrs. Hammerton had taken in the brief interval of time that had elapsed since she had first seen Jacqueline.

Into the clear, truthful eyes she had looked, and had seen within only an honest mind and a clean young soul. Wisdom, too, only lacking in experience, she divined there; and less of wisdom than of intelligence; and less of that than of courage. And it all was so clear, so perfectly apparent to the cold and experienced scrutiny of the woman of the world, that, for a while, she could not entirely believe what she understood at the first glance.

When she was convinced, she surrendered. And never before in all her unbelieving, ironical, and material career had she experienced such a thrill of overwhelming delight as when, that evening at Silverwood, Jacqueline had drawn her head down and had touched her dry forehead with warm, young lips.

Everything about the girl fascinated her—her independence and courage; her adorable bashfulness in matters where experience had made others callous—in such little things, for example, as the response to an invitation, the meeting with fashionable strangers—but it was only the nice, friendly, and thoroughbred shyness of inexperience, not the awkwardness of under-breeding or of that meaner vanity called self-consciousness.

Poor herself, predatory, clever, hard as nails, her beady eyes ever alert for the main chance, she felt for the first time in her life the real bitterness of comparative poverty—which is the inability to give where one loves.

She had no illusions; she knew that what she had to offer the girl would soon pall; that Jacqueline would choose her own friends among the sane and simple and sincere, irrespective of social and worldly considerations; that no glitter, no sham, no tinsel could permanently hold her attention; no lesser ambition seduce her; no folly ever awake her laughter more than once. What the girl saw she would understand; and, in future, she would choose for herself what she cared to see and know of a new world now gradually opening before her.

But in the meantime Jacqueline must see before she could learn, and before she could make up her mind what to discard and what to retain.

So Mrs. Hammerton had planned that Jacqueline should be very busy during March and April; and her patience was sorely tried when she found that, for a week or two, the girl could give her only a very few minutes every other day.

At first it was a grim consolation to her that Jacqueline still remained too busy to see anybody, because that meant that Desboro, too, would be obliged to keep his distance.

For at first Mrs. Hammerton did not believe that the girl could be seriously interested in Desboro; in fact, she had an idea that, so far, all the sentiment was on Desboro's side. And both Jacqueline's reticence and her calm cordiality in speaking of Desboro were at first mistaken by Aunt Hannah for the symptoms of a friendship not sentimentally significant.

But the old lady's doubts soon became aroused; she began to watch Jacqueline askance—began to test her, using all her sly cleverness and skill. Slowly her uncertainty, uneasiness, and suspicion changed to anger and alarm.

If she had been more than angry and suspicious—if she had been positive, she would not have hesitated an instant. For on one matter she was coldly determined; the girl should not marry Desboro, or any such man as Desboro. It made no difference to her whether Desboro might be really in love with her. He was not fit for her; he was a man of weak character, idle, useless, without purpose or ability, who would never amount to anything or be anything except what he already was—an agreeable, graceful, amusing, acceptable item in the sort of society which he decorated.

She knew and despised that breed of youth; New York was full of them, and they were even less endurable to her than the similar species extant in England and on the Continent; for the New York sort were destitute of the traditions which had created the real kind—and there was no excuse for them, not even the sanction of custom. They were merely imitation of a more genuine degeneracy. And she held them in contempt.

She told Jacqueline this, as she was saying good-night on Saturday, and was alarmed and silenced by the girl's deep flush of colour; and she went home in her scrubby brougham, scared and furious by turns, and determined to settle Desboro's business for him without further hesitation.

Sunday Jacqueline could not see her; and the suspicion that the girl might be with Desboro almost drove the old lady crazy. Monday, too, Jacqueline told her over the telephone would be a very busy day; and Aunt Hannah acquiesced grimly, determined to waste no further time at the telephone and take no more chances, but go straight to Jacqueline and take her into her arms and tell her what a mother would tell her about Desboro, and how, at that very hour perhaps, he was with Mrs. Clydesdale; and what the world suspected, and what she herself knew of an intrigue that had been shamelessly carried into the very house which had sheltered Jacqueline within a day or two.

So on Monday morning Mrs. Hammerton went to see Jacqueline; and, learning that the girl had gone out early, marched home again, sat down at her desk, and wrote her a letter.

When she had finished she honestly believed that she had also finished Desboro; and, grimly persuaded that she had done a mother's duty by the motherless, she summoned a messenger and sent off the letter to a girl, who, at that very moment, had returned to her desk, a wife.

The rapid reaction from the thrilling experience of the morning had made Jacqueline nervous and unfit for business, even before she arrived at her office. But she entered the office resolutely and seated herself at her desk, summoning all her reserve of self-control to aid her in concentrating her mind on the business in hand.

First she read her morning's mail and dictated her answers to a red-headed stenographer. Next she received Lionel Sissly, disposed of his ladylike business with her; sent for Mr. Mirk, went over with him his report of the shop sales, revised and approved the list of prices to be ticketed on new acquisitions, re-read the sheaf of dictated letters laid before her by the red-headed stenographer, signed them, and sent down for the first client on the appointment-list.

The first on the list was a Mr. Hyman Dobky; and his three months' note had gone to protest, and Mr. Dobky wept.

She was not very severe with him, because he was a Lexington Avenue dealer just beginning in a small way, and she believed him to be honest at heart. He retired comforted, swabbing his eyes with his cuff.

Then came a furtive pair, Orrin Munger, the "Cubist" poet, and his loud-voiced, swaggering confrère, Adalbert Waudle, author of "Black Roses" and other phenomena which, some people whispered, resembled blackmail.

It had been with greatest reluctance, and only because it was a matter concerning a client, that she had consented to receive the dubious pair. She had not forgotten her experience with the "Cubist," and his suggestion for an informal Italian trip, and had never again desired or expected to see him.

He now offered her an abnormally flat and damp hand; and hers went behind her back and remained there clasped together, as she stood inspecting Mr. Munger with level eyes that harboured lightning.

She said quietly: "My client, Mr. Clydesdale, recently requested my opinion concerning certain jades, crystals and Chinese porcelains purchased by him from you and from Mr. Waudle. I have, so far, examined some twenty specimens. Every specimen examined by me is a forgery."

"Mr. Waudle gaped at her like a fat and expiring fish; the poet ... said not a word"

Mr. Waudle, taken completely by surprise, gaped at her like a fat and expiring fish; the poet turned a dull and muddy red, and said not a word.

"So," added Jacqueline coldly, "at Mr. Clydesdale's request I have asked you to come here and explain the situation to me."

Waudle, writer of "Pithy Points" for the infamous Tattler, recovered his wits first

"Miss Nevers," he said menacingly, "do you mean to insinuate that I am a swindler?"

"Are you, Mr. Waudle?"

"That's actionable. Do you understand?"

"Perfectly. Please explain the forgeries."

The poet, who had sunk down upon a chair, now arose and began to make elaborate gestures preliminary to a fluency of speech which had never yet deserted him in any crisis where a lady was involved.

"My dear child——" he began.

"What!" cut in Jacqueline crisply.

"My—my dear and—and honored, but very youthful and inexperienced young lady," he stammered, a trifle out of countenance under the fierce glimmer in her eyes, "do you, for one moment, suppose that such a writer as Mr. Waudle would imperil his social and literary reputation for the sake of a few wretched dollars!"

"Fifteen thousand," commented Jacqueline quietly.

"Exactly. Fifteen thousand contemptible dollars—inartistically designed," he added, betraying a tendency to wander from the main point; and was generously proceeding to instruct her in the art of coin design when she brought him back to the point with a shock.

"You, also, are involved in this questionable transaction," she said coldly. "Can you explain these forgeries?"

"F-forgeries!" he repeated, forcibly injecting indignation into the exclamation; but his eyes grew very round, as though frightened, and a spinal limpness appeared which threatened the stability of his knees.

But the poet's fluency had not yet deserted him; he opened both arms in a gesture suggesting absolute confidence in a suspicious and inartistic world.

"I am quite guiltless of deception," he said, using a slight tremolo. "Permit me to protest against your inexperienced judgment in the matter of these ancient and precious specimens of Chinese art; I protest!" he exclaimed earnestly. "I protest in the name of that symbol of mystery and beauty—that occult lunar something, my dear young lady, which we both worship, and which the world calls the moon——"

"I beg your pardon——" she interrupted; but the poet was launched and she could not check him.

"I protest," he continued shrilly, "in the name of Art! In the name of all that is worth while, all that matters, all that counts, all that is meaningful, sacred, precious beyond price——"

"Mr. Munger!"

"I protest in the name of——"

"Mr. Munger!"

"Eh!" he said, coming to and rolling his round, washed-out eyes toward her.

"Be kind enough to listen," she said curtly. "I am compelled to interrupt you because to-day I am a very busy person. So I am going to be as brief with you as possible. This, then, is the situation as I understand it. A month or so ago you and your friend, Mr. Waudle, notified Mr. Clydesdale that you had just returned from Pekin with a very unusual collection of ancient Chinese art, purchased by you, as you stated, from a certain Chinese prince."

The faint note of scorn in her voice did not escape the poet, who turned redder and muddier and made a picturesque gesture of world-wide appeal; but no words came from either manufacturer of literary phrases; Waudle only closed his cod-like mouth, and the eyes set in his fat face became small and cunning like something in the farthest corner of a trap.

Jacqueline continued gravely: "At your solicitation, I understand, and depending upon your representations, my client, Mr. Clydesdale, purchased from you this collection——"

"We offered no guarantees with it," interrupted Waudle thickly. "Besides, his wife advised him to buy the collection. I am an old and valued friend of Mrs. Clydesdale. She would never dream of demanding a guarantee from me! Ask her if——"

"What is a guarantee?" inquired Jacqueline. "I'm quite certain that you don't know, Mr. Waudle. And did you and Mr. Munger regard your statement concerning the Chinese prince as poetic license? Or as diverting fiction? Or what? You were not writing romance, you know. You were engaged in business. So I must ask you again who is this prince?"

"There was a prince," retorted Waudle sullenly. "Can you prove there wasn't?"

"There are several princes in China. And now I am obliged to ask you to state distinctly exactly how many of these porcelains, jades and crystals which you sold to Mr. Clydesdale were actually purchased by you from this particular Chinese prince?"

"Most of them," said Waudle, defiantly. "Prove the contrary if you can!"

"Not all of them, then—as you assured Mr. Clydesdale?"

"I didn't say all."

"I am afraid you did, Mr. Waudle. I am afraid you even wrote it—over your own signature."

"Very well," said Waudle, with a large and careless sweep of his hand, "if any doubt remains in Mr. Clydesdale's mind, I am fully prepared to take back whatever specimens may not actually have come from the prince——"

"There were some, then, which did not?"

"One or two, I believe."

"And who is this Chinese prince, Mr. Waudle?" she repeated, not smiling. "What is his name?"

Munger answered; he knew exactly what answer to make, and how to deliver it with flowing gestures. He had practised it long enough:

"When I was travelling with His Excellency T'ang-K'ai-Sun by rail from Szechuan to Pekin to visit Prince——"

"The railroad is not built," interrupted the girl drily. "You could not have travelled that way."

Both men regarded her as though paralysed by her effrontery.

"Continue, please," she nodded.

The poet swallowed nothing very fast and hard, and waved his damp hand at her:

"Tuan-Fang, Viceroy of Wuchang——"

"He happens to be Viceroy of Nanking," observed the girl.

Waudle, frightened, lost his temper and turned on her, exasperated:

"Be careful! Your insinuations involve our honour and are actionable! Do you realise what you are saying?"

"Perfectly."

"I fear not. Do you imagine you are competent to speak with authority about China and its people and its complex and mysterious art when you have never been in the country?"

"I have seen a little of China, Mr. Waudle. But I do not pretend to speak with undue authority about it."

"You say you've been in China?" His tone of disbelief was loud and bullying.

"I was in China with my father when I was a girl of sixteen."

"Oh! Perhaps you speak Chinese!" he sneered.

She looked at him gravely, not answering.

He laughed: "Now, Miss Nevers, you have intimated that we are liars and swindlers. Let's see how much you know for an expert! You pretend to be an authority on things Chinese. You will then understand me when I say: 'Jen chih ch'u, Hsing pen shan——'"

"I do understand you, Mr. Waudle," she cut in contemptuously. "You are repeating the 'three-word-classic,' which every school-child in China knows, and it merely means 'Men when born are naturally good.' I think I may qualify in Chinese as far as San Tzu Ching and his nursery rhymes. And I think we have had enough of this dodging——"

The author flushed hotly.

"Do you speak Wenli?" he demanded, completely flustered.

"Do you?" she retorted impatiently.

"I do," he asserted boldly.

"Indeed!"

"I may even say that I speak very fluently the—the literary language of China —or Wenli, as it is commonly called."

"That is odd," she said, "because the literary language of China, commonly called Wenli, is not and never has been spoken. It is only a written language, Mr. Waudle."

The Cubist had now gone quite to pieces. From his colourless mop of bushy hair to the fringe on his ankle-high trousers, he presented a study in deep dejection. Only his round, pale, parrot-like eyes remained on duty, staring unwinkingly at her.

"Were you ever actually in China?" she asked, looking around at him.

The terrified poet feebly pointed to the author of "Black Roses."

"Oh!" she said. "Were you in China, Mr. Waudle, or only in Japan?"

But Mr. Waudle found nothing further to say.

"Because," she said, "in Japan sometimes one is deceived into buying alleged Chinese jades and crystals and porcelains. I am afraid that you were deceived. I hope you were honestly deceived. What you have sold to Mr. Clydesdale as jade is not jade. And the porcelains are not what you represented them to be."

"That's where you make a mistake!" shouted Waudle loudly. "I've had the inscription on every vase translated, and I can prove it! How much of an expert are you? Hey?"

"If you were an expert," she explained wearily, "you would understand that inscriptions on Chinese porcelains are not trustworthy. Even hundreds of years ago forgeries were perpetrated by the Chinese who desired to have their works of art mistaken for still more ancient masterpieces; and so the ancient and modern makers of porcelains inscribed them accordingly. Only when an antique porcelain itself conforms to the inscription it bears do we venture to accept that inscription. Never otherwise."

Waudle, hypnotised, stood blinking at her, bereft of speech, almost of reason.

The poet piped feebly: "It was not our fault! We were brutally deceived in Japan. And, oh! The bitter deception to me! The cruelty of the awakening!" He got up out of his chair; words and gestures were once again at his command; tears streaked his pasty cheeks.

"Miss Nevers! My dear and honoured young lady! You know—you among all women must realise how precious to me is the moon! Sacred, worshipped, adored—desired far more than the desire for gold—yea, than much fine gold! Sweeter, also, than honey in the honeycomb!" he sobbed. "And it was a pair of moon vases, black as midnight, pearl-orbed, lacquered, mystic, wonderful, that lured me——"

"A damned Japanese in Tokio worked them off on us!" broke out the author of "Black Roses," hoarsely. "That was the beginning. What are you going to do about it? You've got us all right, Miss Nevers. The Jap did us. We did the next man. If you want to send us up, I suppose you can! I don't care. I can't keep soul and body together by selling what I write. I tell you I've starved half my life—and when I hear about the stuff that sells—all these damned best sellers —all this cheap fiction that people buy—while they neglect me—it breaks my heart——"

He turned sharply and passed his hand over his face. It was not an attitude; for a fraction of a second it was the real thing. Yet, even while the astonished poet was peeping sideways at his guilty companion, a verse suggested itself to him; and, quite unconsciously, he began to fumble in his pockets for a pencil, while the tears still glistened on his cheeks.

"Mr. Waudle," said Jacqueline, "I am really sorry for you. Because this is a very serious affair."

There was a silence; then she reseated herself at her desk.

"My client, Mr. Clydesdale, is not vindictive. He has no desire to humiliate you publicly. But he is justly indignant. And I know he will insist that you return to him what money he paid you for your collection."

Waudle started dramatically, forgetting his genuine emotion of the moment before.

"Does this rich man mean to ruin me!" he demanded, making his resonant voice tremble.

"On the contrary," she explained gently, "all he wants is the money he paid you."

As that was the only sort of ruin which Mr. Waudle had been fearing, he pressed his clenched fists into his eyes. He had never before possessed so much money. The mere idea of relinquishing it infuriated him; and he turned savagely on Jacqueline, hesitated, saw it was useless. For there remained nothing further to say to such a she-devil of an expert. He had always detested women anyway; whenever he had any money they had gotten it in one way or another. The seven thousand, his share, would have gone the same way. Now it was going back into a fat, rich man's capacious pockets—unless Mrs. Clydesdale might be persuaded to intervene. She could say that she wanted the collection. Why not? She had aided him before in emergencies—unwillingly, it is true—but what of that? No doubt she'd do it again—if he scared her sufficiently.

Jacqueline waited a moment longer; then rose from her desk in signal that the interview was at an end.

Waudle slouched out first, his oblong, evil head hanging in a picturesque attitude of noble sorrow. The Cubist shambled after him, wrapped in abstraction, his round, pale, bird-like eyes partly sheathed under bluish eyelids that seemed ancient and wrinkled.

He was already quite oblivious to his own moral degradation; his mind was completely obsessed by the dramatic spectacle which the despair of his friend had afforded him, and by the idea for a poem with which the episode had inspired him.

He was still absently fishing for a pencil and bit of paper when his companion jogged his elbow:

"If we fight this business, and if that damn girl sets Clydesdale after us, we'll have to get out. But I don't think it will come to that."

"Can you stop her, Adalbert—and retain the money?"

"By God! I'm beginning to think I can. I believe I'll drop in to see Mrs. Clydesdale about it now. She is a very faithful friend of mine," he added gently. "And sometimes a woman will rush in to help a fellow where angels fear to tread."

The poet looked at him, then looked away, frightened.

"Be careful," he said, nervously.

"Don't worry. I know women. And I have an idea."

The poet of the Cubists shrugged; then, with a vague gesture:

"My mistress, the moon," he said, dreamily, "is more to me than any idea on earth or in Heaven."

"Very fine," sneered Waudle, "but why don't you make her keep you in pin money?"

"Adalbert," retorted the poet, "if you wish to prostitute your art, do so. Anybody can make a mistress of his art and then live off her. But the inviolable moon——"

"Oh, hell!" snapped the author of "Black Roses."

And they wandered on into the busy avenue, side by side, Waudle savagely biting his heavy under-lip, both fists rammed deep into his overcoat pockets; the Cubist wandering along beside him, a little derby hat crowning the bunch of frizzled hair on his head, his soiled drab trousers, ankle high, flapping in the wind.

Jacqueline glanced at them as they passed the window at the end of the corridor, and turned hastily away, remembering the old, unhappy days after her father's death, and how once from a window she had seen the poet as she saw him now, frizzled, soiled, drab, disappearing into murky perspective.

She turned wearily to her desk again. A sense of depression had been impending—but she knew it was only the reaction from excitement and fought it nervously.

They brought luncheon to her desk, but she sent away the tray untouched. People came by appointment and departed, only to give place to others, all equally persistent and wholly absorbed in their own affairs; and she listened patiently, forcing her tired mind to sympathise and comprehend. And, in time, everybody went away satisfied or otherwise, but in no doubt concerning the answer she had given, favourable or unfavourable to their desires. For that was her way in the business of life.

At last, once more looking over her appointment list, she found that only Clydesdale remained; and almost at the same moment, and greatly to her surprise, Mrs. Clydesdale was announced.

"Is Mr. Clydesdale with her?" she asked the clerk, who had also handed her a letter with the visiting card of Mrs. Clydesdale.

"The lady is alone," he said.

Jacqueline glanced at the card again. Then, thoughtfully:

"Please say to Mrs. Clydesdale that I will receive her," she said; laid the card on the desk and picked up the letter.

It was a very thick letter and had arrived by messenger.

The address on the envelope was in Mrs. Hammerton's familiar and vigorous back-stroke writing, and she had marked it "Private! Personal! Important!" As almost every letter from her to Jacqueline bore similar emphatic warnings, the girl smiled to herself and leisurely split the envelope with a paper knife.

She was still intent on the letter, and was still seated at her desk when Mrs. Clydesdale entered. And Jacqueline slowly looked up, dazed and deathly white, as the woman about whom she had at that moment been reading came forward to greet her. Then, with a supreme effort, she rose from her chair, managing to find the ghost of a voice to welcome Elena, who seemed unusually vivacious, and voluble to the verge of excitement.

"'My dear!' she exclaimed. 'What a perfectly charming office!'"

"My dear!" she exclaimed. "What a perfectly charming office! It's really too sweet for words, Miss Nevers! It's enough to drive us all into trade! Are you very much surprised to see me here?"

"A—little."

"It's odd—the coincidence that brought me," said Elena gaily, "—and just a trifle embarrassing to me. And as it is rather a confidential matter——" She drew her chair closer to the desk. "May I speak to you in fullest candour and—and implicit confidence, Miss Nevers?"

"Yes."

"Then—there is a friend of mine in very serious trouble—a man I knew slightly before I was married. Since then I—have come to know him—better. And I am here now to ask you to help him."

"Yes."

"Shall I tell you his name at once?"

"If you wish."

"Then—his name is Adalbert Waudle."

Jacqueline looked up at her in weary surprise.

Elena laughed feverishly: "Adalbert is only a boy—a bad one, perhaps, but—you know that genius is queer—always unbalanced. He came to see me at noon to-day. It's a horrid mess, isn't it—what he did to my husband? I know all about it; and I know that Cary is wild, and that it was an outrageous thing for Adalbert to do. But——"

Her voice trembled a little and she forced a laugh to conceal it: "Adalbert is an old friend, Miss Nevers. I knew him as a boy. But even so, Cary couldn't understand if I pleaded for him. My husband means to send him to jail if he does not return the money. And—and I am sorry for Mrs. Waudle. Besides, I like the porcelains. And I want you to persuade Cary to keep them."

Through the whirling chaos of her thoughts, Jacqueline still strove to understand what this excited woman was saying; made a desperate effort to fix her attention on the words and not on the flushed and restless young wife who was uttering them.

"Will you persuade Cary to keep the collection, Miss Nevers?"

"That is for you to do, Mrs. Clydesdale."

"I tried. I called him up at his office and asked him to keep the jades and porcelains because I liked them. But he was very obstinate. What you have told him about—about being swindled has made him furious. That is why I came here. Something must be done."

"I don't think I understand you."

"There is nothing to understand. I want to keep the collection. I ask you to convince my husband———"

"How?"

"I d—don't know," stammered Elena, crimson again. "You ought to know how to—to do it."

"If Mr. Waudle returns your husband's money, no further action will be taken."

"He can not," said Elena, in a low voice.

"Why?"

"He has spent it."

"Did he tell you that?"

"Yes."

"Then I am afraid that Mr. Clydesdale will have him arrested."

There was an ominous silence. Jacqueline forced her eyes away from the terrible fascination of Elena's ghastly face, and said:

"I am sorry. But I can do nothing for you, Mrs. Clydesdale. The decision rests with your husband."

"You must help me!"

"I cannot."

"You must!" repeated Elena.

"How?"

"I—I don't care how you do it! But you must prevent my husband from prosecuting Mr. Waudle! It—it has got to be done—somehow."

"What do you mean?"

Elena's face was burning and her lips quivered:

"It has got to be done! I can't tell you why."

"Can you not tell your husband?"

"No."

Jacqueline was quivering, too, clinging desperately to her self-control under the menace of an impending horror which had already partly stunned her.

"Are you—afraid of this man?" she asked, with stiffening lips.

Elena bowed her head in desperation.

"What is it? Blackmail?"

"Yes. He once learned something. I have paid him—not to—to write it for the —the Tattler. And to-day he came to me straight from your office and made me understand that I would have to stop my husband from—taking any action —even to recover the money——"

Jacqueline sat nervously clenching and unclenching her hands over the letter which lay under them on the blotter.

"What scandal is it you fear, Mrs. Clydesdale?" she asked, in an icy voice.

Elena coloured furiously: "Is it necessary for me to incriminate myself before you help me? I thought you more generous!"

"I can not help you. There is no way to do so."

"Yes, there is!"

"How?"

"By—by telling my husband that the—the jades are not forgeries!"

Jacqueline's ashy cheeks blazed into colour.

"Mrs. Clydesdale," she said, "I would not do it to save myself—not even to save the dearest friend I have! And do you think I will lie to spare you?"

In the excitement and terror of what now was instantly impending, the girl had risen, clutching Mrs. Hammerton's letter in her hand.

"You need not tell me why you—you are afraid," she stammered, her lovely lips already distorted with fear and horror, "because I—I know! Do you understand? I know what you are—what you have done—what you are doing!"

She fumbled in the pages of Mrs. Hammerton's letter, found an enclosure, and held it out to Elena with shaking fingers.

It was Elena's note to her husband, written on the night she left him, brought by her husband to Silverwood, left on the library table, used as a bookmark by Desboro, discovered and kept by its finder, Mrs. Hammerton, for future emergencies.

Elena re-read it now with sickened senses, and knew that in the eyes of this young girl she was utterly and irretrievably damned.

"Did you write that?" whispered Jacqueline, with lips scarcely under control.

"I—you do not understand——"

"Did you know that when I was a guest under Mr. Desboro's roof everything that he and you said in the library was overheard? Do you know that you have been watched—not by me—but even long before I knew you—watched even at the opera——"

Elena drew a quick, terrified breath; then the surging shame mantled her from brow to throat.

"That was Mrs. Hammerton!" she murmured. "I warned Jim—but he trusted her."

Jacqueline turned cold all over.

"He is your—lover," she said mechanically.

Elena looked at her, hesitated, came a step nearer, still staring. Her visage and her bearing altered subtly. For a moment they gazed at each other. Then Elena said, in a soft, but deadly, voice:

"Suppose he is my lover! Does that concern you?" And, as the girl made no stir or sound: "However, if you think it does, you will scarcely care to know either of us any longer. I am quite satisfied. Do what you please about the man who has blackmailed me. I don't care now. I was frightened for a moment—but I don't care any longer. Because the end of all this nightmare is in sight; and I think Mr. Desboro and I are beginning to awake at last."

Until a few minutes before five Jacqueline remained seated at her desk, motionless, her head buried in her arms. Then she got to her feet somehow, and to her room, where, scarcely conscious of what she was doing, she bathed her face and arranged her hair, and strove to pinch and rub a little colour into her ghastly cheeks.

CHAPTER XIV

Desboro came for her in his car at five and found her standing alone in her office, dressed in a blue travelling dress, hatted and closely veiled. He partly lifted the veil, kissed the cold, unresponsive lips, the pallid cheek, the white-gloved fingers.

"Is Her Royal Shyness ready?" he whispered.

"Yes, Jim."

"All her affairs of state accomplished?" he asked laughingly.

"Yes—the day's work is done."

"Was it a hard day for you, sweetheart?"

"Yes—hard."

"I am so sorry," he murmured.

She rearranged her veil in silence.

Again, as the big car rolled away northward, and they were alone once more in the comfortable limousine, he took possession of her unresisting hand, whispering:

"I am so sorry you have had a hard day, dear. You really look very pale and tired."

"It was a—tiresome day."

He lifted her hand to his lips: "Do you love me, Jacqueline?"

"Yes."

"Above everything?"

"Yes."

"And you know that I love you above everything in the world?"

She was silent.

"Jacqueline!" he urged. "Don't you know it?"

"I—think you—care for me."

He laughed: "Will Your Royal Shyness never unbend! Is that all the credit you give me for my worship and adoration?"

She said, after a silence: "If it lies with me, you really will love me some day."

"Dearest!" he protested, laughing but perplexed. "Don't you know that I love you now—that I am absolutely mad about you?"

She did not answer, and he waited, striving to see her expression through the veil. But when he offered to lift it, she gently avoided him.

"Did you go to business?" she asked quietly.

"I? Oh, yes, I went back to the office. But Lord! Jacqueline, I couldn't keep my attention on the tape or on the silly orders people fired at me over the wire. So I left young Seely in charge and went to lunch with Jack Cairns; and then he and I returned to the office, where I've been fidgeting about ever since. I think it's been the longest day I ever lived."

"It has been a long day," she assented gravely. "Did Mr. Cairns speak to you of Cynthia?"

"He mentioned her, I believe."

"Do you remember what he said about her?"

"Well, yes. I think he spoke about her very nicely—about her being interesting and ambitious and talented—something of that sort—but how could I keep my mind on what he was saying about another girl?"

Jacqueline looked out of the window across a waste of swamp and trestle and squalid buildings toward University Heights. She said presently, without turning:

"Some day, may I ask Cynthia to visit me?"

"Dearest girl! Of course! Isn't it your house——"

"Silverwood?"

"Certainly——"

"No, Jim."

"What on earth do you mean?"

"What I say. Silverwood is not yet even partly mine. It must remain entirely yours—until I know you—better."

"Why on earth do you say such silly——"

"What is yours must remain yours," she repeated, in a low voice, "just as my shop, and office, and my apartment must remain mine—for a time."

"For how long?"

"I can not tell."

"Do you mean for always?"

"I don't know."

"And I don't understand you, dear," he said impatiently.

"You will, Jim."

He smiled uneasily: "For how long must we twain, who are now one, maintain solitary sovereignty over our separate domains?"

"Until I know you better."

"And how long is that going to take?" he asked, smilingly apprehensive and deeply perplexed by her quiet and serious attitude toward him.

"I don't know how long, I wish I did."

"Jacqueline, dear, has anything unpleasant happened to disturb you since I last saw you?"

She made no reply.

"Won't you tell me, dear," he insisted uneasily.

"I will tell you this, Jim. Whatever may have occurred to disturb me is already a matter of the past. Life and its business lie before us; that is all I know. This is our beginning, Jim; and happiness depends on what we make of our lives from now on—from now on."

The stray lock of golden hair had fallen across her cheek, accenting the skin's pallor through the veil. She rested her elbow on the window ledge, her tired head on her hand, and gazed at the sunset behind the Palisades. Far below, over the grey and wrinkled river, smoke from a steamboat drifted, a streak of bronze and purple, in the sunset light.

"What has happened?" he muttered under his breath. And, turning toward her: "You must tell me, Jacqueline. It is now my right to know."

"Don't ask me."

His face hardened; for a moment the lean muscles of the jaw worked visibly.

"Has anybody said anything about me to you?"

No reply.

"Has—has Mrs. Hammerton been to see you?"

"No."

He was silent for a moment, then:

"I'll tell you now, Jacqueline; she did not wish me to marry you. Did you know it?"

"I know it."

"I believe," he said, "that she has been capable of warning you against me. Did she?"

No reply.

"And yet you married me?" he said, after a silence.

She said nothing.

"So you could not have believed her, whatever she may have said," he concluded calmly.

"Jim?"

"Yes, dear."

"I married you because I loved you. I love you still. Remember it when you are impatient with me—when you are hurt—perhaps angry——"

"Angry with you, my darling!"

"You are going to be—very often—I am afraid."

"Angry?"

"I—don't know. I don't know how it will be with us. If only you will remember that I love you—no matter how I seem——"

"Dear, if you tell me that you do love me, I will know that it must be so!"

"I tell you that I do. I could never love anybody else. You are all that I have in the world; all I care for. You are absolutely everything to me. I loved you and married you; I took you for mine just as you were and are. And if I didn't quite understand all that—that you are—I took you, nevertheless—for better or for worse—and I mean to hold you. And I know now that, knowing more about you, I would do the same thing if it were to be done again. I would marry you to-morrow—knowing what I know."

"What more do you know about me than you did this morning, Jacqueline?" he asked, terribly troubled.

But she refused to answer.

He said, reddening: "If you have heard any gossip concerning Mrs. Clydesdale, it is false. Was that what you heard? Because it is an absolute lie."

But she had learned from Mrs. Clydesdale's reckless lips the contrary, and she rested her aching head on her hand and stared out at the endless lines of houses along Broadway, as the car swung into Yonkers, veered to the west past the ancient manor house, then rolled northward again toward Hastings.

"Don't you believe me?" he asked at length. "That gossip is a lie—if that is what you heard."

She thought: "This is how gentlemen are supposed to behave under such circumstances." And she shivered.

"Are you cold?" he asked, with an effort.

"A little."

He drew the fur robe closer around her, and leaned back in his corner, deeply worried, impatient, but helpless in the face of her evident weariness and reticence, which he could not seem to penetrate or comprehend. Only that something ominous had happened—that something was dreadfully wrong—he now thoroughly understood.

In the purposeless career of a man of his sort, there is much that it is well to forget. And in Desboro's brief career there were many things that he would not care to have such a girl as Jacqueline hear about—so much, alas! of folly and stupidity, so much of idleness, so much unworthy, that now in his increasing chagrin and mortification, in the painful reaction from happy pride to alarm and self-contempt, he could not even guess what had occurred, or for which particular folly he was beginning to pay.

Long since, both in his rooms in town, and at Silverwood, he had destroyed the silly souvenirs of idleness and folly. He thought now of the burning sacrifice he had so carelessly made that day in the library—and how the flames had shrivelled up letter and fan, photograph and slipper. And he could not remember that he had left a rag of lace or a perfumed envelope unburned.

Had the ghosts of their owners risen to confront him on his own hearthstone, standing already between him and this young girl he had married?

What whisper had reached her guiltless ears? What rumour, what breath of innuendo? Must a man still be harassed who has done with folly for all time— who aspires to better things—who strives to change his whole mode of life merely for the sake of the woman he loves—merely to be more worthy of her?

As he sat there so silently in the car beside her, his dark thoughts travelled back again along the weary, endless road to yesterday. Since he had known and loved her, his thoughts had often and unwillingly sought that shadowy road where the only company were ghosts—phantoms of dead years that sometimes smiled, sometimes reproached, sometimes menaced him with suddenly remembered eyes and voiceless but familiar words forever printed on his memory.

Out of that grey vista, out of that immaterial waste where only impalpable shapes peopled the void, vanished, grew out of nothing only to reappear, something had come to trouble the peace of mind of the woman he loved— some spectre of folly had arisen and had whispered in her ear, so that, at the mockery, the light had died out in her fearless eyes and her pure mind was clouded and her tender heart was weighted with this thing—whatever it might be—this echo of folly which had returned to mock them both.

"Dearest," he said, drawing her to him so that her cold cheek rested against his, "whatever I was, I am no longer. You said you could forgive."

"I do—forgive."

"Can you not forget, too?"

"I will try—with your help."

"How can I help you? Tell me."

"By letting me love you—as wisely as I can—in my own fashion. By letting me learn more of you—more about men. I don't understand men. I thought I did—but I don't. By letting me find out what is the wisest and the best and the most unselfish way to love you. For I don't know yet. I don't know. All I know is that I am married to the man I loved—the man I still love. But how I am going to love him I—I don't yet know."

He was silent; the hot flush on his face did not seem to warm her cheek where it rested so coldly against his.

"I want to hold you because it is best for us both," she said, as though speaking to herself.

"But—you need make no effort to hold me, Jacqueline!" e protested, amazed.

"I want to hold you, Jim," she repeated. "You are my husband. I—I must hold you. And I don't know how I am to do it. I don't know how."

"My darling! Who has been talking to you? What have they said?"

"It has got to be done, somehow," she interrupted, wearily. "I must learn how to hold you; and you must give me time, Jim———"

"Give you time!" he repeated, exasperated.

"Yes—to learn how to love you best—so I can serve you best. That is why I married you—not selfishly, Jim—and I thought I knew—I thought I knew ———"

Her cheek slipped from his and rested on his shoulder. He put his arm around her and she covered her face with her gloved hands.

"I love you dearly, dearly," he whispered brokenly. "If the whisper of any past stupidity of mine has hurt you, God knows best what punishment He visits on me at this moment! If there were any torture I could endure to spare you, Jacqueline, I would beg for it—welcome it! It is a bitter and a hopeless and a ridiculous thing to say; but if I had only known there was such a woman as you in the world I would have understood better how to live. I suppose many a man understands it when it is too late. I realise now, for the first time, how changeless, how irrevocably fixed, are the truths youth learns to smile at—the immutable laws youth scoffs at———"

He choked, controlled his voice, and went on:

"If youth could only understand it, the truths of childhood are the only truths. The first laws we learn are the eternal ones. And their only meaning is self-discipline. But youth is restive and mistakes curiosity for intelligence, insubordination for the courage of independence. The stupidity of orthodoxy incites revolt. To disregard becomes less difficult; to forget becomes a habit. To think for one's self seems admirable; but when youth attempts that, it thinks only what it pleases or does not think at all. I am not trying to find excuses or to evade my responsibility, dear. I had every chance, no excuse for what I have —sometimes—been. And now—on this day—this most blessed and most solemn day of my life—I can only say to you I am sorry, and that I mean so to live—always—that no man or woman can reproach me."

She lay very silent against his shoulder. Blindly striving to understand him, and men—blindly searching for some clue to the path of duty—the path she must find somehow and follow for his sake—through the obscurity and mental confusion she seemed to hear at moments Elena Clydesdale's shameless and merciless words, and the deadly repetition seemed to stun her.

Vainly she strove against the recurring horror; once or twice, unconsciously, her hands crept upward and closed her ears, as though she could shut out what was dinning in her brain.

With every reserve atom of mental strength and self-control she battled against this thing which was stupefying her, fought it off, held it, drove it back—not very far, but far enough to give her breathing room. But no sooner did she attempt to fix her mind on the man beside her, and begin once more to grope for the clue to duty—how most unselfishly she might serve him for his salvation and her own—than the horror she had driven back stirred stealthily and crawled nearer. And the battle was on once more.

Twilight had fallen over the Westchester hills; a familiar country lay along the road they travelled. In the early darkness, glancing from the windows he divined unseen landmarks, counted the miles unconsciously as the car sped across invisible bridges that clattered or resounded under the heavy wheels.

The stars came out; against them woodlands and hills took shadowy shape, marking for him remembered haunts. And at last, far across the hills the lighted windows of Silverwood glimmered all a-row; the wet gravel crunched under the slowing wheels, tall Norway spruces towered phantomlike on every side; the car stopped.

"Home," he whispered to her; and she rested her arm on his shoulder and drew herself erect.

Every servant and employee on the Desboro estate was there to receive them; she offered her slim hand and spoke to every one. Then, on her husband's arm, and her proud little head held high, she entered the House of Desboro for the first time bearing the family name—entered smiling, with death in her heart.

At last the dinner was at an end. Farris served the coffee and set the silver lamp and cigarettes on the library table, and retired.

Luminous red shadows from the fireplace played over wall and ceiling—the same fireplace where Desboro had made his offering—as though flame could purify and ashes end the things that men have done!

In her frail dinner gown of lace, she lay in a great chair before the blaze, gazing at nothing. He, seated on the rug beside her chair, held her limp hand and rested his face against it, staring at the ashes on the hearth.

And this was marriage! Thus he was beginning his wedded life—here in the house of his fathers, here at the same hearthstone where the dead brides of dead forebears had sat as his bride was sitting now.

But had any bride ever before faced that hearth so silent, so motionless, so pale as was this young girl whose fingers rested so limply in his and whose cold palm grew no warmer against his cheek?

What had he done to her? What had he done to himself—that the joy of things had died out in her eyes—that speech had died on her lips—that nothing in her seemed alive, nothing responded, nothing stirred.

Now, all the bitterness that life and its unwisdom had stored up for him through the swift and reckless years, he tasted. For that cup may not pass. Somewhere, sooner or later, the same lips that have so lightly emptied sweeter draughts must drain this one. None may refuse it, none wave it away until the cup be empty.

"Jacqueline?"

She moved slightly in her chair.

"Tell me," he said, "what is it that can make amends?"

"They—are made."

"But the hurt is still there. What can heal it, dear?"

"I—don't know."

"Time?"

"Perhaps."

"Love?"

"Yes—in time."

"How long?"

"I do not know, Jim."

"Then—what is there for me to do?"

She was silent.

"Could you tell me, Jacqueline?"

"Yes. Have patience—with me."

"With you?"

"It will be necessary."

"How do you mean, dear?"

"I mean you must have patience with me—in many ways. And still be in love with me. And still be loyal to me—and—faithful. I don't know whether a man can do these things. I don't know men. But I know myself—and what I require of men—and of you."

"What you require of me I can be if you love me."

"Then never doubt it. And when I know that you have become what I require you to be, you could not doubt my loving you even if you wished to. Then you will know; until then—you must believe."

He sat thinking before the hearth, the slow flush rising to his temples and remaining.

"What is it you mean to do, Jacqueline?" he asked, in a low voice.

"Nothing, except what I have always done. The business of life remains unchanged; it is always there to be done."

"I mean—are you going to—change—toward me?"

"I have not changed."

"Your confidence in me has gone."

"I have recovered it."

"You believe in me still?"

"Oh, yes—yes!" Her little hand inside his clenched convulsively and her voice broke.

Kneeling beside her, he drew her into his arms and felt her breath suddenly hot and feverish against his shoulder. But if there had been tears in her eyes they dried unshed, for he saw no traces of them when he kissed her.

"In God's name," he whispered, "let the past bury its accursed dead and give me a chance. I love you, worship you, adore you. Give me my chance in life again, Jacqueline!"

"I—I give it to you—as far as in me lies. But it rests with you, Jim, what you will be."

His own philosophy returned to mock him out of the stainless mouth of this young girl! But he said passionately:

"How can I be arbiter of my own fate unless I have all you can give me of love and faith and unswerving loyalty?"

"I give you these."

"Then—as a sign—return the kiss I give you—now."

There was no response.

"Can you not, Jacqueline?"

"Not—yet."

"You—you can not respond!"

"Not—that way—yet."

"Is—have I—has what you know of me killed all feeling, all tenderness in you?"

"No."

"Then—why can you not respond——"

"I can not, Jim—I can not."

He flushed hotly: "Do you—do I inspire you with—do I repel you—physically?"

She caught his hand, cheeks afire, dismayed, striving to check him:

"Please—don't say such—it is—not—true——"

"It seems to be——"

"No! I—I ask you—not to say it—think it——"

"How can I help thinking it—thinking that you only care for me—that the only attraction on your part is—is intellectual——"

She disengaged her hand from his and shrank away into the velvet depths of her chair.

"I can't help it," he said. "I've got to say what I think. Never since I have told you I loved you have you ever hinted at any response, even to the lightest caress. We are married. Whatever—however foolish I may have been—God knows you have made me pay for it this day. How long am I to continue paying? I tell you a man can't remain repentant too long under the stern and chilling eyes of retribution. If you are going to treat me as though I were physically unfit to touch, I can make no further protest. But, Jacqueline, no man was ever aided by a punishment that wounds his self-respect."

"I must consider mine, too," she said, in a ghost of a voice.

"Very well," he said, "if you think you must maintain it at the expense of mine ——"

"Jim!"

The low cry left her lips trembling.

"What?" he said, angrily.

"Have—have you already forgotten what I said?"

"What did you say?"

"I asked—I asked you to be patient with me—because—I love you——"

But the words halted; she bowed her head in her hands, quivering, scarcely conscious that he was on his knees again at her feet, scarcely hearing his broken words of repentance and shame for the sorry and contemptible rôle he had been playing.

No tears came to help her even then, only a dry, still agony possessed her. But the crisis passed and wore away; sight and hearing and the sense of touch returned to her. She saw his head bowed in contrition on her knees, heard his voice, bitter in self-accusation, felt his hands crisping over hers, crushing them till her new rings cut her.

For a while she looked down at him as though dazed; then the real pain from her wedding ring aroused her and she gently withdrew that hand and rested it on his thick, short, curly hair.

For a long while they remained so

. He had ceased to speak; her brooding gaze rested on him, unchanged save for the subtle tenderness of the lips, which still quivered at moments.

Clocks somewhere in the house were striking midnight. A little later a log fell from the dying fire, breaking in ashes.

He felt her stir, change her position slightly; and he lifted his head. After a moment she laid her hand on his arm, and he aided her to rise.

As they moved slowly, side by side, through the house, they saw that it was filled with flowers everywhere, twisted ropes of them on the banisters, too, where they ascended.

Her own maid, who had arrived by train, rose from a seat in the upper corridor to meet her. The two rooms, which were connected by a sitting room, disclosed themselves, almost smothered in flowers.

Jacqueline stood in the sitting room for a moment, gazing vaguely around her at the flowers and steadying herself by one hand on the centre-table, which a great bowlful of white carnations almost covered.

Then, as her maid reappeared at the door of her room, she turned and looked at Desboro.

There was a silence; his face was very white, hers was deathly.

He said: "Shall we say good-night?"

"It is—for you—to say."

"Then—good-night, Jacqueline."

"Good-night."

"She turned ... looked back, hesitated"

She turned, took a step or two—looked back, hesitated, then slowly retraced her steps to where he was standing by the flower-covered table.

From the mass of blossoms she drew a white carnation, touched it to her lips, and, eyes still lowered, offered it to him. In her palm, beside it, lay a key. But he took only the blossom, touching it to his lips as she had done.

She looked at the key, lying in her trembling hand, then lifted her confused eyes to his once more, whispering:

"Good-night—and thank you."

"Good-night," he said, "until to-morrow."

And they went their separate ways.

CHAPTER XV

Une nuit blanche—and the young seem less able to withstand its corroding alchemy than the old. It had left its terrible and pallid mark on Desboro; and on Jacqueline it had set its phantom sign. That youthfully flushed and bright-eyed loveliness which always characterised the girl had whitened to ashes over night.

And now, as she entered the sunny breakfast room in her delicate Chinese morning robes, the change in her was startlingly apparent; for the dead-gold lustre of her hair accented the pallor of a new and strange and transparent beauty; the eyes, tinted by the deeper shadows under them, looked larger and more violet; and she seemed smaller and more slender; and there was a snowy quality to the skin that made the vivid lips appear painted.

Desboro came forward from the recess of the window; and whether in his haggard and altered features she read of his long night's vigil, or whether in his eyes she learned again how she herself had changed, was not plain to either of them; but her eyes suddenly filled and she turned sharply and stood with the back of one slender hand across her eyes.

Neither had spoken; neither spoke for a full minute. Then she walked to the window and looked out. The mating sparrows were very noisy.

Not a tear fell; she touched her eyes with a bit of lace, drew a long, deep, steady breath and turned toward him.

"It is all over—forgive me, Jim. I did not mean to greet you this way. I won't do it again——"

She offered her hand with a faint smile, and he lifted it and touched it to his lips.

"It's all over, all ended," she repeated. "Such a curious phenomenon happened to me at sunrise this morning."

"What?"

"I was born," she said, laughing. "Isn't it odd to be born at my age? So as soon as I realised what had happened, I went and looked out of the window; and there was the world, Jim—a big, round, wonderful planet, all over hills and trees and valleys and brooks! I don't know how I recognised it, having just been born into it, but somehow I did. And I knew the sun, too, the minute I saw it shining on my window and felt it on my face and throat. Isn't that a wonderful way to begin life?"

There was not a tremor in her voice, nothing tremulous in the sweet humour of the lips; and, to his surprise, in her eyes little demons of gaiety seemed to be dancing all at once till they sparkled almost mockingly.

"Dear," he said, under his breath, "I wondered whether you would ever speak to me again."

"Speak to you! You silly boy, I expect to do little else for the rest of my life! I intend to converse and argue and importune and insist and nag and nag. Oh, Jim! Please ring for breakfast. I had no luncheon yesterday and less dinner."

A slight colour glowed under the white skin of her cheeks as Farris entered with the fruit; she lifted a translucent cluster of grapes from the dish, snipped it in half with the silver scissors, glanced at her husband and laughed.

"'That's how hungry I am, Jim. I warned you'"

"That's how hungry I am, Jim. I warned you. Of what are you thinking—with that slight and rather fascinating smile crinkling your eyes?"

She bit into grape after grape, watching him across the table.

"Share with me whatever amuses you, please!" she insisted. "Never with my consent shall you ever again laugh alone."

"You haven't seen last evening's and this morning's papers," he said, amused.

"Have they arrived? Oh, Jim! I wish to see them, please!"

He went into his room and brought out a sheaf of clippings.

"Isn't this all of the papers that you cared to see, Jacqueline?"

"Of course! What do they say about us? Are they brief or redundant, laconic or diffuse? And are they nice to us?"

She was already immersed in a quarter column account of "A Romantic Wedding" at "old St. George's"; and she read with dilated eyes all about the "wealthy, fashionable, and well-known clubman," which she understood must mean her youthful husband, and all about Silverwood and the celebrated collections, and about his lineage and his social activities. And by and by she read about herself, and her charm and beauty and personal accomplishments, and was amazed to learn that she, too, was not only wealthy and fashionable, but that she was a descendant of an ancient and noble family in France, entirely extinguished by the guillotine during the Revolution, except for her immediate progenitors.

Clipping after clipping she read to the end; then the simple notices under "Weddings." Then she looked at Desboro.

"I—I didn't realise what a very grand young man I had married," she said, with a shy smile. "But I am very willing to admit it. Why do they say such foolish and untrue things about me?"

"They meant to honour you by lying about you when the truth about you is far more noble and more wonderful," he said.

"Do you think so?"

"Do you doubt it?"

She remained silent, turning over the clippings in her hand; then, glancing up, found him smiling again.

"Please share with me—because I know your thoughts are pleasant."

"It was seeing you in these pretty Chinese robes," he smiled, "which made me think of that evening in the armoury."

"Oh—when I sat under the dragon, with my lute, and said for your guests some legends of old Cathay?"

"Yes. Seeing you here—in your Chinese robes—made me think of their astonishment when you first dawned on their mental and social horizon. They are worthy people," he added, with a shrug.

"They are as God made them," she said, demurely.

"Only they have always forgotten, as I have, that God merely begins us—and we are expected to do the rest. For, once made, He merely winds us up, sets our hearts ticking, and places us on top of the world. Where we walk to, and how, is our own funeral henceforward. Is that your idea of divine responsibility?"

"I think He continues to protect us after we start to toddle; and after that, too, if we ask Him," she answered, in a low voice.

"Do you believe in prayer, dear?"

"Yes—in unselfish prayer. Not in the acquisitive variety. Such petitions seem ignoble to me."

"I understand."

She said, gravely: "To pray—not for one's self—except that one cause no sorrow—that seems to me a logical petition. But I don't know. And after all, what one does, not what one talks about, counts."

She was occupied with her grapes, glancing up at him from moment to moment with sweet, sincere eyes, sometimes curious, sometimes shy, but always intent on this tall, boyish young fellow who, she vainly tried to realise, belonged to her.

In his morning jacket, somehow, he had become entirely another person; his thick, closely brushed hair, the occult air of freshness from ablutions that left a faint fragrance about him, accented their new intimacy, the strangeness of which threatened at moments to silence her. Nor could she realise that she belonged there at all—there, in her frail morning draperies, at breakfast with him in a house which belonged to him.

Yet, one thing she was becoming vaguely aware of; this tall, young fellow, in his man's intimate attire, was quietly and unvaryingly considerate of her; had entirely changed from the man she seemed to have known; had suddenly changed yesterday at midnight. And now she was aware that he still remained what he had been when he took the white blossom from her hand the night before, and left in her trembling palm, untouched, the symbol of authority which now was his forever.

Even in the fatigue of body and the deadlier mental weariness—in the confused chaos of her very soul, that moment was clearly imprinted on her mind—must remain forever recorded while life lasted.

She divided another grape; there were no seeds; the skin melted in her mouth.

"Men," she said absently, "are good." When he laughed, she came to herself and looked at him with shy, humourous eyes. "They are good, Jim. Even the Chinese knew it thousands of years ago. Have you never heard me recite the three-word-classic of San Tzu Ching? Then listen, white man!

"Jen chih ch'u

Hsing pen shan

Hsing hsiang chin

Hsi hsiang yuan

Kou pu chiao

Hsing nai ch'ien

Chiao chih tao

Kuei i chuan——"

She sat swaying slightly to the rhythm, like a smiling child who recites a rhyme of the nursery, accenting the termination of every line by softly striking her palms together; and the silken Chinese sleeves slipped back, revealing her white arms to the shoulder.

Softly she smote her smooth little palms together, gracefully she swayed; her silks rustled like the sound of slender reeds in a summer wind, and her cadenced voice was softer. Never had he seen her so exquisite.

She stopped capriciously.

"All that is Chinese to me," he said. "You make me feel solitary and ignorant."

And she laughed and tossed the lustrous hair from her cheeks.

"This is all it means, dear:

"Men at their birth

Are naturally good.

Their natures are much the same;

Their habits become widely different.

If they are not taught,

Their natures will deteriorate.

The right way in teaching

Is to attach the utmost importance to thoroughness——

"And so forth, and so forth," she ended gaily.

"Where on earth did you learn Chinese?" he remonstrated. "You know enough without that to scare me to death! Slowly but surely you are overwhelming me, Jacqueline, and some day I shall leave the house, dig a woodchuck hole out on the hill, and crawl into it permanently."

"Then I'll have to crawl in, too, won't I? But, alas, Jim! The three-word-classic is my limit. When father took me to Shanghai, I learned it—three hundred and fifty-six lines of it! But it's all the Chinese I know—except a stray phrase or two. Cheer up, dear; we won't have to look for our shadows on that hill."

Breakfast was soon accomplished; she looked shyly across at him; he nodded, and they rose.

"The question is," she said, "when am I going to find time to read the remainder of the morning paper, and keep myself properly informed from day to day, if you make breakfast so agreeable for me?"

"Have I done that?"

"You know you have," she said lightly. "Suppose you read the paper aloud to me, while I stroll about for the sake of my figure."

They laughed; he picked up the paper and began to read the headlines, and she walked about the room, her hands bracketed on her hips, listening sometimes, sometimes absorbed in her own reflections, now and then glancing out of the window or pausing to rearrange a bowl of flowers.

Little by little, however, her leisurely progress from one point of interest to another became more haphazard, and she moved restlessly, with a tendency to drift in his direction.

Perhaps she realised that, for she halted suddenly.

"Jim, I have enough of politics, thank you. And it's almost time to put on more conventional apparel, isn't it? I have a long and hard day before me at the office."

"As hard as yesterday?" he asked, unthinkingly; then reddened.

She had moved to the window as she spoke; but he had seen the quick, unconscious gesture of pain as her hand flew to her breast; and her smiling courage when she turned toward him did not deceive him.

"That was a hard day, Jim. But I think the worst is over. And you may read your paper if you wish until I am ready. You have only to put on your business coat, haven't you?"

So he tried to fix his mind on the paper, and, failing, laid it aside and went to his room to make ready.

When he was prepared, he returned to their sitting room. She was not there, and the door of her bedroom was open and the window-curtains fluttering.

So he descended to the library, where he found her playing with his assortment of animals, a cat tucked under either arm and a yellow pup on her knees.

"They all came to say good-morning," she explained, "and how could I think of my clothing? Would you ask Farris to fetch a whisk-broom?"

Desboro rang: "A whisk-broom for—for Mrs. Desboro," he said.

Mrs. Desboro!

She had looked up startled; it was the first time she had heard it from his lips, and even the reiteration of her maid had not accustomed her to hear herself so named.

Both had blushed before Farris, both had thrilled as the words had fallen from Desboro's unaccustomed lips; but both attempted to appear perfectly tranquil and undisturbed by what had shocked them as no bomb explosion possibly could. And the old man came back with the whisk-broom, and Desboro dusted the cat fur and puppy hairs from Jacqueline's brand-new gown.

They were going to town by train, not having time to spare.

"It will be full of commuters," he said, teasingly. "You don't know what a godsend a bride is to commuters. I pity you."

"I shall point my nose particularly high, monsieur. Do you suppose I'll know anybody aboard?"

"What if you don't! They'll know who you are! And they'll all read their papers and stare at you from time to time, comparing you with what the papers say about you———"

"Jim! Stop tormenting me. Do I look sallow and horrid? I believe I'll run up to my room and do a little friction on my cheeks———"

"With nail polish?"

"How do you know? Please, Jim, it isn't nice to know so much about the makeshifts indulged in by my sex."

She stood pinching her cheeks and the tiny lobes of her close-set ears, regarding him with beautiful but hostile eyes.

"You know too much, young man. You don't wish to make me afraid of you, do you? Anyway, you are no expert! Once you thought my hair was painted, and my lips, too. If I'd known what you were thinking I'd have made short work of you that rainy afternoon——"

"You did."

She laughed: "You can say nice things, too. Did you really begin to—to care for me that actual afternoon?"

"That actual afternoon."

"A—about what time—if you happen to remember," she asked carelessly.

"About the same second that I first set eyes on you."

"Oh, Jim, you couldn't!"

"Couldn't what?"

"Care for me the actual second you first set eyes on me. Could you?"

"I did."

"Was it that very second?"

"Absolutely."

"You didn't show it."

"Well, you know I couldn't very well kneel down and make you a declaration before I knew your name, could I, dear?"

"You did it altogether too soon as it was. Jim, what did you think of me?"

"You ought to know by this time."

"I don't. I suppose you took one look at me and decided that I was all ready to fall into your arms. Didn't you?"

"You haven't done it yet," he said lightly.

There was a pause; the colour came into her face, and his own reddened. But she pretended to be pleasantly unconscious of the significance, and only interested in reminiscence.

"Do you know what I thought of you, Jim, when you first came in?"

"Not much, I fancy," he conceded.

"Will it spoil you if I tell you?"

"Have you spoiled me very much, Jacqueline?"

"Of course I have," she said hastily. "Listen, and I'll tell you what I thought of you when you first came in. I looked up, and of course I knew at a glance that you were nice; and I was very much impressed——"

"The deuce you were!" he laughed, unbelievingly.

"I was!"

"You didn't show it."

"Only an idiot of a girl would. But I was—very—greatly—impressed," she continued, with a delightfully pompous emphasis on every word, "very—greatly—impressed by the tall and fashionable and elegant and agreeably symmetrical Mr. Desboro, owner of the celebrated collection of arms and armour——"

"I knew it!"

"Knew what?"

"You never even took the trouble to look at me until you found out that the armour belonged to me——"

"That is what ought to have been true. But it wasn't."

"Did you actually——"

"Yes, I did. Not the very second I laid eyes on you——" she added, blushing slightly, "but—when you went away—and afterward—that evening when I was trying to read Grenville on Armour."

"You thought of me, Jacqueline?"

"'It was rather odd, wasn't it, Jim?'"

"Yes—and tried not to. But it was no use; I seemed to see you laughing at me under every helmet in Grenville's plates. It was rather odd, wasn't it, Jim? And to think—to think that now——"

Her smile grew vaguer; she dropped her

head thoughtfully and rested one hand on the library table, where once her catalogue notes had been piled up—where once Elena's letter to her husband had fallen from Clydesdale's heavy hand.

Then, gradually into her remote gaze came something else, something Desboro had learned to dread; and she raised her head abruptly and gazed straight at him with steady, questioning eyes in which there was a hint of trouble of some kind—perhaps unbelief.

"I suppose you are going to your office," she said.

"After I have taken you to yours, dear."

"You will be at leisure before I am, won't you?"

"Unless you knock off work at four o'clock. Can you?"

"I can not. What will you do until five, Jim?"

"There will be nothing for me to do except wait for you."

"Where will you wait?"

He shrugged: "At the club, I suppose."

The car rolled up past the library windows.

"I suppose," she said carelessly, "that it would be too stupid for you to wait chez moi."

"In your office? No, indeed——"

"I meant in my apartment. You could smoke and read—but perhaps you wouldn't care to."

They went out into the hall, where her maid held her ulster for her and Farris put Desboro into his coat.

Then they entered the car which swung around the oval and glided away toward Silverwood station.

"To tell you the truth, dear," he said, "it would be rather slow for me to sit in an empty room until you were ready to join me."

"Of course. You'd find it more amusing at your club."

"I'd rather be with you at your office."

"Thank you. But some of my clients stipulate that no third person shall be present when their business is discussed."

"All right," he said, shortly.

The faint warmth of their morning's rapprochement seemed somehow to have turned colder, now that they were about to separate for the day. Both felt it; neither understood it. But the constraint which perhaps they thought too indefinite to analyse persisted. She did not fully understand it, except that, in the aftermath of the storm which had nigh devastated her young heart, her physical nearness to him seemed to help the tiny seed of faith which she had replanted in agony and tears the night before.

To see him, hear his voice, somehow aided her; and the charm of his personality for a while had reawakened and encouraged in her the courage to love him. The winning smile in his eyes had, for the time, laid the phantoms of doubt; memory had become less sensitive; the demon of distrust which she had fought off so gallantly lay somewhere inert and almost forgotten in the dim chamber of her mind.

But not dead—no; for somewhere in obscurity she had been conscious for an instant that her enemy was stirring.

Must this always be so? Was faith in this man really dead? Was it only the image of faith which her loyalty and courage had set up once more for an altar amid the ruins of her young heart?

And always, always, even when she seemed unaware, even when she had unconsciously deceived herself, her consciousness of the other woman remained alive, like a spark, whitened at moments by its own ashes, yet burning terribly when touched.

Slowly she began to understand that her supposed new belief in this man would endure only while he was within her sight; that the morning's warmth had slowly chilled as the hour of their separation approached; that her mind was becoming troubled and confused, and her heart uncertain and apprehensive.

And as she thought of the future—years and years of it—there seemed no rest for her, only endless effort and strife, only the external exercise of mental and spiritual courage to fight back the creeping shadow which must always threaten her—the shadow that Doubt casts, and which men call Fear.

"Shall we go to town in the car?" he said, looking at his watch. "We have time; the train won't be in for twenty minutes."

"If you like."

He picked up the speaking tube and gave his orders, then lay back again to watch the familiar landscape with worried eyes that saw other things than hills and trees and wintry fields and the meaningless abodes of men.

So this was what Fate had done to him—this! And every unconsidered act of his had been slyly, blandly, maliciously leading him into this valley of humiliation.

He had sometimes thought of marrying, never very definitely, except that, if love were to be the motive, he would have ample time, after that happened, to reform before his wedding day. Also, he had expected to remain in a laudable and permanent state of regeneration, marital treachery not happening to suit his fastidious taste.

That was what he had intended in the improbable event of marriage. And now, suddenly, from a clear sky, the bolt had found him; love, courtship, marriage, had followed with a rapidity he could scarcely realise; and had left him stranded on the shores of yesterday, discredited, distrusted, deeply, wretchedly in love; not only unable to meet on equal terms the young girl who had become his wife, but the involuntary executioner of her tender faith in him!

To this condition the laws of compensation consigned him. The man-made laws which made his complaisance possible could not help him now; the unwritten social law which acknowledges a double standard of purity for man and woman he must invoke in vain. Before the tribunal of her clear, sweet eyes, and before the chastity of her heart and mind, the ignoble beliefs, the lying precedents, the false standards must fall.

There had been no shelter there for him, and he had known it. Reticence, repentance, humble vows for the future—these had been left to him, he supposed.

But the long, dim road to yesterday was thronged with ghosts, and his destiny came swiftly upon him. Tortured, humiliated, helpless, he saw the lash that cut him fall also upon her.

Sooner or later, all that is secret of good or of evil shall be made manifest, here or elsewhere; and the suffering may not be abated. And he began to understand that reticence can not forever hide what has been; that no silence can screen it; no secrecy conceal it; that reaction invariably succeeds action; and not a finger is ever lifted that the universe does not experience the effect.

How he or fate might have spared her, he did not know. What she had learned about him he could not surmise. As far as Elena was concerned, he had been no worse than a fastidious fool dangling about a weaker and less fastidious one. If gossip of that nature had brought this grief upon her, it was damnable.

All he could do was to deny it. He had denied it. But denial, alas, was limited to that particular episode. He could not make it more sweeping; he was not on equal ground with her; he was at a disadvantage. Only spiritual equality dare face its peer, fearless, serene, and of its secrets unafraid.

Yet—she had surmised what he had been; she had known. And, insensibly, he began to feel a vague resentment toward her, almost a bitterness. Because she had accepted him without any illusion concerning him. That had been understood between them. She knew he loved her; she loved him. Already better things had been in sight for him, loftier aspirations, the stirring of ambition. And suddenly, almost at the altar itself, this thing had happened— whatever it was! And all her confidence in him, all her acquiescence in what had been, all her brave words and promises—all except the mere naked love in her breast had crashed earthward under its occult impact, leaving their altar on their wedding night shattered, fireless, and desolate.

He set his teeth and the muscles in his cheeks hardened.

"By God!" he thought. "I'll find out what this thing is, and who has done it. She knew what I was. There is a limit to humiliation. Either she shall again accept me and believe in me, or—or——"

But there seemed to present itself no alternative which he could tolerate; and the thread of thought snapped short.

They were entering the city limits now, and he began to realise that neither had spoken for nearly an hour.

He ventured to glance sideways at her. The exquisitely sad profile against the window thrilled him painfully, almost to the verge of anger. Unwedded, she had been nearer to him. Even in his arms, shy and utterly unresponsive, she had been closer, a more vital thing, than ever she had been since the law had made her his wife.

For a moment the brutality in him stirred, and he felt the heat of blood in his face, and his heart grew restless and beat faster. All that is latent in man of impatience with pain, of intolerance, of passion, of violence, throbbed in every vein.

Then she turned and looked at him. And it was ended as suddenly as it began. Only his sense of helplessness and his resentment remained—resentment against fate, against the unknown people who had done this thing to him and to her; against himself and his folly; even subtly, yet illogically, against her.

"I was thinking," she said, "that we might at least lunch together—if you would care to."

"Would you?" he asked coldly.

"If you would."

His lip began to tremble and he caught it between his teeth; then his anger flared, and before he meant to he had said:

"A jolly luncheon it would be, wouldn't it?"

"What?"

"I said it would be a jolly affair—considering the situation."

"What is the situation, Jim?" she asked, very pale.

"Oh, what I've made of it, I suppose—a failure!"

"I—I thought we were trying to remake it into a success."

"Can we?"

"We must, Jim."

"How?"

She was silent.

"I'll tell you how we can not make a success out of it," he said hotly, "and that's by doing what we have been doing."

"We have—have had scarcely time yet to do anything very much."

"We've done enough to widen the breach between us—however we've managed to accomplish it. That's all I know, Jacqueline."

"I thought the breach was closing."

"I thought so, too, this morning."

"Wounds can not heal over night," she said, in a low voice.

"Wounds can not heal at all if continually irritated."

"I know it. Give me a little time, Jim. It is all so new to me, and there is no precedent to follow—and I haven't very much wisdom. I am only trying to find myself so I shall know how best to serve you———"

"I don't want to be served, Jacqueline! I want you to love me———"

"I do."

"You do in a hurt, reproachful, frightened, don't-touch-me sort of way———"

"Jim!"

"I'm sorry; I don't know what I'm saying. There isn't anything for me to say, I suppose. But I don't seem to have the spirit of endurance in me—humble submission isn't my line; delay makes me impatient. I want things to be settled, no matter what the cost. When I repent, I repent like the devil—just as hard and as fast as I can. Then it's over and done with. But nobody else seems to notice my regeneration."

For a moment her face was a study in mixed emotions, then a troubled smile curved her lips, but her eyes were unconvinced.

"You are only a boy, aren't you?" she said gently. "I know it, somehow, but there is still a little awe of you left in me, and I can't quite understand. Won't you be patient with me, Jim?"

He bent over and caught her hand.

"Only love me, Jacqueline———"

"Oh, I do! I do! And I don't know what to do about it! All my thoughts are concentrated on it, how best to make it strong, enduring, noble! How best to shelter it, bind up its wounds, guard it, defend it. I—I know in my heart that I've got to defend it———"

"What do you mean, my darling?"

"I don't know—I don't know, Jim. Only—if I knew—if I could always know———"

She turned her head swiftly and stared out of the window. On the glass, vaguely, Elena's shadowy features seemed to smile at her.

Was that what tortured her? Was that what she wished to know when she and this man separated for the day—where the woman was? Had her confidence in him been so utterly, so shamefully destroyed that it had lowered her to an ignoble level—hurled down her dignity and self-respect to grovel amid unworthy and contemptible emotions? Was it the vulgar vice of jealousy that was beginning to fasten itself upon her?

Sickened, she closed her eyes a moment; but on the lids was still imprinted the face of the woman; and her words began to ring in her brain. And thought began to gallop again, uncurbed, frantic, stampeding. How could he have done it? How could he have carried on this terrible affair after he had met her, after he had known her, loved her, won her? How could he have received that woman as a guest under the same roof that sheltered her? How could he have made a secret rendezvous with the woman scarcely an hour after he had asked her to marry him?

Even if anybody had come to her and told her of these things she could have found it in her heart to find excuses, to forgive him; she could have believed that he had received Elena and arranged a secret meeting with her merely to tell her that their intrigue was at an end.

She could have accustomed herself to endure the knowledge of this concrete instance. And, whatever else he might have done in the past she could endure; because, to her, it was something too abstract, too vague and foreign to her to seem real.

But the attitude and words of Elena Clydesdale—the unmistakable impression she coolly conveyed that this thing was not yet ended, had poisoned the very spring of her faith in him. And the welling waters were still as bitter as death to her.

What did faith matter to her in the world if she could not trust this man? Of what use was it other than to believe in him? And now she could not. She had tried, and she could not. Only when he was near her—only when she might see him, hear him, could she ever again feel sure of him. And now they were to separate for the day. And—where was he going? And where was the other woman?

And her heart almost stopped in her breast as she thought of the days and days and years and years to come in which she must continue to ask herself these questions.

Yet, in the same quick, agonised breath, she knew she was going to fight for him—do battle in behalf of that broken and fireless altar where love lay wounded.

There were many ways of doing battle, but only one right way. And she had thought of many—confused, frightened, unknowing, praying for unselfishness and for light to guide her.

But there were so many ways; and the easiest had been to forgive him, surrender utterly, cling to him, love him with every tenderness and grace and accomplishment and art and instinct that was hers—with all of her ardent youth, all of her dawning emotion, all of her undeveloped passion.

That had been the easier way in the crisis which stunned and terrified her—to seek shelter, not give it; to surrender, not to withhold.

But whether through wisdom or instinct, she seemed to see farther than the moment—to divine, somehow, that his salvation and hers lay not only in forgiveness and love, but in her power to give or withhold; her freedom to exact what justly was her due; in the preservation of her individuality with all its prerogative, its liberty of choice, its self-respect unshaken, its authority unweakened and undiminished.

To yield when he was not qualified to receive such supreme surrender boded ill for her, and ultimately for him; for it made of her merely an instrument.

Somehow she seemed to know that sometime, for her, would come a moment of final victory; and in that moment only her utter surrender could make the victory eternal and complete.

And until that moment came she would not surrender prematurely. She had a fight on her hands; she knew it; she must do her best, though her own heart were a sword that pierced her with every throb. For his sake she would deny; for his sake remain aloof from the lesser love, inviolate, powerful, mistress of herself and of her destiny.

And yet—she was his wife. And, after all was said and done, she understood that no dual sovereignty ever is possible; that one or the other must have the final decision; and that if, when it came to that, his ultimate authority failed him, then their spiritual union was a failure, though the material one might endure for a while.

And so, believing this, honest with herself and with him, she had offered him her fealty—a white blossom and her key lying beside it in the palm of her hand—in acknowledgment that the supreme decision lay with him.

He had not failed her; the final authority still lay with him. Only that knowledge had sustained her during the long night.

The car stopped at her establishment; she came out of her painful abstraction with a slight start, flushed, and looked at him.

"Will you lunch with me, Jim?"

"I think I'll lunch at the club," he said, coolly.

"Very well. Will you bring the car around at five?"

"The car will be here for you."

"And—you?" She tried to smile.

"Probably."

"Oh! If you have any engagements——"

"I might make one between now and five," he said carelessly. "If I do, I'll come up on the train."

She had not been prepared for this attitude. But there was nothing to say. He got out and aided her to descend, and took her to the door. His manners were always faultless.

"I hope you will come for me," she said, almost timidly.

"I hope so," he said.

And that was all; she offered her hand; he took it, smiled, and replaced his hat after the shop door closed behind her.

Then he went back to the car.

"Drive me to Mrs. Hammerton's," he said curtly; got in, and slammed the door.

"Dearest?"

He could feel her trembling.

After a long while he said, very gently: "Come back and say good-night to me when you are ready, dear." And quietly released her.

And she went away slowly to her room, not looking at him. And did not return.

So at one o'clock he turned off the lights and went into his own room. It was bright with moonlight. On his dresser lay a white carnation and a key. But he did not see them.

Far away in the woods he heard the stream rushing, bank full, through the darkness, and he listened as he moved about in the moonlight. Tranquil, he looked out at the night for a moment, then quietly composed himself to slumber, not doubting, serene, happy, convinced that her love was his.

For a long while he thought of her; and, thinking, dreamed of her at last—so vividly that into his vision stole the perfume of her hair and the faint fresh scent of her hands, as when he had kissed the slender fingers. And the warmth of her, too, seemed real, and the sweetness of her breath.

His eyes unclosed. She lay there, in her frail Chinese robe, curled up beside him in the moonlight, her splendid hair framing a face as pale as the flower that had fallen from her half-closed hand. And at first he thought she was asleep.

Then, in the moonlight, her eyes opened divinely, met his, lingered unafraid, and were slowly veiled again. Neither stirred until, at last, her arms stole up around his neck and her lips whispered his name as though it were a holy name, loved, honoured, and adored.

THE END

www.ingramcontent.com/pod-product-compliance
Lightning Source LLC
Chambersburg PA
CBHW080907190726
48294CB00008B/1996